ONCE UPON A TIME IN DOLLYWOOD

ASHLEY JORDAN

BERKLEY ROMANCE
New York

BERKLEY ROMANCE
Published by Berkley
An imprint of Penguin Random House LLC
1745 Broadway, New York, NY 10019
penguinrandomhouse.com

Book design by Ashley Tucker

Library of Congress Cataloging-in-Publication Data

Names: Jordan, Ashley, 1987- author
Title: Once upon a time in Dollywood / Ashley Jordan.
Description: First edition. | New York: Berkley Romance, 2025.
Identifiers: LCCN 2025006657 (print) | LCCN 2025006658 (ebook) |
ISBN 9780593819128 trade paperback | ISBN 9780593819135 ebook
Subjects: LCGFT: Romance fiction | Novels
Classification: LCC PS3610.O65524 O53 2025 (print) |
LCC PS3610.O65524 (ebook) | DDC 813/.6—dc23/eng/20250514
LC record available at https://lccn.loc.gov/2025006657
LC ebook record available at https://lccn.loc.gov/2025006658

First Edition: August 2025

Printed in the United States of America
1st Printing

The authorized representative in the EU for product safety and compliance is Penguin Random House Ireland, Morrison Chambers, 32 Nassau Street, Dublin D02 YH68, Ireland, https://eu-contact.penguin.ie.

To all the Black girls and women mistaken for difficult when they just needed to be seen.

And to the village of Black women who not only raised me, but lifted me—Mom, Portland, Stefani, Brenda, Wylene, Janet, Annie Ruth, Lula, Ruby Jean, Phyllis, Stephanie, Dianne, Anita, Barbara, Shirley, Soneni, and Miss Hattie—I love you.

Pain is important: how we evade it, how we succumb to it, how we deal with it, how we transcend it.

—Audre Lorde

Dear Reader,

I won't lie—this isn't exactly a light story. While it is absolutely a romance, and I do think there is quite a bit to laugh (or at least chuckle) about, it's not what I'd call a rom-com. I want you to go into this knowing that I cried while writing parts of this novel, and low-key (maybe high-key), I hope you cry a little reading it! So, with that in mind, there are some heavy themes you should be aware of before you dive in: fertility issues, infidelity, teenage pregnancy and childhood trauma, adoption, divorce, and battles with depression and anxiety. Like many love stories, this is a book about our beautiful, ordinary lives and the many dark and bright spots within. I hope you're willing to go on this ride—I like to think it'll be worth it—but more important, I hope you take care of yourself.

Warmly,
Ashley

ONCE
UPON
A TIME IN
DOLLYWOOD

CHAPTER 1

Unoriginal Sin

EVE

Eve's thoughts were swirling. Running rampant. She wasn't entirely sure she wasn't drowning—in her feelings, at least—as she sat silent and helpless in front of her fiancé and his therapist, watching them talk about her as if she weren't in the room. She wished she weren't in the room.

I just lost my baby, and now I'm losing my mind.

There were no windows. Why no windows? She might as well have been sitting in a box. That might have made more sense—this sensation of feeling trapped. Instead, Eve just sat there, studying the taupe walls, decorated with little more than degrees and other accolades, counting the minutes until she could escape. There was one piece of art within eyeshot, a chart alleging the correlation between success in therapy and stepping outside one's comfort zone. Eve rolled her eyes.

"She's such a trooper," Leo said, shaking his head. He sighed, the notion ostensibly too heavy to bear, and then followed it up with a half smile in her direction, as if that would somehow console her; as if they wouldn't still be going home with this heartbreak hanging over their heads.

Eve was vexed by his unending affability—something no one would ever accuse her of—knowing he was going to take her hand any second now. And she was going to have to pretend that she wasn't revolted by the thought of being touched in that moment. She would have to force herself not to physically recoil, lest her future husband and his psychiatrist realize just how shitty a person she was.

"I just feel like I'm failing her, because I don't know what to say," Leo continued. "I can't fix it. I wonder if I'm just making shit worse sometimes."

Eve felt herself glaring at him as he pensively rubbed his graying beard, performing his guilt.

That wasn't fair to say. He probably did feel guilty on some level. But it just gave Eve another reason to feel bad, and she already had plenty. The physical ache was enough, but the mental anguish hung on her like lead. It was why she hadn't left the house for the last two weeks. She only came to this appointment so Leo would shut up about it. But if she'd known he'd sit here and effectively blame her for not knowing how to make him feel better, she would've just stayed in bed.

"Eve, do you want to say more about how you've been feeling?" Dr. Hawthorne asked. "Leo wanted you to have a safe space, too."

Eve knew all too well that there were no safe spaces. If there were, this wouldn't keep happening. She wouldn't be mourning the loss of a third embryo, when all she'd wanted, for seventeen years now, was a child.

"I feel broken," she said, and then corrected herself: "Barren."

The doctor nodded. "But you know you're not, right? That

your worth, your sense of self, is not wrapped up in carrying a baby to term?"

It was Leo's turn to chime in, apparently. "It's what I've been trying to tell her for a year now. And that we have other options, too, if she wants to try 'em."

Eve nodded back, understanding the logic, and she could see their mouths continue to move, the two of them attempting to explain her own feelings to her. But a rush of emotions left the room spinning, all their words turned to white noise, an incessant scraping at her ears. The dizziness gave way to panic, a feeling as if she'd been pushed off a cliff. A sudden loss of control, both physical and emotional, as pangs of dread thumped in her chest. She felt simultaneously exposed and smothered, cold and hot. The edges of the room went dark, leaving Eve with only her frenzied and conflicting musings. She'd experienced this before, this need to dissociate, to somehow get outside of her own body, but never quite so acutely. She could not sit still any longer.

As Leo indeed reached across the small space between them, taking her hand, Eve disentangled her fingers from his grip and stood from her seat unsteadily.

She grabbed her purse from the back of her chair and left the airless room without a word. If either of them called after her, she didn't hear it.

She continued out of the office and into the late-June midday sun, wishing she had the forethought to have a Lyft waiting before exiting. The heat—the humidity, really—was somehow even more suffocating than the sense of failure that had wrapped itself around her the moment she realized she'd miscarried *again*. Trying to talk through it with Leo's therapist was a compromise for his sake, but therapy only made her feel broken open. And nothing was going to assuage this feeling—a particularly demoralizing confluence of pain and emptiness.

Eve held back tears as a bright green cab passed and she inwardly cursed herself for not hailing it. Leo would be following her outside soon, and she simply did not have the energy to be normal for him. But the entrance to Prospect Park sat just a few steps from Dr. Hawthorne's office, and it would be easy enough to vanish there.

Eve hurried across the street, dodging traffic and passersby, until she reached the majestic old arch that welcomed her into the park. It was busy for a random Wednesday, kids running rampant in their summer freedom. It wasn't ideal for Eve, a hundred little reminders of what she'd lost. But on hot days like this, she liked to head to the Ravine, where it was cooler than probably anywhere else in the city, full of footbridges and unique little waterfalls, enclosed in a parcel of trees. It was Brooklyn's only forest, small as it was, but enough to be pacifying.

As she approached a small boulder to claim as her seat, she felt her phone vibrating in her purse. She retrieved it, knowing it was Leo, knowing she wouldn't answer, but took note of the string of texts he'd sent in the five minutes they'd been apart: six varying versions of *What the fuck?*

Instead of replying, Eve went to her favorite contacts, where her mother sat at the top of the list, her best friend just below, letting her thumb hover over the entries as she wrestled with whom to call. Conversations with her mother had a fifty-fifty chance of going awry, and Eve was already in a foul mood. But Maya was working, and she didn't want to dampen her day yet again.

Before Eve could make a decision, drops of water dotted her

touch screen, and she halfway wondered if an impromptu rain shower was the culprit, despite the beating sun. But instead of fighting the onslaught of emotion, she bowed her head and let her tears fall, sobbing quietly as the sound of children's laughter in the background haunted her.

"Well, you look good for someone who ain't left the house since Memorial Day."

Eve suppressed what would've been a genuine but self-effacing smile as she entered her best friend's studio. While she appreciated that Maya noticed what little effort she put into her appearance—from her little black sundress to the high pony she'd fashioned her box braids into—she was loath to encourage any more backhanded compliments.

"Hello to you, too," Eve said. She claimed the plush chartreuse couch set opposite her friend and practically nestled into it like it was her bed. She would've fallen asleep there if it weren't for the crazy eyes boring into her. "What?"

Maya shut down her computer and crossed her arms. "Why did your texts make it sound like you're a fugitive?"

Eve shifted to her back, lying like she was in a psychiatrist's office—ironically—and stared at the textured ceiling. "I guess I kinda am," she said. She used the knuckle of her thumb to massage the bridge of her nose in a useless attempt at tempering the headache that had formed in the thirty minutes since she left Leo. "I have to get out of this place."

"You told me that much," Maya said. "How do we get you outta here?"

"You don't even wanna know why?"

Maya shook her head. "Don't matter why."

Eve didn't hold back her smile this time, the ceaseless comfort of Maya's New Orleans inflection doing its job. "I feel like I can't breathe here," she said.

"Okay. So where can you breathe?"

Eve wasn't sure that such a place existed. Everything felt suffocating if she had enough time to think about it. "I wish I could go back to college," she said. She didn't realize it until long after she was gone, but her time in Atlanta was her first, and perhaps last, experience with freedom. Away from her parents, cocooned from the noise of her mistakes. "I don't know," she eventually appended. "Anywhere but here."

"You want me to take you to the airport in the morning?" Maya asked. "We can just choose from the departure boards."

Eve admired the thought, but her neurosis would never allow her to be *that* spontaneous. Planning a trip with a day's notice was pushing her limits, but she could not, would not set foot on a plane without having accommodations at her destination. "Did you forget who you're talking to?"

"I'm just trying to get you outta here as efficiently as possible," Maya said. "So you can try to get your happy back."

Sounded nice, but Eve couldn't remember the last time she concerned herself with being happy. She just wanted to be . . . not sad.

"Maybe . . ." Eve paused before letting her suggestion into the air, knowing that once it was out there, she was probably going to follow it. There were so many places she could go to take a break. A couple of weeks in Los Angeles always did her well. The openness of it all. The antithesis of home, the high-strung havoc of New York. Or she could go to Paris for a bit. She'd always had an abstract dream of escaping to the City of Light and James Baldwining it up for a year or two. The way her bank account was set up, she couldn't quite afford that luxury, and again, she was not someone who could live on whims. But she could do it for about a month.

Mostly, Eve wanted to drop off the grid, and the one place that kept coming back to her mind was some cabin in the middle of nowhere, where she could grieve and write—in no particular order—all by herself.

"I think I'm going to Gatlinburg," she finally said. She gazed at Maya, awaiting her approval—or lack thereof.

Maya only raised an eyebrow. "You *sure* you wanna go back there?"

Eve shrugged. "Can't hurt any more than I already do."

"Damn."

"That was a long time ago anyway."

Maya gave her a knowing look, clear that Eve was in denial, at best, and lying, at worst.

"I sort of already knew what I was gonna do before I got here," Eve admitted. She pulled out her phone, where she had started her search for flights on the ride there, and lamented that she would have to fly out of LaGuardia if she wanted a nonstop route. "I guess I just wanted to see your face before I left," she added.

"Bitch, why are you being so dramatic? How long you goin' for?"

"I don't know."

"A year?" Maya asked, cocking her head as if to challenge Eve.

"Probably not, but . . ."

"It better not be a year."

"I said I don't know," Eve said.

"So you gon' sit up in your grandmama's old cabin by yourself for a year? Shut up."

"I can't stand you," Eve said, holding back her amusement.

"A second ago, you couldn't live without my face."

"When I don't call you for a year, I want you to recall this moment as the reason why."

"I will hunt you down in Tennessee before I let that happen," Maya said.

"You can try."

"And you better not need money while you're there, because you will starve messin' around with me."

Maya's immaculate smile evolved into a laugh, and Eve responded in kind. A small one, but a laugh, nonetheless. Which was precisely why she wanted to see her best friend. She wasn't in a laughing mood, and hadn't been for the last few weeks, but Maya would bring her to a place where she could at least fathom it for a couple of minutes. She always took the pain away.

"I just hope a change of pace will let me feel something different," Eve said, sobering.

Maya nodded. "It's the hope that kills you, you know."

"No shit." It was all this time, the *years* she'd spent hoping for a baby, that left her feeling like this.

The last pregnancy test she took had been on her opening night at Playwrights Horizons, with Maya waiting on the other side of a bathroom stall as Eve anxiously peed on a stick. They spent the requisite three-minute wait reminiscing, as they often did when they didn't want to face the complexities of present-day adult life. They cried with a muted delight when the result came back positive, after Eve spent the better part of the holidays trying to get over her second miscarriage. She hoped upon hope that the third time would be the charm. And so, this one only felt heavier. Crueler.

Maya sat back in her chair, her arms folded over her chest again like a judgmental auntie. "I don't like it. But I guess I'm gonna be an adult about this. Go . . . get better. Write a play about it. Shit's way cheaper than therapy." She let out a somber chuckle and so did Eve. "But then bring your ass home."

Eve replied with a strained smile. But Maya wasn't wrong—writing had been far more therapeutic than any time she'd spent on a psychologist's couch. It would be nice if she could write her way through this. If she could fix herself. "I'll try."

When Eve walked into her parents' Strivers' Row brownstone, she shouldn't have been surprised to find Leo waiting there. He was like a stray puppy, desperate for affection from the human who abandoned it. She often wished she had a dog, but Leo was allergic. So she accepted his unconditional love, regretful that she didn't have the same to give to him. He'd called her four times, and texted twice more, and she ignored nearly all of them. *I'm ok* was her only response after his third attempt, and even that was a lie. Depression, even when exacerbated by what they were going through, wasn't a good excuse for treating loved ones badly. But she would use it, and he would take it.

"You found me." She said it as a simple statement of fact, too numb to even be annoyed.

"Maya told me where you were headed."

Eve made a mental note to curse her out next time they

spoke, then continued into the kitchen, where she found her mother hovering over the Crock-Pot on the island counter. She couldn't help but notice how the white marble top matched her mother's gray locs, and she welcomed the distraction from the heavier things on her mind. The unmistakable aroma of stewing oxtails brought Eve a modicum of much-needed comfort.

"I thought I heard your voice," Joan greeted her. She embraced Eve with a quick kiss to her cheek and then studied her face, undoubtedly looking for something to comment on. To criticize. "You would look so nice with a bit of color on your lips," she decided. "A nice red would bring out your beautiful skin."

"Where's Daddy?" Eve asked, resisting the urge to argue.

Joan resumed stirring and seasoning as Eve looked on. "He's around here somewhere."

Eve surveyed the bright space—a pot of rice sat on the stove, a half-mixed salad on the counter closest to the refrigerator, the dinner china waiting just beside the slow cooker, with an assortment of silverware resting on the top plate. She spotted a set of keys sitting near the landline at the entryway. "Are those for me?"

"Oh, yes." Joan gestured for her to take them. "I realized that her car would still be there, too. You're going to need one while you're there."

Eve had been relieved that her mother didn't make a big deal when she called to ask for the keys to her grandmother's cabin. No superfluous questions disguised as concern, none of her typical meddling. Just an agreement that the cabin would be a great place to write her next play. It did come with a bit of unsolicited advice: *You need to strike while the iron is hot, sweetheart.* But Eve took the empty platitude in stride because she'd been expecting worse. Which was why Eve wasn't surprised when she went to retrieve the key ring and found a church bulletin sitting directly underneath it.

"Ask and it will be given to you, knock and the door shall be opened." True prayer is a personal dialogue with God in which we trust in God's mercy and kindness.

Eve rolled her eyes. The Parish of St. Charles Borromeo had become something of a thorn in her side as she found herself outgrowing her Catholic upbringing.

"How old is that car anyway?" Eve asked, ignoring the provocation. She rejoined her mother to take in the sights and smells of the oxtails.

"Oh goodness." Joan paused to think about it. "Probably . . . twenty years old now."

"Jesus."

She flicked her daughter for the mild blasphemy and went on, "It's a sturdy car. It'll get you where you need to go."

"I don't think I'll be going too many places, but it'll be nice to have," Eve said. "Thanks, Ma."

"You're staying for dinner?"

Eve stopped herself from pointing out that her mother's questions often sounded like demands. "I'm not really hungry." She was lying.

"Nonsense. Your fiancé is here. You're going out of town. You can have a meal with your parents."

"Okay, but Leo doesn't need—"

"Roger!"

"Mom, I—"

"By the way, your father is very excited that you're finally writing something new."

"Finally?" Eve huffed and rubbed her face as she tried to process the idea of sitting down to dinner with her parents and fiancé, when all she wanted to do was find somewhere to be alone and cry. Now, she would have to paint on the happy face she'd tried to avoid all day with Leo. It probably served her right for leaving him that way.

She forced a smile as she heard her father's footsteps approach. "Where's my Tennessee girl?" Roger asked.

"Hi, Daddy," Eve replied. She wrapped her arms around his tall, sturdy frame as he left a kiss atop her braids, the way he did when she was little. She and her mother were similar in shape and size—slender and on the tall side of average—but fit in his arms in decidedly different ways. "How are you?" she asked.

"Oh, I'm good, Tètè." His grin, with its tiny gap between the front two teeth, was identical to hers. "Sounds like you are as well?"

"I can't complain," Eve said, meaning it literally. She hadn't told her parents about the pregnancy—for a number of reasons—and she certainly wasn't going to open that can of worms now. So no, she couldn't tell her father that she actually felt like crawling inside a hole and dying at that very moment.

Roger nodded. "I told you you would come up with something for your next play. You just needed to soak up a little more of the world."

Eve was convinced that the semi-success of her current play was the first time her parents deigned to be proud of her. When she got her PhD, their response was basically, *Took you long enough.* Nothing special in a family of academics. Her little production hadn't even sniffed Broadway, barely filling ninety seats a night in Clinton Hill nowadays. But it was external validation, at least. Eve understood why they were looking to recapture that. Adamant that she not be a half-hit wonder. A failure.

"We'll see what happens," she said, her smile tightening. "I won't even know if it's worth anything 'til I see it on a stage."

"But you'll tell us what it's about?" Joan asked, pulling a series of glasses from an upper cabinet. "Leonardo, come set the table," she added in another shout.

"I don't think I'm ready for that, Ma." She wasn't even sure she knew what it was about yet.

"It's that superstition where you cannot tell someone your wish before it comes true," Roger said, chuckling. "You can tell us about it when you're ready."

Lacking any substantive response, Eve went to retrieve pitchers of water and sweet tea from the refrigerator.

"Do you know how long you'll be in Tennessee then?" he asked.

"Who's going to Tennessee?" Leo asked, entering the kitchen.

Eve avoided his eye as she pointed him in the direction of the plates. "I am."

"Oh . . ."

"Writing retreat," Joan said. "God knows she needs it."

"For how long?"

"I don't know," Eve said. Guilt was swallowing her whole, and she wasn't in the mood to be honest with herself about why. "Maybe for the summer. Come back in September. If I don't get bored and come back sooner, of course."

"Wow," Leo said.

"That's so long," Joan said. "Will Leo visit you on the weekends?"

"I think I would have to," he said.

Eve choked out an awkward laugh, unable to tell him that she would rather have her nails plucked out than have him visit.

"Do you have enough money to be gone that long?" Roger asked.

"Yes, Daddy." She gave her mother a knowing glance. The night she got engaged, Joan impressed upon her just how important it was to keep her own secret stash of money. Just in case. The implication was in case *Leo* turned out to be terrible. She never imagined she'd end up using it because she was the loathly one.

The kitchen became chaotic as plates and bowls, platters and serving dishes were passed back and forth, making their way to the dining room. The table there made her think of her grandmother; it was something her mother had coveted for years and brought back from Tennessee after the funeral. It was wide and sturdy, in a beautiful tobacco color, its legs made up of spheres descending in size. Had she been willing to go to the funeral, Eve might've tried to keep this particular heirloom for herself.

Once they were finally seated, her parents at the head and foot of the table, Eve and Leo across from each other, she could no longer avoid her fiancé's dubious stare.

"When are you leaving?" he asked. His brown eyes were sad, practically pleading.

Eve purposely began shoveling rice onto her plate as if the action would block out his question. "In the morning," she finally said. "And I don't want you to come visit me," she added in a mumble that was likely audible only to her father, who had hearing like a bat. She could never even sneak midnight snacks as a kid, because he would know the second she opened the fridge or pantry.

"What was that?" Joan asked.

Leo eyed Eve long enough for her to understand that he heard her loud and clear. And he was hurt. She bit the inside of her cheek, realizing just how sudden and shitty this was, her thoughtlessness once again rearing its ugly head. "I'm sorry," she whispered.

"Sorry for what?" Joan pressed. "What is going on?"

"I'm pretty sure your daughter is breaking up with me in the middle of dinner," Leo said flatly.

"What?"

"Eve?" Roger eyed her as if he were willing her to be brave and not embrace the streak of cowardice that was trying to force her up from the table. The one sending her running once again.

"Don't do this," Leo said. Begged.

"I'm so sorry," Eve said, brushing away a stubborn tear as she indeed rose from her seat. She felt tinges of déjà vu as she left the table, blocking out everything except that throbbing impulse to escape. It was a terrible thing to do to anyone, much less to a man who had never done anything but love her. And for much of their time together, she'd loved him, too—or she'd tried to. But she could no longer care about him more than she did herself. She was running for her life here. With her grandmother's keys in hand, Eve left the apartment without another word.

CHAPTER 2

Stuck in the Mud

JAMIE

The courtroom was a smothering kind of stale, barely large enough to fit the nine people in it. Jamie glanced at his lawyer apprehensively, and then back at the judge, both of them wearing unreadable expressions that only managed to make his heart beat faster as he awaited the ruling. He had never been particularly good at reading people. Women, especially. It was probably why he was sitting there in the first place. But it was hard not to believe that all these inscrutable faces weren't there just to taunt him.

"I know this isn't easy on anyone," Judge Schiff said, "and I appreciate both your candor and patience today, Ms. Ewen, Mr. Gallagher." She peered across the room at each of them like a disappointed parent. "Now as you both know, it is the court's job to make a decision in the best interest of the child. I still wish that you could've come to a compromise on your own. I've seen nothing here to indicate that you couldn't, other than sheer stubbornness. As you move forward, Mom and Dad are going to *have* to *communicate*."

"Yes, Your Honor." Jamie offered a meek nod as he gripped the vinyl armrests of his chair for dear life and the sweat that claimed his palms for the better part of an hour made its way to his back. When he glanced to his left, Lucy looked equally abashed, at least.

"I understand, Your Honor," she said.

"That said, in light of the information shared today, Ms. Ewen, I cannot say that I am comfortable having Jack in your home primarily at this time," the judge told Lucy. "When you can show that you're able to maintain your household without Mr. Gallagher's financial support, I am happy to revisit this. Until then, it is the court's order that you will share joint legal custody of Jackson Gallagher. Mr. Gallagher will retain physical custody, and Ms. Ewen will be allowed visitation on weekends. Any further visits will be at Mr. Gallagher's discretion."

Jamie let out the breath he'd been holding for the entire proceedings as he felt his brother's strong hand squeeze his shoulder from behind. "Thank you, Your Honor," he croaked out, just before the emotion could clog his throat.

Morgan, his lawyer, offered him a sparkling grin as she placed a comforting hand over his. "I told you," she said.

"Thank you both for your appearances," Judge Schiff said, all of the reprimand and authority suddenly gone from her tone.

As everyone rose from their seats and the judge disappeared, Jamie snuck another peek at Lucy, whose boyfriend (or more accurately, her fiancé, apparently) consoled her. Pesky remnants of regret churned in Jamie's stomach, and he looked away in the hope of pushing it all down.

"So you'll get the official order in the mail," Morgan explained as they began their exit. "It'll be probably about a week. In the meantime, she may try to fight you, but you do not have to do anything you don't feel comfortable with."

"Wait, so there's no paperwork he can have today?" Jamie's brother cut in. "In case she tries to kidnap the kiddo?"

Jamie rolled his eyes at Casey's input. "She's not gonna do that."

"You don't know that."

"Go to the car," Jamie said, handing over the keys to his truck before Casey could protest. "I'll be right there." As Casey took off, his typically chaotic energy dissipating, Jamie offered his lawyer his most earnest half smile. "Thank you."

"You did most of the work. You've been doing most of the work, and I'm just happy the judge saw that."

Jamie nodded, squinting at the sun high in the sky, the sudden heat wave that came with it making Nashville feel like a personal hell. More than it did already anyway. "Hopefully, I won't need you much more after this."

Morgan grinned at him again and left him with a conservative hug. "I hope not, too. You take care of yourself."

"I will."

Jamie continued to stand on the steps of the Davidson County General Sessions Court, and he wasn't sure whether he was waiting for Lucy or for the will to keep moving, but he ended up staying until she appeared with her small entourage. Ever the perpetual victim, she was still wiping tears as she approached Jamie.

"You waited to gloat?" Lucy asked with a hint of playfulness in her tone.

"Nothing of the sort."

"No, I know," she said soberly. "But congratulations to you."

Jamie's eye couldn't help catching the diamond now adorning her left hand. It was small but elegant. Fitting for her thin fingers. "It's not how I wanted it," he said.

Lucy bit her lip. "I know that, too. But thank you for being generous anyway. There were a lot of things you could've said in there, and I appreciate you holding back."

"Luce, I never wanted to go to court in the first place."

"And when I pushed, you could've made it ugly, and you didn't, so . . . I'm thanking you."

"Fair enough."

"And I'm sorry," Lucy said, her light brown eyes studying his. "That you had to find out about the engagement this way. We wanted to tell Jack first. It all just . . . sort of . . . happened."

Jamie grimaced at that bit of information, wondering how a proposal, complete with a ring, just *happens*. Ten years together, and nothing of the sort ever *happened* to them. "Right. Well. I'm glad you're finally happy."

Lucy looked pained by the statement, briefly at least. But then she went on. "I know what the judge said, but is it still okay if I have Jack this week?"

"Of course. What we agreed to this summer is still fine with me."

"Okay."

Jamie noticed, again, Lucy's fiancé waiting for her at the bottom of the steps. "So . . . I'll drop off Jack around six?"

"Oh . . ."

"What?"

"Well, I was hoping I could pick him up from camp today."

"I'd actually . . . I'd rather have him for a couple of hours," Jamie said. "If that's okay with you."

"You already won, Jamie. Can't you just give me this?"

"Lucy."

"I'm sorry," she repeated, brushing her wispy brown bangs from her eyes. "I know you're being kind. I just—"

"Can't we both just enjoy that this is finally over?" he asked, and he knew it sounded like begging. That was all he'd done for the past six months, beg her to be civil.

"Yes, I know how you hate fighting."

Jamie caught the sarcasm but ignored it, because he couldn't stand in front of her and that ring much longer. "I'll see you at six, Lucy."

Separately, the two of them descended the steps, Lucy heading to the left with Tyler, while Jamie went to the right, toward his car and his brother. And when a tear slipped down his cheek, he wiped it as quickly as he could, happy to pretend it was more sweat rather than whatever feelings he had left for this woman. When he reached his old pine-green Silverado and saw Casey propped against it looking like a rebel without a cause, he reminded himself that despite everything, he'd had a good day.

"What did the Wicked Witch of Middle Tennessee have to say for herself?" Casey asked.

Jamie shook his head, suppressing a laugh as he hopped into the driver's side. "I got a couple more hours with Jack, mostly for your benefit, and then she has him the rest of the week."

"That's cool. I'm just here for the day anyway."

Jamie gazed at his younger brother in search of something meaningful to say, something to express how grateful he was that he flew into town just to support him through the inanity of this custody battle. But Casey already knew. He'd watched Jamie go through hell for the better part of a year, in this entanglement with Lucy and Tyler, all while trying to hold on to his sanity for Jack's sake. When another tear trickled down his cheek, Jamie didn't bother hiding it this time.

"Hey." Casey reached out, gently wiping Jamie's face. "You did everything right, dude."

Jamie let out a quiet sigh. "Not everything."

"It truly wounds my soul that you don't know what a catch you are."

"Stop."

"If you could just be, like, a little bit gay, I have someone who'd be *perfect* for you," Casey joked. "He works with Jelani, but he's *nice*. He shares your brand of nontoxic masculinity. Great with kids. He pays his own bills . . ."

Jamie let out an unexpected, genuine laugh at the fact that his brother and brother-in-law never tired of trying to indoctrinate him. "Sometimes, I wish I was."

"No matter. I'm gonna find you someone. Someone who's gonna make you forget you ever knew Lucy fucking Ewen."

Jamie looked at him. "That's obviously not gonna happen."

"I mean, yeah, Jack. Of course. But besides that . . ."

"Right." Try as he might, Jamie couldn't hide his amusement with his brother. Because quietly, he wanted nothing more than to forget he ever knew, or loved, Lucy fucking Ewen.

"Hey, Dad?"

"Yeah, bud?" Jamie glanced at his eight-year-old in the back seat, bracing himself for whatever might be on the other end of his query. With Jack, it could be anything from a request for a napkin to a deep dive into existentialism. After the day he'd had, Jamie prayed for the former, but he would give his best if it were the latter.

"Would it be okay if you take me to camp in the mornings and Mom picks me up?"

Jamie chuckled uneasily. "You don't want your mom to take you to camp?"

"It's not that I don't want her to. It's just . . . we're always late when she takes me, and I miss out on breakfast and then I get the worst seat in class, away from all my friends."

"I see."

"And they don't let them save seats. You know Riley would save a seat for me if she could."

"Of course . . ."

"So if you could take me and Mom picks me up, that would just be a better start to my day, I think."

Jamie paused to deliberate, to devise the correct combination of words to share the big news with his son. In the process, he grabbed a napkin from the glove compartment for Jack before his ice cream could melt all over his hand. "Your mom and I discussed things, and you're actually gonna spend more time with her during the summer," he said. "So the only time I'll be taking you to camp is on Monday mornings."

Jack scrunched his face at the unusual arrangement. "Oh."

"Is that all right with you?"

"I guess," Jack said. "So I'll be at Mom's all week?"

"For the most part. 'Til school starts again."

Jack continued to eat his ice cream with a thoughtful look on his freckled face. "And what are you gonna do?"

Jamie wished he knew. "I'm gonna work. Rest. Maybe do some traveling."

"Yeah, right, Dad."

"Oh, you think I can't go anywhere without you?"

"You never have before," Jack retorted coolly as he bit into his cone. "Where would you even go?"

"I don't know," Jamie said, laughing at his kid as he turned in to Lucy's subdivision. "You're too smart for your own good, you know."

"Tyler says that, too."

Jamie didn't respond, beyond his grip tightening on the steering wheel, always working not to let on how much he hated that guy. "I'll talk to your mom about getting you to camp on time. I don't want you worrying about that."

"Thanks, Dad." As they pulled up to Lucy's Brentwood home, Jack brightened at the sight of the gold SUV at the top of the driveway. "Cool, Tyler's here."

Jamie felt inclined to tell his son that Tyler would always be there, as the guy was now moving into this home he was still paying for, but that wasn't his information to share, and he didn't want to burst Lucy's engagement bubble. Instead, he retrieved Jack and Jack's things and they headed up to the front door, where Lucy was there to greet them before Jack could ring the bell.

"Well, look at you," she said, grinning warmly. She cupped his face, which was covered in chocolate ice cream, and kissed his forehead. "Run inside and let me talk to your dad for a minute, okay?"

Jack turned to say his goodbye, wrapping his little arms around Jamie's waist. "See you later, Dad. Tell Uncle Casey bye for me."

"I will," Jamie said, ruffling his dark brown locks. "Be good. And I'll see you next Friday."

"Don't get too lonely without me."

Jamie watched Jack scamper off while he waited for Lucy to find some new way to ruin his day.

She started off gingerly. "Tyler and I have been talking and . . . we're going to need a little more time before we can take on this mortgage. Is there any way we can—"

"It's fine," Jamie said. He didn't want to talk anymore, not to Lucy, and not about this. They'd spent hours upon hours, with lawyers, trying to come to compromises, and he was exhausted from the conversation. Even when they were together, money seemed to be an unending discussion. He was glad those days were over. "I got it," he said. "How's December?"

Lucy grinned, her hazel eyes gleaming with gratitude. "Thank you." She reached out to affectionately touch his arm. "Thank you, Jamie."

"It's nothin'." He averted his eyes, looking down at the threshold between them; he noticed her bare feet and the fresh French pedicure that decorated her toes. "I'm, um, probably gonna be at the cabin in Gatlinburg for the week. In case you need anything."

Lucy offered another genuine smile. "I think that'll be good for you. You never take time for yourself."

"Hard to do that when you have a kid to raise."

"Well. Now you get to have a life, too. You deserve that."

Jamie chewed the inside of his cheek, hating the way her

Southern lilt still calmed him sometimes. He hated that he had anything left for her at all, after . . . everything. "I'm gonna get going," he said. "I've gotta take Casey to the airport, and then it's a long drive."

"Yeah."

"Oh, by the way, Jack would like it if you could get him to camp on time."

"I'm trying. I keep forgetting there's traffic."

"Right." Jamie could hear Jack laughing in the background with Tyler, and that was his explicit cue to leave. He loved the sound, of course, and Jack was generous with it, happy to share his joy with anyone who'd take it. But a small, petty part of Jamie hated that it had nothing to do with him, that some stranger was getting to experience it. It made him ache.

If there was a bright side, at least Tyler sounded entertained by him. He was invested in Jack, which was probably the most Jamie could hope for in this situation. If Lucy had to be with someone else, he was relieved it was someone who treated their son well. If that laughter meant Jack was okay, Jamie could deal with the heartache.

But maybe, hopefully, some time away from the city (and from Lucy) would dull the pain.

Jamie looked forward to trying to be happy again.

CHAPTER 3

Neighborhood Watch

EVE

Wed, Jun 25 8:04 PM

Leo Coletti: Can we please talk?

Wed, Jun 25 11:56 PM

Leo Coletti: What the fuck Eve at least answer the phone

Jesus Christ

Here I thought I was the asshole in this relationship

Thu, Jun 26 7:12 AM

Leo Coletti: This is not how you treat someone after five years

Thu, Jun 26 10:18 AM

Daddy: Be safe, cheri mwen. We want you back in one piece.

Daddy: Last night was difficult but necessary. I am proud of you. Bondye Bon!!

Thu, Jun 26 11:09 AM

Daddy: Your mother is upset today. I advise you to call her soon.

Thu, Jun 26 1:48 PM

Maya Baudin: Hey boo! Call me when you get there.

With the sun low in the sky, Eve pulled up to her grandmother's Tennessee mountain home, a small cabin perched within the peaks of the Great Smoky Mountains, a few miles from the northern edge of the national park. The place was more beautiful than seventeen-year-old Eve had cared to remember—she used to hate the rustic feel of the Appalachian-style home, but now it looked like a painting to her, constructed of rich, dark brown logs, surrounded by nothing but trees. The porch jutted out to meet her at the end of a short cobblestone walkway, and the shrubbery along the way, while overgrown, was the brightest and greenest she'd ever seen.

Inside was dusty but spacious, and sparsely decorated, thanks to her mother and aunt claiming all the good pieces for themselves. The only remaining items were a small cherrywood coffee table and an old mustard-colored wool sofa in the living area.

Eve smiled at the fireplace encased in stone below the staircase. She remembered the locals bringing her grandmother firewood, because everyone knew and loved her, and in small towns like Gatlinburg, where there were exactly twenty-one Black people, it wasn't unusual for them all to take care of each other. It was cool for June, so Eve imagined she'd spend many evenings by the hearth, just like she used to.

A narrow flight of steps led up to the bedroom Eve used during her previous nine-month stint there. The full-sized bed remained in the exact same spot, evoking the many nights she'd cry herself to sleep, feeling abandoned by her parents and quite literally sick to her stomach as her belly swelled with a child she would never be able to keep. As a minor act of rebellion, she'd carved her initials in the wooden bedpost; she tittered seeing it there now. Her grandmother rarely went up there, the steps too arduous as she grew older, but Eve would've bet her weight in gold that Hazel Beasley knew about the carving all the same.

"I miss you, lady," Eve said out loud, her words riddled with her contrition.

In the end, Eve didn't call enough. Never came to visit after she got away, too inundated with unpleasant memories to ever consider returning. Her grandmother came to New York twice but hated it as much as teenage Eve had hated Gatlinburg. Hazel had found the city frenetic—which most visitors would likely agree with, but it was especially true for a seventy-year-old woman used to being alone. Twenty years ago, this was the only house for several miles, and Hazel liked it that way. The closest grocery store was a ten-minute drive, and it was just about the only reason she would get into her car. Anything beyond that and she risked crossing paths with all the tourists. Eve would always ask to go down to Dollywood, desperate, like Ariel, to be where the people were. Wanderin' free, etc. But her grandmother, with her aversion to the amusement park crowd, would perpetually refuse. *Ain't nobody takin' you down there with all them folks.*

Now, Eve treasured this empty space. New York City *was* frenetic. Between her parents and Leo, it was far too crowded for her grief. She relished the idea of locking herself away in her grandmother's home and shutting out the world if she wanted to.

And she really wanted to.

Within the hour, Eve had finished unpacking the two carry-on-sized suitcases meant to sustain her for the next few weeks, maybe months. They were full of mostly light sweaters and leggings. She wouldn't need much else to sit around alone, and she'd be headed back to New York before it got unbearably cold.

After finding some candles and matches to get her through the night, Eve briefly considered calling her mother, per her father's request, but she was too tired by the drive and, well, life to feign cordiality. She opted for a quick text, just to let them know she'd arrived safely, but when it didn't go through, she remembered her mother's warning of how bad the reception was up here.

Shit. This was the kind of thing horror movies were made of. Last house on the left, indeed.

Eve roamed the ground floor in search of a bar, maybe two, padding from the kitchen to the master bedroom and back to the front door. She continued down the short staircase of the porch and into the yard, the message not going through until she was nearly at the mailbox. It was soon followed by an influx of missed texts and calls from her friends—most notably her bestie, imploring her to check in.

Defenseless against Maya's overbearing ways, Eve walked into the middle of the street, hoping the signal would somehow improve enough to make a call. Four rings before being met with

Maya's sunny voicemail greeting, and she held the phone close to her face as if it could mimic the feeling of a hug from her friend.

"It's me," Eve spoke after the beep. "I just got here. I'm fine." She sighed at the lie she was telling herself as she surveyed the vacant landscape ahead. "The reception is awful here, so catch me if you can. Love you."

Eve ended the call, stuffed her phone in her pocket, and took off for a walk, wanting to reacquaint herself with the lay of the land. The neighborhood was nearly silent, save for a few chirping birds and leaves whispering in the wind, and as she continued down the road, making her way to the bottom of a steep hill, the faint burble of running water tickled the air. She'd noticed the creek on her way in, but as she came to a bridge in the road, she spotted the small waterfall.

In the distance, the mountain range made for a splendid backdrop to it all. The sky was a crisp blue, the mountains a blanket of forest green beneath it. Eve's friend Brian was an amateur photographer, and he would've had a field day soaking up this place. She *almost* took out her phone to take some pictures for him but wasn't ready for the conversation it would prompt.

Instead, Eve followed the bridge's path, allowing it to take her straight down to the creek. There was a charming little painted sign on the way that read "Fishin' Hole," which made her grin.

Eve tiptoed through the high grass until she was at the edge of the moss-colored water. She took a seat where the grass was the shortest, closed her eyes, and inhaled the fresh air, the rippling sound filling her mind. And for a few quiet minutes, she let herself believe that it wasn't utterly reprehensible to leave New York the way she did.

A spectator might've assumed she was meditating. A previous version of herself probably would have been praying. *Bless me, Father, for I have sinned. My last confession was seventeen years ago. I led a man to believe I was going to marry him because I was too scared to be alone and then I dumped him unceremoniously because I ran out of the bandwidth to pretend.*

Eve was thankful when her phone began to vibrate. Maya, as always, a welcome distraction.

"I'm not about to be playing phone tag with you for the next however many months," Maya greeted her.

Eve laughed as she wiped her eyes. "Unless I'm supposed to build a cell phone tower, I'm not sure what you want me to do." On second thought, Maya probably would expect as much.

"I'mma need you to share your location with me indefinitely, just in case you get locked in somebody's basement," Maya said.

"Absolutely the fuck not. Next thing I know, you'll be moving in here with me," Eve said as she hiked her way up the hill back to her grandmother's cabin. "And there's no one around here to put me in their basement anyway."

"That makes it even worse!"

"No, actually, you're right. You know it's only white people in this part of the state." In fact, Eve would've been smart to just stay inside. Even if the neighborhood was empty, she was not in New York anymore. She couldn't go exploring some random neighborhood in the middle of Bumfuck, Tennessee, and think her Black ass was safe.

"And you don't think you need to share your location?"

They were both joking, supposedly, but Eve did put her friend on speakerphone while she updated her settings for the time being. In the process, she made sure to remove Leo from the list of family members who could potentially find her iPhone.

"You know I don't even agree with this trip in the first place, so unless you want me to harass you the entire time you're there . . ."

"I'm sharing it," Eve nearly shouted into the phone.

As she returned to her temporary home, it seemed she would be eating her own words as she spotted a lone figure lurking near the righthand side of her small cabin.

"What the fuck," Eve mumbled, stopping in her tracks. She checked her signal to make sure she'd be able to keep Maya on the line. "Girl, there's someone at this house."

"At *your* house?" Maya sounded more panicked than Eve felt. "Bitch, see? What did I tell you?"

"Shhhut up," Eve hissed, taking her off speakerphone as she tried to get a better view of the culprit. It was a willowy white guy with far too much hair on his face and head; he looked like he'd spent most of his time in the sun, his peachy skin bearing a golden glow. His T-shirt and jeans were tattered but clung to his body as if they knew it well. "I think he might be homeless," Eve said.

"Girl, he was probably staying at your grandma's and you done kicked him out. Squatters have rights, you know."

"Girl, shut up." Eve immediately tensed when the presumed vagrant spotted her and began walking toward her. "Shit, he sees me."

"Maybe you should run."

Eve strongly considered it, but where was she supposed to go? "Stay on the phone," she said.

"Can I help you?" the man asked.

Eve was taken aback by his manner, talking to her as if *he* owned the place. She peered at him as he moseyed her way, and something about his gait made her question her initial assumptions. He didn't seem to be lacking anything—certainly not confidence.

"I think I should be asking you that," she said, deciding to match his gall.

"Well this is private property, ma'am. Are you lost?"

Now there's a loaded question. "I'm aware this is private property," Eve said. And suddenly, she wondered if she'd gotten something wrong. She was positive she had the right house, but maybe her aunt had sold the property and hadn't bothered to tell anyone. This man seemed so self-assured, he really had her questioning her sanity. "Are you saying you own this place?"

"A friend of mine does," he said. "Or . . . did."

Eve frowned.

"So can I help you with anything? Are you looking for the park?"

"Was this 'friend' of yours Hazel Beasley?" Eve asked.

He eyed her as if to question a story she hadn't even told yet. "You know her?"

"I'm her granddaughter."

"Oh shit." The skepticism on this strange man's face seemed to recede, replaced by recognition, like they'd known each other in some other life. "Evie," he said. "Of course."

It was Eve's turn to be wary, responding with narrowed eyes, unreasonably rattled by the idea that this person could've known her grandmother. Caught off guard by the familiarity of it all. Her grandmother loved to add an *ie* to anyone's name she could. Her mother was Joanie; her aunt, Annie; and Eve was, well . . . Evie. She'd forgotten about it until now. She'd forgotten so much. And she liked it better that way.

"Eve," she said.

"I'm Jamie."

The man moved closer to extend his hand, and Eve ignored everything in her that wanted to retreat. She returned the handshake and even felt some measure of comfort when their eyes finally locked. His were the color of the sky, and she imagined there might've been an attractive guy hiding somewhere under all that hair. He had a Southern drawl that managed to make her feel warm, not unlike her grandmother, and she fought the urge to smile.

"So why are you lurking around my grandmother's house?" Eve asked, her typical New York brusqueness punctuating her words.

"I wasn't lurking," he said. "I was surveying. I've been taking care of the place for the last year or so. Mowing the lawn, pruning the hedges . . ."

Eve scanned the yard, taking special note of the grass hitting their shins, and stared back at him. "You're doing a great job."

Jamie grinned in a way that made his eyes twinkle. "I know. I haven't been around the last few months, and I'm sorry about that."

Eve averted his gleaming gaze then, mostly out of guilt, because she was the last person who could blame someone for not being around. "Well. Don't worry about it. I'm here now."

"You're gonna cut the grass?"

"Are you implying I can't?"

"No, ma'am. I just didn't think Miss Hazel had a lawn mower."

Eve hadn't considered that part—she never had a lawn to worry about in Brooklyn—but refused to show it. "Well . . . I'm sure I can buy one."

"At least borrow mine," Jamie offered. "I can drive it down here for you now."

Eve was reluctant to let this strange man with the smiling eyes any further into her life than she already had, loath to give the impression that she was friendly or anything like it. "I'll pay you," she said. "How much does something like that usually cost?"

"For the whole acre?" He looked around and shrugged casually. "Seventy bucks an hour, and it'll take about four hours."

Eve nearly choked on her tongue. That would really cut into her budget, considering she wouldn't be collecting much of a paycheck for the next few months. "I thought it was supposed to be cheaper in the South," she said.

"Well, I was gonna do it for free until you and your pride jumped in."

Eve had forgotten Maya was still waiting on the phone until she detected the faint but unmistakable sound of her cackling in the background. "I hate you so much," she muttered.

"I'm sorry?" Jamie asked.

Eve shook her head. "You're welcome to do whatever you want. But don't feel obligated." She was already heading toward the porch, desperate to get away from this man and whatever he'd done to turn her into a bumbling idiot. "I have to get back inside."

"Right. Well, I'm sorry about all the confusion," Jamie said, seeming to detect her unease. "It's rare to see another face but mine up here, so I thought you were trespassing."

Eve found that encouraging—she wouldn't have to worry about park visitors wandering around. "I'll be sure to stay out of your way," she said.

"Oh, that wasn't what I meant—"

"You're welcome to stay out of my way then."

"Got it," Jamie said, nodding. Though that damn twinkle told her he was more amused than offended by her statement, which, in turn, piqued her curiosity more than it irritated her.

"Well, if you need me in the meantime, I'm right down the hill," he said.

Eve only responded with a slight wave as she realized the big cabin she'd spotted earlier when she sat at the creek belonged to Jamie. She watched him walk away, because in the two minutes they'd spent together, she realized she enjoyed his walk. And for the short time that she was in his presence, that overwhelming sense of grief seemed to take a break.

She unenthusiastically returned to her phone call, finding Maya still giggling. "Why are you like this?"

"I should be asking you that," Maya said. "Not you out here embarrassing the whole bloodline."

"He caught me off guard."

"It's hard to believe somebody gave you three whole degrees. What was that?" Maya continued, still snickering as she spoke.

"He caught me off guard," Eve said, louder this time, and she hoped Jamie had gotten too far away to hear. She hated the idea of him knowing he'd managed to fluster her and, seemingly, without trying.

"Well, he sounds MAGA, so it's probably best if you keep your distance anyway."

"Looked it, too," Eve said. But if he really had known her grandma well enough to recognize her, she trusted that he wasn't. "I think he's harmless, though."

She hoped so anyway. She could see Jamie being annoying. Maybe even showing up at her door unannounced, obtrusive in the way that Southern people mistook for friendly. But beyond that, he seemed innocuous. Even safe. And she looked forward to staying as far away from him as possible.

CHAPTER 4

Mindful

JAMIE

Thu, Jun 26 3:01 PM

Lucy Ewen: Hey you around?

Jamie Gallagher: Am I around in Nashville? No.

Lucy Ewen: I had a favor to ask.

Jamie Gallagher: What?

Lucy Ewen: Would you mind terribly if I kept Jack an extra day next week?

Lucy Ewen: I know you only have weekends right now and here I go cutting those short. But Jack overheard me talking about the 4th of July kayak race and of course he wants to go.

Lucy Ewen: I'd hate to disappoint him.

Jamie Gallagher: Of course you would.

Lucy Ewen: I'm so sorry for the short notice.

Lucy Ewen: You can keep him until Tues if that works for your schedule.

Jamie Gallagher: It's fine. I'll see you then.

Lucy Ewen: You're the best! See you then.

Lucy Ewen: And try to have fun with your free time. :)

Lucy's patronizing texts should have annoyed Jamie, but it was borderline funny at this point. It hadn't even been a week and she was already infringing on the court's orders. Jamie's friends used to refer to Lucy as a "habitual line-stepper," which had just amused him at the time. It wasn't until the breakup that he recognized the painful accuracy, how her lack of boundaries should have been a red flag long ago. But behind rose-colored glasses . . . well, everyone knows how that goes.

But Gatlinburg seemed like the best place to try getting over her. His airy cabin had always been his place of respite, a space where he could be quiet without feeling strange about it. And he needed that now more than ever. Lucy had grown bored with him over the years, and Jamie would find himself wanting to be more adventurous for her. But in truth, it was draining. Antithetical to his introverted tendencies. It was much easier to escape to this place when they were in the throes of their shitty relationship. Up here in the woods, he could just be.

But he hadn't been out here in months now. Mostly because he'd been busy with Jack and with custody hearings, which didn't leave him with the desire to enjoy anything, much less the time to do so. But there was another piece of it that he hadn't quite considered until he was back in the neighborhood and flooded with memories of his time there: It wasn't the same without Hazel Beasley.

He had such a vivid memory of their first meeting, nearly a decade prior, when he got the keys to his place. Miss Hazel was walking the neighborhood with her little cairn terrier, Tip, and stopped by to tell Jamie he better not come around making a lot of noise. She said this was a quiet neighborhood, and come hell or high water, it would stay that way. Jamie understood why she was dubious of some twenty-five-year-old white kid appearing and possibly disturbing her peace, but he assured her the most noise he'd make would be sawing wood.

They became fast friends when he volunteered to make her a bear box to keep her trash cans safe between garbage pickups, and as a thank-you, she made him a peach cobbler that he still dreamed about from time to time. Miss Hazel loved baseball, and although Jamie had had a messy breakup with the sport, she was the one person he didn't mind discussing it with; they'd reminisce about how much they loved the Atlanta Braves in their heyday, and they relished in the team's recent resurgence. She met Jack only once, but she often sent Jamie home with something for him: a blanket she'd knitted, some cookies she'd made, an old book her granddaughter used to love. When Tip died, Jamie buried him for her. And they drank some gin and sat quietly at her kitchen table while she mourned her beloved pet.

He and Hazel Beasley were friends, and he missed her. He

hadn't been back since he learned she was gone. Not until now. And he didn't know whether it was some cosmic interference that had him cross paths with Hazel's granddaughter within just a few minutes of his grand return, but he appreciated it all the same. Evie was just as beautiful as Miss Hazel often said. And she made him smile. All of it was a more than welcome surprise when he figured he would be nothing but alone for the next several days.

Jamie hoped *he* wasn't line-stepping by showing up at Eve's home unannounced after she specifically told him to keep out of her way. He had no intention of staying, but he did feel he owed her a better welcome than the one they started with. And the last time he decided to be a good neighbor to the person living there, he ended up making a good friend.

When Eve opened the door, Jamie wondered if he'd interrupted a nap, her glasses and sloppy bun denoting coziness. "You're back," she said flatly.

"I come bearing gifts," Jamie announced. He'd gone down to Food City to pick up some staples for himself for the next couple of weeks, and he considered Eve might need some of those same items.

"What . . . is this?" she asked as he handed over the first of several shopping bags. "If this is some kind of weird scam, I'm not into it."

Jamie chuckled at her skepticism as she attempted to return the bag. "You really are from New York, huh?"

"Excuse me?"

"I just assumed you didn't have food or electricity since this place has been empty for so long. Thought I'd bring you some things to get you through the night."

She looked taken aback by the small gesture, but she did finally accept another one of the proffered totes. "You can come in," she said, opening the door wider for him. "Thank you."

Jamie was tickled at how unenthused she was, and he appreciated that she didn't bother to pretend. "I hope I'm not overstepping," he said as he entered the dim cabin. But he paused, realizing only then how off-putting it may have been for some random guy to keep showing up at her grandmother's home. She had no way of knowing whether he and his intentions were benign. "I can just leave this at the door if you want," he said, careful not to move too far inside.

"It's fine," Eve said. "I didn't have anything to eat, so you were right."

Charily, Jamie headed for the kitchen and set the woven bags on the table. He looked around at the familiar space as he fished the receipt from his pocket, noting how different the room looked without Miss Hazel in it. "This is a list of everything I got." He handed over the paper as if it might be the key to her trusting him. "I paid in cash, so you can get a refund for anything you might not want."

"I'm not gonna do that," she said, though she did take a moment to peruse the receipt. "Why did you get so many sandwiches?"

"Well, I figured they were the best bet, assuming you don't have any gas to cook with. So I got ham. And then I thought you might not eat pork, so I got turkey. And then I thought you might not eat meat, so I got the tuna and the egg salad. And if you're a vegan, I'm sorry. There's plenty of fruit."

With that, Eve released a full giggle, instantly brightening the room and Jamie's own muted mood. "That's insane, you know," she said.

"Just tryin' to be accommodating."

Eve began to rifle through the bag containing the assortment of deli sandwiches, plucking out the turkey and tuna for herself. "I do eat meat. But I don't have a working refrigerator yet, so you can take the rest of these."

"Shit, I should've brought you a cooler."

"I think you've done more than enough," she replied, continuing to unpack the things in the bag she presumably wanted to keep. She paused when she got to a small, unadorned birthday cake. "Is this for me, too?"

Jamie shrugged. "I figured you can't really go wrong with yellow cake." He felt a twinge of satisfaction when she removed the container from the bag and set it in the middle of the table.

"I prefer chocolate, but . . . you're not wrong."

Jamie nodded, surveying the room one more time as it grew darker by the minute, dusk settling over their little corner of the mountains, and he inwardly cursed himself for not thinking to bring batteries for flashlights. "Do you have candles?"

"I do." She was staring at him like she was waiting for him to annoy her with another question.

"I just wanna make sure you have what you need."

"I didn't say anything."

"Your face is saying everything."

Eve cocked her head. "You want me to perform for you? I told you I appreciate it."

Jamie nodded, and he hoped he wasn't suddenly blushing. "You're right. I'm gonna go now."

"You sure? You don't wanna give me some cash to have a pizza delivered?"

"If you want a pizza, I can . . ."

"Jesus," she sighed. "I understand that I perhaps didn't give the impression earlier today, but I am a full-grown woman."

Jamie stepped back and raised his hands in surrender. "Sorry."

"You don't have to apologize. But you don't have to save me either."

"I promise I won't try to help you again."

She smiled that smile again. "Good."

"I'll see you around," he said, turning back toward the door. He really wanted to leave her the rest of those sandwiches, but he ignored his instincts in favor of her instructions and opened the door. He was surprised when Eve stopped him before he could take a step.

"Jamie?"

He liked the way she said his name. He spun on his heel to see her face one more time as she spoke. "Yeah?"

"Thank you. Seriously."

"You're more than welcome," he said, grinning. But then, the tiny glint in her eyes reminded him of something. "Can I add one more thing?"

"Oh my god." She was shaking her head, but Jamie could tell there was levity wrapped up in her exasperation. "What is it?"

"Keep an eye out for the fireflies."

"What?"

"The fireflies," he repeated. "This is the time of year for the synchronous light show at Elkmont. I talked to some folks at the grocery store, and they confirmed it hasn't happened yet."

"Oh, yeah." Eve's dark brown eyes flashed with a hint of cognizance, maybe an old, fond memory. "I thought that usually happened in spring."

Jamie shrugged. "Climate change?"

"Likely culprit," Eve agreed, and the weary sigh that followed felt like an allusion to the profuse weight of the world these days.

"At any rate, you oughta have a good view of the mountain from your backyard," he said. "Won't be the best view from the distance, but you'll see the waves. It's a beautiful sight."

Eve replied with a subtle nod and a slow smile. "That sounds nice . . ."

"It is," he said.

Jamie would have been fine on his own in Gatlinburg. He'd been looking forward to it, even. A summer of remembering what it felt like to be still. Away from the business. Time off from Dad duty. Maybe get reacquainted with the guy who willingly wore those rose-colored glasses way back when. Reunite with the optimist who disappeared in the fog of the last year.

He didn't know what Eve's plans were. He didn't know whether she'd be receptive to spending even another minute in his company. But either way, it was nice to know that he wasn't alone up here.

"Have a good night, Eve."

CHAPTER 5

Hateithere

EVE

Hey, Ma." Eve greeted her mother with a little wave despite the FaceTime screen displaying only the bottom left half of her mother's face. Like a typical Boomer, she held her phone much too close to her mouth, using it as a speakerphone instead of a camera. But Eve did get a few glimpses of her mom's Sunday best, from her shamrock green dress to her favorite tortoise-print cat-eye specs.

"Hello, Eve," Joan returned loudly. Her tone was already a combination of cross and concerned. "Are you okay?"

"I am," Eve said, glancing back at her surroundings. She wasn't quite *comfortable* in the foreign space that was her grandmother's cabin—not yet—but it still didn't feel like a mistake. And even if it did, she was unlikely to let her mother know. "It's quiet here, but—"

"Well, that's what you wanted, right?"

"Right," Eve said. "That's what I was going to say."

"Well, the way you disappeared, I assumed you'd be more excited about your little trip. Since you clearly couldn't wait to leave."

Eve refrained from reacting, going so far as to cover her mouth with her hand as she weighed her response. "I am excited," she eventually said—unconvincingly. "I'm just . . . tired."

"You've been there almost three days now. You haven't gotten any rest?"

"Not much. Got in late Thursday, and I spent most of the last two days trying to get set up and clean up."

"Are you saying your grandmother's home was messy? It shouldn't have been. In fact, I'm certain we left it pristine."

"Ma, no." Eve sighed in an effort to hold on to her composure. But between her mother's expression of her dismay and her own convoluted feelings surrounding being back in Gatlinburg, Eve was finding it difficult to appear unbothered. "I'm saying no one's been here in over a year and it was dusty. There's no food or amenities. There was work to do."

"That's why I offered to come down with you and help you get set up. But again, I know you were in a rush."

"I'm so sorry that my overactive emotions ruined your dinner," Eve mumbled. "I'm fine."

"You don't like it there," Joan said, her knowing tone feeling even more condescending than usual.

"I'm fine."

"You can come back home," she said. "You don't have to force yourself to stay there just because you left the way you did."

"I haven't been here long enough to know how I feel about it," Eve insisted. It was entirely possible she was saying it more for herself than trying to convince her mother of anything, but she could not let her mother's arrogance trick her into thinking it was already time to give up on whatever this plan was. "I'm gonna stick it out for at least a week," she said.

"If you feel like you can't go home to your husband, you can always come here," Joan appended. "You're not alone, sweetheart."

Eve exhaled sharply and dropped her phone onto the kitchen table. Her mother was clearly uninterested in anything she had to say. The fact that she insisted on calling Leo her husband when they were only engaged, and Eve had effectively ended their relationship altogether . . . "I *want* to be alone. That's the whole point." She was roughly two sentences from shouting.

"I'm sorry," Joan said. "I was under the impression that the point was to write. Forgive me for being confused."

"You're forgiven."

"I just want you to know that you can change your mind. Nothing has happened that can't be undone."

With her phone on the table, Eve felt slightly more comfortable rolling her eyes now. "Where's Dad?" she asked instead. While he was undoubtedly confused by her actions as well, he at least wasn't acting like a dunce about it.

"He's out back tending to his little garden," Joan said, chuckling as she so often did whenever the topic of Roger's favorite hobby arose. In the warmer months, he spent more time with his catmints, hydrangeas, and Japanese cypresses than at work or with his wife. "You want to talk to him?"

"If he's not too busy," Eve said. She picked up her phone in anticipation of seeing her father, thinking—or perhaps hoping—that his quieting presence could be valuable in the moment. She'd been seesawing between sadness and anger since she arrived—save for the few moments when the guy down the street distracted her—and talking to her mother only sharpened those feelings. She wished she had the courage to say what she really wanted to say, to hold her mother accountable for all the awful memories Eve had attached to this place. But she didn't have the energy to even try to argue. And her father tended to bring down the temperature and act as a mediator between them.

Eve watched the screen as her mother and her phone whooshed through their home, and she tried not to feel homesick for a place where she had no desire to be. It was a mere matter of seconds before he appeared in the frame, properly holding the camera an appropriate few inches from his face.

"Hi, my darling girl," Roger greeted her warmly, a big smile to match.

"Hi, Daddy." Eve waved at him, his happiness managing to affect her marginally. Hearing his beautiful Kreyol-tinged accent always made her feel like a kid again, leaving her grinning as she gazed at him. "Just wanted to show proof of life," she said.

"Well, that part is debatable, but it is good to see your face," he joked. "I am sure you are doing better than your fiancé."

Eve knew he was kidding, as was his way; her father straddled the line between stern and droll incredibly well. But she was not in the headspace to confront her actions, even jocularly. "Daddy . . ."

"Oh, lighten up. You cannot be so bold as to leave that man sitting dumfounded in our home and think I will not rib you about it."

"Okay, well, that's fine. I didn't want anything anyway—"

Before Eve could complete her goodbye spiel, her father cut her off to go on his typical Sunday tangent about the people who annoyed him at Mass that day. It was funny how church was supposed to be about betterment of spirit, yet he turned into a gossiping old goat whenever he spent more than an hour there. And she was supposed to feel bad about severing her ties with it?

"Deacon Withers supposedly took over at the Kennedy Community Center, he is supervising our food pantry, and he is leader of the altar servers. But my question is how he has all of these jobs when he does none of them well?" Roger's laugh came from deep in his belly, as it often did when he amused himself, as his smile, contrasting with his ebony skin, lit up the screen. "I am sure you have people like that in your department, hmm?"

Eve was likely that person in her department. "I do," she said.

"I shall pray for us both then," he said, still chuckling. "By the way, have you watched *Lupin* yet?"

"Daddy, I'm the one who told *you* to watch *Lupin*."

"Are you sure? I don't think so. It was recommended to me by Deacon Brown."

"Yes. Several years ago." With that, Eve effectively checked out of the conversation as he went on about catching up with the series over the weekend. She reached for the little non-birthday birthday cake Jamie brought her the other day, not bothering to cut it into any discernible slices or even find a fork. She snatched a chunk using her thumb and forefinger like the depressed mess she was. Though, to be fair, the cake was quite tasty for a grocery store variety, rivaled only by Publix, in her estimation. Eve began to reminisce on her college days, and the genuine delight that was their regular escapades to Publix. A couple of Pub subs, some fried chicken, and a pound cake would make her whole weekend. She made a mental note to research the nearest location now that she was back in the South.

In the background, Eve could hear the faint sounds of a lawn mower, and she assumed it was Jamie tending to his yard after taking care of hers. She wondered how long it would take him to find his way back to her door, and what excuse he would bring with him. She'd take pretty much anything that would get her off this phone.

As Roger went on to regale her with his tales of solving Saturday's *NYT* crossword, Eve would nod every thirty seconds or so and then submit a well-placed "Mm-hmm" or "Wow, that's crazy" to give the impression she was engaged in whatever he was saying, but it was becoming impossible to hide her boredom. Her lack of focus was getting to be a problem. And she didn't know whether she could blame it on her parents—and Leo, for that matter—or if this was something else to add to her ever-growing list of neuroses.

"What is that you're eating?" Roger asked, just as her mind had wandered all the way out of their conversation.

"Cake," Eve replied with a mouth full of it.

"She doesn't have any real food in that house?" her mother asked in the background. "Tell her to get some real food."

"Your mother says you need some real food."

"Yes, I heard," Eve muttered. "I have real food." It was a lie; she had been living solely on what Jamie brought over Thursday, too lazy to actually fill her refrigerator after going through the trouble of turning on the electricity for it.

"She looks like she hasn't been eating," Joan said.

"Your mother says you look like you haven't been eating."

"I heard," Eve said tersely, utterly unamused by this tag-team shtick they were doing. She wasn't sure where mothers perfected the art of death by a thousand cuts—probably from their mothers—but now that her father was playing along, it was definitely time to go. Eve surreptitiously swiped to the Wi-Fi option on her phone and disabled it, knowing her weak cellular signal would end the call before she could hear another passive-aggressive word.

She did, however, take the time to text them and apologize for the mishap. Because, thanks to her mother, she was also learned in the art of passive aggression.

Sun, Jun 29 10:56 AM

Eve Ambroise: Sorry about that! The wifi went out! I can call you back when it returns

Mom: No need. We are going to brunch with Harriett and Calvin in a bit.

Mom: You make sure you eat something. Will talk soon.

Eve Ambroise: I will ♥

CHAPTER 6

Roll With It

JAMIE

It was a cool and overcast Thursday, just before 9:00 a.m., when Jamie pulled up to his favorite breakfast spot, Crockett's Breakfast Camp. Despite the unfortunate name, and the tacky faux cabin decor, it had the best food in eastern Tennessee, and when he was in town, he always made sure to stop by for some pecan-smoked bacon and a fried cinnamon roll. They did no favors to his waistline, which was only increasingly difficult to control the farther he got from thirty, but he'd decided a couple of years ago they were worth the extra inches. Luckily, he had no one to impress these days anyway.

When he walked into Crockett's, he immediately spotted Eve, as she was literally too beautiful to miss, her skin dark, like midnight, but rivaling the sun in brilliance, and her hair in long braids that fell past her waist. It had been almost a week since they met, but he'd thought of her often in the intervening days. He instantly and instinctively smiled at the sight of her in line at the register. He'd kept his promise to stay out of her way, but seeing her in public, purely by coincidence, seemed like a good excuse to initiate another conversation.

Jamie called out to her a couple of times before tapping her on the shoulder, receiving a confounded scowl when she turned his way. She removed one of her AirPods when she finally seemed to recognize him.

"Oh," Eve said, holding on to a smile. "Hey."

He'd obviously startled her and took a step back to give her some space. "Sorry," he said, and gestured to the earbud she was clutching. "I'd been calling your name, but I guess you couldn't hear me." He wondered what song had her so engrossed. She seemed like someone who would put on Sade for a day like this.

Eve only stared at him. "Did you . . . need something?"

"No, I just . . . It's good to see you again." He hoped he wasn't coming off too eager. He was a pretty low-key guy, but she had a way of making him feel like he was constantly doing too much.

"Well, I'll . . . probably see you again at some point," she said plainly as she turned back to the register.

"I'm sure you will." Jamie smiled at the back of her head wryly. If she was uninterested in furthering the conversation, he would leave it at that, but his eyes stayed on her as she went through the motions of making (or rather, avoiding) small talk with Jill, the cashier. She was kinda awkward, closed off in a way that he didn't quite understand but that he liked. The opposite of Hazel Beasley, but he could see the older woman in her when he looked long enough.

". . . They say it might get up to about seventy today," Jill was saying to her, oblivious to Eve's indifference. "If it's seventy up here, I can only imagine how hot it is at lower elevation. Probably ninety-somethin' down there."

"Well, it is almost July," Eve said.

"How long are you visiting for?" the cashier asked. Jamie's ears perked up as he waited for Eve's reply.

"I'll be here awhile."

"Oh, yeah?"

"That's the plan," Eve said.

It wasn't until she finished the transaction that Jill asked the question clearly sitting on her lips, her eyes searching for the answer on their own. "Aren't you Hazel's girl? From New York City?"

Eve replied with a curt "No" before practically running away once her receipt was in her possession.

"She's like that with everyone," Jamie said, stepping forward to place his order. "Don't take it personally."

"I wasn't going to," Jill said, eyeing him now. "People in pain aren't always the best communicators."

Jamie raised an eyebrow, wondering if she knew something he didn't. It would be an understatement to call Jill nosy; it was entirely possible she had Eve's entire backstory in her pocket. But there was also a melancholy about Eve that was perhaps more noticeable than he thought. At least it wasn't just in his mind. "I guess that's true." He was perusing the take-out menu when he noticed his neighbor's debit card in the reader.

"Can't remember the last time I saw you here on a weekday," Jill said as he gazed out of the exit. "Everything okay with *you*?"

Jamie kind of enjoyed that Jill couldn't help herself from prying. It was a hallmark of tiny towns like Gatlinburg, charming when it wasn't annoying. "Everything's fine," he said. "I'll have a fried cinnamon roll and a small coffee."

She smiled at him sweetly. "No bacon today?"

"And bacon," he said, glancing outside again. He handed

over a twenty-dollar bill and grabbed Eve's card. "I'll be right back." He rushed out of the restaurant to catch Eve before she could take off, spotting her at the back of the moderately full lot, unlocking Hazel's champagne-colored Honda Accord. "Eve," he called out, careful not to surprise her yet again. But as he reached the car, he realized that she was leaning against the vehicle for support. "You . . . okay?"

"What do you want?" Her tone still lacked any of the playful indignation of their introduction.

"You left this inside." Jamie gingerly handed over the red, orange, and yellow Wells Fargo card but retreated like a skittish puppy when Eve dropped her bag to the ground and appeared to double over in pain. He could hear her mutter a series of expletives as she rested her hands on her knees and shook her head. "Eve . . ." He said her name as delicately as he could, warning her that he was moving closer.

"Don't touch me," she said.

"I won't." He halted in his tracks and watched as she frantically tried to remove the hoodie she was wearing. "I just wanna know if you're all right."

Eve tried to cover her face, but he'd already caught the tears rolling down her cheeks as she began to hyperventilate.

"Can I help you take this off?" Jamie remained calm, recognizing the signs of a panic attack. He'd been through this a few times with Jack, and it never got any easier watching his kid devolve into a fit of sweats and trembles while gasping for air. Especially when they seemed to coincide with some of his worst fights with Lucy. Luckily, Eve seemed amenable as he assisted in getting her sweatshirt over her head.

"I feel like I'm not breathing right," she said through tears.

She was massaging her throat with her fingertips as if trying to coax air from it. "What the fuck?"

"I know," Jamie said. "It's scary, but I can help you get through it." When she didn't protest, he moved to stand directly in front of her, taking care not to touch her any more than necessary. "Close your eyes and try to think about three things you can hear right now. My voice. The birds. That car pulling off." When Eve nodded, he gave her a moment to focus before moving on. "Now, put your hand flat on your stomach. Just above your belly button." She immediately followed his instruction. "And I want you to take a big, long inhale through your nose, and then exhale slowly . . . *slowly* . . . through your mouth." He nodded along as she completed the task, her eyes squeezed shut as she drew in big gulps of air and softly released them. "Just breathe," he said. He wanted to wipe her tears, but that wasn't a boundary worth crossing just as she was regaining her bearings. "Keep breathing."

When Eve's breaths seemed to quicken after a few minutes, Jamie interjected again. "Think about two things you can smell right now," he said. "Think about something you can taste. Whatever you just had for breakfast."

Eve nodded again, seeming to focus on those tiny diversions until the worst of the attack began to subside. She kept her right hand on her stomach and was wiping her face with her left when she finally reopened her eyes.

"You okay?" Jamie asked.

"I think so." She continued to rest against her grandmother's car, which left him dubious of her claim.

"You wanna go back inside and sit down?"

"No," she said. She looked down at her feet as if in deep contemplation before speaking again. "That's never happened before."

"This was your first panic attack?"

She looked like she wanted to argue but didn't. "It's never been so debilitating before, I guess. If what I've been having are panic attacks, they were much more composed. Elevated heart rate. Maybe tingling or shivering. But this literally felt like my throat was closing up."

Jamie wished he had something useful to offer, but nothing would allay just how terrifying that must have been. "Did something trigger it?"

Eve stared out to the horizon as she shook her head. "I don't know. Feels like everything about this place is a trigger."

He wondered what that meant; he also knew better than to ask. "You sure you're okay? You wanna go to a hospital, maybe?"

She seemed to consider it, at least. "Is that little one still in Pigeon Forge? I think it was called Crestwood . . . something?"

"I haven't heard of it," Jamie said. "Closest one to here is Covenant over in Sevierville."

Eve made a face, and he had a pretty good idea of why, considering the demographics of the area. At least on this side of town, visitors to Dollywood and the national park gave the illusion of some diversity.

"I can take you to Knoxville if that would make you more comfortable," he said.

"No offense. Truly. I appreciate you talking me down," Eve said. She finally stood up without the aid of her grandmother's car. "But that would make me exponentially more *un*comfortable."

"Understood." Jamie extended a small smile and a bit more

space now that she seemed beyond the attack, at least. "But I wouldn't feel right just leaving you here like this. So what's our move?"

"*Our* move?" She matched his grin with one of her own, and all at once, it felt like the sun was shining on their dreary day. "So in a situation where *I* have a panic attack, *your* comfort trumps mine? Is that what's happening here?"

"I'm afraid so." Jamie was prepared to go head-to-head if she wanted, as it was what he enjoyed most about their first interaction. And if she was in the mood to banter, maybe he didn't have to worry about her as much as he presumed. But he also hoped, as his smile grew wider, too, that she recognized he was joking and wasn't truly trying to encroach on her boundaries.

"In that case, I guess I could afford to go back inside and sit down for a few minutes," Eve said. "I assume you came here to have breakfast and not tend to a crazy lady."

"I did." Jamie motioned toward the restaurant entrance, cuing her to go ahead of him. "Lucky for us, I can do both."

CHAPTER 7

All Shook Up

EVE

Much to Eve's chagrin, she was relieved Jamie had been around to keep her panic attack from spiraling into an all-out war in her brain. Even more to her chagrin, she enjoyed having some company after nearly a week of spending her days with only herself. Ostensibly, it was what she wanted—to be alone—but that came with the sobering realization that alone was distressingly lonely. And Jamie appearing practically out of thin air seemed like the universe's way of throwing her a bone.

As much as she hated that he'd seen her in such a vulnerable state, it couldn't hurt to have someone give a shit about her well-being. Someone other than Maya and her parents, all of them a two-hour flight away.

It was why she returned to the kitschy diner with the pushy cashier and sat in silence while Jamie made his way through his breakfast. Eve had a few sips of coffee before determining that the caffeine may have contributed to her hysteria in the first place, and she decided to just people watch. The number of kids in the area seemed endless. But then, she was the dumbass who moved to a place known for its parks. Gatlinburg was a humble town of maybe four thousand people, but visitors came in droves. Millions every year. Eve hadn't considered it until it was too late.

When Jamie asked to take her home, she didn't protest. Eve wasn't particularly comfortable with driving anyway—she only learned because she needed to get around in college, and Atlanta's public transportation was . . . lacking, to put it nicely. But if she had it her way, she would never get behind a wheel again. It was anxiety inducing on its own, and doubly so in the mountains, with the threat of another panic attack looming over her.

Sitting in the passenger seat of Jamie's Chevy truck, Eve found the roar of his engine rather agitating, and the butter-soft seats the opposite. His car was old—old enough to be in high school, if she had to guess—but it was well cared for, the cab so spotless she worried about touching anything. He had one of those Little Trees air fresheners hanging from the rearview, reminding her of New York in a way she didn't mind. Her father drove a taxi as a side hustle when she was younger, and she could still recall the aroma of citrus and bergamot that dwelled in his vehicle. Jamie's was the standard pine scent, which fit into the box of what little she knew about him. He was Classic Coke. Original Levi's 501s. Vintage.

"How you doing over there?" Jamie asked.

Despite the noise of the car, Eve had gotten comfortable enough to close her eyes and was on her way to a light sleep when Jamie's voice startled her alert. "I was fine until you woke me up," she said.

"I figured you might've just been pretending to sleep so you wouldn't have to make conversation."

Eve wanted to be annoyed that he thought so little of her, even if it was absolutely something she would do. "We don't know each other well enough for you to be talking this much shit," she said.

Jamie smiled in that way of his. She could see the mirth in his eyes just from his profile. "I guess you really are all right," he said.

As they fell back into a comfortable silence, Eve resorted to scrolling through her phone, mindlessly liking everything that popped up on her Instagram feed. She forgot that it was a signal to people that she was alive and well enough for social media, thereby prompting a couple of direct messages from friends whose texts she had ignored. Jamie turned his radio to some station playing an old Outkast song, leaving her wondering if he was like those Uber drivers who set their music to hip-hop whenever a Black person set foot in their car. She never complained, because, well, the playlists usually slapped, but she was never not at least slightly annoyed by it.

"You can play whatever you usually listen to," Eve said.

"And what makes you think this isn't what I usually listen to?" Without thinking, she eyed him and he laughed. "I'm thirty-four and grew up in Memphis. I listen to Outkast."

She supposed that was fair. Just because Leo only liked jazz—or pretended to—didn't mean every white guy she came across was the same.

"I probably know more about Outkast than you do, New York," Jamie added. He was instigating, but she was going to take the bait anyway.

"Not you trying to play me. I went to school in Atlanta. Where Outkast was *born*."

He glanced at her as if impressed. "Is that right?"

Eve shrugged. Her time at Spelman was nothing to write

home about. She was a mess for three of her four years. But it was where she met Maya. And where she learned to hone her flair for the dramatic. "The start of my dramaturgical journey," she said. "And my lifelong affair with André Benjamin."

"Well, the truth is, I just turned on the radio because the only CD I have in the car right now is the *Encanto* soundtrack."

She chuckled at the idea of still using CDs in the year 2025. "You know, most people have music on their phones nowadays."

"Well, I'm not most people," Jamie said. He pulled out a little LG flip phone as proof, which made Eve smile so hard she started giggling.

"Wow . . ."

"It does what I need it to do."

"Unless you need to listen to something other than *Encanto*," Eve said, still tittering. "Why are you listening to Disney soundtracks at your big age anyway?"

"First of all, Disney soundtracks are timeless."

"Fair," she said. Though she was having a harder time imagining him belting out "A Whole New World" than rapping along to "Elevators (Me & You)" now. "You're just full of surprises, huh?"

"I'm kidding," Jamie said. "My son is obsessed with *Encanto* right now, so that's *all* we've been listening to lately."

Eve physically recoiled, her elbow knocking against the passenger door as if her body had attempted to jump out of the car and simultaneously been splashed with a pitcher of cold water. She flashed back to the son who had been taken away from her all those years ago, and she hated Jamie for reminding her—even though she never actually stopped thinking of him. She'd allowed herself to enjoy his company, only for the record to scratch as soon as she stopped being afraid of that fact.

"You have a son?" she asked. He could've punched her in the chest and she would've been less flummoxed.

"Yeah. Jack." He glanced back at her for longer than she was comfortable with, considering he was driving, but she couldn't blame him for likely wondering why she was losing her fucking mind. "Is that okay?"

"It's fine," she said, trying to regain her poise. She shook her head as if to knock away the intrusive thoughts. "It just—it didn't occur to me."

"He lives in Nashville," Jamie explained. "His mom and I share custody."

Eve wanted to detach herself from the gory details. It occurred to her that Jamie was probably divorced, and he wasn't old enough to be divorced long, so he probably had some baggage he was dealing with. She didn't like baggage. She had too much of her own and no space for anyone else's. She started to fish in her purse for her AirPods case, figuring he'd at least get the hint, even if it would be remarkably rude.

"He's eight," Jamie went on while she continued rummaging frantically. "Goin' on about twenty, though."

"I have to call my mom," Eve blurted out, desperate to make him shut up. And while she did owe her mother a call, Eve had no intention of dialing her up. Upon locating her AirPods, she simply pretended, leaving a fake voicemail after a realistic enough waiting period. The entire act was inane, but that was how badly Eve needed to end this conversation.

Jamie seemed to understand that she was no longer in a chatty mood, so he let the silence speak for the bulk of the ride. Surprisingly, it didn't feel awkward, though it should've. He had every right to check her for being an asshole, but he left her to it.

Perhaps he'd had enough of her brand of unhinged for one morning. Either way, she was grateful.

"I don't know what your plans are for the rest of the day," Jamie said as their ride ascended to their tiny neck of the woods, "but you're welcome to come by for dinner. I'll be cooking either way."

"Oh." Feeling trapped again, Eve cursed herself for not just biting the bullet and driving herself home. "I think I'll be okay. But thank you." She imagined that if Jamie hadn't mentioned his son, she would've accepted his invitation, and who knows where that would've led, so in a way, it was best that he brought her crashing back down to earth.

When they pulled up to her grandmother's cabin, Eve was struck by what a good job he'd done with the landscaping, turning the year of neglect into an idyllic little cottage to house all her issues.

"Thank you," she said sincerely. "For everything."

"You're welcome," he said. Jamie put the car in park and then turned to her expectantly, his blue eyes searching for something she clearly didn't have to give.

"But I don't think I'm someone you wanna be friends with," Eve said.

Jamie nodded as he looked down at the console between them. "Maybe I *am* somebody *you* wanna be friends with."

Eve smiled. He was probably right. But if she could help it, she would never find out. She grabbed her things and piled out of the truck before he could undoubtedly do the gentlemanly thing and help her out of it. "I'll see you around, Jamie."

CHAPTER 8

Tennessee Whiskey

EVE

Later that afternoon, Eve was sitting in her cabin, now fully functional, stocked, and redecorated, waiting for inspiration to strike. She had yet to come up with anything specific to write about, which was why she spent the week prior renovating her little summer space. She'd removed the ugly mint-green window treatments, replacing them with sleek, light-filtering shades. She traded the mustard-colored couch for a more modern sectional, the color of oatmeal, to complement the floors. She'd even assembled it herself, along with a square taupe cocktail table, which all seemed near impossible when she started, then became an unexpected point of pride once it was done. With electricity, water, and Wi-Fi in place, her grandmother's cabin had turned into somewhere she didn't mind living.

Of course, upon completion, Eve wished she hadn't finished so quickly, because redecorating had been exactly the diversion she needed. The only cure for her listlessness so far. In fact, if she went back to New York anytime soon, she was seriously considering signing up for one of those apps where she could complete tasks for other people. She welcomed the idea of being useful to someone—especially if it kept her mind busy.

This was precisely why she'd spent the bulk of the day considering and reconsidering Jamie's dinner invitation. Thinking about all the things that could go wrong if she spent a significant, concentrated amount of time with this man. What she would do when he brought his son around. If the kid was anything like his father, he would most certainly show up at her door uninvited, and Eve would have to try not to spontaneously weep at the mere sight of him.

Perhaps, at worst, Jamie would get a full grasp of just how weird and sad she was and stop trying to befriend her. At best, maybe he'd make her laugh. He had a way of doing that that she wasn't used to.

She just hoped she wouldn't regret it.

For that matter, she hoped *he* wouldn't regret it.

And so, without much thought to her tatty leggings and flamboyant pink Beychella hoodie, Eve marched down the hill and over the bridge and trespassed into her neighbor's yard, much like she'd done the first day she was here. She followed the grass path along the pond until she reached his driveway. Unsure where to go next, she opted for a rather steep flight of steps that she hoped led to the entrance. Once she got to the top, she knocked tentatively at the door and gazed out to the water as she waited for Jamie to answer.

In a matter of seconds, he greeted her, sounding nonplussed by her appearance. "Uh . . . hey . . ."

"There's a deer," Eve remarked, answering a question he hadn't asked. It seemed to be limping, which troubled her more than it should've, and she couldn't take her eyes off it. "I think it's injured."

"Oh, yeah. That's Buckley," Jamie said, stepping onto his porch to join her. He smelled of pine, like his car, and it made Eve smile internally. But then she gave him a strange, obviously perplexed look, wondering what kind of Sleeping Beauty arrangement he had with the animals around there if he knew this deer's name, and Jamie grinned. "Jack named him," he said.

Eve tried not to visibly react at the mention of Jamie's son. "So this deer comes around often?"

"Not *often*. But enough for me to still recognize him," he said, leaning against his balcony's railing to watch with her. "He's kinda squirrelly, so we don't get close. But he seems to think he's safe around here."

"Or maybe he knows you've got his mom in your freezer," Eve said wryly. After mowing her lawn the week prior, Jamie mentioned that he was preparing venison, and she never quite let it leave her mind.

"Did you need somethin', or did you just come over to judge me?"

"I . . . came for dinner," Eve said. "If the offer is still open."

"'Course it is."

Jamie headed back inside, leaving Eve to follow; she did so guardedly, hesitant to go beyond the threshold, scanning his place from where she stood. It appeared that his vast home was just an open-concept room—kitchen, living area, and bedroom all in one—and standing in Jamie's bedroom was a bridge farther than she was ready for.

"You can come inside," Jamie said, chuckling when he caught her gawking from the doorway.

Eve gradually moved farther inside, studying the space like she was at an open house. Wood paneling covered every inch of the room, but it was a deep, dark wood that didn't bother her here as much as it did at her grandmother's. The kitchen sat at the far end of the house, partitioned from the rest of the room by a chic high-top dining set for two. The table was rectangular, and its matching chairs seemed to fit underneath it like puzzle pieces. The appliances were white, matching nothing else in the room, and NeNe Leakes's voice echoed in Eve's head, melodramatically bemoaning the very existence of *a white refrigerator, honey.*

Nevertheless. Jamie's cabin was quaint and charming, warm, and a little dark—a bit like Jamie.

As Eve finished her exploration, she moved back toward the door, a bar sitting adjacent to the exit. It was beautifully designed, made of a rich wood she could only assume was mahogany, its surface boasting a shine so impeccable she was scared to mark it with her fingerprints. Everything in his place was like that, all the pieces elegantly crafted. Even the floating television stand was splendid.

"Where did you get all this stuff?" she asked, running her finger along the smooth edge of the cabinet, almost magnetically drawn to it. "It's beautiful."

"Oh, thank you. I um . . . I actually made it," Jamie said.

Eve was a little bit stunned and a little bit skeptical. Then again, it made some sense that the guy with the Jesus beard was a carpenter. "Really?"

"I figure why buy it when you can make it?"

"Indeed," she agreed, still meandering around the open space. She was unable to ignore his stunning bedframe—partly because it sat so prominently at the front of the room, but mainly because it was just gorgeous. It was a tatami platform bed in a dark, almost black wood, flanked by matching miniature nightstands, their sleek design not really fitting the image she had of Jamie. "You made these, too?" she asked. Likely a silly question, but she was bewitched by the idea that he was this good with his hands.

"All of it," he confirmed with a laugh. "I made all of it."

Genuinely impressed, Eve went ahead and made herself a drink at his instruction. He'd offered wine, but she was going to need more than that to get through the foreignness of prolonged one-on-one interaction. She helped herself to the bottle of Jack Daniel's, figuring it appropriate for the locale, and poured it neat. She turned and watched Jamie at work in his kitchen, looking different to her in the glow of the evening. He wore a nice denim shirt that managed to bring out the already striking blue of his eyes, with dark jeans that fit his trim frame well. She discovered that it was a chore to tear her eyes from him.

"So Miss Hazel told me you're a college professor?" Jamie asked, not looking up from his task of chopping vegetables.

"I'm a playwright, actually," she said, illogically annoyed with her grandmother—and so, with him—for not knowing.

He stopped chopping long enough to cock his head, regarding her with a confounded smile. "Really?"

His disbelieving tone echoed hers when she learned of his job. But it was a familiar response. Most people, when they said, *Really?* were asking whether she was successful. *You write plays . . . for a living?* "Really," she said. "Without going into a lot of boring details, that's my day job. But I do teach at NYU to keep the lights on. Not this year, but usually."

Jamie resumed work on their dinner, seeming to ignore that a stranger was making her way around his home. "What if I wanna hear the boring details?" he asked.

"You don't," Eve said. "People's eyes tend to glaze over when I talk about my plays."

"Well, now I'm really interested."

"Fine." She sighed, already knowing how this conversation would end. "By any chance, do you know who Sandra Bland is?"

"Of course I do."

She replied with further disbelief, her eyes narrowing before reflexively roaming downward until they landed on his forearms. "Who is she?"

"She was a young Black woman in . . . Texas, if I recall correctly? She was arrested after a traffic stop, and then she died, supposedly by suicide, in jail."

Eve was waiting to find fault with his account, to detect some hint of bias that she could use as an excuse to get out of there as soon as possible, but he was simply accurate. It eased her apprehension, even if only slightly. "Well, my most recent play is about her. It's called *Gamba Adisa,* which is the Yoruba name Audre Lorde adopted before she died, and it means 'the she-warrior who makes herself clear,' which felt apropos for Ms. Bland. It's about her life before that arrest."

"You don't include that part?"

"I've had many debates about it, but I was adamant that this story be about her life. The sort of mundaneness of it. Not the tragedy of its ending," Eve said. "We tend to martyrize victims of police brutality. But we don't have to be extraordinary to have value. She was in jail because of a police officer with a superiority complex and a history of pretextual traffic stops. I didn't want that to be the totality of her story."

"I see."

"It dovetails into other stories about Black women taken

from us too soon. Sonya Massey, Dominique Fells, Oluwatoyin Salau. Unfortunately, the list is endless," Eve said, receiving a pensive gaze from Jamie. "But it just opened in Chicago, which is where she was from, and it's doing well, so that's been . . . I don't know. Gratifying, I guess. And the reviews have been kind, although part of me worries that it's because white people are just reticent to critique Black art, especially if it has to do with race . . ." Eve realized she was talking about a mile a minute—showing signs of life—and slowed down. "At any rate . . . everyone keeps telling me I need to get to work on the next one, so . . . here I am . . ."

"You sound excited," Jamie said, beaming. "Granted, there's absolutely nothing I can add to this conversation. But I liked hearin' you say it."

She hated that his accent made her ears perk up, his deep drawl feeling warm like the whiskey. "You probably say that to all the girls."

"I don't have any girls. And I wouldn't've said it if I didn't mean it."

Eve tried to hold his gaze once it landed on her, but she couldn't, getting lost in him and his flirtatious-ass tone. She turned away, taking a nip of her drink as she continued slowly around the room, a covered structure in the corner near the balcony catching her eye. A hot tub? "A hot tub?" she asked, tickled by the notion.

"Now that, I didn't build. Came with the house."

"Have you ever used it?"

"Not yet." He was placing silverware and condiments on the dining table, his footsteps sounding like a soft drumbeat against the hardwood floors as he walked.

"And how long have you lived here?"

"Well, I don't really . . . live here . . ."

"Oh God." She knew he looked homeless that day they met. "Who lives here?"

"No, it's my house." He laughed at the panic that had surely claimed her face. "But it's sort of a vacation home kinda thing. Which is why I hadn't been out here recently. My son seems to think it's cool, though," he said. "The hot tub, I mean."

"Oh." Eve nodded, but the mention of his son again reminded her that she couldn't afford to forge a real friendship here; he was a distraction and nothing more. She needed to just eat her food and go. If she played her cards right, she could be in bed by nine. "What's for dinner?"

"Just some pork chops and roasted potatoes. Figured you weren't ready for venison quite yet."

Eve replied with a small smile, appreciating that more than she would say. She took her seat at the table, where an arugula salad sat in the middle and Jamie served a bone-in pork chop, fried and lightly smothered in a brown gravy, with a side of golden potatoes and onions, all of it sprinkled with parsley.

"This looks so good."

"You sound surprised," he said, taking his seat across from her.

"I didn't know what to expect."

"Well, I hope it tastes as good as it looks." He raised his glass to her. "Bon appétit."

"Mèsi. Bon apeti," she replied in her Haitian Creole dialect. They cut into their pork chops in unison, a stiff silence washing over them for several bites, leaving only the sound of silverware clinking against plates.

Jamie was the one to break first. "So you said you're here to work on your next play? Does it take place in the woods or something?"

"Oh. No." Eve covered her mouth as she laughed. She was going to have to be more forthcoming if her story was going to make any sense. "I'm using my grandma's as sort of a retreat. I had a lot going on in my home life, and I needed to get away from it."

"A lot like what?"

"Oh." His inquisitiveness was disarming, but Eve wouldn't be sharing those details with him—the only safety in being around Jamie was that he didn't know her whole sad story. He had no reason to pity her, no motive to suggest she try again, stop letting her grief drown her. He had nothing to do with her real life, and she intended to keep it that way. "Just . . . everyday drudgery," she said. "I wanted to get away from all the noise of New York and just . . . write."

Jamie's brooding expression conveyed empathy, perhaps deliberately. Perhaps not. "My girlfriend of nearly a decade cheated on me," he confessed between bites. "She's with the guy now. *Engaged,* apparently." He spit the *engaged* like it was the most disgusting thing he'd ever said. "Drives me fuckin' crazy."

Eve smiled sympathetically. "*You* don't seem crazy."

"I'm just good at hiding it," he said. "But I came here because I needed to get away, too. So . . . I understand."

Eve was at a loss for any type of meaningful response, unequipped with whatever he seemed to be looking for. "I was with my boyfriend for five years," she decided to say. Calling him her boyfriend was a lie, meant to make the relationship sound less meaningful somehow. "Blame it on the alcohol if this is too forward to ask, but is there a reason you didn't get married after so long?" Eve searched his face for a reaction before he could respond. "Not that you needed to be, but most people . . ."

"No, I wanted to be," Jamie said, stabbing at his pork chop as he spoke. He took a bite and chewed for several beats before continuing. "At a certain point, I thought it was basically inevitable. But she just . . . never wanted it. Felt like the commitment was enough."

"Well, obviously not," Eve said, then gasped, immediately wishing she could take back the droll retort. "I'm so sorry."

"No, it was funny." He nodded with a small grin on his pink lips.

"I thought so, but then I realized I should probably know you a little better before I make cracks about your ex." She grinned at his smile—the way it grew wider as he swallowed his food. "I'm sorry."

"Maybe on the second date," Jamie said.

Eve sent him a pointed stare, her eyebrows raised when she replied, "This isn't a date."

CHAPTER 9

No Chaser

JAMIE

It was nothing short of astonishing when Eve showed up at Jamie's door for dinner. After the awkward start and abrupt end to their morning, he didn't expect to see her again for at least another week, and only if he sought her out first. But she'd arrived in a pleasant enough mood, happily making small talk for a while. In fact, he'd learned that she was much more charismatic than their first few interactions would've led anyone to believe.

However, as they sat there eating, Jamie had to wonder *why* she'd shown up. He couldn't figure out whether she was enjoying herself. One minute, she was regaling him with the details of her job, and her face, already gleaming in the dim room, absolutely lit up as she spoke. But in the next breath, she was downing her tumbler of whiskey and snapping at his joke, like the very idea of being on a date with him was insulting.

"I was kidding, but it's good to know where I stand," he said in response. He traded his fork for his water, his eyes staying on hers as he took a long sip. "If it's not too forward for *me* to ask, how long have you and your boyfriend been broken up?"

Eve paused before answering. "Not long." She seemed to be

avoiding him as she picked up the tongs and added more salad to her plate. "We should've broken up months ago, but neither one of us could bring ourselves to do it."

"Why's that?"

"Honestly, I don't know. Maybe it was easier to pretend we were happy. When in the end, it just . . . it drove us insane. Or me, at least."

Jamie felt as though he could see that in her. It explained that oddness that he liked so much. "Was it a bad breakup?"

"The worst." She stood from her chair, empty glass in hand, off to find his liquor cabinet again. "Can I get you anything?"

"I should be asking you that," he said, peering at her as she shuffled across the room. "But no, I'm good."

"I wish you'd drink with me so I don't have to feel like a lush." She said it as she generously poured herself another glass of brown liquor, which he found rather funny. "How about a shot?"

"I'm good." He raised his glass of water as if to prove it. "I didn't realize we had to drink to have a good time."

"If you insist on talking about past relationships, we're gonna have to drink."

"I wasn't insisting on anything." He laughed again, nervously this time, feeling as though they were both being put on the spot. "I thought we were just talking." Eve repeatedly steered the conversation away from anything too personal. She had a wall up, and Jack Daniel's seemed to be its reinforcement. "We can talk more about your job, if you'd like."

She removed the bubblegum-pink hoodie she was wearing—a different one from that morning—leaving her in a black tank top and leggings, allowing Jamie an unobstructed view of her many curves. The ones in her muscular arms stole his attention first, and he would've guessed she was an Olympic runner before anything, which just made her all the more compelling.

"What about you?" she asked, returning to their dinner. "You make these things for a living?" She tapped on the table. "Or is this a hobby?"

He was entertained by the way her speech seemed to hasten the more she drank. "It's my job." He wiped his mouth with his napkin before going on about how he was in the business of bespoke woodcraft, mostly for rich folks back in Nashville, but he had customers all over the country these days. He pointed out his liquor cabinet, as he'd noticed her admiring it earlier. "That was supposed to go to one guy who passed away suddenly. Most of the things here are just designs I wanted to try out."

Eve's eyes widened. "And it's just you?"

"I have a small staff. Including a couple of guys who do really great work."

"And you're the boss?"

Jamie shook his head. "I wouldn't call it that. If you met Floyd Hicks, you'd know he doesn't take orders from anyone."

"Floyd Hicks," she repeated loudly, failing to contain her amusement and, therefore, her giggles. "Now that's a country-ass name."

"That's a pretty normal name in Tennessee. I once did work for this guy named Reynolds Boderham."

Eve burst into laughter. Loud, genuine laughter. "Shut up."

"I'm serious. His wife's name was Bonnie."

"You're making this up."

"I swear it. They had this little Pomeranian named Peaches that she carried everywhere. It was somethin' out of an *SNL* sketch."

"That is hilarious."

"I've definitely met some characters along the way," he agreed, still smiling at the joy she got from this simple thing. "Your grandmother was one of 'em."

Eve raised an eyebrow. "She was one of your customers?"

"A repeat customer," Jamie said proudly, hearing the disbelief in Eve's slight New York accent. "There was the table in the kitchen, a chest upstairs, and I redid the front door. I also fixed a leak on that downstairs bathroom sink. And I ended up giving her a couple of maple end tables I didn't need."

Eve cracked the tiniest of smiles, and it looked like there was a bit of regret attached to it. "I'm, like, ninety percent sure my mom took that kitchen table after the funeral."

"Is that right?"

"The one with the legs?" Eve used her hands to make the shape of an orb, and he nodded in confirmation. "Yeah, she actually drove that table to New York herself, because she 'didn't trust the shipping process,'" she said.

Jamie laughed again, imagining someone who looked like Hazel and Evie saying something like that. "Miss Hazel talked about all of y'all pretty often, but especially you," he said. He remembered how proud she was to say her only granddaughter had gotten her doctorate. "She would say how you worried her."

Eve looked down. "I'm just surprised she let you in her house," she said, her dark brown eyes twinkling.

"Yeah . . ." Jamie was well aware that Hazel Beasley would talk to white people all day long, but they didn't get past that threshold if she could help it. "If it makes you feel any better, she made sure I knew she had her derringer handy at all times."

"I bet she did," Eve said, giggling.

He turned solemn thinking of how Hazel had just disappeared from his life. "I wasn't here as often as I liked after business picked up. I was heartbroken hearing she passed."

"I can't remember the last time I was here," Eve said. "I'm glad you were."

Jamie considered it something of an honor to hear that.

Conversation comfortably ceased as Eve began to slowly cut the rest of her pork chop into big chunks, not unlike the way he would for Jack. It felt like she was on the verge of opening up to him, and he was at a loss for words, fearing the wrong ones might ruin the moment. When his phone vibrated loudly in the silence, he took it as a sign not to force it.

"Sorry." He pulled his LG from his pocket to see Lucy's name scrolling across the front screen. "I gotta take this."

"Of course."

He slipped outside to take the good-night call from Jack, with it coming the news that Lucy and Tyler had gotten him a dog. A beagle that Jack named Bucky. Jamie had to convince himself that it wasn't some shameless attempt to curry favor with an eight-year-old. But when he glanced inside to see Eve gone from the table, he realized he was being rude and ended the call, which kept him from dwelling on it.

Inside, he found that Eve (and her drink) had drifted across the room, landing in front of his bookshelf. It was a cabinet he'd made of Panamanian rosewood, about a foot taller than her, with a glass door that allowed her to see the contents inside. He watched her scan the titles, noticing that she'd paused on the second row, containing the Unfortunate Events and Dark Materials of the world. She then lingered on the fourth row, which boasted works from Jane Austen and George Orwell, James Baldwin and Octavia Butler. She stopped and opened the bookcase at the fifth, as if the Broken Earth series had physically summoned her, which sat beside some newer greats like Brit Bennett, Colson Whitehead, and Roxane Gay. She looked back at Jamie then, her expression seeming to convey surprise, as though she thought he'd written all those books himself.

"Sorry about that," he said, holding up his phone before stuffing it back into his pocket. "I talk to Jack every night before bed, and I was late."

"Not a problem." She set her glass on top of the bookcase and pulled out the Black Panther novel about Shuri, which he recognized as one of Jack's favorites. This was his second copy, in fact. "You've read all these?" she asked.

"Most of 'em," he said, joining her. "Some with Jack. Some I didn't finish." He pointed to a couple of titles that he hadn't chosen for himself. "My brother-in-law sends me some things, too. He's one of those intellectual types, so I try to listen to him."

Eve stared at the selection a bit longer before returning the Shuri book to its rightful spot. "So . . . does any dessert come with this dinner?" she asked, handing over her emptied glass. "Because an important thing to know about me is that I love dessert."

"I do have some ice cream." He headed off to the kitchen to retrieve it. "You ever been to that ice cream parlor down near Dollywood? Old Mill Creamery?" Eve appeared to be distracted as she continued to study his books and his furniture, and he wished he knew what she thought of it all. She seemed impressed, which was encouraging; he craved her approval for reasons unknown. "Eve?"

She turned back to him. "Huh?"

He held up two white tubs of ice cream for her to see. "You wanted dessert? Banana pudding or whiskey ribbon?"

"Oh." She shook her head and made a face. "Does it have real whiskey in it?" Her voice lowered as she asked, like the question was an inappropriate one. As if she hadn't been chugging the very same liquor all night.

"Moonshine," he confirmed, matching her tone with an impish smile. He grabbed a couple of bowls and returned to the counter, directing her to follow. "Come here."

Eve joined him in the kitchen, where he was already digging into a pint-sized plastic container of vanilla ice cream with chocolate and whiskey ripples throughout.

"Is this legal?" she asked.

Jamie laughed. "Of course it's legal. It's not like we're makin' it."

"Oh, well, I'm sorry I don't know the alcohol laws."

"Here." He offered her a small scoop of the banana pudding first, figuring she'd like it less than the other.

He watched as she relished in the rich, creamy banana and vanilla wafer flavors, and she let out a gentle moan before taking the spoon from him to lick clean. "That's good," she said. "That's *really* good."

"I know." He grabbed a spoon for himself before offering her the whiskey ribbon. "They're all good there, but these are my favorites."

He waited for Eve's reaction as she sampled the second one, but he couldn't help fixating on her lips as she licked remnants of ivory cream from them. She had the most beautiful mouth he'd ever seen. Lips for days, with a Cupid's bow that rivaled Rihanna's. It was a wonder he hadn't spent the entire evening just staring at her mouth. And now that he had the idea, he couldn't be sure that he wouldn't.

"That one's good, too," Eve said. She slid into the space beside him to steal another spoonful. "Mmm."

"You're gonna have to stop making that sound if you don't wanna call this a date."

She giggled loudly, her smile lighting up the room as she glanced at him. "Sorry." Eve was beautiful like this. Not that she wasn't gorgeous every other way, but her entire face managed to smile when she was happy, and it was enchanting. *She* was enchanting when she dropped that guard even a little bit. Like a flower trying to blossom.

Jamie went for another spoon of ice cream, feeling Eve's gaze on him as he moved. He liked the idea that she was perhaps as intrigued by him as he was by her, so he didn't shy away. He faced her as he devoured another dollop of the dessert, their eyes locking as he slowly pulled the spoon from his mouth. They stared at each other for far too long, and he knew it. He was internally yelling at himself, *Look away,* but he couldn't. Like some magnetic pull between them, forcing him to acknowledge his attraction to this woman.

He licked his lips, his breathing labored as his mind went haywire. His stare danced downward to her collarbone, mesmerized by her dark skin paired with the most gorgeous bone structure and decorated by a dainty gold chain—like dunes in a desert beneath the sun.

But before he knew it, before his imagination could take him too far into a fantasy, a loud clunk knocked him from his trance, his spoon having fallen out of his hand.

Thankful for the interruption, Jamie picked it up and went to a separate corner, his common sense telling him that now wasn't the time. And that was assuming there ever would be one. But it surely wasn't when she was clearly intoxicated and he was just barely hanging on to his own faculties.

Eve also seemed relieved by the interruption, as she averted his gaze and buried herself in the banana pudding. "I'm gonna eat this whole tub, okay?"

Jamie chuckled, believing her. "You mind if I put on some music?" he asked, taking another helping for himself before sauntering to his stereo.

She sent a coy smile his way. "You gonna play me some Outkast?"

"I might," he shot back.

In reality, he went with what was already sitting in the CD player, and within a few seconds, Ella Fitzgerald's silky voice filled the open room. Jamie and Eve took that as an opportunity to let the music be the conversation, taking their ice cream and retiring to the couch, side by side.

The minutes progressed into an hour, then close to two, as they lost track of the time. Ice cream was finished, more drinks consumed, mostly by Eve, and evening turned to night. They spoke of favorite singers and albums—Jamie eventually landing on Prince after much internal debate, while Eve decided on Nina Simone. They shared similar opinions about TV shows; Eve asked him about several plays that he knew only by name. They argued, amicably, about "SpottieOttieDopaliscious" being Outkast's best work. But mainly, the quiet prevailed.

Jamie wasn't surprised when he looked over to find his neighbor curled up against the arm of the couch, fast asleep. Something in him was glad she felt relaxed enough, or maybe just drunk enough, to do so. Then again, maybe her willingness to be drunk with him was a sign of comfort itself.

He figured it unlikely she'd wake up anytime soon, so like any good host, he made sure his home was hers. Gently and deftly, he lifted Eve from the couch and carried her to his bed. He untied her boots, leaving them neatly beneath the bed's platform, then found the hoodie she came in with and covered her with it, ensuring she had all of her things close in case she did wake in the middle of the night and want to leave. He gazed at her for just a moment, her serene expression giving him hope that she had a good evening, that she'd found some respite from what anguished her. Then he turned off the bedside lamp, leaving her to rest.

CHAPTER 10

C U Next Tuesday

EVE

Eve awoke with a sharp inhale and an aching neck. She didn't know where she was, but it wasn't any version of home. She sat up in the strange bed, her head spinning from the quick movement, and as the room came into slow focus, she recognized the place where she had dinner the night before. Jamie's home. And her head went from spinning to pounding as it all came crashing back.

How much she liked his place. How cozy it was. How cozy *he* was. The way he spoke so fondly of her grandmother. And how good it felt to speak to someone who knew her grandmother and nothing else.

She remembered studying Jamie's bookcase like she was going to buy something from it. A conversation about moonshine. And ice cream. And being powerless to resist watching Jamie as he ate said ice cream.

More vividly, she remembered wanting to kiss him. It was the alcohol talking, of course—she no longer liked kissing or anything else sexual, so it had to be her drunkenness speaking for her—but she distinctly recalled the urge all the same, a flutter that moved haphazardly between her chest and the pit of her stomach all night long.

Eve surveyed herself and the rest of the bed, relieved to find that she was still fully clothed and appeared to have slept alone. She scolded herself for drinking so much that she couldn't be sure. She scanned the room for Jamie, but there was no sign of him other than a neatly folded blanket at the edge of his dark leather sofa. She couldn't believe she'd been so imposing.

As Eve untangled from his sheets, she spotted a note left just beside her boots. She smiled faintly at his use of the name Evie but braced for some cutesy message about going to pick up breakfast.

Hope you slept well. I had to leave and didn't want to wake you. I've got Jack the next few days, so I'm headed to Nashville 'til Tues. I arranged for Hitch-A-Ride to pick you up around 10:00 and take you back to your car. When you leave, just give the bottom lock a turn. And if you need me by any chance, my number is 615-555-0167. Have a good weekend.

By the way, there's green tea above the fridge. For the hangover.

—JG

"What the fuck?" Eve whispered, pouting at the message. There was nothing cute about it, and no breakfast to speak of. Only the sobering reminder that Jamie had a son, and she'd acted an entire fool because of it.

She looked around, waiting for the punch line to what had to be a joke. What kind of person would leave a sleeping stranger in their home for the week? Then again, she was the deranged woman who'd passed out here in the first place. He probably pitied her.

On second thought, it was a relief that Jamie had disappeared into the night. Hopefully, a few days apart would help him forget her behavior. In her more clearheaded reflection, she'd become uncomfortable with the things she'd started to feel in his presence. Attraction? In this economy? No, she hadn't signed up for that, and so she was completely unprepared for even the seeds of it. Sparks. Whatever it was, she didn't want it. Not now. She couldn't.

When Eve arrived at Crockett's to pick up her car, she decided she might as well stay for breakfast—and hope it didn't come with a side of panic attack this time. Business seemed to have picked up from the day before. As she rattled off her order to the server, she caught mention of "the Fourth of July crowd," and she had to wonder if they were really that close to the holiday already. The month of June had been such a blur, she wasn't even sure what day it was.

Once she received her coffee and strawberry-orange juice, Eve turned to a podcast to drown out the hum of the restaurant and pulled out her iPad to get to work. Half listening to an episode of *The Read,* she made her first attempt at outlining her next play, settling on the working title *Down from Dover,* based on a Dolly Parton song. Seemed fitting for the setting.

Eve looked up from her tablet when she noticed a figure taking shape across from her. She could feel her heart beating faster with the hope that it was somehow Jamie, but her eye caught the feminine hands resting on the table, and her anticipation went down as quickly as it had gone up. Instead, it was the cashier Eve had embarrassed herself in front of the day before—Jill, according to her name tag. Eve removed her earbud, worried she'd done something else foolish.

"You look like Hazel," Jill said.

"Yeah," Eve admitted, her eyes averting Jill's as the shame washed over her. *Aren't you Hazel's girl?* Eve had bristled at the question previously, and she couldn't be sure it wasn't what triggered her panic. She hated that people knew her before she could speak. That her face immediately summoned the memory of her grandmother. *Hazel's girl. The one who came down here pregnant at seventeen.* "I'm sorry I said I wasn't."

"I shouldn't have asked," Jill said. "You looked so familiar, it just slipped out."

Eve smiled weakly and regarded Jill again. She was an attractive older white woman with a slender face and soft rosy cheeks, her olive eyes both welcoming and inquisitive. She had the most beautiful gray hair, the short, wavy strands ranging from pewter to platinum. Eve wondered if Jill had grandchildren somewhere not calling or visiting her enough.

"What brings you down this way?" Jill asked. "It's been, what, a year since she passed?"

"Just about," Eve said. "I actually . . . I came to write." She held up her iPad. "A play."

"Hazel mentioned that you did that," Jill said, seeming to remember as she said it out loud. "Glad you're still at it."

Eve looked down again, unready to engage in a discussion about her plays and why she was in Gatlinburg to write one.

"Were you friends with my grandmother?" Her voice sounded small outside of her body.

"I like to think so," Jill said with a rueful grin. "She didn't come by very often. Especially at . . . you know, the end. But I would bring her things. Do her grocery shopping when it got a little harder for her to move around."

Eve scratched the corner of her eye, stopping a tear before it could form. She was such a piece of shit for abandoning the woman who took care of her when her parents refused to.

"You okay, honey?"

"Yeah," Eve lied. She exhaled her emotions and forced another unconvincing smile in their place. "I just miss her."

"Well, I don't mean to keep you." Jill reached across the table, briefly resting her hand over Eve's, and Eve closed her eyes at the simple, tender touch. "Just wanted you to know that I'm right here if you need anything."

"Oh." Eve had done nothing to deserve Jill's kindness, and she doubted she would be needing her for anything, but she received her words with a small nod.

As Jill departed from the table, the familiar ding of a text message rattled Eve out of her feelings. It was her agent, Stella, directing her to check her emails. Eve took one look at the daunting little red badge in the corner of her Gmail app, the one that told her she had 2,063 unread emails, and let out a huff. She had been avoiding her inbox for a good three weeks now, too scared of the incessant updates still coming in from BabyCenter.com, because she was also too scared to complete the simple task of unsubscribing. Unable to admit the defeat of losing another embryo. Leo was right about her being a coward.

Finally, she bit the bullet and opened the app, and of course, right at the top sat the weekly bulletin from that fucking website. My Pregnancy This Week: 8 WEEKS, DAY 1.

Fuck me.

Nevertheless, just a few lines below, there was, indeed, an email from her agent. Eve reread the subject line and the preview for far longer than was rational, as opening the email would answer any questions she had about it. But she was convinced she was either dreaming or her eyes had rendered some alternate images beyond what was on her screen, because this simply could not be correct.

From: Stella Fischer-Fox

Date: July 2, 2025

Subject: THE PUBLIC THEATER

Eve,

Some happy news I couldn't wait to share: The Public wants *Gamba Adisa*! We do have some logistics to figure out, but I think we can make this work. I have a Zoom scheduled for Tuesday to talk dates and casting, and then I'll give you a call. Until then, I hope you can enjoy your holiday with this on your mind!

Warmly,

Stella

"Eve! New York misses you already," Stella was practically yelling into her mic. "How long are you planning to be gone?"

Eve had already grown weary of explaining her leave of absence to everyone she knew; still, she laughed as though she hadn't just had this conversation with two of her friends via FaceTime in the hour since she returned to her cabin. It was her own fault for taking off without any notice. She turned down the volume on her computer as she replied, "I'll try to be back in September." It tasted like a lie every time she said it—she had no idea how she would adhere to that deadline—but it seemed to placate everyone who asked.

"Jeez Louise." Stella sighed. "But if you're writing, I'm not complaining. If *Gamba Adisa* makes it to the Public, the people are gonna be clamoring for your next one. *Clamoring*."

"That's very—"

"So when do we think we'll have a first draft ready?"

"Oh." She had barely written a first word; she couldn't imagine having a first draft anytime soon. That was what the summer was for. "Well. I was thinking October . . ."

"Okay . . ." Stella bobbed her head as she took a long sip from her iced coffee, but her brown-green eyes relayed something much less relaxed. Trepidation would be putting it mildly. "So how about this. Why don't we meet at the end of August to see exactly where we are? The Public is looking at a late spring debut, which means come January, you are gonna be one busy bee. I don't want you to have to split your focus."

Eve forced another smile, but the dread of all that responsibility was already filling her lungs. This was unmistakably good news, but in the moment, with reality setting in, it was simply overwhelming. "I know you'll be talking to them next week, but how confident are we that this is happening?"

Stella's eternal megawatt smile fell slightly as she admitted,

"It's not a *done* deal. But I feel good about it, Eve. The fact that they reached out to me is a very good sign. I wouldn't have told you about it otherwise."

"Okay." Eve exhaled.

"Don't worry, my dear. You are on your way." Stella barely paused to take a breath before continuing. "Oh, and did we talk about Gigi Alvarez being on board to produce? You know she got *Black Coffee* on Broadway *and* they're extending their run." Eve tried to reply, but Stella steamrolled through her thoughts. "I can't remember whether I put it in my email, but I also have some directors for you to consider. I know you mentioned Zindzi was a dream get, but I have some equally interesting names from Lukas at the Public." Stella somehow seemed even more stressed out than Eve as she pulled her jet-black hair from its sloppy bun atop her head and then readjusted it into the exact same style. "It would be great if you were in the city right now," she said. "I get it. *I get it.* I'm just saying it would be helpful."

Eve felt like a Stepford wife, grinning broadly while internally trying to swat away her doubts. Maybe she'd left New York at the exact wrong time—just as her professional dreams were starting to come true. But her mind had been telling her she *needed* this break, and her body seemed to be following suit. "I had a panic attack yesterday." Eve said it out loud, uncertain she meant to.

"Oh my god, Eve! You need to take care of yourself." Stella was uttering the right words, but to Eve's anxious ear, it sounded like she meant the opposite of them. "I know this is a lot. We're just gonna take it one day at a time."

"O—"

"Just know that once we start rehearsals, I *need* you here, lady."

"I know," Eve said.

"Eve, I need you to be more excited!" Stella was shouting again. She had always been the peppy to Eve's cool—it was one of the reasons Eve chose her as an agent—but they were really existing at opposite ends of the spectrum about this prospect.

"I'm excited," Eve promised. But when she glanced at herself in the Zoom window, it was clear that her facial expressions were betraying her. "I'm nervous."

"Nothing to be nervous about, Eve. You already know people love the show. You're just getting a bigger stage."

Eve nodded, but she was on the verge of tears she couldn't understand. To be delighted, apprehensive, honored, and enervated, all at once, was a heady tonic.

Stella sent her a genuine, warm smile. "It astounds me that after all this time, you still don't know how good you are."

And that was it. The compliment was more than Eve could handle—particularly when she felt quite the contrary. Not only did she consider herself a terrible person at least every other day, but impostor syndrome was kicking her ass. She wasn't good at all. And the dam broke, all of her emotions leaking out in one pitiful sob.

"Eve?" Stella called out to her.

"I'm sorry," Eve whispered through the tears she uselessly tried to hold back.

"Do you wanna talk about it?"

The concern in Stella's voice only cracked her further. "This is so unprofessional," Eve said. Though, in truth, Stella probably would have loved nothing more than for Eve to open up like this—for the last four years, she had been trying to crack Eve's hardened, withdrawn shell, but Eve would never actually let her.

"No, no, it's okay," Stella said. "I just don't want you to feel like you have to do anything you're uncomfortable with."

Eve didn't know what to say, fearing her contradicting feelings would make her sound unstable if she unleashed them. "It's not discomfort," Eve said. Eve lied. "I just need some time. To feel like myself again."

"Well, take the weekend. I'll have more information after that and then we can . . . regroup."

"Okay." Eve was wiping at her face as if it would expel the embarrassment.

"All right, babe. Until then, please take care of yourself?"

"I will," Eve said.

The two of them waved at each other until the Zoom screen swooshed out of sight. As soon as she was sure Stella was gone, Eve allowed herself to fully deflate. Their conversation left her less motivated to write than she was when she started the day. In fact, she just wanted to lie down.

Ordinarily, she would have called Maya for a short pep talk that would have turned into a long discussion on everything they'd missed over the week. But her friend was on holiday somewhere on the Italian coast, and Eve was loath to interrupt, debating with herself about time zones and whether a text would be appropriately unobtrusive. Of course, she wasn't sure there was ever a time when *Hey, sis, how did you figure out your depression wasn't temporary?* wouldn't be obtrusive.

Maya had always been the enlightened one between them. Therapy actually worked for her—a concept Eve simply could not wrap her head around. She'd tried twice aside from her latest failed attempt at joint therapy: once in grad school, and again just after she met Leo—back when she still wanted them to work. She figured if he found it worthwhile with all the shit he had to sort through, she could at least give it a try. But Eve hated the way therapy made her feel cut open. Her doctors seemed simultaneously disapproving and dismissive. The psychiatrist she'd seen the second time relied mainly on SSRIs, which Eve quit cold turkey after two months of feeling like there was a muzzle on her brain.

Sniffling through her tears, Eve stared at her computer screen, the Final Draft app containing the opening scene she'd written earlier. She hated every letter, resenting the instant feeling of despair they ignited in her. Writing a play about her own experiences seemed like a good idea on paper. Religion. Teenage pregnancy. The trauma some parents are willing to inflict on their children in the name of Jesus, Joseph, and Mary. Great topics for theater. But being back in the same house, the same room, where she'd been sent all those years ago only sharpened the pain, making it impossible to write.

She was starting to realize just how silly this mission was; the idea of being alone with nothing but her mind was absurd. And she'd gotten an out in the form of Jamie, a kind, attractive man, willing to keep her company, and she couldn't help but shit all over that, too.

"Fuck!" Eve shouted. She was exhausted with herself. "Fuck, fuck, fuck."

In the few hours since her call with Stella, Eve had settled deep into her feelings—with the help of some wine. Scrolling through her texts, most of them annoying her, it was best to hold off until she was in a better mood; Eve ignored this logic and wrapped herself in her nearest cozy cardigan, nestled into her couch, and called her parents first. She was surprised when it took them more than a couple of rings to answer, as they were rarely farther than their couch on weekends, but maybe they had holiday plans.

"Hey, Ma. Just returning your call."

"Oh, hi, sweetheart. We didn't think we'd hear from you to-night. Thought you might be out on the town."

"You've been to this town. Not a lot to go out on."

"Now that's not true. There's a whole world down there once you get out of the mountains. Downtown Gatlinburg is beauti-ful."

Eve made a face as she pictured the so-called downtown area, which was really just a strip of chintzy shops and cheesy attrac-tions. She had no designs on spending her days at the Pancake Pantry or Ripley's Believe It or Not! "That would defeat the purpose of coming here to write, wouldn't it?"

"Well, surely you need a break sometimes." An under-statement if there ever was one. "Maybe you can go to Mass tomorrow. I'm sure you remember St. Mary's. They're very wel-coming."

Eve chewed at her bottom lip as she tried to hold her tongue. Her parents—her mother, especially—never grew tired of trying to proselytize her. It was almost impressive that they could still poke her from seven hundred miles away. But all it really did was rekindle a bunch of uncomfortable feelings, forcing her to con-front this thing constantly weighing on her.

"Anyway," Joan continued, "I'm assuming you got my mes-sage. Your father and I just cannot figure out this website at this theater. They say we have to register, and we have, and then they put us in some kind of room to buy tickets, but it won't let us out of it. And I can only imagine this is impacting your ticket sales. Y—"

"Ma," Eve cut in, unwilling to go along on this tangent with her.

"Yes?"

"Why did you send me here?"

"Eve, I'm *quite* sure this was your idea. Matter of fact, I wanted you to wait until I could come with you to help you clean up."

"You know that's not what I'm talking about."

"Well, then what?"

"Why . . ." Eve took a deep breath. "Why did you make me give up my baby?"

Joan sighed into the phone. "Please, don't start this again. You made a mistake, and we fixed it. So you could have your life."

"And what life is that?"

"So now we're going to pretend you have nothing?"

"I don't have anything," Eve mumbled.

"You have degrees from two of the best schools in this country. You have a wonderful career that is flourishing. You think you'd be 'doctor' of anything with a baby on your hip?" Joan said. "You *had* a fiancé who adored you, and I'm sure he'd be willing to—"

Eve cut her off again. "You sent me away and I have *never* recovered. You still don't understand that the only reason I went to school for ten years straight was to get away from you. That I chose writing because it was the easiest way to pretend that what happened didn't happen."

"Well, you certainly chose the right profession with these

histrionics," Joan said. "I don't know if this is part of a play or if you've been drinking or what, but I'm not doing this with you tonight. Talk to your father."

"Ma . . ."

The next thing Eve knew, her father's rich baritone was on the other end of the line. "What have you done to your mother, Tètè?"

"All I did was ask a question neither of you have ever been willing to give an adequate answer to."

"Must we do this tonight? Ban m zòrèy mwen. Please."

"You don't have to listen to me. You never do."

"What more is there to say? It was an unfortunate situation, but we did what we thought was best."

"You thought sending me to nowhere to carry a child I would never be able to know was *best* for me?"

"We did." Roger's voice turned soft, hints of sincerity and regret apparent. "You deserved to *be* a child, Eve. Go to college, figure out your career. You were never going to be able to do that *with* a child."

"But you don't know what I could've done. You didn't give me a chance." She angrily wiped away a tear. "And now, *all* I think about is what was taken."

Eve ended the call, too emotional and too tipsy to realize she was hanging up on her parents—a criminal offense in any Black household. But after nearly two weeks of stewing in her feelings, she was no less exasperated with her life and feeling a little nihilistic as a result.

She missed Jamie. She was annoyed with him for leaving, but much more with herself for not being more inviting. He'd even offered his number if she wanted it, but she was too stupid and stubborn to take it. Serves her right for being an asshole.

Against her better judgment, Eve poured another big glass of the cheap Chardonnay she'd found at Whole Foods and returned to her perch at the edge of the couch, where her tenuous Wi-Fi signal seemed to work best. She forged ahead with one more call, finally dialing her ex-fiancé at his behest.

"I thought surely you were dead," Leo answered flatly. She could hear the hum of some restaurant or lounge in the background. If she knew Leo, he was at his favorite hipster beer garden in Williamsburg, and Eve was halfway relieved he wasn't sitting at home sulking, like her. One less thing to feel guilty about.

"Stop texting me," she said loudly.

"Stop ignoring me," he said, not missing a beat—a rarity for him. He was smart, sure, but no one would describe Leo as quick-witted.

"I don't have anything to say." She absently rubbed her eyes, ignoring the very real possibility of her contacts slipping out. "You can't harass me because I don't wanna do this anymore."

"Asking for an explanation is not harassment, Eve. I'd think you owed me that much, at least."

"Why do I owe you anything? Have I not done enough?"

Just the thought of Leo drained her now. Their relationship started as a meet-cute at a little Italian restaurant near NYU, Eve enjoying the way he was so immediately infatuated with her. And she was intrigued by him, too, always dressed to the nines, like some old-school, golden age movie star. But after his father died, Leo was a shell of himself, and based on what little she knew of their abusive relationship, she understood it. She pitied it. And so she protected him. Tended to him.

But now, she no longer had a grip on her own sanity, and there was just no way she could worry about his, too.

Leo released a mocking chuckle. "I sat by the phone for days, thinking just maybe you'd do me a simple kindness, as the man you were about to marry, and give me a damn phone call. That's all I asked for. I wasn't trying to make you come back. I wasn't gonna make you feel like shit for leaving. I just thought, at the very least, I could get an explanation," he said. "And now, you call? Did it take you a whole fucking week to find my phone number? Did you maybe realize you were being a fucking asshole? No, of course not. You're calling me on the Fourth of fucking July, drunk and belligerent, just to twist the knife. Do me a favor and go to hell, Eve."

The line went silent before she could even pretend she had a defense. Whatever damage she'd done to him was likely irrevocable. There's not much you can say when someone wants you in hell.

Lucky for Leo, Eve felt like she was already there.

CHAPTER 11

Red, White & Blue

JAMIE

Fri, Jul 4 2:42 PM

Lucy Ewen: Hi hi hi. So sorry but we got caught up and are running a little late. Can we meet at four instead?

Jamie Gallagher: Sure. I need to stop by my office anyway. I'll swing by after that.

Lucy Ewen: You're the best

Fri, Jul 4 4:42 PM

Jamie Gallagher: Hey, I'm at the house. Where are you?

Jamie should've intervened when Lucy told him she wanted to paint the house red. He didn't say anything at the time because he was no longer living there, so the fight felt both futile and petty. But . . . it looked like a barn. Complete with white accents and an American flag posted above the door.

And ordinarily, he wouldn't have thought twice about it. The only time he spent there was picking up his son. Except that particular day, he'd been sitting in Lucy's driveway for a full hour before Tyler's greige Cherokee finally pulled up beside him. So he had nothing but time to stew over what had become of this unsightly home he was still paying for.

Lucy hopped out of the driver's side before the engine was off, as Jamie exited his own vehicle, taking care to keep his irritation at bay. But he was doing a bad job of it.

"I'm *so* sorry," Lucy said as she approached. "I know."

"It is five thirty, Lucy. You said you were running a *little* late."

"I know. I know. We just got caught up and lost track of the time. And then I didn't realize my phone died until we were back in the car . . ."

Jamie shook his head. "It's always something with you."

"Hey, it's not on purpose. I'm acknowledging it, and I'm saying I'm sorry for it."

"Apologizing doesn't mean I'm obligated to forgive you," he said, his statement loaded with the weight of their past. "But I have somewhere to be, so I'd like to get Jack and go."

"It's okay if you're mad," she said gently. She tried to smile as if to comfort him. "I just needed you to know that it wasn't intentional."

"Thank you for your permission." Jamie went to retrieve his son, but not before adding, "I hope you keep in mind that my generosity is the only thing allowing you to spend this extra time with Jack. Please don't take it for granted."

"And here I thought you were doing what was best for Jack."

"Well, God knows it's not you," Jamie muttered.

"What was that?"

"Forget it." Jamie was never one to start arguments, but surely not around Jack.

Lucy, on the other hand . . . "Don't mumble it, Jamie. Just say it."

He turned back to her, intending to heave some pithy retort her way, but that goddamn ring of hers stopped him cold. He bristled whenever he saw it, but it felt especially conspicuous when he was peeved.

"You never asked," Lucy said, noticing his gaze.

"Well, you might not recall, but . . . you were a little busy."

Jamie suddenly felt heavy but recomposed himself as he turned and opened the car door to greet his son. They exchanged their typical fist bump, and Jamie added a forehead kiss for good measure. Jack's hair was so wet it looked black, and his freckled cheeks were sunburnt.

"You look like you had a good time," he said, grinning at the image. He grabbed Jack's blue-and-orange backpack, which was heavier than it looked, meaning his sopping wet bathing suit and towel were likely inside. "You have anything you need to get out of the house?"

Jack shook his head and sent a quick wave to his mom's fiancé. "Bye, Tyler!"

"All right, little man. We'll see you in a couple days."

"Tyler's gonna take me and Riley to the Titans training camp," Jack informed Jamie as they headed back up the driveway hand in hand.

"Whoa. That's gonna be so much fun," Jamie said brightly, wishing he could make his mood match his tone.

Soon enough, Jack was strapped safely into the back seat of

Jamie's truck, and they were headed east on I-24 toward Smyrna. Away from Lucy's bullshit.

Jamie spent the better part of eight years training himself to let go of the minor things that bothered him about her; he owed it to their son to keep things on an even keel. But as their relationship dwindled to nothing, those small things seemed to only grow bigger over time, and his dislike for her was turning him into someone he didn't want to be. Cold. Angry. Tired.

"Dad, where are we going?" Jack asked.

In the rearview, Jack was gazing out the window at the unfamiliar route, and it brought an instant smile to Jamie's face. A few short years ago, Jack was oblivious to such things, all the roads and streets practically identical to a five-year-old. The time was going by so quickly. Too quickly.

"I told Miss Grace we'd stop by her house for a bit. She's having a barbecue."

"Oh, cool. I like Miss Grace."

"You like everybody," Jamie said. He hoped his son would be able to hold on to that.

"Not *every*body. Remember Mrs. Vanderpool?"

"You just didn't like her because she wouldn't let you draw in your textbooks."

"I think that's a perfectly good reason not to like someone, Dad."

"You're right," Jamie said, his amusement with his son sitting in his eyes. "You don't *have* to like anyone. So long as you're not being prejudiced, you won't hear an argument from me."

There was a natural pause in the conversation as Jamie navigated through a slight buildup in traffic due to construction. He was anxious about being late, because he was never late, but at least he could blame some of it on holiday traffic instead of having to explain how his son's mother had no regard for his time.

"Hey, Dad?"

Jamie already knew he wasn't going to like the question on the other end of his son's familiar inflection, but he was all ears, as always. "Yeah, bud?"

"What were you and Mom arguing about?"

"We weren't really . . . arguing." Jamie pinched the bridge of his nose, lifting his sunglasses in the process, as he tried to concoct a tactful explanation. "We just had a misunderstanding. About when you guys'd get back."

"It was my fault we were late," Jack said. "Mom said it was time to go, but I wanted to do the Stage Dive again, and the line was super long."

"Jack . . ."

"I'm sorry, Dad."

"No, it's not . . . I just don't want you worrying about this stuff." Now he felt like an asshole for making his son feel bad, which only amplified his resentment for Lucy. "Nothing is anyone's *fault*. It's all just gonna take some time to get used to. You know what I mean?"

Jack nodded, but there was obviously more on his mind, his brows still knitted over his thoughtful blue stare.

"What is it?"

"Will it be okay with you if I like Tyler?" Jack asked carefully. "Because I kinda . . . do."

Jamie laughed, mostly to disguise that it felt like he'd been punched in the gut. As much as he wanted to be mature about this whole thing, trying so desperately to be big after Lucy made him feel so inadequate and small, he still wasn't ready for this part.

"Of course you can," he said, glancing back at his son. Those four words went against every thought circulating in his brain, but it was the right answer. "Your mom and I won't bring anyone into your life that we don't want you to like. And they have to like you, or no deal."

"Have you ever thought about getting a new girlfriend?"

Jamie laughed again at the way he said it, like it was that simple. Just think about it and she'd appear. Eve was the only woman he'd met outside of work, and from everything he'd seen, she was less ready than he was for anything resembling a relationship. "It's not a priority for me right now," he said.

"Priority?"

"It's not a big deal to me." Jack was so astute, Jamie sometimes forgot he was only eight. "I'm not looking for a girlfriend right now. But if I find one, you'll be the first to know. Okay?"

"Okay."

It was close to 11:00 p.m. when Jamie pulled into his apartment's designated parking space, Jack tuckered out in the back seat. He'd spent most of his evening frolicking in and around Grace's pool with the other kids, and then stuffed down enough hot dogs to keep him full until August. Jamie had to carry him out like a tiny drunk from the local bar, a scene he wasn't exactly a stranger to, once upon a time. But he was glad the kid had fun, at least.

On the dry end of the barbecue, Grace had made her second and, hopefully, final attempt at setting up Jamie with one of her church friends. Grace was his office manager and invaluable to business operations, but if he let her, she would've been happy to take charge of his entire life.

The woman Grace introduced him to, Elena something, was nice enough, and attractive enough, but he was already harboring a bad mood, thanks to Lucy, and he wasn't up to feigning friendliness, much less interest, all evening. It actually just highlighted how much he'd enjoyed his time with Eve, who didn't believe in cordiality, it seemed, and was fine with silence. Probably preferred it. And he appreciated someone who understood that quiet wasn't a symptom of something amiss, but rather a sign of comfort.

Once Jack was tucked in, Jamie settled in his living room, stretching out on his big cornflower-blue sofa with a plate of leftovers from Grace's and the remote control. He'd been in his condo for about a year now but still wasn't used to the frill of it all. He didn't decorate it himself, because then it would've looked like his cabin back in Gatlinburg: drab and disparate. So he let his brother make sense of the space. Casey had done an excellent job, if his friends had anything to say about it. They marveled over the color schemes, the accents of chartreuse in the kitchen spilling out into the dining area, which featured a table Jamie made himself. Casey surrounded the table with a rainbow of acrylic chairs, making the place look more like an art class than a home. It was beautiful, but it all felt too bright for Jamie's general malaise since the breakup.

He pretended to be interested in Wimbledon highlights for all of two minutes before deciding to call his brother, as anything tennis automatically invoked thoughts of Casey, who used to refer to himself as a "Serena Williams stan," whatever that meant.

"Now what are *you* doing up at midnight?" Casey answered the phone in his honey-laced Tennessee twang.

"It's eleven here," Jamie reminded him. He set his plate on the nearest end table and sat up straighter. "I'm surprised you're not at a party in some speakeasy in an underground bunker."

"I'm afraid I've become as boring as you in my old age."

"I'm sure your aching joints appreciate it," Jamie joked. "How's Jelani?"

"Snoring. Loudly."

Jamie halfway wished he were doing the same. "Well, I didn't mean to bother you," he said. "I've just had a lot on my mind the last few days . . . you know I'm supposed to be in Rachael and Nick's wedding soon, and . . . I guess it's got me thinking about Dad."

Casey exhaled sharply into the phone. "That's never good."

"I just wonder . . ." Jamie absently scratched his beard as he tried to find a diplomatic way to talk shit about their father. "Why do you think he never dated anyone after Mom?"

"Have you met our dad? Who would want him?" The two of them laughed for several beats before Casey soberly continued, "If I had to guess, he was probably too afraid to put himself out there. Easier to just focus on us."

Jamie bridled at the idea that he was some walking cliché, reliving his own father's hellish story, thirty years later. "I can relate."

"Well no shit, Jameson," Casey said. "You were blessed with Dad's tender heart. But it means you also got stuck with his unabating martyr complex."

"It's actually annoying how smug you are sometimes," Jamie said, chuckling. "Guess you got that from Mom."

"Oh, absolutely. Her flightiness, too."

Shaking his head, Jamie traded the comfort of his couch for

the warmth of his terrace, overlooking his trendy Nashville suburb. Despite mostly quitting years ago, back when Lucy was pregnant, something about standing out there made him ache for the gratifying buzz of a cigarette. A bad habit he'd picked up from Diane Gallagher. "Well. Despite inheriting her worst traits, I'd say you turned out okay," he told Casey.

"We both did."

"I guess."

"Why'd Rachael's wedding make you think about Dad anyway?"

"I don't know." Jamie yawned, leaning against the railing to view the fireworks that started to flash in the air above him. Of course, people had been setting them off throughout the city since sunset, but he never tired of watching those blasts of color fill the sky. "After the last year, I thought I'd feel relieved to be out of this fight," he said. "But I feel like I'm still struggling with something. I don't know if it's listlessness, depression, or just plain old heartbreak . . . but I don't wanna be like Dad."

Casey chuckled in a way that sounded dismissive. "You should move to New York. That inexplicable ennui would be like catnip here."

"Jesus, you really are like Mom," Jamie said.

"Listen, just because Dad is back with her doesn't mean you're gonna end up with Lucy again. Or at least, it doesn't have to."

Jamie felt his face contorting to a scowl. "What . . . ?"

"You're not deterministically fated to end up just like your father. You get to do whatever you want, you know."

"No. What do you mean 'Dad is back with her'?" he demanded. "You're not talking about Mom, are you?"

"Shit."

"Spit it out, Case."

"I thought you knew," Casey said. "I thought that's why you were brooding. Trust me, I had *no* plans on being the one to break this news to you."

Jamie exhaled, feeling something like a headache forming. His mother was probably the worst person he knew, which was saying a lot considering how he felt about Lucy during the last year. "How long has this been goin' on?"

Casey hemmed and hawed before giving a noncommittal "A while, I guess?"

"What's 'a while'?"

"Since Easter?"

"For months? Why the fuck didn't you tell me?" Jamie was shouting, and while he would've liked to pretend it was because of the fireworks, he was simply irate.

"Yes, you're taking it so well, and don't seem unhinged at all. I don't know what I was thinking."

"You're an ass."

"You've had so much going on," Casey said, the sarcasm gone from his voice. "I genuinely didn't think it would help to add this."

Jamie let out a low grumble, unable to argue with that. "Jesus," he said, sighing again. "Why would Dad do this?"

"Maybe because being alone sucks. Weren't you just lamenting him spending the last two decades without someone?"

"Yeah, but not her."

"Maybe he loves her, Jamie."

"I find that hard to believe."

"Yeah, well, you spent ten years with Maleficent, so I'm not sure you should be judging Dad for anything."

"Why . . . do I talk to you?"

"Because you know I'm right. And honestly, it's time to get over this feud with Mom," he added pointedly. "She didn't ruin your life. You chose to stay." Jamie opened his mouth to protest, but Casey beat him to the punch. "And I know you did it for me. Lord knows I love you for that more than words will ever be adequate enough to express. But, Jamie, *you* chose that. And *you* chose Lucy."

"I don't blame her for me choosing Lucy."

Casey laughed as he replied, "Yes, you do. But at the end of the day, let's be real. You are loved. You are successful. You have an awesome kid, which basically eclipses everything else. What are you so mad at our mother for?"

Jamie couldn't believe what he was hearing. Her lies, selfishness, and unwillingness to be their mother wasn't enough? "She destroyed our family," Jamie said. He stated it as a fact, impossible for Casey to dispute.

"And yet, here you are."

"You were too young. You wouldn't understand."

"I understand, Jamie. I carried that grudge right along with you for more than half my life. Which is how I know . . . You've gotta let some things go, bro. That shit you're holding on to will swallow you whole."

CHAPTER 12

Let the Flames Begin

EVE

It was Tuesday, finally. And despite all of Eve's efforts to be unaffected by that fact, all she could think about was what it meant: Jamie would return soon. The days crawled by without him, and even more so after the shitty weekend she'd had. Leo's last words hung over her head like an anvil, her hollowness amplified.

And the only thing that had made her feel a little less empty was Jamie. Granted, she'd known him only a matter of days, and if someone asked her his last name, she would've had to make one up. But she liked the way she felt around him. And if he was okay with being around her, perhaps she wasn't as fucked up as her self-doubt would have her believe. So she could admit, at least to herself, that she looked forward to seeing him again.

After spending all afternoon waiting for the sound of Jamie's charmingly loud truck, Eve opted to stop by his house and invite him to dinner. Sure, it would seem eager, maybe even thirsty, showing up so soon, hat in hand, but . . . much of her pride had been stamped out already anyway. And she'd promised herself that if Jamie returned, she would stop acting like such a jackass.

Making him a meal felt like a good first step toward that resolution.

Jamie arrived at 7:00 p.m. to a three-course meal of bruschetta, beef braciole, and poached cherries. By eight, he was telling Eve it was the best meal he'd ever had. She wasn't sure she believed him, but it was a compliment either way. Eve wasn't exactly known for her kitchen skills—that was Leo's pursuit—but she'd mastered this one dinner, at least. Braciole, aka *involtini* in Italy, was made of sirloin and prosciutto, parsley and garlic, three different cheeses, and pine nuts, with homemade breadcrumbs as the filling. It was a labor of love, standing over the stove while it cooked for two hours in a tomato sauce with red wine. For their dessert, she'd cooked some Rainier cherries in Tempranillo and brown sugar, then topped it with a dollop of honeycomb custard. It wasn't as good as whatever magic Jamie served at his place, but it did the job.

"Did you go to cooking school while you were gettin' all your other degrees?" Jamie wondered.

Eve grinned at the way he dropped his *g*'s every now and then. "Definitely not. Got these recipes from a coworker."

Jamie accepted that answer as he scraped up the last bits of cherry and brown sugar. "I think I'd pay you to make this for us every week."

"Well, I don't come cheap, so I hope you're prepared if I decide to take you up on that." Eve didn't miss his use of *us*, and something within her liked that he was including her in his plans. Something else within her was terrified of it.

"I'm prepared." He grabbed his wineglass and finished what was left of it. "So you've been here for almost two weeks now. How are you liking it? . . . Or not liking it?"

"I actually . . . I'm getting used to it." She reflexively scanned her grandmother's home. While he was gone, it was all she had, and she was coming around to really loving her space. "This feels more like me now," she said, gesturing generally. "And I'm getting more comfortable with the town. I don't feel quite as lost."

"So you've been to places other than Crockett's?"

"Well . . . no."

"Not even Food City?"

"I literally drove to Knoxville for a Whole Foods."

Jamie laughed, presumably at how bougie she sounded, and Eve was grateful he didn't seem to take it too seriously.

"Better than nowhere," he said.

"Safe to say you'll be my only entertainment for a while."

"I'm not gonna complain about that," he said, grinning. As she rose from the table, taking both of their emptied bowls to the sink, he added, "It's nice talking to you without the aid of three glasses of whiskey."

Eve's face grew warm, and it wasn't from alcohol this time, but sheer embarrassment. "I don't think it was three." She hoped it wasn't anyway.

"Shit, was it four?"

She tried and failed to suppress a laugh. "It wasn't my finest hour."

Jamie joined her in the kitchen, bringing their stemware with him. "I like to think you're getting used to me."

Eve rolled her eyes. "You want more wine?"

He responded by pushing his glass toward her. "You're like a puzzle I don't have all the pieces to yet."

She ignored his comment, along with the tingling in her

cheeks, to pour his drink. She could feel his gaze flirting with her until she could no longer stand the heat, forcing her to turn away. "Come," she instructed, taking off before he could reply.

Without protest, Jamie followed her up the staircase that led to the extra bedroom—Eve's room. She'd bedecked the space in mostly white, turning the old-fashioned space into her modern personal oasis, including a new queen-sized bed to replace the tiny wooden one, complete with complementing nightstands. She'd also converted one half of the angled ceiling into a wall of warm lights that made her room glow like Christmas. She admired her own work as she guided Jamie through, but she noticed his footsteps grow more tentative as they moved farther in.

"Can I ask what we're doing?"

Eve laughed at the unease in his question. For the first time in their short history, she felt like she was the steady one between them. "Are you nervous?"

"More like . . . curious."

She boasted a self-satisfied smile as they reached the balcony, hoping the scenery would satiate his curiosity. "I just thought we could hang out here," she said, showing off her view. Even in the darkness of dusk, those Great Smoky Mountains were stunning. "Sorry I don't have chairs . . ."

"No, it's fine." He leaned against the railing with his glass. "This is nice."

She smiled at the side of Jamie's face, pleased that he agreed. She was having a bit of déjà vu as she gazed at his splendid profile, enjoying the shape of his nose and the way his dark hair curled around his ears. But this time, she detected a hint of melancholy.

"You okay?" she asked.

"Yeah . . ." He sighed and stood up straighter, relieving the balustrade of its duty. "Wine makes me sleepy."

It felt like he was being evasive, but she didn't know him well enough to push the issue. "Well. If you wanna talk, I'm here. And if you don't wanna talk, I'm here."

Jamie looked at her. "Is that right?"

"Don't say it like it's so unbelievable. I'm a good listener. When I wanna be."

"I guess there's still time to prove that."

Eve smiled again, relishing in his wit. Most men didn't have the range, but Jamie rolled with her thorny punches, and maybe even considered them a challenge. It just made her want to talk to him even more. Eager to see what he'd say next.

"It's my mom," Jamie announced as he swirled the contents of his glass. "Or . . . I don't know. I guess it's my ex."

"It's alarming that you don't know the difference."

He chuckled. "You're not wrong."

"What did she . . . or they . . . do?"

"It's a long, sordid story. But I guess I just feel . . . stuck. Resenting both of them for ruining everything and still getting to be happy. I don't know."

Eve gazed at him pensively. It wasn't obvious at first glance, as he seemed so at ease. But this was that hint of darkness she'd detected in him. There was a little gloom there. Probably what kept drawing her to him.

"You don't feel like you're happy?"

"I feel like I'm fine. My kid is amazing. I could go through my entire life the way it is now and probably be okay with it," he said, finishing off his wine. "But I don't know that I'd call myself happy."

Eve automatically recalled Don Draper delivering the line *What is happiness? It's a moment before you need more happiness.* She was a bit fascinated by the way white people—white men, especially—found it to be so elusive. Black folks rarely got to concern themselves with their version of happy. Didn't ask for much beyond safety, financial stability, and family. Black happiness was too often rooted in plain old survival. White people seemed to define it by avoiding boredom.

"Maybe happy is overrated," she offered.

"I don't know about that. Maybe it's fleeting, but . . . I gotta believe there's somethin' more. Some people reach self-actualization, right?"

"You think your ex has?"

"Probably not what Maslow had in mind. But her version of it, maybe." He bit his bottom lip contemplatively before adding, "Maybe half the battle is just finding someone and something you like."

Eve looked down at the balcony floor, Jamie's comment managing to send her to Leo. It was that simple: She didn't like him. She loved him. At some point. But if she ever really liked him, it didn't last long; it was a wonder they lasted for as many years as they did.

"Maybe so." She swatted a tear that appeared on her cheek, hoping Jamie hadn't noticed.

"Sorry. I didn't mean to bring down the mood."

"No, I asked. And I get it. When everyone around you seems okay, it's hard not to wonder where you went wrong."

Jamie nodded, his blue eyes focused on the black abyss in front of them. "We can move on to easier subjects."

"Easier subjects like what?"

He looked at her then. "You got any book recommendations?"

"I should be asking you that," Eve said, recalling his eclectic bookshelf. "I've only been rereading. Maya Angelou. For work."

"Oh yeah. I saw *Mom & Me & Mom* on your coffee table."

Eve met his gaze, mildly surprised that he'd noticed.

"You using that for your play?"

She shrugged. "It's a long, sordid story."

He grinned at her joke, though she was only about half kidding. "Well, if you feel like reading about the rise of the Islamic State, that's what I just finished," he said.

Eve laughed at first, but her face quickly contorted into concern when she realized he was serious.

"I just try to know about the world." He smiled again, this time with a more wistful tint. "I didn't go to college, which I feel insecure about sometimes. Especially when my kid comes home with math problems that look like Greek to me. So I learn what I can."

Eve was further surprised to hear that he was insecure about anything; prior to this conversation, he seemed so self-possessed.

"Even standing here talking to you is a little intimidating," he said.

"Me? Why?"

"You have how many degrees?"

"Please." Eve snickered at the thought. "I promise you don't need a degree to learn anything I know."

"Why'd you get 'em then?"

"I didn't really have a choice. My parents wouldn't have allowed anything less. Nor would the world." When his eyebrows furrowed, she added, "I'm a Black woman, so a degree is generally the only way to get my foot in the door. They'll let you in with little more than a nice smile."

Jamie nodded slowly. "Fair enough."

"It's not fair at all," Eve mumbled, sipping her wine again. "But y'know, whiteness."

"I got it," he said, his eyes landing on her, and she was thankful there was amusement in them. He was a good sport. "No college for me, I guess."

"If it's something you wanna do, I would never tell you not to," Eve said. "But you shouldn't feel intimidated by me. I can't remember the last time I enjoyed talking to anyone this much."

He answered with a ghost of a smile on his lips, the warmth in his eyes only growing warmer as he regarded her. "Likewise," he said.

Eve looked away, fearing getting lost in his stare. Then, in the distance, she noticed a pattern of faintly flashing lights dotting the darkness, and her initial instinct was to wonder if she was seeing little fires somehow igniting in the mountains. But no, the much likelier culprit was the lore of the Great Smoky Mountains, which Jamie had been kind enough to remind her of on her first night there. "Are those fireflies?" she wondered out loud.

Jamie turned his head, peering into the dark until there was a spark of recognition dancing in his blue gaze. "Yeah, they are," he said, clearly awed by the magical sight. "They're late this year, but that's definitely them."

It wasn't long before the mountains echoed like a stadium shimmering with cell phone flashes. The fact that pure nature was putting on a light show, as if just for the two of them, left Eve in pure wonderment, feeling as though she could reach out and touch the stars. "It's beautiful," she said, wishing she had something more valuable to add to the moment. Instead, she stared, for minutes on end, Jamie watching with her, as the fireflies did their coordinated caper through the sky. Hundreds, maybe thousands, of tiny beacons of light. It felt surreal and intimate and exhilarating, and much to Eve's surprise, she was elated she had someone to share it with.

Eve wasn't sure what was happening. Why she couldn't ignore these prickles of emotion that materialized whenever she was close to Jamie. There was an attraction there, yes, and she wanted to be mad that it wouldn't go away. But it was more than that. It was the simple act of being close to someone when she felt so disconnected from her real life. She wore a facade like armor, but Jamie was so willing to be vulnerable anyway. She'd known this man for all of two weeks, but she trusted him. On the lowest of keys, she wanted him to trust her. It was such a peculiar and unwelcome feeling, but she didn't know how to fight it. And maybe she wasn't supposed to.

"You remember that boyfriend I told you about?" she asked.

"Yeah . . ."

"He was my fiancé." Her brown eyes were wide and pleading, waiting for him to react, but he didn't. "His mother taught me to make that braciole." She paused, recalling the many Sundays spent in the kitchen with Greta Coletti helping her perfect the dish. "And he loved me so much that I thought I would suffocate. So I left."

Jamie didn't speak—perhaps he was speechless—and instead simply watched her.

"I came here because I couldn't spend another minute in that brownstone. I couldn't pretend I cared anymore."

He nodded, but it was still a long time before he said anything, needing the space to digest all of her lies, if she had to guess.

"It feels like this is the first time you've been honest with me," Jamie said, his voice just above a whisper.

Eve closed her eyes, feeling like he was seeing right through her. She wanted so badly not to feel things and thought he was going to be the distraction she needed. But instead, he just made her feel different things. *Kouri pou lapli, tonbe nan larivyè,* as her father would say. Running from the rain, falling in the river. It didn't change the fact that Jamie gave her butterflies. Maybe fireflies. He opened her up without even trying. It made her want to run for her life. But there she stood.

"Jamie," she whispered back, her voice breaking as a new tear slipped down her cheek.

He moved to wipe it from her face, and the two of them were suddenly standing so close, she could feel his warm, wine-scented breath touch her skin.

"I'm glad you came here," he said. He allowed his thumb to slip down to her bottom lip, caressing her soft, wet flesh as their eyes locked, and time seemed to stop.

Eve's mind was screaming, *Do it, just kiss him,* as her body so clearly wanted. Despite the cool outside air, she felt hot, her nervous energy seeming to wrap its fingers around her throat, rendering her stock-still, unable to make the first move.

She was thankful when Jamie did, his graceful fingers caressing her jaw. She exhaled a wobbly breath, an expression of her excitement and uncertainty, just before he leaned in with the kiss. His lips were gloriously soft, and she liked the tickle of his beard against her face. His kiss was gentle. As her tongue touched his, he moved his hand to the small of her back, pulling her closer, their bodies melting together, leaving Eve feeling more alive than she had in months. Probably years.

As the two of them separated for air, Eve pinned against the balcony railing as Jamie's face flushed, the unexpected moment leaving her a bit dizzy, she was already kicking herself for the words that were about to come out of her mouth next.

"You wanna have sex?"

She asked it plainly, devoid of any romance or even emotion—which, to be fair, she wasn't looking for. Quite the opposite, really. It had been a long time since she even wanted anything in the realm of physical intimacy, after years of associating sex with trauma. But as they stood there, chest to chest, her lips tingling from his, she became acutely aware that she wanted *him*.

Jamie forced his gaze from her mouth and looked her in the eye, his eyebrow quirked with what she hoped was intrigue and not him thinking she was out of her mind. Even if she was. "Is . . . that what you want?"

Eve nodded eagerly before pulling him in for another kiss. Her fingers enmeshed in his beard, obsessed with the fuzzy feeling against her fingertips, his hot tongue lashing against hers, she led him back inside with her lips.

The two of them stumbled blindly through the unfamiliar terrain as they attempted to undress each other. As Eve's shirt went over her head, the backs of her legs hit the bed, sending her falling into the mattress with a tiny, surprised gasp; that gasp soon turned into a shy smile when Jamie joined her, grinning mischievously as he straddled her.

He threw her Henley to the floor and began to fervently kiss her neck, giving her velvety skin a series of long, slow licks that made her shiver, and he smiled. His tongue explored the curves of her collarbone and worked his way down, past her bra to her torso, where he could lick through the ripples of her taut stomach as he unbuttoned her jeans.

"Kiss me again," Eve whispered, needing a few more minutes to adjust to the idea of being naked. Plus, she liked the way he kissed. He was tender and good with his tongue, letting it dance with hers instead of the typical wrestle. As he indulged her request, she ran her fingers through his curls, so soft they felt like feathers in her hand.

She began to unbutton his shirt, feeling more butterflies when her fingers found his skin, the hardness of his stomach surprising her. She whimpered when he broke their kiss, and then she licked her lips as his tanned skin and broad, muscled shoulders came into view. She watched him like a movie as he pulled his arms from the sleeves, the veins of his forearms leaving her squirming. She wanted to lick every inch of him. She imagined him tasting like that banana pudding ice cream she'd become such a fan of.

"You okay?" he asked.

Eve nodded. She wiggled her feet, still clad in her Timbs. "Take off my shoes?"

Jamie did so with a smile, hopping off the bed to kick off his own boots as he untied hers. "I should probably mention that I haven't done this in a while," he said, just as her shoes made two big thuds hitting the wood floor.

She wanted to say that she hadn't, either, but decided against it. She was about to share more than enough with him for one night.

Eve felt disarmed by the way Jamie stared at her body. Did he notice the stretch marks, all the scars she'd always obsessed over? Evidence of her past, with no baby to show for it. She wasn't even naked yet, but he made her feel like she was. Constantly.

"Take off your pants," she said.

He unzipped his jeans and allowed them to fall as she crawled to the edge of the bed to meet him. "I think it's your turn," he said, smirking at her as his finger traced the underside of her bra, seemingly waiting for permission to remove it.

Eve unhooked the brassiere for herself, letting her full breasts spill from the cups before throwing it to their pile of clothes collected on the floor. She distinctly remembered keeping her bra on the last time she had sex—sometime in May. An anxious sigh fell from her lips as that fact washed over her.

"Kiss me again?" she asked.

Jamie went in for another, inhaling sharply as her soft chest pressed against him, his lips pressed against hers. Eve enjoyed the way their noses smashed together when they were close enough, his narrow where hers was wide—they fit together well. His hands spanned her toned back, tickling her hot skin before roaming south. He slipped his fingers into the back of her opened jeans, and then inside her panties, palming her backside, squeezing her flesh as he brought her closer.

Eve was pulsating as Jamie's bulge pushed against her. She moaned desperately as she deepened their kiss, her fingers gripping at his hair, luring him back onto the bed. Jamie and his wet pecks moved lower, Eve only getting wetter as he landed on her tits. He lapped and sucked her stiffened nipples, smiling up at her when she responded with gentle purrs. His tongue circled her navel as he skillfully peeled off her jeans, his lips never breaking contact with her skin.

"Stop," Eve whimpered, tugging gently at his curls.

Jamie immediately halted, sitting up on his knees to gaze at her, his chest still heaving, teasing her. "You're not ready for this?"

"It's not that," she said. She appreciated his concern. But he was journeying toward oral sex, and she wasn't ready for *that* level of intimacy. "I don't need the foreplay," she said. "I just . . . I'd rather just the sex."

"Oh."

She clumsily added, "If that's okay with you . . ."

"I'm fine with whatever you want . . ."

He was so kind. Maybe even too kind. But it was very much the reason that she liked him as much as she did. "Okay," she said, a sheepish smile telling him to proceed.

Eve lifted her hips from the bed to assist in removing her pants. Suddenly, she was aware of how quiet the room was, just the rustling sound of clothing being removed. It was all so awkward, even innocent. He looked at her like she was the most beautiful thing on earth. Meanwhile, she was self-conscious because she hadn't shaved in far too long, not even her legs, and she was allowing this man to see her stark naked. She fidgeted on the bed as he removed his boxers, swallowing hard when she got a glimpse of him. Her nipples tightened into knots again, conveying her arousal, and her stomach was doing backflips as it contracted. Maybe she wasn't ready for this.

Jamie gave himself a few strokes before returning his attention to Eve, licking his full lips as he positioned himself between Eve's thighs. "You're sure you're good?" he asked, caressing her left leg.

"If you ask me that again, I'm gonna go find someone else," she said.

"Good luck with that," he said. The smile that came with his statement made her insides tingle even more.

Resuming their kiss, he began to finger her, familiarizing himself with the most intimate parts of her body. The levity in the room was all but gone, replaced by pure heat as the head of his length flirted with her opening. They both moaned quietly, their lip-lock turning sloppy once he found his way in.

"Right there," Eve whispered as he pushed into her with a soft grunt. Filling her up, pressed against her walls, he felt good. So maddeningly good.

Jamie began to thrust with slow, sensual rolls of his hips that managed to hit several spots at once, his tongue hot against her throat as he sucked her flesh. Eve felt like she was on a ride, and she wasn't sure whether she should want to get off.

"Wait, wait, wait," she said, breathless as she squeezed his bare shoulder, the firmness of it telling her to ignore her instincts and keep going. But alas . . . "Do you have a condom?"

Jamie immediately stopped thrusting and kissing long enough to realize their mistake. "Shit." He heaved a sharp and clearly frustrated sigh. "I don't even have any at home."

"Fuck," Eve said. She whined.

"I mean . . . I can always pull out . . ."

As desperate as she was to climax—for once—Eve wasn't going to take that chance. She gestured for him to move. "Just let me do you."

"What?"

"I can finish you off . . ." She licked her lips as her eyes averted his, hoping he would get the picture without her having to ask to suck his dick.

"O-okay . . ."

Carefully, Jamie pulled out and repositioned onto his back, allowing Eve to mount him.

"You good?" Eve asked. In truth, she was out of practice and questioning whether *she* was good at that point.

"Oh, so you can ask me that, but I can't ask you?"

"You asked me, like, twelve times."

"Excuse me for making sure you were comfortable."

"And now I'm doing the same."

"I'm good," he said, his eyes, a darker blue than usual, dancing down her body.

Eve expelled a long breath as she ran her fingers along his thighs and traced them up his stomach, trying to work up the gumption to begin. This was much easier when he was doing all the work.

"What's wrong?" Jamie asked, all the teasing gone from his tone.

"I don't know. I think you made it weird by talking so much."

He smiled. "I assure you it was weird anyway."

Eve wanted to argue with that, but she had no leg to stand on. Of course, sex was inherently awkward, and especially with a new partner, but this was really taking the cake. Due in large part to the fact that she had no idea what she wanted. She wanted everything and nothing. She wanted to feel *something* without being forced to think about all the things she'd tried so hard to push down. And she had yet to master how to actually do any of it. "Yeah. I guess it was . . ."

"Did you know this was what you wanted when you invited me over?"

Eve cocked her head. "Does it seem like I had a plan here?"

"No," he said, still grinning. "But we can just lie here if you want. I don't . . . need this."

He didn't do anything to make this easier on her. She could try forever to be uninvolved and seem unaffected, but everything he did, damn near every word he said, just chipped away at that. The first time they met, she was impolite and idiotic; their second encounter, she had a panic attack; and the third, she drank herself into a stupor. But here he was, still trying with her.

"I don't know, it seems like you do need this," she said suggestively.

Jamie shrugged. "I'll live."

Sure he would, but she didn't want to leave him like this. Just because she was still figuring out what she wanted didn't mean he should go to sleep horny and frustrated. "So you're saying you *don't* want me to suck your dick?"

"I mean . . ." He matched her impish smile as he shook his head. "If you want to, I'm sure as hell not gonna say no."

Eve bit her plump bottom lip as her gaze slipped down his lithe frame, landing back on his erection. "Are you gonna say yes?"

Jamie sat up to meet her with another kiss, and she appreciated that he recognized how much she enjoyed them. He cupped her face, his wet mouth claiming hers, briefly but sweetly, before answering in a whisper, "Yes."

CHAPTER 13

Wed, Jul 9 12:25 PM

Jamie Gallagher: So . . . should we talk about last night?

Wed, Jul 9 12:31 PM

Eve Ambroise: Please let's not.

Jamie Gallagher: Why not?

Eve Ambroise: Making a fool of myself isn't punishment enough? You're gonna make me stand in the mirror and face it too?

Jamie Gallagher: Lol you didn't make a fool of yourself. I just want to know what we're doing.

Eve Ambroise: Why do we have to be doing anything?

Eve Ambroise: Did you enjoy it?

Jamie Gallagher: I did.

Eve Ambroise: So can't we leave it at that?

Jamie Gallagher: Ok. But. Are we leaving it at that?

Eve Ambroise: Why are you like this?

Jamie Gallagher: So sorry for being an adult.

Eve Ambroise: Ugh, I don't know. 😩

Eve Ambroise: Do you wanna leave it at that?

Jamie Gallagher: Well no, not really.

Eve Ambroise: Okay.

Eve Ambroise: So we'll begin with that and see where it goes

Eve Ambroise: Not that it's going to go further than this anytime soon.

Eve Ambroise: I would just prefer if we feel it out rather than having to talk about it.

Jamie Gallagher: Lol ok.

Wed, Jul 9 1:07 PM

Eve Ambroise: Are you really ending this incredibly disconcerting conversation with "lol ok"?

Jamie Gallagher: Why not? What else was there to say?

Eve Ambroise: I don't know. Nothing, I suppose.

Eve Ambroise: Just feels like this deserved something more substantial.

Jamie Gallagher: You want me to draw up a contract?

Eve Ambroise: Bye Jamie.

Jamie Gallagher: ☺ See you tonight, I hope.

Eve Ambroise: lol ok.

CHAPTER 14

Late Night Tip

JAMIE

Thu, Jul 31 8:04 PM

Eve Ambroise: I'm on my way over. Please tell me you cooked something.

Jamie Gallagher: I didn't. But I do have plenty to eat.

Eve Ambroise: Ew. Don't be crass.

Jamie Gallagher: Lol I wasn't. Weirdo. Picked up some BBQ from Preacher's.

Eve Ambroise: Oop. Leaving rn.

Jamie Gallagher: Keep an eye out for bears.

Eve Ambroise: . . .

"Evie . . ."

With Eve's tongue rendering Jamie speechless, his unfinished thought hung in the air, as his mouth had been agape for the last ten minutes. He squeezed the fistful of her ponytail he'd been clutching as she licked him like a lollipop. He tried to watch, but in the haze of his euphoria, his eyes wouldn't even stay open.

"Shit," he whispered.

With her hand wrapped around his length, Eve continued to pump him gently as her mouth worked the tip. She alternated between long, delicate kisses that made his breath hitch, and flicking her tongue against him, making his entire body quiver. She seemed unhurried in her mission to torture him, surely getting her own pleasure from watching him twitch beneath her, listening to her name repeatedly fall from his lips in a dazed mumble. It had only been a few weeks of the two of them doing this weird little dance, but he knew that much about her.

In fact, Jamie had learned a lot about Eve through their semi-sexual relationship. Or not-quite relationship. A situation? Situationship.

She liked to kiss. It was unexpected for someone so guarded. But then, so was all of this. Her kisses were hungry, like she was looking for something, and Jamie hopelessly wanted to be the thing that she found.

She needed to be in control, but she was trying to let go. Figuring out how to be free. And he wanted that for her, too.

She hated being cold.

She wasn't exactly comfortable being naked, and it was a shame, because her body was exquisite. He marveled at it all that first night: from the majesty of her muscles to the elegance of her long fingers and the roundness of her backside. He fantasized about drinking from the curve of her back and then feasting on her pussy for dessert.

Eve was an enigma that he delighted in trying to unravel. He told her she was a puzzle, and he meant it, beguiled by how much she confounded him. And while he still didn't have all the pieces, he was definitely starting to see a clearer picture.

"Let me know when," Eve said. He'd also learned that she didn't quite like surprises.

"*When,*" Jamie blurted, and it was immediately followed by a gruff and unceremonious grunt to signal his release. His hips reflexively bucked upward as his thighs went numb, but she didn't stop sucking and stroking until he was empty.

She was gentle but efficient, and once certain he was done, she massaged him back into his boxers, leaving him only semi-erect. She pulled her shirt back into place and sat up on her knees to gaze upon her work: He was frozen in place, a sated smile dangling from his lips.

"God," Jamie said in one growly breath, lacking any other coherent thoughts as he lay there senseless from the waist down. Eve seemed to approach this whole thing like a series of to-do boxes that needed to be checked, but he supposed that was part of her charm.

Eve simpered, clearly satisfied with herself. "It was good?" she asked. She crawled up to her side of the bed, falling into the spot beside him.

"I'm convinced this is some elaborate ploy to kill me."

Eve nodded as she wiped her mouth. "It's not," she said, "but I appreciate the confidence boost."

Jamie turned onto his side and adjusted his pillow to see Eve's face. "Can I return the favor yet?" He asked the question already figuring the answer, as it had been the same for more than two weeks now. Still, he reached out to her waist, his fingers playing with the elastic lining of her panties, just waiting for permission to pull them off.

"No." She denied him with a smile and used her index finger to push his face back in the other direction. "You better go get yourself some ice cream if you want something to eat."

He laughed as he rolled back to his side of the bed; he enjoyed her playfulness and the fact that he'd gotten to see a lot more of it lately. It was how he learned that she had a tiny dimple in her right cheek when she let her giggle loose.

"All right," Jamie said, "but you know I won't be here during the week anymore, so this'll be your last chance for a while."

Eve sighed, and he detected a flash of disappointment somewhere in it. "I'm aware," she said. "I'll be busy writing, and not at all thinking about you. So don't worry."

As she spoke, she repositioned sideways across the bed, using Jamie's torso as her headrest. The week before, she'd mentioned that she liked feeling the warmth of his body against the back of her neck. And that she didn't usually sleep well, but she did next to him. She'd become comfortable with him, the effortlessness of their first few interactions swelling into familiarity already. He wondered what she would do now that he'd be gone more often than not.

"I wasn't worried," Jamie said once she got settled. "Just thought you'd like to know."

"Mm." Clearly checked out of the conversation, Eve pointed to his nightstand, a cue to hand over her book. She'd taken him up on his offer to read about the Islamic State, a decidedly strange thing to pick up every night after something like sex, but it had become part of their routine. He'd be there beside her, reading whatever she'd picked out for him: He was currently deep into Kiese Laymon's most recent novel; before that, a collection of Nikki Giovanni's poems. Then they'd fall asleep, usually him before her, but not always.

"I'm gonna try to finish tonight," Jamie said. "I've got just two chapters left."

"You're gonna fall asleep," Eve said knowingly. She'd obviously learned some things about him, too. "But godspeed, my friend."

Jamie smiled at being called her friend and opened his book to the place he left off. As he set his bookmark aside, he thought of his son. Jack had given him the placeholder years ago, something he made at school. Kindergarten. Now he was starting third grade, and it was unfathomable how quickly it was all happening.

Even when he was with Eve, time didn't quite make sense. Jamie had known her only about a month, but in some ways, it felt like she'd always been there. This pattern they'd settled into seemed to curb whatever had been aching in him. Knowing that he would get to see her at the end of every day. Keeping her company while she worked on her play. Over at her cabin, she had constructed a corkboard and filled it with Post-it notes, some of which were connected by multicolored string, reminding him of that one scene with Charlie from *It's Always Sunny in Philadelphia*. But it really had been a privilege to see her work, watching her turn simple words into a work of art.

And he didn't want to ruin it by asking for more from Eve, by asking for anything, really, but it did feel like there was still something opaque sitting between them. Maybe not quite a wall, but a curtain, maybe a screen door. He didn't know if it was due to his having a kid, if her ex was still in her way, or if it was related to whatever triggered her panic attack. But Jamie questioned whether he would ever manage to get her to let her guard all the way down.

"You're tense," Eve said, turning the page on her paperback.

"What?"

"You feel tense," she repeated. "What part are you on?"

"Oh, it's not the book," he said. "I was just . . . daydreaming, I guess."

She seemed to accept that answer until a few minutes later, when she started to yawn. "Daydreaming about what?"

"Just trying to remember if I have enough gas," he lied.

"What time will you leave in the morning?"

"Probably around six," he said, failing to stifle his own yawn. "I'll try not to wake you."

"Oh. Okay."

They went quiet again for several more minutes, only the faint noise of crickets chirping in the distance intruding on the comfortable silence between them. The room was cool, but Jamie felt hot with Eve lying against him. At one point, she let her fingertips skim his leg hair, and he knew she was just trying to keep herself awake.

"You travel to Africa often?" he asked. It was in the interest of keeping her up, but he was also curious.

Eve's eyes rolled up at him as she replied, "You know I'm American, right?"

"Of course I know that." He was disappointed that she thought so little of him. He knew she was from New York, and had lived in Atlanta and DC, and he'd even inferred that her dad was from Haiti. "I was asking because you mentioned it earlier, spending a few months in Nigeria and Ghana. And you're supposedly a doctor of African studies."

"Oh."

"Yeah, *oh*."

"Well, no, not often," she said. "I've only been to six countries, eight cities so far. And it was all for research, so I didn't get to enjoy any as much as I would've liked."

"I've never even left the US," Jamie said, a wistful regret in his words. And he was talking to someone who'd been everywhere, which only made him feel more uncultured. "Not even to the Caribbean."

She looked up at him again, intrigue replacing whatever was there before. "Why not?"

"When I was younger, we never had the money to go anywhere. Now? I guess I just haven't had a reason to go."

"You don't need a reason."

"I know." He recommenced reading and then stopped again. "But sometimes you need a push, you know?"

Eve nodded against him, offering a commiserating smile. "I do know . . ."

The two of them went back to their books, but before much longer, Jamie felt Eve shift, all her body heat gone from his chest as she moved back to her side of the bed.

"Callin' it a night?"

"You wore me out," she said, settling onto her stomach and nestling into her pillow.

"I haven't done anything yet," he mumbled, and even though he knew this, he still felt a tinge of pride that he was a lot of work for her.

Eve drifted away while Jamie continued his book, determined to finish this fantastic voyage before leaving Gatlinburg for the week. He'd have little time for leisure reading once Jack was in school again, back to early morning drop-offs and karate on Tuesdays, toiling through homework, and the daily challenge of satisfying his son's picky palate. But there was a buzzing sound that thwarted his plans to keep reading, Eve's iPhone rattling against his nightstand, the illuminated screen grabbing his attention like blinking neon. The name Leo Coletti accompanied a picture of a handsome white guy with short black hair and a graying goatee, wearing dark-rimmed glasses and a wide, perfect smile. The buzzing stopped almost as quickly as it started, which confused Jamie as much as it disquieted him; he could take a wild guess at who that was.

Nonetheless, he promptly turned to Eve. "You just got a call," he whispered. He slipped his hand beneath the sheets to gently squeeze her thigh. "Evie . . ."

Eve moaned at the nuisance, but she was too deep in her sleep to take heed.

Jamie could only leave it at that. But he couldn't pretend it wouldn't bother him. It was bad enough he wouldn't see her for a couple of weeks, but now, he'd have to worry about some mystery man taking the space he was leaving.

When the phone lit up again with the notification of a text, Jamie caught all the other missed messages and call notifications sitting on her home screen, most of which were attributed to a Stella Fischer. Eve's agent was named Stella, but why would she be ignoring her for what appeared to be several weeks now? It wasn't like she was doing anything particularly important with him. Dinner and silence didn't qualify as busy.

Jamie didn't know how to parse it, and Eve would likely shut down before he could even broach the topic. But it did leave him wondering. And with that, he set his unfinished book back on the nightstand.

Morning came swiftly, and with rain attached, leaving Jamie even less enthused about the drive back to Nashville than usual. It would've been a perfect day to just lie in bed, but alas, he'd already scheduled Jack's back-to-school haircut for that afternoon, and with his not-quite-best friend's wedding the following week, he had a number of groomsman duties he had to attend to, including a bachelor party, for which he was already dreading having to be sociable.

When he stepped out of the bathroom, freshly showered, Eve was awake, much to his relief, as he had no interest in sneaking out without a goodbye.

"Mornin'," he greeted her. Morning suited her—even this gloomy version of it. The white sheets and her tank top absorbed the light, making for a beautiful and striking contrast against her dark skin. "The way you were snoring, I just knew you were still gonna be asleep when I left," he said, deciding not to reveal his kinder musings.

"Nice try, but I don't snore."

She was staring at her phone, which was so unlike her, he could only surmise that it had to do with that late-night call from "Leo." He waited a few minutes, going on to find underwear and a cleanish pair of jeans to throw on before returning his focus to her. "Everything okay?"

"Everything's fine."

From her vacant responses, Jamie knew she was holding something back, but he also knew better than to press her on it. She would tell him only what she wanted him to know, and she would do so only when she was ready. If he were being honest with himself, he wasn't ready to confront his fears about whoever this guy was. Not after everything he'd been through with Lucy. Instead, he took a seat on the bed, needing to address a different elephant in the room.

"So when I come back, we're gonna have to do something about this arrangement."

Eve stared at him tentatively, and when he placed his hand on her bare foot, his thumb running across her toes, she wriggled out of his grasp. "'Something' like what?"

"Eve, as much as I enjoy you . . . doing what you're doing, I'm not exactly liking the disparity here."

"If anyone's gonna complain about that, it should be me," she said, laughing in a way that sounded like a scoff.

"Which makes me wonder why you're not," he said. "Not that I'm trying to pressure you, or even . . . if you don't wanna talk about it, we don't have to. But I am curious."

Eve shook her head. "I . . . just . . . don't feel comfortable. Yet." She recoiled, as if to prove her point, and crossed her arms over her chest, covering what her thin tank top failed to conceal. "When we tried, I was so inside my head, I couldn't even enjoy it."

"In your head about what?"

"I don't know," she said, and he imagined her face had crimsoned beneath all her melanin. "I don't know that I deserve to feel . . . good."

"Eve, why—"

"I know that's not true," she quickly added. "It's just . . . I've got shit I need to sort out. And sex is a big part of that shit, I guess. It's easier to focus on you. I like doing it."

Jamie nodded back, appreciative of her honesty. He'd figured out a lot of this along the way, but he was still missing the why of it all. Still, it was nice to hear the words, to know that she was trying to trust him.

"You think it's possible we can help you through that?"

" 'We'?" She smiled timidly.

"I mean, we're doing this . . . whatever it is. I don't wanna be in a relationship, sexual or otherwise, where you do all the work. Even if you like it, it doesn't sit right with me. And I think if we could knock down this wall you have up, we'd both be better off for it."

Eve rolled her eyes and exhaled heavily. "I don't wanna make you uncomfortable," she said. "If you want to, we can just go back to being neighbors who don't engage in sexual activity."

"You know that's not what I want." He stood from the bed to finally finish dressing; he got the feeling that being so close was adding to her discomfort. "I want us to navigate whatever your insecurity is so we can actually have sex." As he found a gray T-shirt in his dresser and made quick work of pulling it on, he kept his gaze on her, watching for a physical response if he wasn't going to get a verbal one. "If that's what you want."

"And if it's not what I want?"

"Then I guess we do go back to being *neighbors* who don't have sex."

"Fine. Friends. You know what I meant."

"I did. But I didn't wanna overwhelm you with labels," he joked.

"Right." She bit her lip, seemingly to stop herself from laughing. "I'll think about it."

"That's all I ask."

"And I don't like oral, so don't expect too much there. But I'll *think* about it."

Jamie frowned at that last tidbit as he went to the kitchen to retrieve a new water bottle and an apple for his drive. "You don't like the way it feels?"

"Not necessarily." Her brows also furrowed, as if she weren't sure of the answer. "It just feels very intimate to have someone's face between your thighs."

He chuckled, understanding the issue now; she obviously didn't mind when the roles were reversed. "You don't wanna give up control. Got it."

"That's not what I said."

"It's what you meant." She opened her mouth to rebut, but when nothing came out, he took the reins of the conversation. "I'm good at it. I'll ease you into it."

Eve let out a sigh that sounded unsteady as it flew past her lips. "You should get outta here," she said. "It's gonna be a long drive in this weather."

Jamie grinned smugly as he moseyed across the room, positive he'd struck a nerve there. "Do I get a kiss goodbye?"

"You know that's not what this is," she said, a broad smile sitting on her fresh face.

"You haven't brushed your teeth yet, so it's probably for the best," he said. "I'll see you in a few weeks."

"Okay, okay, get over here."

"Nope, that's not what this is," he mocked her, continuing to the door to retrieve his keys.

And Jamie would've walked out, happy to leave it at that, perfectly fine with sarcasm being her love language. But there were a couple of books sitting on the table beside the door; they were beneath his keys so he'd know to take them, he presumed. *A Parent's Survival Guide to Common Core Math* and *Never Too Late: The*

Adult Student's Guide to College. They stopped him in his tracks, and he turned back to Eve, practically beaming as he imagined her browsing Amazon on his behalf. He was never sure what she got from all of his rambling, if anything, but maybe the college professor in her took notice when he mentioned how Jack's math confounded him and latched on to his abstract desire for a degree.

Another thing he'd learned about Eve: She wasn't necessarily nice, unconcerned with that superficial layer of pleasantness that ran rampant in the South, but she was thoughtful. She was kind, actually.

"Look at you, caring about me," Jamie said.

"Yeah, don't get used to it," Eve said, obviously suppressing a smile as he crawled across the bed to get to her. "I just didn't want you calling me for help while you're gone."

"You would love it if I called you for help."

He planted a grateful peck on her lips and felt a swell of satisfaction when he tasted the gentle tug of her returning the kiss.

He probably shouldn't have liked her as much as he did. He was reminded every time she tried to pull away from him. With every white lie she told. Her unwillingness to define them should've been a big red flag. But then she would do something like this, or in a rare show of candor, confess to missing him while he was gone, and suddenly, it didn't matter that she would rather give him a blow job than have a conversation; that she liked being close to him, but still did her best to maintain a healthy distance. He was going to ignore the red flags. Because whatever this was (or wasn't), it was starting to feel like something. And he needed something.

CHAPTER 15

Sorry, Mom

JAMIE

The gradual approach of fall was one of Jamie's favorite times of year, not only because it would soon stop being so goddamn hot outside, but also because he valued the potential that came attached to every new school year. He simultaneously loved and loathed seeing his son get older, but he got true fulfillment from witnessing his growth . . . as a person, as a student, and even as an athlete.

Jamie was sitting toward the top of the bleachers of Williamson County's soccer complex, under a beating sun, watching a crop of eight- and nine-year-olds scramble across the field. He envied their energy. Though he did notice that Jack seemed uncharacteristically sluggish and wondered whether he was feeling ill or just uninspired by his new position as a fullback. He'd excelled as a center midfielder last season, but the coach was adamant about reconstructing the team for the sake of diversifying the kids' skills.

Jamie told Jack he didn't have to keep playing soccer if he didn't want to, which only prompted a lecture from the eight-year-old about the importance of follow-through. "You played sports when you were my age, right?" he'd asked. "So you know you can't just quit when you don't like something."

Jamie adored Jack's idealism. He contemplated telling Jack about his former love affair with baseball, all its ups and downs and in-betweens, but there was no reason to crush his jaunty spirit just yet. In fact, Jamie didn't talk about that part of his past with anyone, stingy about sharing his disappointments, not wanting to be judged for their superficiality. Some people had real problems, and not playing a sport for a few extra years was barely one.

And really, it was a sore spot to this day. Back in high school, Jamie had been accepted to a few different colleges, including his first choice, Vanderbilt, with a preferred walk-on status for their illustrious baseball team. But he hadn't received any full scholarships, and with his dad barely hanging on, both financially and emotionally after the divorce, Jamie thought it better to stick around and get a job instead of adding an extra financial burden. Pick up the slack his mom left. There was no rush; it wasn't like he was going to be drafted into the majors. He could go to college when Casey went.

Of course, then he didn't. He'd made enough money as a handyman to help his dad as needed. Enough to send Casey to Duke, with some financial aid. And Jamie found purpose elsewhere. He'd convinced himself that college wasn't for him, and as he started making real money, he'd grown to believe it.

Over the years, his dad encouraged him to try baseball again, just for fun. Find some local team he could occupy his time with. But he never even watched the sport anymore. It actively bothered him. The pesky ache that surfaced every time he considered whether he'd given up too easily. Lucy used to chide him about that. How readily he walked away. He didn't like to fight. Not with her, but not even *for* things he wanted. Maybe he'd be happy, whatever that meant, if he tried a little harder to follow that dream, no matter how impractical.

With all of this on his mind, Jamie headed down to the field to keep a closer eye on Jack, persisting through whatever seemed to be bothering him. As Jamie took his new seat, his phone began to vibrate in his pocket, and although he couldn't place the number, he answered hastily, the 901 area code eliciting immediate concern for his father.

But he instantly regretted it upon recognizing the voice on the other end. Speak of the devil and she will undoubtedly appear.

"Jamie? Are you busy?" It was his mother, with her pompous drawl that people used to liken to Julia Sugarbaker, more Savannah than Memphis.

"I am," Jamie replied curtly. His tone was especially impolite considering they hadn't spoken in at least four years. But that was on her. "What do you want?"

"Well." She took a deep breath, presumably bracing herself for his rebuff. "Your father and I will be having a get-together for Labor Day. Nothing fancy, just a little barbecue. And I thought it would be nice if you and Jack could come out for the occasion."

Jamie instinctively scoffed at the invitation, thinking she couldn't possibly be serious. But then, Diane Gallagher was nothing if not audacious. "Did Casey put you up to this?"

"Of course not. I asked him if he thought you would be amenable, and he actually said no. But with my birthday comin' up, and things . . . the way they are now, I think it would be a nice time to reconcile."

What the hell did she mean by "things the way they are now"? He was, of course, too stubborn to ask, unwilling to give the impression that he cared. "I don't know if I'm ready for that," he said. "Dad and Casey may be happy to forgive you, but I haven't found a reason to."

"Understandable," Diane said quietly. "But I would very much like to see my grandson."

"You haven't seen him in five years. Why are you pretending to care now?"

"I'm not pretending." She chuckled in a way that sounded almost pained. "I can't make amends if you won't allow me to even see you all."

"But I don't owe you that," Jamie said, speaking in a hushed tone. "I don't owe you anything. You've had how long to 'make amends'? And instead of giving a shit, you gave up at the first sign of difficulty." Jamie paused when he recognized how familiar that sounded; but it wasn't his job, as a teenager, to make her feel better about what she'd done to their family. It was always on her to atone for her sins, and he didn't appreciate her suddenly reappearing, seventeen years later, to guilt him into fixing what *she* broke. He didn't even understand how his brother and father were okay with this.

Diane began to speak again, surely something in her own defense, but Jamie's capacity for her ceased as soon as he noticed Jack running off the field, headed straight for him. He wondered, worried, whether this was a panic attack or something somehow worse.

"I have to go," he told his mother, hanging up the phone as Jack approached. "You okay, bud?" Jamie called out to him.

Jack was signaling for water, but before he could even reach the outfield, he confirmed Jamie's suspicions as he bent over, his hands on his knees, and retched into the grass.

Funny enough, hearing from Diane had Jamie feeling the exact same way.

CHAPTER 16

Let Her Cook

EVE

Jamie being gone during the week had really forced Eve to acclimate to her general existence in Tennessee. She wouldn't pretend she didn't miss her friend, but she also no longer minded the forty-minute drive to Knoxville if it meant having some creature comforts like farmers' markets and big-box stores. And she'd found something of a groove in her writing, allowing her to pass much of her time doing what she came to do in the first place.

She also continued to frequent Crockett's for breakfast, not only for the bacon, but because Eve learned very quickly that the happenings there made for great theater fodder. She'd been sitting in the restaurant one afternoon, quite a while after closing, when the waitstaff learned of a new policy that meant they'd have to pool all of their tips to share with other support staff. Considering tipped employees made only $2.13 an hour in Tennessee, all hell broke loose, and rightfully so. That was when Eve decided to make Crockett's the backdrop of the second act of her play. Her teenage heroine would work there during her summer break, navigating through everything from petty squabbles over aprons to major dilemmas about how she would support a baby on less than minimum wage.

Eve had even made a couple of friends at the restaurant, including one of the waitresses, Abbey, who rocked a blue-and-blond Mohawk and spoke in a chirpy Southern accent like Kristin Chenoweth. Abbey had invited her to a nearby bar for drinks and karaoke with the locals, but one google of the place and Eve decided she was better off declining. She still had her limits, and trying to do too much too soon would probably backfire.

Then, there was the kind but nosy cashier, Jill, who made for good company, it turned out. On Saturdays, Eve would go to the diner later than usual. She started doing so to avoid the weekend rush, and all the kids who came with it, but now and then, if she asked nicely, Jill would join her for lunch and bring along leftover food from the kitchen that day.

Jill always looked at her suspiciously when she showed up without Jamie—which had been often, as of late—but she rarely said much about it. Eve was endlessly amused that Jill didn't even know his name, because he always paid in cash.

"What kind of person only carries cash in this day and age?" she'd asked.

Eve laughed at her, agreeing that Jamie was certainly singular. He carried a flip phone and read authors most white people had never heard of, and she got the feeling he had much more money than his car or wardrobe would lead anyone to believe. Against all odds, he was uneasy about getting head without being able to give it, which only mystified her, thereby making her more interested in him.

"Where is he anyway?" Jill demanded. "It's the weekend. He should be with you."

"I don't keep tabs on him," Eve said, even though she knew full well he was back in Nashville for Dad duty. But that wasn't a can of worms she intended to open up with someone as inquisitive as Jill. "I'm sure he's wherever he needs to be."

"Pretty as you are, I didn't sit here just to stare at you," Jill said, stuffing her mouth with corned beef hash. "So what do you wanna talk about?"

Eve suppressed a laugh, but she really cherished Jill's company. She was direct in a manner similar to Maya, and Eve had missed that. She had to remind herself not to call this woman *bitch* in the playful way she did with her best friend. "Well, excuse me for thinking you just wanted to have lunch with me."

"I have lunch at home," Jill replied. "I'm here to sit with you. To talk to you. So talk."

"Okay . . ." Eve expelled a heavy breath, trying to think of something other than her grandmother to discuss. At their last meal, Jill was the driving force of the conversation, revealing that she was a retired nurse; she worked at the diner because it allowed her to still take care of people, minus the interminable hours. Now it was Eve's turn to pretend she did anything remotely as valiant or interesting as being on the front lines of health care.

"Let's talk about your play," Jill suggested. "How's it going?"

"It's going slowly," Eve said. "I have a shoddy version of most of the first act, but I haven't figured out whether I like it."

"So you have nothing."

Eve laughed, supposing that was true. Another lie to add to the list. Soon, she would no longer be able to tell people she was here to write. "I was too arrogant to realize that this one would be harder to write than the last few."

"Is it autobiographical?"

Eve pursed her lips and gave her dining companion a knowing look.

"Well . . ." Jill shrugged. "*I* would think it took a lot of guts for someone to come back here and try to muster up all those old feelings."

"You're kind to say that." Eve tried to smile. "It was cowardice that kept me away so long." As the guilt tried to resurface, she began to break apart cold pieces of French toast, inhaling one after the other.

Jill did that thing where she reached across the table and managed to calm every anxiety that seemed intent on coursing through Eve's body whenever she thought about her grandmother for too long. "Hazel loved you so much," she said. "I'm sorry she didn't protect you."

Eve shook her head, knowing Hazel couldn't have. She'd tried. She'd prayed. Even she was convinced that abortion was their best route, believing God would forgive them. Her grandmother's version of God was less about vengeance and more about justice—which left Eve to wonder how her mother turned out the way she did. Nonetheless, her parents had made their decision, and no amount of haranguing or guilt-tripping would change their minds. "It wasn't on her," Eve said.

"Do you know who the baby went to? Have you been able to see him or her, at least?"

Eve shook her head. "It was a closed adoption," she said. "I've read that that makes it 'easier' to move forward." She played with the handle of her coffee mug, debating whether to pick it up and "accidentally" spill the lukewarm liquid on herself just to evade this conversation.

"Oh, honey," Jill returned, her soft voice full of sympathy, her green eyes projecting pity.

And there it was. The look Eve had come to Tennessee to avoid. Because everyone in New York had it. Every person she passed seemed to detect the misery that haunted her. It was why she couldn't talk to Leo, and why she would never tell Jamie.

It was also why when Eve arrived home that day, she launched into her yearly ritual of trolling adoption websites for any morsel of information that might connect her to her seventeen-year-old baby. He would soon be older than she was when she had him; meanwhile, she felt stunted, stuck in the heart and mind of that scared, much-too-young girl whose newborn was snatched from her arms.

Adoption Database, Adoption Network, Adoption.com, Adopted.com, even Tennessee's Department of Children's Services. She'd been at this for seven years now, getting the idea from a short film by one of her Howard classmates. But it was all based on the ghost of a hope that her son was as interested in finding her as she was in finding him. That he'd go to one of those websites, looking for his birth family, and in a minor miracle, they'd match each other. And every year, she'd have to remind herself—convince herself—that he was with some family that loved him better than she ever could've. That her parents were right, and it was heedless to want him simply to quell her own inadequacies.

That didn't mean it hurt any less when, every year, the search came up empty.

But that day was the first time in seven years she didn't shatter upon seeing those results.

While Jamie was gone, Eve generally spent her evenings with Hulu, her favorite episodes of *Living Single* keeping her company for dinner and at bedtime. She texted Jamie on occasion—on one late night in particular, they had a brief back-and-forth about his neighbor asking him on a date, which tickled Eve as much as it annoyed her. Her father sent emails that she refused to respond to, though she did send the read receipts so he'd know she was alive. Still no word from her mother. Leo had called late one night but texted to say it was a mistake, so she left it at that, deciding that after their last conversation, she couldn't care, even if it was a lie.

And despite her successful entry to life in Tennessee, Eve still hadn't brought herself to call Stella since she'd embarrassed herself on Zoom more than a month ago. There weren't many people she would cry in front of anyway, but she definitely never planned for Stella to be one of them. And considering the only topic they had to discuss was the possibility of Eve debuting at the most notable Off-Broadway venue in New York—the place where *Hair* and *Hamilton* premiered—she simply did not know how to talk to her without the threat of another panic attack coming with it.

But sometime midweek, Jamie told her she should stop avoiding her agent, and for some reason, she took heed. Perhaps because she trusted him more than most, or maybe she just didn't want to disappoint him, but she finally called Stella on Thursday and made it through their short but productive conversation unscathed. No tears, no panic attacks. Just a few errant pangs of guilt for avoiding Stella in the first place. By Friday morning, they were on a conference call with the Public, and much of the anxiety that shrouded Eve was dissipating with every suggestion she received from her new colleagues.

"So, Eve, you can tell us how you feel about it, but we were looking at an early May debut," said Hassan, one of the three associate artistic directors at the theater. He had an imposing mien, his features dark and beautiful, and whenever he flashed his immaculate pearly whites, it felt like the sun was shining. "Ideally, we would like to do eight weeks, so you'd be kicking off our summer season. And we'd promote it in tandem with Shakespeare in the Park."

Eve was nodding, albeit skeptically, while wondering if he really thought she would demur. "So long as there's central air in the theater," she said, joking. Mercifully, everyone on the call laughed.

"So Stella thought Martinson, which has a capacity of one ninety-nine. LuEsther is currently still open, if you're uncomfortable with that many. But we need to decide quickly. Like, right now."

"And LuEsther is one sixty, right?" Stella asked.

"Correct."

"Eve, it's up to you," Stella said. "But based on Chicago and San Diego numbers, I don't think you'll have an issue getting two hundred a night."

Eve felt that sense of panic creeping up her throat, and she took a long sip of water in hopes of pushing it back down. She wished she were as confident as Stella that she could find two hundred people a night, for eight weeks, to be interested in her play. When she opened at BAM in Brooklyn, yes, it was two hundred fifty seats, but she had to fill them for only a week.

"What are the implications for the budget between the two

theaters?" Eve asked, pretending she was feeling any semblance of control over her spiraling worries.

"About forty thousand difference," said A'ja, the "numbers person," as she'd been introduced.

"But Ms. Alvarez and her team are fine with the difference if Martinson is what you want," Hassan said.

"We'd make back the difference in ticket sales."

Yeah, if we actually sell them.

"Don't overthink it, Eve," Stella said.

That was like telling Eve not to breathe. She was already imagining the ledes about her little activist project struggling to sell half the theater each night and closing early. This was a make-or-break moment—her shot to be on Broadway, if it went well. But if it didn't, she could very well be knocking on obsolescence, forever a fledgling playwright who was almost successful. She could already hear what her mother's disappointment would sound like as she avoided talking about her failure of a daughter among her friends.

"We wouldn't be offering these theaters if we didn't think this work could sell them," Hassan said. And again, his smile comforted Eve in a moment when she absolutely needed it.

Eve sighed and said a silent prayer that she wouldn't live to regret it. "Let's go with Martinson then," she said.

The other five people on the call cheered as if she'd just announced she was giving them money instead of spending theirs, but she grinned at their response, a tinge of relief coming along with it. She was scared of this undertaking, but it wouldn't be the worst thing in the world to have this challenge awaiting her whenever she went home.

The rest of the call went much easier as they settled on a director and discussed casting options. Eve didn't technically have a say in any of those things—she was still considered up-and-coming and didn't have the cachet to bring in anyone, much less her dream actors. But when she told them that Amina Pearson was her dream cast for the role of Sandra, they were enthusiastic about the idea. Amina recently won an Emmy for her role in a Netflix limited series, meaning she was booked and busy, but no one thought she would be an impossible get, which bolstered Eve through the rest of the conversation. Even after she found out that her dream director, Zindzi Jeffers, had already taken on a project in London.

"As long as the director is a Black woman," Eve said, and she was adamant about it. She remembered when *Eclipsed* premiered as the first Broadway play to feature a cast and creative team of only Black women; it was a distinction Eve admired and vowed to continue.

"We'll make it happen," Stella said. Eve took it as an oath, knowing that Stella would do everything in her white woman power to bring Eve's dreams to fruition. They'd gotten this far precisely because Stella didn't make promises or proclamations she couldn't stand behind. In fact, Stella said the Public was a great venue for this piece the first time she read it. And now, here they were.

When they finally released Eve from the Teams call, with most of her misgivings at bay, she immediately texted Jamie to let him know of her triumph.

Fri, Aug 8 11:24 AM

Eve Ambroise: It didn't go terribly. And I now have a tentative opening date of May 7.

Eve snorted at the text message bubble turning green as it sent and threw her phone to her coffee table as she returned to her laptop. Her rough draft for *Down from Dover* was, indeed, rough, but the conversation with the Public left her feeling inspired and even a little excited, seeing firsthand that their belief in her was real. If things worked out the way she was willing to admit she wanted, this play could debut right after *Gamba Adisa* completed its run. But that would mean finishing it—as in, as close to a final draft as possible—by the end of the year. That was a much more onerous proposition.

Luckily, Jamie texted back before she could spiral again.

Fri, Aug 8 11:31 AM

Jamie Gallagher: Is it too soon to say 'I told you so'?

Eve grinned at his response, knowing he would say something along those lines. In the few weeks they'd been . . . hanging out, she'd come to appreciate that he was not only confident, but also a little cocky every now and then.

Eve Ambroise: Please know that there's never a right time to say "I told you so" to me.

Jamie Gallagher: Sounds like a defense mechanism for someone who's used to being wrong . . .

Eve Ambroise: . . . Why do I talk to you?

Jamie Gallagher: Seriously, doesn't it feel good to have that weight off your chest?

Eve Ambroise: I don't know that it's gone. I'm still scared out of my mind. But it feels good to move forward, at least.

Eve Ambroise: I feel like I've been stuck for a long time.

Jamie Gallagher: What are you so scared of?

Eve Ambroise: Failing.

Jamie Gallagher: Can I ask why you're fantasizing about failing when you're smack dab in the middle of succeeding?

Eve balked at his latest text, the wisdom taking her by surprise. Not because she thought Jamie was being vapid or anything close to it—he was possibly the most thoughtful person she knew—but she simply did not expect him to read her like that. Why *was* she skipping over the good to worry about the bad?

Eve Ambroise: How about you mind your business lol.

Jamie Gallagher: If I'm right, you can just say that.

Eve Ambroise: You're not right! It's not that simple.

Eve Ambroise: (But you're right.)

CHAPTER 17

Love's Lookin' Good on You

JAMIE

Fri, Aug 15 12:07 PM

Chris G: Gentlemen, all appointments are officially confirmed. Collins & Co. at 5. Marsh House at 8. (Meet at my house at 3.)

Marcus Thompson: Bet.

Jamie Gallagher: Gonna be a great weekend.

Nick Serrano: the best.

Travis Murphy: I got the Cubans on the way!!

Chris G: Maybe we should refrain from talking about committing crimes in the group chat?

Marcus Thompson: Taking notes on a criminal fucking conspiracy lol

Jamie Gallagher: Lmao

Travis Murphy: My fault. Strike that from the record.

Nick Serrano: lol I cant wait to see yall.

At some point in his life, Jamie did enjoy weddings. And not just attending them, but he could once upon a time remember being vaguely flattered when a friend would ask him to take part in the festivities. It was an honor to stand by someone he loved as they made eternal promises to someone they loved. And despite whatever protestations he might have had about dancing in front of strangers, weddings were fun. The Electric Slide was fun. So he wasn't sure when the tides turned and he began to genuinely hate the very concept of a wedding. When his oldest friend from high school, Rachael Horton, got engaged, his second thought, after *Fucking finally* (because she and Nick Serrano had been together since *high school*) was the dread associated with being in the wedding. He liked to believe it was Lucy's fault, having ruined all of his notions of love and anything involving it, but that just wasn't true. Even if Lucy had deigned to marry him, he wouldn't have wanted a wedding. Maybe he had just become curmudgeonly in his old age, announcing how uncomfortable he was to anyone who'd listen.

"God, I hate weddings." It was the third time he'd said it out loud in the last twenty-four hours, at least.

Jamie's friend Marcus snickered at his comment but elbowed him. "Everybody hates weddings," he said. "At least you get to make the most of this shit."

Jamie sent a sidelong glance to his friend as they waited for the photographer to direct them in the next photo. "What?"

"I'm not saying I'm not happy with Kira. I am. Hundred percent. But I am saying weddings are only useful when you're single."

Jamie hadn't been single in so long, he was failing to make sense of the logic. He peered at Marcus, studying his face for hints as to what the hell he was talking about. But he got nothing but his usual playful expression, a glint in his dark eyes as he watched his wife posing with the bride.

"And why's that?" Jamie finally asked.

Marcus gestured to two of the bridesmaids currently lining up on either side of the bride, all of them looking like sister wives in their matching saffron dresses. "Amy *and* Chloe have had their eyes on you since rehearsal."

"What?"

"Don't pretend you haven't noticed."

"I'm not pretending," Jamie said, containing his smile. This was legitimate news to him, though he didn't have the chops to act as though the information wasn't gratifying. Chloe and Amy were Rachael's coworkers, and the only two members of the wedding party he hadn't known for at least a decade. They were both conventionally attractive, though much more outgoing than his speed would allow. Of course, he wasn't looking for anything. Hell, he barely had a handle on whatever was happening with Eve. But after the tumult of his time with Lucy, the idea that anyone was looking his way was indeed nice to hear.

Just as he was about to share this information with Marcus, the maid of honor, Robin, was approaching and wearing an expression that said she was on a mission. Then again, that was usually her face. He'd always appreciated Robin's no-bullshit approach to life. She took it upon herself to fix Jamie's sunflower boutonniere ahead of the next round of pictures.

"Why is he blushing?" she asked Marcus.

"He just found out a girl likes him."

"No," Jamie replied. "It's just hot as hell out here." He attempted to prove as much by wiping nonexistent sweat from his hairline.

It was actually a mild day for August. Warm, but not oppressive, especially once the sun slipped below the horizon. The moment their friends announced the venue would be a barn, he'd been worried about relying on cross ventilation alone to keep them from sweating through their suits and dresses. But it all ended up working out spectacularly. Even with his ex and her boyfriend sitting a mere few feet away. In fact, he could've used Lucy's presence as a legitimate excuse for his ruddy hue, but in truth, he wasn't particularly bothered to see her there. He wasn't ready to say he was over the situation, but it was starting to feel like he was no longer emotionally shackled to whatever she had going on. He was thinking more about Eve than Lucy clinging to Tyler's arm all day.

Once the newlyweds had taken all their pictures against the backdrop of the sunset, it was the bridal party's turn. All twelve of them smiled through a number of poses, from serious to silly, surrounding the pond, at the stables, and lined up along the grassy knoll just beyond the outbuilding. They all piled inside a decked-out vintage Volkswagen camper that wasn't really large enough to fit them all but would undoubtedly make for the most memorable photos, a series of action shots of impossibly beautiful people laughing at nothing in particular. Not that Jamie considered himself particularly winsome, but he cleaned up nicely. He'd gotten a haircut and a shave for the occasion, and Nick, the groom, made certain that their sapphire-blue suits were tailored to a tee.

While they completed their photo shoot, the barn had been converted into a reception area, rustic and chic like the ceremony before it, trimmed in wood and white, with chandeliers that looked like clusters of diamonds hanging from the rafters and sheer white curtains festooning every doorway and window.

Like a good groomsman, Jamie grinned through dinner conversations and toasts, including his own, and more pictures than anyone could ever possibly need. But by the time everyone was on the dance floor, he found himself sitting at the bar by himself, trying to convince himself not to text Eve. He always wondered what she did with her Saturday nights. Soon enough, he would find out. But he refrained from asking, careful not to seem suffocating, trying to strike the balance between invested and aloof, as she did so adeptly. So he sat at the bar, drinking his old-fashioned, watching in amusement as the white people in the room tried to keep up with everyone else on the Cupid Shuffle.

"Are you alone?"

He glanced at the redhead looming near him, her white skin rosy, her green eyes already dancing with him as she waited for his answer. "Am I alone?" he repeated, the question sounding foreign in the air. What did that mean? "As in right now?" At the wedding? In general?

"I'd been watching you," she said, pointing toward the opposite end of the room, where the wedding party's table had emptied out, "and I was just wondering if you were with that bridesmaid you were talking to."

"Natasha?" Jamie made a face, the idea genuinely perplexing. "No."

"Oh." She grinned at him, flashing a perfect smile; he sent a polite one back and returned to his drink before the ice could water it down. "Okay . . ."

When he turned to order another, he realized the woman was still standing there, watching him, waiting. She was tall and lithe, with the figure and face of a model. Someone he'd never imagine noticing him, even with her standing there expectantly. "Did you want me to get you a drink?" he asked.

She chuckled. "It's an open bar."

"I . . . realize that."

She looked around and then offered her hand. "I'm Bree."

"Jamie."

"I know who you are."

"I'm so sorry, have we met before?" He was so confused.

"No . . ." She laughed again, and it was really starting to feel like there was some joke he wasn't in on. "Like I said, I've been paying attention to you all night."

"Ah. Well . . . it's nice to meet you, Bree." He resumed placing his order, leaving a ten-dollar tip for the bartender's trouble. As much as he'd been amused when Marcus mentioned Amy's and Chloe's interest, he didn't actually know what to do with this kind of attention. He wouldn't anyway, but not now, not considering his . . . situation with Eve. Maybe she wouldn't care one way or another. But maybe she would. Maybe he wasn't alone.

"So, Jamie, any chance I can convince you to dance?" Bree asked, just as some thumping, up-tempo song overtook the room, every woman there seeming to know the words. Even Bree was already singing along as she tried to coax him to the floor.

"I . . . don't dance," he said with an awkward chuckle.

"Seriously?"

He shrugged. "Seriously."

"That's disappointing. I'm disappointed in you."

"Better now than later." He punctuated his statement with a matching wry grin.

She sent him another smile as she disappeared into the crowd on the dance floor, and he could feel the stranglehold of apprehension unwrapping itself from his neck. He was in no way prepared to turn down this woman, and especially not when he barely had a reason to. *Sorry, I have a situation*? Genuine disinterest was valid, of course, but he couldn't truthfully say that was the case. He was perhaps simply more interested in someone else.

He abandoned his resolution not to bother Eve, feeling like he needed the reassurance that he wasn't stupid for rebuffing Bree's advances.

Sat, Aug 16 8:46 PM

Jamie Gallagher: So, I'm at a wedding and I've been propositioned twice now. If I get a third, I should accept, right?

"She was flirting with you, Gallagher."

Jamie immediately recognized Robin's voice and turned to his left, finding the bride's sister smirking and clutching two glasses of wine, one red and one white, which she seemed to be enjoying in equal measure.

"Believe it or not, I did recognize that," he replied, moving down the bar a few inches to close the space between them. "Eventually."

"Then what the hell?" Robin was loud, and her Tennessee accent only exaggerated everything she said. "She was hot as fuck."

Jamie chuckled, unable to deny that.

"Don't tell me you're still hung up on Lucy." She looked pained by the statement as she made it, scrunching her face until she'd rendered her beautiful makeup useless. "She's one of my best friends, and if you tell her I said this, I'll cut off all that pretty hair of yours. But, dude." She shook her head, expelled a long, weary sigh, and then lowered her voice to a whisper. "You can do better."

"Oh." He wasn't expecting that, but he could admit he liked hearing it. "Well, no, I'm not still hung up on Lucy."

"Then what?" Her greenish eyes scanned his, seeming to beg him to make sense of this.

He could only shrug. "I just . . . wasn't interested."

"Do you know what kind of message that sends? If you're not interested in her, then the rest of us don't have a fuckin' chance."

"I don't know who you think you're foolin'. You could have anyone in this room, and you know it."

"You're not gonna flatter your way outta this, Gallagher. This is a giant blow to my self-esteem."

"You're drunk," he noted, watching her finish one glass and move on to the next. "And where's your date? He should be the arbiter of your self-esteem tonight, not me."

Robin grinned at him, her twinkling gaze flitting across his face and then descending slowly until it landed on his wrist. "Excuse me, sir. Is that a Patek?" She pulled his arm in her direction, examining the alligator leather and gleaming gold timepiece. "Holy shit."

"It is," he said, laughing at her reaction.

"The checks from RH have been clearing, I see."

Sheepish about the topic, Jamie searched for a way to downplay just how good business had been. While partnering with Restoration Hardware a few years ago was an undeniable boon to his bank account, it changed his relationship with his work. He never necessarily loved it, but lately, he found himself wondering whether he even liked it. In fact, he hadn't told anyone that he'd just turned down an A-list celebrity requesting some custom pieces. It would surely sound ridiculous to just about anyone who understood anything about capitalism. Except maybe Eve.

"Things are okay," he said. "I decided to take a break for the summer."

"Shit, obviously you can afford to." She was still inspecting his Calatrava like she might be able to telepathically transfer it to her own wrist if she tried hard enough. "I mentioned to my mom you were charging thirteen grand for a table these days. She said you and your family always were uppity."

He laughed again. His family went way back with Rachael and Robin's, all the way to Memphis, where his mother and their mother had been best friends before any of them were born. His dad was quite the opposite of anything resembling *uppity,* but that was probably an apt descriptor of Diane. It was surely one of the reasons she left in the first place.

"Your mom said she was surprised I made it to the rehearsal dinner," he said with a knowing nod. "Now I get it."

"That's nice," Robin said. She finally released his hand but continued to gaze at the timepiece. "I'm happy for you."

The two of them returned to their respective drinks: Robin to her wine, and Jamie to his whiskey. "Hey, can I ask you something kinda personal?" he said, thinking of Eve and the fact that she'd yet to reply to his text.

"Luckily, I'm too tipsy to care about couth." She grinned, brushing her falling wavy brown hair from her slender face. "Shoot."

"When you were dating that guy, Brendan? How did it go when you told him about Liv?"

"Oh." She frowned as if she had to work to recall her last long-term relationship. "Well, his daughter and mine were in the same gymnastics class. That's how we met. So he always knew about Liv."

Jamie took in a sharp breath. "That is deeply unhelpful."

"Is that why you didn't flirt back with that girl?" Robin asked and sighed again. "Can you just be an adult and have a one-night stand for once? You don't have to fall in love with everyone you fuck. Jesus Christ, Gallagher."

"As much as I'm enjoying you jumping to all these wrong conclusions, no, that is not why I'm asking." He was on the edge of needing a cigarette. "Just trying to figure out how to handle it once I do start dating."

"Well, you and Jack are inseparable anyway, so it's not like you can avoid the topic." She was staring at his watch again as she spoke. "And whoever she is, if she's gonna be worth it, she's gotta be open to having a super-dedicated single dad in her life."

Jamie nodded, even as his heart sank to his stomach, wondering what that meant for Eve and the fact that she clammed up whenever he even mentioned Jack's name.

"Somebody better for you than Lucy was," she added. "I cannot stress that enough."

Amused, he sipped his drink just as his pocket buzzed, and he was relieved to find that Eve had finally replied:

Sat, Aug 16 9:01 PM

Eve Ambroise: So what you're saying is I'm not enough for you?

Jamie grinned more at her text than he had all night.

Jamie Gallagher: I didn't know you were an option

Eve Ambroise: Oh, is that why you've spent the last two weeks propositioning *me*?

Jamie Gallagher: Lol, you're such an asshole.

Eve Ambroise: Enjoy your wedding. Just not too much.

"Look at that smile." Robin leaned into him drunkenly, amusement evident in her typically piercing eyes and crimsoned cheeks. "*Now* I see why you turned down the model."

Jamie also reddened as he set his phone down. "It's not like that."

"Uh-huh."

"It's not."

"So if I tell you I don't feel like going home alone tonight . . ."

Jamie frowned at what appeared to be his third pass of the night. "We're not really trying to go back down that road, are we?"

"Don't be such a girl. It wasn't a road. It was friends with benefits, at best."

"It was a long time ago," he reminded her. He wasn't sure if intoxication was speaking for Robin or actual desire, but either way, she was right. He couldn't bring himself to acquiesce.

Maybe because of Eve, maybe not. There was too much going on for him to parse it all now.

"That's what I thought," Robin said. "What's her name?"

He made another face. "I don't know if I'm ready to say yet. I don't know if it's going anywhere. She's just here for the summer."

"What, like she's in day camp?"

"Like she's on vacation," he said, his serious tone starkly contrasting with Robin's silliness. "She's a playwright from New York. So she's here writing."

Robin looked impressed by that statement, and it made Jamie smile. Eve was definitely an impressive person.

"You want it to go somewhere," she said with a knowingness in her eyes.

Jamie could feel his cheeks grow warm, his stomach doing backflips as he thought about the nights he spent with Eve. The nights he wanted to spend with Eve. He pretended to be rubbing at his cheek in an effort to hide the smile trying to burst past his lips. "I don't know that I've felt this way about anyone. It wasn't *love,* but I don't know . . . maybe *like* at first sight? Is that a thing?"

"Sounds like it was," Robin said. Her smile seemed sad but supportive as she raised her nearly empty glass to him. "So I'm not sure why you're wastin' your ticking clock sittin' here with me."

Jamie considered that for a moment. He and Eve had a little more than a month? Which translated to four or five stolen weekends, and here he was, hanging around a wedding he didn't really want to be at, long after his duties as groomsman were over. Why *was* he sitting there? He silently raised his glass in agreement, finished it, and shot up from his seat.

"I gotta go."

CHAPTER 18

Strawberry Bubblegum

EVE

Even when Jamie was out of town, Eve enjoyed being at his cabin. She hated him being gone, but she'd sit on his porch during the day with her laptop, trying to turn her teenage pregnancy into capital-*T* theater. Jamie had a set of rocking chairs that sat at the east end of his second-story porch, and she felt at peace up there, eye level with the trees, the creek burbling beneath her.

That evening, she made herself a light salad for dinner, accompanied by some red wine. She got settled with a blanket and a book to keep her mind off the fact that Jamie was at some wedding, flirting with God knows who, and maybe going home with them, because she was too stubborn and scared to take their relationship to the natural next level.

She tingled with delight when he sent her some silly text to alert her to these facts. Knowing she was on his mind meant more to her than she was prepared to admit.

Thirty minutes later, he sent another text to let her know he was heading back to Gatlinburg, and she could not stop smiling.

She hated that, and she didn't know what to do with her feelings about it, so she did what any girl in her position would do—she consulted her best friend.

Sun, Aug 17 12:52 AM

Eve Ambroise: Remember MAGA?

Maya Baudin: Your lil' neighbor who read you like a book when y'all met? Yeah

Eve Ambroise: So yeah. I think I like him. 😖

Eve punctuated her sentence with the scrunched-face emoji, because that was precisely how she felt about it. And seeing the words in text only made it that much more difficult to make sense of. She was six weeks out of a five-year engagement; she had no business liking someone. But fuck if she couldn't wait until she heard that truck of his roar into his driveway.

Maya Baudin: No shit

Maya Baudin: I knew that when you told me you were goin to dinner by his house

Maya Baudin: You don't be hanging out with just anybody

Eve Ambroise: No, I mean I *like* him like him.

Eve Ambroise: Like we've seen each other naked kinda like.

Eve was not at all surprised when her phone immediately vibrated, though the buzz did feel louder and more conspicuous than usual—perhaps because she knew she had so much explaining to do. She laughed as she answered, equally unsurprised when Maya's salutation was "Bitch . . ."

Eve did her best to make sense of why she hadn't updated Maya since she and Jamie started their semi-sexual relationship, but as she spoke, she realized it was because she liked keeping him to herself. She'd found something, not precious, but close to it, and they existed in their own little world up here in the mountains and the trees. And some part of her worried the bubble would burst if she dared share her secret with the world. Telling Maya would start to make it real, and she was enjoying the fantasy. The giddiness of liking someone, the magic of starting a new story. She wanted to hold on to that. And it was why she hung up the phone as soon as humanly possible the moment she knew Jamie was home.

Eve unraveled herself from her blanket and headed down the steps to meet him, the nearly full moon casting a gentle white glow over their quiet neighborhood. They reunited at the edge of the driveway, and as Jamie came into view, Eve wasn't sure that glow hadn't blinded her.

She knew he'd been at a wedding but somehow hadn't connected the dots to a haircut and shave. Now, she wished she'd prepared herself for the sight of Jamie without a beard. His long curls had been chopped to a more refined length, leaving waves instead of the fluffy tendrils that typically adorned his neck. His facial hair was nonexistent, just a slight five-o'clock shadow left to show off his dimpled cheeks and the fullness of his lips. A Disney prince come to life. Her very own Prince Eric.

She stared for much longer than appropriate, awed by the

fact that he was even more attractive than she bargained for under all that hair. "I . . . You look so different." It was a silly thing to state—obviously, he knew that—but she had nothing of import to say in the moment. His bone structure had rendered her speechless.

Jamie smiled back bashfully. "I thought it was best not to scare folks at the wedding."

He was wearing a slim-fitting pair of blue trousers that emphasized just how bowlegged he was and a matching vest to accentuate his lean physique. She could only imagine how handsome he looked among all the other groomsmen, that crisp blue making his eyes sparkle in the midnight.

Eve approached him gingerly, wanting a closer look, but his gaze caught hers first, their eyes doing a flirtatious dance, leaving her pondering whether to kiss him. She felt nervous about it, so she didn't. Instead, again, she replied with the first thing on her mind. "Here I was looking forward to feeling that beard between my thighs."

His eyebrows raised in surprise, followed by the acknowledgment of her simple outfit. She also looked different from the way he most often saw her—leggings and a tank top, sometimes accompanied by a sweater. Today, she'd slipped into a maxi dress for the occasion. It was heather gray—a color that did her no justice, but it was the only thing she'd packed in the realm of sexy, as the fabric did its job of hugging her slight curves and showed just enough cleavage to hopefully whet his appetite.

"I didn't realize you'd be waiting for me," Jamie said as she led him up the stairs. As he removed his vest and tie, Eve made her way into the kitchen, where she poured herself a big glass of the wine she'd brought over, and he joined her. "I went over to your place first."

Eve looked at him, amused, wanting to tell him she liked his place better than hers. But tonight, in particular, she'd stayed because she wanted to make it easier for him to find her. "I thought you'd come here first."

"Not on the same page."

"We were," she said, taking a sip of her wine before offering him the glass. "We were so eager to see each other, we tried to plan ahead."

He smiled, and she hoped it was because he appreciated her ceaseless efficiency. But as he drank from their glass, his cheeks reddened, leaving her to wonder what on earth was on his mind. If perhaps it was the same thing on hers.

"Can I touch it?" she asked, her voice thin, nervous to speak her desire out loud.

"What?" He chuckled, flashing dimples she didn't know existed until today.

"Your face," she said. She realized what an odd request it was, but he just looked so handsome, his skin so soft, her hands were tingling to feel it. Like electricity coursing through her, her attraction to him pushing through to her fingertips.

He nodded for her to do so, their eyes locking as she moved in close and pressed her warm hand to his face. She caressed him, her lips curling into a demure smile as she studied his beardless visage. She combed her fingers through his hair, examining the full length of it, as if for her approval. Her gaze dropped to his mouth and her hand innately followed, her thumb tracing the line of his pink bottom lip.

Jamie set their wineglass back on the counter, pinning her against it in the process, and went in for a kiss. Gentle but hungry, he sucked at her plump lips like they were his sustenance.

Her tongue met his within seconds, drawing an unexpected moan from both of them as they melted into one another. His right hand snaked down her back until it reached her ass, giving it a soft squeeze as he pulled her in.

Eve's tongue lashed against his, tasting the red wine, but feeling drunk from him, their bodies so close they were practically one. When they pulled apart for air, her chest heaving against his, she gave him a small, knowing smile. She reluctantly left Jamie's embrace to go and sit on the bed like she owned the place, waiting for Jamie to catch up.

"Oh," he said with surprise. He eyed the condom packets she'd placed on his nightstand, and then her. "You're sure?" he asked.

"Don't start this again," she said, recalling their first attempt. His need to make sure she was okay was part of why she realized she wasn't. And while that was something she should've been thankful for, she wanted to enjoy this without overthinking it. "I'm sure that I trust you. And I wanna give it another try." She sat back so that she was squarely in the middle of the mattress. "So get over here."

Without another word, Jamie crossed to the bed with a mischievous gleam in his eyes as he began to unbutton his shirt. He climbed on top of her, between her legs and into her arms, and he kissed her again. Harder, more passionately this time, his mouth forcing hers open and pulling all the air from her lungs.

He wasted no time, but still, he took what he needed, giving attention to every part of her, his lips brushing across her chin before moving down her neck. He sucked at her skin like candy, giving it three little licks before taking a soft bite, making her moan his name. He paused only briefly to pull off his shirt, then continued across her collarbone and down her chest, tugging at the straps of her dress to leave her shoulders bare.

As he kissed and lapped at her décolletage, Eve ran her fingers through his feathery hair, trying to keep her thoughts on it, as opposed to everything else that wanted to consume her. She was scared to reveal too much of herself still. Too unwilling to divulge that her issues with sex were vast and complicated, and stemmed from the ignominy of getting pregnant after losing her virginity. And how mad she was, mostly at herself, because she'd somehow found the perfect man—while she was the most emotionally unavailable she'd ever been.

The farther his kisses moved south, the more her anxiety grew, her heart racing as he touched the hem of her dress. She worried as if this were her first time—how would it feel? How would she taste to him? What if she did something embarrassing while he was down there? She thought she was ready, even making sure to shave for the occasion, but as he exposed more of her flesh, in what felt like slow motion, she realized she was trembling. Quivering as he kissed between her thighs, licking and biting at her dark brown skin as if it were actual chocolate, her breathing intensified as he moved higher.

Predictably, he pulled back to look at her. "Eve, maybe we should talk—"

"I'm fine," she said, sitting up on her elbows. "Keep going."

"You don't seem fine," he said. "If you're doing all this because of the girl at the wedding, I wasn't really gonna go home with her."

"I haven't had an orgasm in eight months," she blurted out, her thoughts soaring past the many times she'd pretended with

Leo just to get it over with. "I don't think I've ever really had sex for pleasure."

Jamie sat up on his knees, obviously speechless. "What?"

"I shouldn't say *never.* But with my last . . . with my fiancé, it was usually . . . practical." She drew a long breath before going on. "It's hard for me not to feel . . . I don't know. Shame. My mother made sure of that," she said. "I don't even pleasure myself."

"I see . . ."

"I know. I didn't mean to drop all this in your lap."

"No, I'm glad you told me," Jamie said, his brow line straightened, leaving a thoughtful mien. "I just . . . I wish it was different for you."

"You're different for me," Eve said, offering her sweetest smile. "You are."

"You don't have to be ashamed with me." His earnest gaze and deep voice made her feel safe, in a way she never had before in bed. "If you're nervous . . . if you're downright scared," he said, "we don't have to do anything. Ever. But there's nothin' to be ashamed of, Evie."

Eve nodded, and in the back of her mind, she hoped it would knock away the tears that were trying to surface. "I am nervous," she said. "But I'm ready." She pulled up her dress so that she was naked from the waist down and bit her bottom lip. She was eager to get rid of this cloud hanging over her head. "Don't stop unless I tell you to."

Jamie swallowed visibly at the sight of all her skin on display, licking his lips before pushing her legs apart. He dove in head-first, starting with a kiss to her warm flesh, her entire body twitching in response, then turned his attention to her clit. She silently encouraged him to go deeper, her thighs widening for him, a quiet moan escaping her lips. But he continued to tease her with short, soft licks to her sensitive bud, then followed them with prolonged draws that quickened her breath and tightened her grip on his hair.

"Jamie," Eve hummed, her body already feeling like it was on fire. Within minutes, he had her squirming, on the brink of an orgasm. His tongue was inside her, dipping in and out of her, while his long, deft fingers rubbed her tenderly, working her most delicate nerves like he was getting paid for it.

"You okay?" he asked from between her legs.

"Yeah," she answered with a quick, breathless nod.

As her body tensed, he moved his kisses down her thighs, meticulously covering every inch of her skin, apparently intent on giving special attention to her scars and stretch marks. He licked across the ripples of her stomach, his tongue circling and kissing her navel before heading back down. His fingers gently penetrated her, his mouth doing the rest of the work, all of it making her hips lift from the bed.

Eve's own mouth was watering as she listened to the sounds of him eating her like she was a three-course meal. As the hum of his gentle moans reverberated against her, she felt a rush of ecstasy in her core. A little explosion. She moaned loudly and unabashedly as she experienced her first orgasm in far too long. "Jamie," she whispered, unsure whether she wanted him to stop or keep going. But when he began to run his tongue sideways across her slit, as if he didn't even notice her climax, she tried her best to go with it. Squeezing a fistful of his curls in her hand, her thighs shaking and periodically closing on him, his skin feeling warm against them, she relished in his tongue work. She closed her eyes and bit her lip and let him take her to heaven.

"Fuck."

"I told you," he mumbled.

"Shut up," she hissed, writhing beneath him. Her other hand gripped the sheets as he pushed her legs so far back, they were damn near over her head, and she almost combusted at just the thought of him getting any deeper. "Jamie," she groaned.

His only response was to keep going, and she adored that he not only enjoyed this, but he wasn't shy about broadcasting his delight, his whiskey-like timbre softening into deep moans. He made out with her lips, pushing his tongue between them as if she could return the kiss. He used his entire face to pleasure her, his nose working her nerves, his fingers finding her G-spot, leaving her whimpering and gripping his hair so hard, it was a wonder she hadn't pulled any out.

"Jamie . . ." she whined, feeling his tongue circling, another happy ending on its way. "Shit." Her toes locked, her breathing labored, and she erupted with another delicious orgasm, leaving her a puddle of delighted bliss.

Jamie continued to moan through it as he finished her off, leaving her wet for the next round. Before he would allow her legs back down, he kissed and sucked at her left cheek, then the right, then made his way up her thigh, his lips leaving little damp spots along the way. All while Eve tried to find some way to process what had just happened.

She gazed at the ceiling in a daze, her hand still clutching the sheets with a death grip as Jamie rolled onto the bed beside her. She turned her head to steal a glance of this perfect man. His face was flushed, and he was still licking his swollen lips, making her insides prickle.

He sat up and looked over at her, still splayed across the bed with her dress around her waist, exhausted. "You need a break?"

Eve could only nod and watch helplessly as he left the room with that walk that drove her so crazy.

She was stupid for not doing this sooner. She wanted to feel something other than pain, and the remedy was here all along. Jamie and his magic tongue. She could tell this wasn't a chore for him; he treated it like an art, in fact. And unfortunately, that was yet another thing to like about him.

Damn it.

Jamie returned from the bathroom several minutes later, Eve in the exact position he left her. She enjoyed the cockiness of his little smile as he strolled across the room to the bar. He poured some gin while Eve watched, wondering why he still had pants on. She questioned why she was still wearing her dress and sat up from the bed, finally, to pull it off.

"You want somethin'?" Jamie asked, already retrieving a glass for her.

Wordlessly, Eve grabbed a condom and went to join him at the bar that she'd admired so much on her first visit. Every time she was there, she thought about how beautiful it was, marveling at Jamie's immaculate work. And now, her only interest was in defiling it.

She wrapped her arms around his waist, showing off the gold wrapper in her hand. She pressed her chest against his bare back, her forehead resting against his cool skin, and said, "I want you."

Jamie set down his glass and turned to face her, licking his lips. In one swift motion, he grabbed her by the hips and picked her up, sitting her on the cabinet for easy access. She yelped in surprise but caught up rather quickly, pulling him in for a kiss as she reached for his belt, desperate to undo those pants. Their tongues wrestled as he squeezed her tits, his thumbs fondling her stiffened nipples to make her moan. She could already feel his bulging erection as she got him down to his boxers.

Eve lowered his underwear with her toes while he fumbled to open the condom wrapper. The rise and fall of her breasts teasing him, he stopped to wrap his mouth around one, sucking at her hard nipple with hot, lingering licks until it went soft again, devouring her flesh as she massaged his dick.

He released her breast to finish the job of unwrapping the condom, and the two of them locked eyes as he pulled her hips to the edge of the cabinet, the head of his length pressed against her. Eve gripped his arm for leverage and nodded for him to go on. She was ready this time.

A delighted sigh fell from her lips as he pushed inside her, accompanied by a grunt from Jamie as they acclimated. When he picked up his pace, Eve had to clutch his shoulders and neck, her short nails scratching his skin as her back beat against the wall behind them. He felt so damn good, his erection filling her up, sliding past her walls and back out again. The fluidity of his stroke left absolutely nothing to be desired. His tongue had her mind ajumble. Her hair had come out of its high ponytail, her braids falling into her face, practically blinding her. The glasses clinking around them only amplified the heat of it all.

"Fuck," Eve growled into his skin. She'd been waiting to be dicked down like this all her life. She could hear herself whimpering his name, and she both loved and loathed the way he made her do that. He had her in the palm of his hand, just trying to stay upright while he fucked her sideways.

"I'm gonna come," Jamie breathed into her neck.

She nodded, feeling her heartbeat in her ears, her sight just a blur of this gorgeous man. He had her feeling brave enough to start rolling her hips to meet his, the result sublime. They had a chemistry that couldn't be concocted—she'd been hiding from it, but she felt it the first time they met. Turns out, it made for fantastic sex. The kind that came with sloppy kisses and unattractive grunts, little scratches and bites and breathless, nonsensical expletives as their eyes rolled to the back of their heads.

As Eve came for the third time that night, Jamie slowed his grinding to a near halt, releasing with a hard groan as the smell of their sex filled the warm room. He finally allowed himself to rest, his forehead touching hers, while his hands continued to massage her backside affectionately. Their heavy breaths were the soundtrack to their orgasms.

"God . . ." Eve exhaled, rubbing at his back. She could already feel the raised welts in his skin that would undoubtedly leave marks the next day.

Jamie smiled, leaving slow kisses along her clavicle. "You saw Him, too?"

She playfully swatted his lower back, admonishing him for the blasphemous joke. Though in the back of her mind, she wasn't entirely sure she hadn't. "I'm glad you encouraged me to face this," she said seriously. "I can't believe I would've missed out on you."

He grinned a bit bashfully. Just when he was returning to his normal color, she made him blush again. He ran his thumb up the side of her torso and back down as he nodded. "We broke your dry spell."

She worked hard to hold on to her smile, but it burst past her lips anyway. "We did." He'd broken through more than that—her sadness, her supposedly impenetrable walls . . .

Jamie offered her another kiss, slow and almost chaste, despite the erotic scene. Eve closed her eyes, happy to get lost in him and his lips for the night, but as their tongues did their tango, there was a silent prayer echoing in the back of her mind. She wasn't religious, not anymore, but she hoped someone up there could hear her plea: *Please, God, don't let me fall in love with this man.*

CHAPTER 19

Memphis City Blues

JAMIE

Sun, Aug 17 7:05 AM

Casey Gallagher: Don't be alarmed, but Dad had a (minor?) accident. Was in the ER, but he's home now. I was thinking if you have time this weekend, you could drive out to see him? I know he'd like that.

Jamie hated having a phone. If it weren't for Jack, he wouldn't; and if it weren't for Jack, he wouldn't be predisposed to noticing every instance of it buzzing, chiming, or ringing, no matter when or how far away. And he wouldn't be staring at a text from his brother, guilting him out of his cozy spot in bed, just beside, or rather, underneath, Eve. He didn't want to move. Hell, after the night they'd just had, he wasn't sure that he *could* move. But he'd had every intention of basking in the afterglow of their time together. He'd already imagined morning sex and coffee, in no particular order, and the nonpareil bliss of lying in bed naked all day.

But alas, duty as the elder brother, and the one who stayed

close to home, was calling, and he would never be able to justify hanging around doing nothing when his father had been in the emergency room. He was at that precarious age when concerns about parents and kids converged, and he seemed to exist in a constant state of latent distress. Seeing his dad in the flesh would relieve some of that, at least.

He whispered Eve's name and gently ran his fingertips along her back in an effort to stir her, only reminding him how soft her skin was. She was warm to the touch and barely twitched in response. "Evie . . ."

She woke up with a groan. "What are you doing, man? The sun isn't even up yet."

"I know." His sigh was full of regret as he continued to coax her awake. "But I gotta go."

That got her up. Even if she was glaring at him. "You 'gotta go' where?"

He smiled at the demand in her voice, making it clear that for once, she really didn't want him to leave. "Come here." He reached out to pull her back into his arms, hoping to reassure her that he wasn't taking off because he wanted to. "My brother just texted to let me know our dad had an accident. He's okay," he added when he felt her concern give way to tension in her back. "But I really should go see him."

"Oh." She sounded disappointed, but she nodded anyway. "Of course."

"I'm sorry."

"You don't need to apologize." She turned her head in his direction. "Unless you're lying."

Jamie laughed before kissing her cheek. "I'm not."

"So the sex wasn't bad and you're not running away because you don't know how to tell me?"

Jamie couldn't even fathom the idea that the sex was bad. It was transcendent. It was taking every ounce of his own resolve not to ask for another round now that she was awake. "I'm not gonna dignify that with a response." He did plant another series of kisses along the crook of her neck as she giggled, and the sound of her laugh was somehow just as arousing as her naked body. They'd just started doing . . . this, and already, he was going to miss it.

"Do you have a little more time for me before you go?" Eve asked.

He'd never seen her so demure before. Sex really brought out the tender side of this woman who'd done her best to hide her soft spots.

"A little," he rationalized between kisses, figuring another hour wouldn't change much about his four-hundred-mile drive to Memphis.

"Any chance you can come back before Friday this week? Just to make up for our lost time?"

"Or maybe you can come with me," he said, pausing his kisses. He was always painfully aware of their limited time together, and it seemed that she was, too, but still, he was wary of asking for too much. And inviting her along to meet his dad was exactly the opposite, but after the last night and the way his feelings had ballooned into something much more serious than a situation, he had to try. "It's not because I want you to meet my dad, but . . . because weekends are all we have, and I don't wanna lose this one . . ." His words trailed into silence as she contorted out of his embrace.

"You want me to come home with you? Right now?" She pulled the sheets up around her body as she shifted to the edge of the bed. "Jamie . . ."

If this was her reaction to a simple road trip, he could only imagine how she would react whenever he wanted her to meet Jack. "Not if you don't want to, Eve. It was just a suggestion."

She nodded, but it was clear that the curtain around her had somehow gone back up in a matter of seconds. *Just* when he'd managed to get it down.

"I don't think I'm ready for that," she said. "But I hope everything's okay. With your dad."

Jamie had nothing substantive to say, his euphoria replaced with diffidence. He offered a half-hearted smile and nod, but he, too, hoped everything was okay.

With Eve.

Half past 2:00 p.m., Jamie arrived in Collierville, the little Memphis suburb where he grew up. His dad's place was a typical middle-class Tennessee home, nothing particularly special about it, other than the childhood memories it evoked. Jamie's upbringing reflected the conventional nuclear family: two parents, two kids, and a dog, complete with a picket fence. Until their mother, the human wrecking ball, sent it all crashing down.

He was nearly finished with high school when he learned of his mom's affair, but Casey was barely an adolescent, and Jamie felt particularly affronted on his behalf. He carried that betrayal as his own personal baggage, so of course he ended up with someone who did the same. The cliché of it all only added insult to the injuries.

Jamie let himself into the house, not wanting to disturb his quasi-incapacitated father, and instantly detected the sound of laughter emanating from the living room. He smiled at the sound until he recognized the culprit: Diane Gallagher, speak of the devil, sitting just beside his father, a lit cigarette propped between her manicured fingers, the red nail polish and her square face giving him shades of a Disney villain.

She grinned as their eyes met and put out her smoke. "Jamie. Hello."

He was suddenly gripping his keys tighter, the ridges practically threatening to draw blood. "I didn't realize you were here," he said flatly.

"I'm the one who suggested Casey text you," she said. She stood from the couch, looking more like a housewife now than she ever did, dressed in a silky blouse and cropped pants; her curly hair was fully gray now and chin length. She looked elegant, and the falsity of it all made Jamie recoil when she approached.

"Dad, what happened?" he asked, brushing past his mother to examine his father. His dad had an ugly bruise above his left cheek, morphing into something like a black eye. His pale face was splotchy all around, Jamie noticed, as he touched the stitched lacerations along his forehead. "Jesus."

Sam sighed at the contact. "It's nothin', kid. Just missed a step." Jamie knew Sam hated to be fussed over, but Jamie couldn't help himself. His dad was relatively fit for his age, yet suddenly, he looked frail. "I'm fine. Embarrassed more than anything."

Jamie caught sight of his newly chipped tooth, one of the upper incisors missing a small chunk. "You said it wasn't bad," he said, scrutinizing his other teeth for further damage. "That looks pretty fuckin' bad."

"It looks worse than it feels."

"It was a little spill," Diane said, gliding across the room to join his dad on the couch again. "The doctor says he took it well. The dentist will be able to see him on Monday." She flashed her own grin at Sam, nicotine stains and all, in a way that felt flirtatious, and Jamie felt vaguely sick to his stomach. "He'll be good as new."

"Where's Jack?" his dad asked, seeming eager to switch subjects.

"He's with his mother," Jamie said, eyeing the two of them. "She has weekends."

"I'm surprised she agreed to that," Diane said.

"It was court ordered," Jamie mumbled as he went to investigate the staircase. As if it were the culprit in his father's fall, rather than time and lack of coordination catching up to him. "Dad, was it late when it happened? Or early in the morning?"

"It was the middle of the night, Jamie," his mother said. "What does that matter?"

"Can he speak for himself?"

"Jamie . . ." His father's blue eyes pleaded for his civility.

"Was she here when it happened?"

"I was."

Jamie shook his head. "You two are unbelievable." He wanted to turn and leave, but he didn't drive six hours to see his dad just for his mother to run him off. "This is really what you want?"

Sam rubbed at his gray stubble the same way Jamie often did when he was ill at ease. "What do you want me to say, kid?"

"I want you to say that you remember how she treated you.

Us. She couldn't just leave like a normal person; she had to cheat on you for *years*."

"And she's apologized. She wasn't happy."

"Nobody is fucking happy," Jamie shouted. He felt like a child, screaming into that void where parents think their children are too young and too dumb to listen to. "That's not a reason to treat people like shit."

"Jamie," Diane cut in, "I was young. And selfish—"

"She's gonna do the same thing again," he said, leaping into her sentence. "And I know you know it. That's why you kept it from me." Jamie scoffed at his father's lack of reply and rubbed his hand over his stress-riddled face. "I can't believe I drove out here for this."

"We kept it from you because you're so goddamned judgmental," his mother said. Her voice was even, but her stare wavered.

"Excuse me?"

"No one can make a mistake around you. You see flaws like a bull's-eye, and it's the only thing you focus on."

Jamie scowled at her. "That's not true. And how would you even know?"

"Because you're the reason we don't have a relationship," she said. "You preferred drinking yourself to embarrassment than accepting that your mother wasn't perfect. Skipped college and martyred yourself. Twenty years later, you can't fathom that I've changed, because you haven't. You'd rather your father be unhappy than know that he forgave me."

He looked to his dad for some form of rebuttal, a futility considering he was clearly in on this ridiculous charade. And maybe Casey was, too, because his mother sounded just like him.

Jamie could understand his mother feeling trapped in a family she was never ready for. Parenthood was an excruciating undertaking for him now, in his financially secure thirties; for an eighteen-year-old, forced to rely on a man for everything, it must have felt impossible. But she made the worst available decisions at every turn, and she'd never been accountable for them. Leaving his father to pick up the pieces.

All this time, Jamie believed their dad tolerated her narcissism for the sake of the kids. It was why he worked so hard to preserve an amity with Lucy. He always appreciated his father's brand of stoicism, his quiet determination to be a good dad. Especially now that he knew the difficulties of single parenthood. But maybe it came down to the fact that his father loved his mother; the pain of what she did refused to erase that.

"I need some air," he said. He escaped the increasingly stuffy room, trading it for the backyard.

In the time since his last visit, sometime around Christmas, he noticed the patio had been converted into something much more charming than the bare canvas there before. Now, there were flowers planted along the courtyard, yellow, pink, and orange begonias livening the space. There were some nice wicker sectionals and a matching dining set, complete with a lighted umbrella, the beige color giving off posh when it should have seemed dull. Jamie knew this was his mother's doing; she and Casey had this talent in common. Their father's taste was more classic, to put it kindly, and less trendy than this setup suggested. But Jamie had to admit it looked far better than its previous iteration. Having someone around to take care of his dad, even if it was Diane, for however temporarily she'd be around, perhaps wasn't the worst thing in the world.

"God." Jamie sighed. Making excuses for her again.

His mother had been right about one thing: She did drive him to drink. And today, he was itching for something, that little buzz to dull the razor-sharp edges of his anger. He loathed that this was his reaction to her. When she wasn't around, so long as she remained some abstract idea, he could almost laugh off her selfishness. He and Casey joked about their awful mother often. But whenever he was in the same room with her, a rarity by his own design, this ire bubbled back to the surface. He probably needed a therapist, but whiskey always worked much faster.

His dad kept a fifth of Jameson in his den, making it easy for Jamie to summon his younger self and sneak in to get it. He sat at Sam's desk, vacantly thumbing through the neatly filed paperwork, mostly bills and bank statements, before finding the liquor.

"Now what the hell are you doin'?"

Speaking of his younger self, he startled like a child at the sound of his father's heavy twang catching him in some delinquent act. "I just need a little somethin'," Jamie said.

"Why do you start sounding like an alcoholic whenever your mama's around? It ain't healthy."

"Neither is your relationship with her."

"You don't know a damn thing about my relationship with her," Sam said.

Jamie wanted to argue, but his father was right, and he was being petulant. He relented, setting the bottle back in its drawer, and stood from his chair, allowing Sam to take the seat. "I gotta get a handle on how I react to her," he said, using the edge of the desk as his stool. "I don't know what it is."

"I think you think that if she hadn't done what she did, your life would've been different. And that might be true, Jamie, but ain't no proof that it would be better."

"I don't want better," he said. "But different might've been nice."

"People think that . . ."

"Come on, Dad. You never wondered about your life if you hadn't been saddled with two kids alone?"

Sam immediately dismissed the thought with a guffaw. "You two are the only good thing I ever did."

"We have to say that," Jamie replied. "But seriously . . ."

"I've thought about it," Sam said. "And the truth is I think I would've been a lot less happy without y'all around."

Jamie nodded.

"I'm glad you stayed, Jameson, God knows I am. But if I'd known you'd regret it, I would've kicked you out of this house myself."

"What?"

"When you decided not to go to Vandy . . ."

"Well, I didn't decide on my own. We couldn't afford it."

"But you could've gone somewhere," Sam said. "I wish I'd had the forethought to make you go. All these regrets ain't good for you."

Jamie sighed. "I'm fine, Dad."

"You're not. You're mad at yourself. You're mad at me for not being mad at your mama. Of course I wish she hadn't done what she did. But what good does it do to hold it against her? People are human. Another truth is that I was a bad husband."

Jamie narrowed his eyes at his dad, offended on his behalf.

"I was. Being a good parent and a good spouse are two different things. And I didn't give your mother what she needed either. Nothin' in a relationship is ever just one person's fault."

Jamie looked to the floor, wanting to believe that, but he refused to take the blame for Lucy's infidelity. He'd done his best to understand it, but he drew the line at shouldering that responsibility with her.

"I understand forgiving her, if you really needed to, but why did you have to get back together?" Jamie asked. If in twenty years, he considered running back to Lucy, he hoped to God that Casey would cut off his feet first.

"I don't know what to tell you, kid. We had unfinished business."

Jamie sighed. Maybe that was why he was so inexplicably drawn to Eve. He couldn't make sense of it, but it felt like there was something there worth exploring. "I met this woman out in Gatlinburg," he said, figuring it would be nice to talk about it with *someone*. "She's the most beautiful person I've ever seen, and somehow, she enjoys my company. But she's also messy and . . . withdrawn. Half the time, I'm not even sure she likes me." He chuckled at his own description, recognizing that Casey was correct that he had no business judging anyone. "I know she's not some magic cure to all the things that've gone wrong in my life, but . . . fuck if the world doesn't seem better when I'm with her." He looked at his dad, searching for recognition in his eyes. "Is that Mom? For you?"

Sam smiled, audaciously showing off his broken tooth. "Always has been."

"Then . . . I guess I get it."

Just then, Jamie felt the recognizable sensation of his phone vibrating in his pocket, and as always, he checked the message in case it involved Jack. Instead, it was Eve, speak of the devil, doing her best to render everything he'd just said absolutely fucking pointless.

Sun, Aug 17 2:14 pm

Eve Ambroise: Hey. I hate to do this this way, but it's the only way I can maintain my resolve. I have to finish this play and my focus isn't where it needs to be. It would be best for me if we put a pause on it all. I hope you understand. And take care of yourself in the meantime. xo

CHAPTER 20

What's Love Got to Do with It?

EVE

Sun, Aug 17 2:20 PM

Jamie Gallagher: If that's what you need, of course. How long do you think this pause is gonna be?

Mon, Aug 18 9:04 AM

Jamie Gallagher: Hello?

Wed, Aug 20 12:56 PM

Jamie Gallagher: Are you seriously ignoring me?

Fri, Aug 22 10:10 PM

Jamie Gallagher: I guess no answer is an answer, but I was thinking about driving out tomorrow. If you don't want me to, I won't, of course. But I would like to see you.

Sun, Aug 24 11:13 AM

Jamie Gallagher: Ok, I guess this is what we're doing. You take care of yourself too, Eve.

"I think I might've done something stupid."

"Okay," Maya said, looking utterly unfazed by the news. "Well, that's a step up from you not doing anything at all, so what's up?"

"Wait, where are you?" Eve asked. She was squinting at her phone, trying to discern the background of Maya's side of the call, a seemingly endless scape of green behind her.

"Girl, Siobhan got us out here golfing again." She tilted her camera so that Eve could see her ensemble, a pair of cropped plaid pants, teal and navy blue, with a white top. She also had a dark blue ivy cap perched on top of her 3C curls, which should've been a dead giveaway to her whereabouts. Maya then showed Eve the view of her girlfriend putting, in her pink skort, top, and green visor, looking like a Black Barbie—AKA Edition.

"Are y'all in the city?" Eve asked, as the place looked too sprawling to be anywhere near Brooklyn.

"Oh, so you went to Tennessee and just forgot all about everything, huh?"

Eve frowned, unsure what that meant until she recalled the date—August was the time of year their friend group congregated in Martha's Vineyard for a few weeks.

Eve used to think *The Inkwell* was just a Jada Pinkett movie, but as it turned out, it was a real destination spot for the Black elite and middle class alike. Maya's girlfriend secured a cute little cottage near the beach back in grad school—her family wasn't wealthy, but close enough—and so it had become tradition. They didn't go every year—mainly because Maya was usually playing basketball—but they'd made tentative plans for this summer, as their friend Adebimbola had a documentary premiering at the film festival there. But Maya was right—it had completely slipped

Eve's mind. She was going to blame that on Jamie, along with everything else she'd forsaken because she'd started liking him a little too much.

"Damn, I really did forget," Eve said, feeling even worse now. "Why didn't you remind me?"

Maya gave her a knowing look. "You said you needed to get away. I didn't think Martha's Vineyard was gon' stop you."

"Well, how's it going?"

"It's hot and I don't know how to play golf," Maya deadpanned. "Oh, but guess who we saw out here this morning."

"An Obama?" Eve predicted. She wasn't sure whether to guess Barack or Michelle, Malia or Sasha, but at least one of them was spotted in Oak Bluffs every single year.

"Girl, don't nobody care about them no more. Stacey Abrams."

"Oh, shit."

"Just hanging out at breakfast, being all effervescent and shit."

"Did you meet her?"

"I just waved. You know I don't like to bother nobody."

Eve narrowed her eyes at what could only be deemed a lie. Granted, Maya's job involved being around notable people often, and she was generally chill about it. But when it came to someone she really wanted to meet—namely, Rihanna—she lost her goddamn mind. "Listen, both of us can't be delusional right now. Not when I need your help."

"Hold on, lemme take my shot," Maya said before handing off the phone to Siobhan.

"Eve Antoinette Ambroise!" Siobhan greeted her cheerfully. "I miss your face, girl."

"I miss yours, too," Eve said, waving at her friend. It was a bit ironic they were saying as much, since most people said they looked alike. Though Siobhan had picked up a bit of a tan out there on the beach, her dark skin rich and glowing like gold under mahogany. "The category is melanin," Eve exclaimed, snapping her fingers.

"Listen." Siobhan giggled, proudly flipping her long straight hair. "Seriously, though, how are you?"

Eve sighed. "I don't know. Better in some ways, worse in others."

"Maya says you got a new boo down there. Must be the reason you are positively glowing, sis."

Eve tried not to smile as she tried not to think about Jamie, but neither her mouth nor her mind cooperated. "I wouldn't call him that. Maybe boo-adjacent. I don't even know what to call what we've been doing, but it feels like it only just got started last night."

"Okay, but it's good, I take it?"

At that point, Maya had come running back to the conversation, both of their pretty faces squeezed into the frame like they were taking a selfie.

"Obviously it was good," Maya said. "Look at her."

"So why is he boo-adjacent?" Siobhan asked.

"Because she did something stupid," Maya said. When Eve started to protest, Maya stopped her. "Your words."

"Well, he started it," Eve said, sounding like someone too immature to be having sex with anyone.

"Watch this," Maya said to Siobhan, then redirected to Eve. "What he do?"

"He asked me to come with him to Memphis."

Both Maya and Siobhan stared blankly at the screen, leaving Eve to wonder whether the call had frozen.

"What's wrong with that?" Siobhan said.

"Was it for a Black Lives Matter protest or something?" Maya asked.

"That would be weird," Siobhan said. "Unless he already planned to go before he met you, I guess."

Maya made a face. "Even then."

Siobhan nodded. "Performative. Yeah."

"Can we focus," Eve said. "He's *from* Memphis. His dad had some kind of accident, and he was going to visit him."

"And he asked you to come with him," Siobhan said. "And that's a problem."

"It was a few hours after we had sex for the first time. So yes."

The two of them continued to stare at Eve like she was stupid. "This is giving straight people problems," Siobhan said.

And Eve realized then that she probably did sound ridiculous to two queer Black women who would've given anything for the privilege to meet each other's parents. But Siobhan's conservative upbringing and Maya's issues with her dad—ones that weren't related to homophobia, at least—meant that wasn't going to happen anytime soon.

"Maybe we should call Nikole," Siobhan suggested.

"I'm not bothering her at the beach with this," Maya said. "Eve, why are you playing on my phone?"

"I'm not playing! I recognize that I maybe overreacted. Especially when I texted to tell him I needed a break."

Both Maya and Siobhan shouted variations of "Oh my god!" at the screen while Eve covered her face in embarrassment. While she had certainly allowed that she was being irrational—which was why she called Maya in the first place—she didn't think she was being so obtuse that her friends would literally be screaming at her about it.

"I hate y'all," Eve said, pretending to pout.

Maya took control of the phone while Siobhan, Eve presumed, went off to take her next shot. "A few nights ago, you were all 'my man, my man, my man.' To the point where you hung up on me," Maya recounted. "Don't think I forgot about that. And now you say it's over . . . because he asked you to go to Memphis."

"You're oversimplifying it to make me sound moronic. No, bitch, it's over because I have shit to do. It's season two, I'm Carmy, Jamie is Claire, and my play is the Bear."

"Eve, you know damn well I don't know what you talking 'bout."

"I told you to watch *The Bear* like a year ago."

"It's too many shows. I can't keep up," Maya said. It was the same answer she gave a year ago when everyone was watching *The Bear* and she felt left out. "How 'bout you give me the gist?"

"The gist is that I told Stella I'd have a new play for her in December. This is after I told her I'd have it in October. So clearly, Jamie is just a big-ass distraction. And I don't need him to be."

"That's exactly what you said you wanted him to be." Maya peered at Eve. "Don't be rolling your eyes at me. That's what you said."

"I know what the fuck I said. And now I'm taking it back."

"All because he wanted you to go over by his daddy's house. *Like I said*. Girl, get off my phone."

"Maya."

"Eve, what do you want me to do with this information?"

"I want you to tell me what to do!"

"Sistren. You got this far without any input from me. Try just trusting your instincts."

Eve huffed at the useless advice. If her instincts were working, she wouldn't be in this predicament in the first place. "Those haven't done what they're supposed to do since I met Jamie."

Maya was giving that blank stare again. "You want me to come down there? We can fight for real if that's what you want. You know I got your address."

"I absolutely do not want that," Eve said. Maya was five feet ten inches of mostly muscle. That battle would end worse than Kendrick v. Drake. "Stay right there in Oak Bluffs."

"Matter fact, your birthday is coming up. Let me see what these flights talkin' about."

"Maya, do not do it," Eve was practically yelling at her phone.

"Then stop crashing out over this," Maya said, turning halfway serious. "Let that man fuck you the way you deserve to be fucked. And then bring your ass home."

But therein lay the problem. If Eve continued down this path with Jamie, and not just in terms of sex, but in spending any marked time with him at all, she wasn't going to want to come home. She already didn't. And she had no clue what she was going to do about it.

Cheri. Tètè. Your mother and I send this card with love. We send this card with the hope that you will reach back out. The silence of the last two months has been deafening. Disrespectful. We do not ask much and do not wish for anything more or less than your happiness. You have done nothing but wrestle with us for it. Please call. Please write. Please anything. It is your birthday to do with as you please, but remember that we are the reason for your birth. Be grateful. You are a beautiful human being with much to offer the world. Do not run away from it. Do not hide it. Be present. Everyone has a past and everyone has a path forward. In this 34th year of your life, we hope you are able to find yours and march down it proudly. Be you.

Bondye Bon!
Dad & Mom

Sitting on her porch steps under the setting sun, Eve stared at the week-early birthday card from her parents. She ran her fingers over the dark red rose and rosary embossed on the front before rereading the verse beneath it: *May the God of hope fill you with all joy and peace in believing, so that you may grow rich in hope by the power of the Holy Spirit.—Romans 15:13. Happy Birthday!*

Her eyes pricked with the sting of tears as the gesture tugged at an unexpected, unexplainable ache. She wasn't sure whether she actually missed her parents or just the familiarity of her life in New York. Her home. Her mother's nagging disguised as advice. *You need more rice in your diet; you're getting too thin. A degree in political science would be much more useful than theater. I don't know why you like those fake braids when you have such beautiful hair. The money you spent on "Coa-chello" could've gone into a place you can own.* Constantly having your life choices put into question was psychological warfare, yes, but she was used to it, at least. In her lowest, loneliest moments, she yearned for the comfort of what she was accustomed to.

Eve did consider calling her parents, as requested, but for the time being, her father's barely legible lecture was enough. Instead, she scanned and rescanned the hodgepodge of words, hearing his deep, velvety voice and all the hints of Haiti in his intonation. They meant well. She knew that. They loved her, which was much more than some could say. She wished that were enough.

"Hey."

Startled, Eve looked up to see Jamie standing in front of her, donning his typical ensemble of jeans and a button-down with the sleeves rolled to his elbows. She'd been distracted, so she was unsurprised that she missed the approach of his footsteps, but she definitely hadn't expected to see him anytime soon.

"What are you doing here?" she asked.

His gaze was sympathetic as he nodded to the contents in her hands. "You okay?"

She fixed her face and stuffed the card back in its mauve envelope. "I'm fine," she said. "Why are you here?"

"May I?"

Eve gestured for him to take a seat, which he accepted, claiming a lateral spot on the steps. "You didn't answer any of my texts."

"Most people would've taken that as a message in itself . . ."

Jamie appeared disappointed by her answer, his small smile flattening into nothing. Understandably. "I guess I just wanted to make sure this was over before I gave up on it," he said.

Eve stared at the ground, studying the shape of the cobblestones in the walkway, the unevenness in some places, smooth in others. "How's your dad?" she asked.

Jamie chewed at his bottom lip contemplatively before answering. "I think he's as fine as he's gonna be."

"What does that mean?"

"I don't know. Nothin'."

His response was disquieting, leaving Eve fidgeting with her envelope while Jamie sat there as composed as ever. "Well, is he okay? Is he in the hospital?" she asked.

"Oh. Yeah. No, nothing like that. Just your run-of-the-mill clash-of-the-parent-with-the-adult-child kinda thing."

Eve nodded, wishing she couldn't relate. She showed off her envelope to Jamie. "Birthday card from mine."

Jamie grimaced, his dark brows knitting over his light eyes. "It's your birthday?"

"Not until the beginning of the month. They're just weird."

"They wanted to make sure it got to you in time."

Eve pushed a long breath through her lips before shaking her head. "The thing I hate about our relationship is I'm never sure whether I'm the disappointment or if they are."

Jamie scratched at his bearded cheek before replying. "I would think it's a little bit of both for all of us. And not just with our parents, but for me, it's every relationship I have. It's that push and pull, give and take, am I getting this right? Am I accepting too little? Doing too much?" He shook his head, too, and then rested it against the banister, his eye catching hers and not letting go. "I never know the answer."

Eve's gaze softened under his, and she regretted that she didn't have one for him. She wished she were better at this. Better for him. "I don't know if I can make this make sense to you, but . . . you weren't in my plans," she said. "This"—she gestured between them—"wasn't in my plans."

"No, I get that. I didn't come here expecting to find you either. But we're here now. And I guess I don't understand why we can't just . . . see where things go. I don't really know what the issue is, and I don't think it's fair for you to just disappear without even explaining it to me."

"It's not an *issue*. It's me. I don't know what I'm doing here. But asking me to meet your parents four hours after we have sex for the first time is a lot. It's too much."

"I wasn't asking you to *meet my parents*." He frowned and then sighed. "I just wanted to spend more time with you," he said.

Eve felt herself internally melting at his earnestness. None of this was good for her resolve, her sanity, or anything in between.

"I can see how a request like that would sound overwhelming," he conceded. "But that doesn't mean you just stop communicating with me. You can't just cut me off like that, Eve."

"I told you I needed time. I don't owe you more than that."

"You owe me the respect I'd give to you. God knows you've had a wall up from day one, but I still communicate."

"You can't force me to be who you want me to be. I've never been unclear about who I am."

Jamie opened his mouth, but then paused. "You're right," he said. He nodded as he stared out to the trees ahead, still biting at his lip as a quiet breeze inserted itself into the conversation. "I expected too much," he said eventually.

"That's not what I'm saying, Jamie."

"That sounds like exactly what you're saying."

"I'm saying . . . that I'm scared. Because I like you." Eve exhaled, the confession taking her by surprise. She already knew it—and said as much to Maya a couple of weeks ago—but she never imagined sharing that news with him. "And the truth is . . . I just wanna spend more time with you, too."

Jamie looked to Eve once more, his blue eyes dancing with hers, both of them instinctively basking in the excitement of requited like.

"Yeah?" Jamie asked.

"I shouldn't like you," Eve said. "I didn't mean to."

"So ignoring me all week was your attempt to what? Undo it all?"

"Whatever it was, it didn't work." Eve smiled in spite of herself, her gaze flitting back to the card from her parents, and she wondered whether their wishes for her happiness would ever align with what actually made her happy.

Going forward, she would hold on to her pointless prayers about not falling in love with Jamie. She still didn't want to, but she could feel it happening anyway. Now, she simply hoped, she prayed, that she wouldn't disappoint him. That he wouldn't disappoint her. That somehow, they would both simply make it out of this thing, whatever it was, whatever it turned out to be, unscathed.

CHAPTER 21

Something He Can Feel

JAMIE

"Can I ask you something?"

Jamie opened his eyes to the sound of Eve's voice. "Ask me anything."

She started with a deep, tense sigh. Then: "What's it like for you? Being a parent."

Jamie chuckled uneasily, the question feeling far too heavy for the lightness of the moment. He inhaled as he considered his answer, the ambrosial scent of Eve's downy curls filling his nose. Soft, citrusy, and woodsy. For this, among other reasons, he loved that she liked to cuddle after sex; another surprise in a long list of things he didn't quite understand about her. Including this question.

"I don't know how to describe it," he said, absently running his thumb along her upper back. "It's terrifying. It's exhilarating. It can be annoying. But at the end of the day, trite as it might sound, it's made me a better man."

"Annoying?" she repeated, raising her chin to stare at him.

"Maybe that's the wrong word. It's just, I don't know what I'm doing half the time. Sometimes I think I got lost in the last eight years." He stopped short when she looked down, and he wondered if some part of her identified with that feeling. "I just mean, I've spent a lot of time being Jack's dad. At some point, I stopped letting myself have my own identity."

Eve looked up again, her exquisitely arched eyebrows furrowed. "Wow."

"What?"

"I hear of women feeling that way. Vanishing into motherhood. I'm not sure I've heard that from a dad's perspective."

"I'm not complaining about it," he was quick to add. "I just—"

"No, I know." She nodded and affectionately ran her knuckle along his jaw. "I appreciate the honesty."

He had never said that out loud before, not even to Lucy, even though he imagined she had some similar feelings. But he appreciated the question, and especially coming from Eve, who had never once initiated a conversation in the realm of Jack. She often cut them off at the pass. He wondered if that meant she was opening herself up to the possibility of hearing more about him. Maybe even meeting him one day.

More than likely, he was getting ahead of himself. Eve would be back in New York sooner than later, so the idea of this being more than what it was was pure delusion. More than likely.

"I know it's probably impolite to ask this, especially of a woman, but . . . do you ever think about having kids?"

"No." Her answer was even drier than her usual deadpan.

Jamie peered at her as if he could see into her brain if he tried hard enough. "Do you just not like kids?"

Eve let out what he could only describe as a chortle. "Would that be a deal-breaker?"

"It would depend on the deal."

She chuckled again, resting her face against his chest. "I guess that's true."

"In your mind, what is this, Eve?"

"I honestly don't know." Before the words were out of her mouth, she'd slipped out of his arms and rolled across the bed to grab her water glass. Jamie watched, his eyes drawn to her muscles as she stretched and contorted along the mattress, her deep complexion a shade of blue in the dark room. She seemed more comfortable with nudity now, but the veneer had remained in place, and so he was still waiting to see her naked.

Eve left the bed altogether, off to brush her teeth and tie up her hair. When she returned, she claimed her usual spot in bed, their postcoital cuddle finished, he supposed. He rolled onto his side to gaze at her, studying the side of her face as he ruminated over asking the question that had set up shop in his mind since that night Leo Coletti's name flashed across her iPhone.

It was a simple question. *Is your ex really your ex?* But it was loaded with the weight of distrust and insecurity. Did she care if he didn't trust her? Probably not. But it was boorish to ask. And still . . .

"Is your ex really your ex?"

"Yes," Eve said, reaching out to touch his face. "I wouldn't do that to you." She studied him right back, and Jamie wondered if she recognized the vulnerability that sat in his eyes. "Lucy really did a number on you, huh?"

Jamie scoffed at the mention of her name. He gazed at Eve, the warmth of her hand on his cheek making him feel protected. "Can I tell you something?"

"Of course."

"Little over a year ago, I was coming home with Jack early one morning," he said. He assumed she would withdraw again at the mention of Jack's name, but she only nodded, encouraging him to continue. "We'd been up here for the weekend, and he didn't feel well, so I thought I'd get an early start on the road," he explained. "We got back to the house before sunrise, and there was a strange car sitting in our driveway, so I gave Lucy a call to make sure everything was all right." He rolled his eyes at the thought now. "I knew what it was, probably even before that moment, but I still walked in that house . . . I don't know, thinking wishfully, I guess.

"I walk in with Jack fast asleep in my arms," he went on, "and Lucy and this guy are knocked out on the couch. On *our* couch." He expelled a soft breath. "I took Jack to his room and just laid down with him. I didn't know what else to do."

"Jamie . . ."

"The thing that really got me, though . . . when she finally realized what happened, that I'd come home and caught her, she got mad at *me*. I was over it, but she wanted to fight. Told me to ask myself whether I really even loved her." He smirked at the ridiculous notion, cynicism taking hold of his thoughts. "She really tried to convince me that I was in the wrong. And for a while, I wondered if she was right." He gazed at Eve. "So yeah, she did a number on me."

Eve shook her head against her pillow. "How could anyone cheat on you?"

"Who knows why people do what they do."

He went on to tell Eve of his mother doing the same to his father. How he'd caught her with their neighbor and kept the secret for months because he'd been too afraid to break his dad's heart. How he hated her for that, not just then, but still, and he was trying not to, for his own sake. How he often failed at that mission.

"I always ask myself how I ended up with someone just like my mother." He exhaled deeply as Eve continued to rub her thumb along his cheek, listening. "And just like Lucy, my mom resented me for knowing."

"Shout-out to gaslighting," Eve said.

"I hate how much the two of them have molded who I am," he said. "But I spent twenty years getting over my mom, and only about a year moving on from Lucy, so . . . progress?"

Eve's gaze faltered, and she took that opportunity to turn away, lying on her back to stare at the angled ceiling.

"Do you trust me?" she eventually asked.

Jamie continued to watch her. "Do you want me to?"

"I don't know." She thoughtfully rubbed her lower lip as she confessed, "I can't decide whether to want nothing from you, or absolutely everything."

Jamie kept his eyes only on her. He watched as a tear slipped out of her eye, following its path down the side of her face until it seeped into her pillow. Then another tear followed. And another after that. And in that moment, it felt like he was finally seeing her naked.

"I trust you," he whispered. "I just don't wanna fall in love with someone who's taken."

"Please don't fall in love with me." She turned to him, her dark eyes both searching and pleading.

Jamie was starting to think it was already too late. What was supposed to be a summer situationship had turned into something far more significant. "If I were a smarter man, I wouldn't."

Eve smiled. "Just keep in mind what you said about the other two women in your life."

"Maybe the third time's the charm."

"Maybe it's a disaster waiting to happen."

"Until you leave me, at least," Jamie said. He hated that she was there only for the summer, Labor Day marking the unofficial end of the season. But he was trying to keep her imminent departure in mind, despite his heart wanting to ignore the facts.

"Not you trying to get rid of me after you just begged me to let you in."

"I begged you," he said, chuckling. "Okay."

Eve gazed at him. "I'm not ready to fall in love," she said. "But I'm not ready to leave you either."

Jamie could feel his heart start to beat faster at her admission, his face growing warm with that familiar concoction of excitement and relief. Anyone with sense would've just let this go. But Jamie had yet to discover anything sensible about love, like, or in between. "Don't you have to?" he asked, forcing himself back down to earth. "What about Stella? The Public Theater?"

"I'll still have a draft for Stella." She didn't sound confident, but rather like she was rationalizing. But Jamie didn't know enough about the theater industry to push back in any meaningful way. Especially when all he wanted was for her to stay in Tennessee forever.

"So you're gonna stick around?" he asked.

Eve nodded, her flirtatious expression irresistible. "Yeah."

"Until when?"

"I don't know yet," she said. "But I wanna stay in the fantasy a little longer."

CHAPTER 22

Ballad of a Teenage Queen

EVE

Eve Ambroise

Oct 7

Subject: DOWN FROM DOVER

Hi Stella,

Not sure that I'll be able to finish by December, but I'm still working on it. The attached is my first draft for the end of Act I. Please send along any/all thoughts, good or bad. I know you like the opening as is, but I'm not sure that I do. In fact, I'm feeling directionless beyond this and wondering if I should scratch what I have altogether and simply focus on the Tennessee aspects of the show.

Please help!

Eve

ACT I
SCENE EIGHT

At the Marcelin apartment, teenager's bedroom. Next day, after work. CELESTE is lying across her bed, flipping through Seventeen *magazine. TAMARA is sitting at the desk, cross-legged, painting her nails dark blue.*

CELESTE: Make sure you take that with you when you leave. Last thing I need is Gwendolyn thinking that's mine.

TAMARA: (*Sighing as she wipes excess polish from her cuticle.*) Is there anything your mom doesn't find demonic?

CELESTE: If I ever find out, I'll let you know.

TAMARA: I'm surprised she's even letting you go on this trip. It seems like if the devil were gonna be anywhere, it'd be Paris.

CELESTE: (*Pauses for a beat.*) Well she did try to sign up as a chaperone. Thank God it was too late.

TAMARA: (*Mocking.*) "Don't you dare take the Lord's name in vain!"

CELESTE: I can't tell if that's supposed to be my mother or if it's Sister Lydia.

TAMARA: What's the difference?

CELESTE: (*Snorts loudly.*) Faaacts.

(CELESTE and TAMARA giggle for several beats when the slam of the front door startles them. CELESTE frowns and goes to investigate. GWENDOLYN is storming into the apartment. EMMANUEL is following gingerly behind her.)

CELESTE: (*Entering the living room.*) Ma? What's wrong?

GWENDOLYN: (*Glaring.*) Little girl, you have tried me for the last time.

CELESTE: (*Sensing the brewing storm, turns back to her room to get her friend out of there.*) Tam—

(Before CELESTE can leave—or finish her sentence—GWENDOLYN forcefully pulls her daughter back into the room by her forearm. It sends her crashing to the floor.)

EMMANUEL: Gwen! (*He goes to his daughter to help her up.*) Temper cannot solve this.

TAMARA: (*Hearing the commotion, she runs into the living room, shocked to find the chaos that has already unfolded.*)

GWENDOLYN: (*To TAMARA, tersely.*) Go home, Tamara.

TAMARA: (*Stammering.*) I—my mom isn't—I left my key and my mom isn't home yet.

GWENDOLYN: I need you out of this house right now.

EMMANUEL: (*Stepping between GWENDOLYN and TAMARA. To TAMARA.*) Please. Go next door. Celeste cannot have company at this time.

(*CELESTE and TAMARA exchange glances as TAMARA scampers off, retrieving her backpack from the kitchen table. In the background, TAMARA can be heard banging on the neighbors' door.*)

GWENDOLYN: (*Approaches a distracted CELESTE. Her tone is combative.*) Who do you think you are?

CELESTE: I'm not sure—

GWENDOLYN: (*Yelling.*) WHO DO YOU THINK YOU ARE?

EMMANUEL: (*Gently pulls GWENDOLYN out of CELESTE's personal space.*) Gwendie, please.

GWENDOLYN: (*To CELESTE.*) I oughta slap that silly little smirk off your face.

CELESTE: I'm not smirking, Ma. I just don't know what this is about.

GWENDOLYN: Your auntie told me!

CELESTE: (*Visibly shaken, she retreats, now in fear of actually being slapped.*) I— What did she tell you? I didn't tell her anything.

EMMANUEL: (*Calm but direct, to CELESTE.*) She found the test, cheri.

CELESTE: (*Tears welling, eyes wide with realization, the innocence of her inner child seeps out.*) Mommy. I didn't . . .

GWENDOLYN: You didn't what!

CELESTE: (*Silent for several beats, she stares at her shoes.*) I'm sorry.

GWENDOLYN: When did you start having sex?

CELESTE: (*Blinking.*) I don't know.

GWENDOLYN: When did you find out?

CELESTE: Um. (*Trying to recount the last several days.*) Monday.

EMMANUEL: (*Disappointed.*) How long did you think you could keep this from us?

GWENDOLYN: Who is the boy?

CELESTE: (*Quietly.*) Rashad.

EMMANUEL: The boy from prom?

CELESTE: (*Nodding.*) Yes.

GWENDOLYN: When did you start having sex?

CELESTE: It was just the one time.

GWENDOLYN: WHEN?

CELESTE: (*Quietly, again.*) After prom.

GWENDOLYN: Sweet heart of Mary, be my salvation. (*To EMMANUEL.*) I told you we could not trust her. Always been grown. Always been fast. (*To CELESTE.*) You thought you could hide this from us?

CELESTE: (*Averting her mother's gaze.*) I don't know what I thought.

GWENDOLYN: What am I supposed to do with you?

CELESTE: I can get—

GWENDOLYN: I'm calling his parents. (*Starts toward the kitchen drawer containing the school directory. She finds the book and immediately starts thumbing through.*) What was his last name again? Brooks? Brunson?

CELESTE: Please don't, Mommy. He's gone for the summer. He doesn't even know.

GWENDOLYN: (*Slams the drawer shut.*) Of course he doesn't. (*To EMMANUEL.*) What are we supposed to do with her?

EMMANUEL: (*Calmly.*) We'll start by taking her to the doctor. We can ask her to recommend adoption agencies, next steps.

CELESTE: Wait—

GWENDOLYN: (*To EMMANUEL.*) Until then, you need to take her door off the hinges.

CELESTE: But—

GWENDOLYN: (*To CELESTE.*) You have abdicated all rights to privacy.

CELESTE: Mom—

GWENDOLYN: Don't even think about Paris.

CELESTE: I know, but—

GWENDOLYN: (*To EMMANUEL.*) That's it for Spelman.

CELESTE: Why—

GWENDOLYN: Can you imagine her waddling her narrow behind around campus eight months pregnant?

EMMANUEL: Don't be cruel. She can defer her acceptance.

GWENDOLYN: Well we clearly can't trust her that far away from us. She can go to Fordham. Somewhere in state where I can keep an eye on her.

CELESTE: (*Shouting to no one in particular.*) You cannot be serious right now!

GWENDOLYN: (*Approaches CELESTE, forcefully grabbing her face.*) Who do you think you're talking to?

CELESTE: (*Tears falling freely now.*) Please let me go.

GWENDOLYN: (*Staring into her daughter's eyes, searching for the little girl she raised.*) God, what did I do to deserve this?

EMMANUEL: (*Intervening to pull them apart.*)

GWENDOLYN: (*Drops to her knees to pray. Melodramatic, comedic.*) O Lord, please shine your glorious light on this girl. Please bring this child back into your embrace. I don't know where I went wrong, Lord. I tried to give her everything. I tried to instill her with sense and with strength and she has neither, Lord. I am sending you to open her eyes, that she may turn from darkness to light and from the power of Satan to God. Eternal Father, I offer Thee the Most Precious Blood of Thy Divine Son, Jesus, in union with the Masses said throughout the world today, for all the holy souls in purgatory, for sinners everywhere, for sinners in the universal church, THOSE IN MY OWN HOME AND FAMILY. Amen.

EMMANUEL: (*To CELESTE while GWENDOLYN prays.*) Come, cheri. Go to your room. We will talk soon.

CELESTE: (*Internalizing her mother's words, she trudges to her bedroom. There, she finds that Tamara not only left her nail polish, but the dark liquid has spilled onto her desk and is dripping on* *the floor. CELESTE closes her door while she still can.)*

Stella Fischer-Fox
Oct 7
Subject: Re: DOWN FROM DOVER

Eve!

I don't know where you're pulling this from, but everything in Act I so far has been soul-searing! That concoction of rage and disappointment from Gwendolyn! And the empathy you have for Celeste is palpable on the page. I personally think her full journey is so worth telling. Because from what you've described, this scene is the crux of her story. I want you to squeeze everything you can from it. Even if you don't end up using it all, maybe just see where it takes you, you know?

If you want to work on the Tennessee aspects while you're in Tennessee, I think that's a great idea. Especially if writer's block is getting in the way elsewhere. But please don't discard anything before you even know what it is. Just keep swimming! Incredible work you're doing here.

By the way, regarding *Gamba Adisa*, I happened to run into Stefani at *Jordans* last night. ('Twas amazing, by the way, but you already know that.) She mentioned that she loved your notes and would really like to have your input on auditions. I told her you would definitely be at rehearsals, but I wasn't sure how involved you wanted to be in casting. Thoughts?

Talk soon!
Warmly,
Stella

CHAPTER 23

You Done Lost Your Good Thing Now

EVE

Fishing was something of a spiritual experience—at least according to Jamie Gallagher. Eve learned this in the wee hours of one fall morning when she caught him sneaking out of bed and he claimed he was going to catch some crappie. She asked to accompany him, and the way he wavered, one would've thought she asked him to hand over his firstborn.

"I don't take just anyone fishing," he'd said.

At the time, Eve took umbrage at the idea of being *just anyone,* and the declination only made her want to try it more. But after she'd been standing on the bank of Gallagher Pond for the better part of two hours, in utter silence, she understood why he felt that way. Fishing was a test of patience, and bringing someone along for that ride was an act of trust. To stand in stillness with someone for hours on end was not for the faint of heart. And it was an honor for Eve to be brought into Jamie's inner sanctum—one he'd previously reserved only for his dad.

The last several weeks had been full of experiences like that—things she never thought she'd do, never thought *to* do. Summer had turned to autumn, and she'd fallen into a routine.

She spent her weekdays working on her plays—Zoom sessions with her *Gamba Adisa* production crew, auditions for the cast impending, and she was still ironing out the first two acts of *Down from Dover*—while her weekends were all Jamie.

He would teach her things like how to shoot a crossbow or forage for edible nuts and berries, and then they'd come home and devour each other. After, they'd get lost in their own little worlds of words, and sometimes, but not always, discuss the things they read. And then they'd devour each other again. She learned how to field dress a deer, and she taught him how to make her braciole. They'd made a table together—granted, he did most of the work—and she helped him find adult degree programs for universities in and around Nashville. Eve encouraged him to expand his horizons and look into schools in Atlanta, maybe Chicago, or even NYU's School of Professional Studies—it wasn't like he *needed* a degree, so he would have been able to attend school at his own pace, and maybe be with her in New York in the process—but he was determined not to exist outside the state lines of Tennessee, it seemed.

When he was gone, they tried phone sex, which was initially distressing to Eve, as were most things concerning sex. She had only ever tried it once, in grad school, when her boyfriend at the time was desperate for some form of intimacy when she had none to give. But her shyness got the best of her, and he gave up on it—and her—soon thereafter. But Jamie, as always, made her feel confident in her vulnerability. It was illuminating, embracing her desire—learning to speak it out loud without feeling foolish. Phone sex evolved into the occasional nude, ranging from R- to X-rated, and it wasn't difficult to convince Jamie to upgrade his shitty flip phone to an iPhone that would allow him to fully appreciate her body of work. From there, they didn't hesitate to try FaceTime sex, which was, surprisingly, sublime. Far more satisfying than she ever deemed it could be. Everything about Eve's time in Tennessee had been that way. She'd come there looking for peace, not expecting to actually find it.

But maybe she had.

That particular evening, Jamie and Eve celebrated their successful fishing outing with a dip in the hot tub. The temperature outside had dropped to almost freezing, which was apparently normal for October, but inside, they had a fire roaring, along with a little alcohol, and it wasn't long before the two were quite cozy. Eve was sitting across from Jamie, her feet resting in his lap as she took a long sip of her rum-tinged apple cider. The brew had been mulling all day long, leaving his entire cabin smelling of cinnamon and cloves.

"This is nice," Eve said, setting her mug on the ledge of the tub.

Jamie let out a contented sigh, the lazy smile on his face and his hoarse reply telling her that he felt the same.

She wished this were her real life.

"We oughta just do this forever," Jamie said, reading her mind.

Eve knew better than to respond, because whenever she thought of anything beyond their quiet little neighborhood, worry wanted to consume her. There was a latent tension surrounding the idea that she would eventually have to go back to New York, but she was going to ignore it for exactly as long as she could.

One early November morning, Jill asked her when she would be heading home, which, of course, forced her to consider the notion once again.

"You sound like my agent," Eve told her in response. "The truth is, I don't know."

Jill looked at her as if she were dense, which was fair—it was a stupid answer. "Your friends and family must miss you . . ."

"And I miss my friends," Eve admitted, thinking of Maya. She ached for the simple solace that came with sitting on her best friend's couch talking shit. She missed impromptu get-togethers with their crew. A nice, long dinner at some cute little restaurant on Smith Street. "Family, not so much."

"Do any of them know about Jamie?"

Eve instinctively smiled at the mention of his name. "Maya does, of course." She chewed on a cherry as she considered what Joan and Roger would think. Her dad would like Jamie, for sure; both her parents would hate the situation. Her mother, on the other hand, only liked Leo because he was vaguely Catholic—Jamie and his out-of-wedlock kid would send her guard right on up. Like mother, like daughter.

"What do people do for Thanksgiving around here?" Eve wondered. "Are you all open?"

"We are." Jill cocked her head, as if worried. "You're gonna be *here*?"

Eve shrugged. "Pretty sure, yeah."

"Well, I won't," she said, grinning in a way that made her green eyes glimmer. "But I can let the kitchen know to take care of you."

"And where are you going?" Eve smiled back.

"To mind my business."

"Fair enough," she laughed, while also envying Jill's commitment to a life well lived.

"Does this mean you're thinking about staying in Gatlinburg permanently? Or is this just a long detour?"

Eve's instinct was to say no, but the words didn't make it out of her mouth. Because why not? She had broken up with her fiancé, so she didn't exactly have a home to go back to. Plenty of people worked remotely now, and she was only a two-hour flight from New York if she really needed to be there. She could find reasons to justify making Gatlinburg her home base. After conversations with Jamie and Jill, she even went so far as looking for jobs at the University of Tennessee. Just in case.

Maybe she was dreaming, but every time she tried to imagine her life without Jamie, she hated the picture, so she was allowing herself to exist in some unreality where they had a real chance.

That weekend, Jamie and Eve were in the woods again, fully immersed in the chill of autumn in the Tennessee mountains. They were chopping wood for the upcoming week, as Eve's need for it only increased as the days went by. The daily highs barely reached forty in November, and at night, the twenty-degree temperatures left her little cabin icy.

"Your nose is red," Eve observed with a grin. Jamie was wearing a suede bomber jacket, which made him look both soft and menacing somehow—perhaps because she'd just watched him work with a hatchet for the last several hours—but his ears and nose pinkened from the cold decidedly swayed him to the softer side. "You ready to go?"

"Yes, ma'am." He was already trampling through the leaves to retrieve his chain saw. "You wanna take this?" he asked, holding up the machinery. "Or the wood?"

"Well, the wood has wheels, so that," Eve said. "But I appreciate you offering both options."

"You know I'm all about equity."

"You are," Eve said, grinning. She followed him down the path back toward his truck, glad that he took the lead so she wouldn't have to admit she had no idea where she was going. "It's one of the reasons I trust you," she added.

He looked back at her. "Is that right?"

"It is." She stayed close behind him, highlighting her point. And as they reached his truck, the sun getting low in the sky, she knew it would be dark before long. "Do we have something to make for dinner tonight?" she asked.

"I have some ground beef," Jamie said after a moment of thought. "You want chili?"

"We should've started on that earlier . . ." she said. "But I guess we could have a late dinner."

"Yes, we can do somethin' outside of our usual routine."

Eve watched as Jamie loaded his truck with their supplies, and she meant to help, but she was dumbstruck by both his statement and his tone. "Are you implying that I'm boring?" she asked.

Jamie chuckled. "I'm not. At all." When she cocked her head in disbelief, he added, "I think you can be rigid. It's difficult for you to move outside your comfort zone. And that's fine."

She nodded tersely, glad to know how he felt, if nothing else. But it was ironic coming from someone who had never even left the contiguous United States. And more than that, everything about the two of them was outside her comfort zone, and that deserved some acknowledgment. But she would take the criticism on the chin.

"Hey," Jamie called out to her.

Eve had commenced filling the back of his pickup with wood as she mindlessly responded, "Hey."

"What would you say . . . if I asked you to come to Nashville?" When she finally paused and looked back at him, he replied with a little nod. "Not tomorrow or anything. But maybe for Thanksgiving."

Eve wrinkled her nose, thinking Thanksgiving *was* practically tomorrow. "Really?" she said, solely because she was too unprepared to respond with an outright *no.* The last time he asked her to leave the confines of their little neighborhood, she responded by ghosting him. He was testing her rigidity, and she was going to fail.

"Me and Lucy are splitting Jack's Thanksgiving break, and he asked to meet you. I thought maybe a group dinner would ease the tension . . ."

"You told your son about me." It was a question, but it had come out as a statement.

"Did you think I wouldn't?"

"I hadn't thought about it," she said, shaking her head. She'd done everything in her power not to think about it. Or any of the realities of their situation.

"We've been at this for months now," Jamie said.

"I know."

"So yeah, I'm gonna mention you to my son," he said with a tense chuckle. "He just thinks we're friends."

Eve was full on scowling by then, still trying to process the idea that he wanted her to come to Nashville and interact with his child. On a family holiday, of all things. Would she be meeting his ex, too? And Tyler? It all felt dangerously close to a real relationship.

"How old is your son again?" She was deflecting. She knew he was eight. That fact didn't leave her mind, because it often sent it wandering to what her own son would've looked like at that age. At every age. She'd only gotten a glimpse after delivering him, and with her exhaustion and sorrow, she was never sure she remembered him quite correctly. Through her blur of tears, she had a picture in her head of a round face, cinnamon skin, and a head full of soft black hair. She squeezed her eyes shut, needing to block it out.

"He's eight," Jamie said. "It's fine if you don't want to. I just thought, since he asked, and he's the most important person in my life, you might be interested at this point."

Eve rolled her eyes at his attempt to emotionally manipulate her. "Don't do that passive-aggressive shit," she said, slamming the tailgate shut. "You're better than that."

"I'm not being passive-aggressive. I'm being honest."

"Jamie, we're not . . ." She ran a frustrated hand over her face. "What we have is working as is. I don't know why you can't leave it at that. Keep your kid out of it."

He visibly bristled in response, his jaw clenching as he looked to the treescape ahead of them, and Eve knew she was fucking this up.

It had been such a good day. They awoke to the sun shining through the bare trees, had sex for breakfast, and ate pancakes for lunch. They'd gone grocery shopping and then wood chopping. And if this conversation had gone well, they would've retired to his cabin and cuddled up together to read their separate books—he was in the middle of *1984,* while she was rereading some Tayari Jones for inspiration—as was their typical Saturday routine. But Eve was just a couple of wrong words from making their evening an uncomfortable one.

She wanted to give in. She wanted to tell him about the child she birthed and the ones she couldn't. That she'd spent so much of the past year, the past decade and a half, aching for the little boy she never got to meet, she didn't think she'd ever feel normal again. That was until she met Jamie.

But she'd rather him think she hated kids than find out she was just pathetic.

"I can take a lot, Eve," Jamie said. "I dealt with you ignoring me. I'm fine with going slow. But you can't disregard my son and expect me to play along."

"I'm . . . not sure what to say here," she said, attempting to tread lightly.

"Maybe you should sleep at your house until you figure it out," he said, his twang uncharacteristically hushed.

Eve was taken aback, dismayed by the idea of him being down the road and them sleeping apart. The last time that happened, they were still strangers. "No," she said. It wasn't exactly optional, but she wasn't ready to be pushed away. "I'll sleep on the couch if you really want me to, but I don't think we should be apart."

"So I guess this is only a relationship when you want it to be," Jamie said, heading to the driver's side of his truck.

Eve didn't respond, partly—maybe mostly—because she knew he was, yet again, correct, and there was nothing to respond with. She listened to his engine roar, some part of her wondering if he was going to leave her there, the other part unable to blame him if he did.

She let out a heavy, quaking sigh. She was on the verge of ruining the one really good thing she'd somehow managed to find in her mess of a life. But she just wasn't ready to open the can of worms that included children.

"Fuck, fuck, *fuck*!" she hissed.

"Are you coming?" Jamie asked through his window.

Eve shook her head. "I'll walk. Back to my place."

Eve awoke the next morning on her own couch, discombobulated and cold. The night before, she'd been too defeated to kindle a fire, so she drank some wine and curled up with a couple of fleece blankets. She was paying for it now, feeling like she'd slept in an igloo, not to mention the ache in her back and joints, her thirty-four years hastily catching up to her.

She forced herself up and started on breakfast, mainly in hopes of warming up the house. But it was still early—still dark—so she would make some biscuits and bring them to Jamie before he left for the week. A sort of peace offering.

By the time her kitchen counters were covered in flour and the biscuits were in the oven, Jamie was knocking at the door. When she greeted him, she noticed that he'd driven over, which likely meant he was about to leave for Nashville.

"I didn't even hear your truck," she said, leaving him to follow her to the kitchen.

Jamie did follow, but not too far. "Just wanted to let you know that I probably won't be out here next weekend," he said evenly. "Figure I should use that time to prepare for the holiday."

Eve made a concerted effort not to visibly react and simply

looked at him. He stood in the middle of her living room as if afraid to get too close.

"Okay," she said. She returned to her task of cleaning off the counters, unwilling to play whatever game this was.

"This is really how you wanna do this?"

"Jamie, I woke up this morning thinking we could start on a new page, because obviously we ended up on different ones last night," she said, pointing toward her mess of a kitchen. "You're the one who came over here to continue your tantrum."

"I came over here because I didn't wanna be immature and leave without saying anything. But I'm not gonna pretend I'm not bothered by this whole thing."

"Well . . . have a safe trip home." She offered a strained smile as the period at the end of her sentence.

Jamie nodded. "You said you didn't wanna push me away, but that's what you're doing."

"Don't throw that back at me," she said. She stopped cleaning and planted herself in the corner of her kitchen, coolly crossing her arms over her chest as she rested against the counter. "What do you want?"

"Why don't you like kids?"

Eve rolled her eyes. "I don't wanna have this conversation again."

"We barely had one the first time."

"Meeting your son makes this serious, and I'm not ready to be serious."

"Well, maybe I should stop driving out here every weekend for something that's not serious."

"If you had somewhere better to be every weekend, I'm sure you would've been there."

Jamie's chuckle sounded so mocking it felt caustic. "All right," he said.

"So I shouldn't expect you anytime soon?"

"You're just gonna spend Thanksgiving here? Alone?"

Eve shrugged. She was supposed to be home by now anyway. Jamie was the reason she didn't have an exit plan. She'd been enjoying her new life so much, it was easy to ignore the old one. Until now. "I have a play to finish."

With his hands stuffed in the pockets of his coat, Jamie finally walked toward Eve until he was closer than she wanted him to be. He pulled a scrap of paper from his right pocket and set it on the counter in front of her.

"Whatever this is you're doing, you don't have to do it by yourself," he said, his voice soft but clear. "People don't exist . . . *I* don't exist to distract you from whatever you're running from. I'm a person, Eve. Not a fantasy."

Eve should've left it at that. She wanted to. But he couldn't leave well enough alone, and she couldn't either. "Maybe you should've listened to me when I told you what this was."

At the end of summer, she'd asked Jamie not to fall in love with her—not because she was taken, but because she was unavailable. This was always going to be the end result, her disappointing him in some way.

Jamie nodded again, his eyes scanning her face before turning for the door. "I wish I could turn it all off as easily as you do," he said. "I'll see you around, Eve."

CHAPTER 24

It's All Wrong, but It's All Right

JAMIE

Thu, Nov 27 4:44 PM

Dad: Jamie. It's your mother. There's a bit of traffic on the 40 but we're on our way. Should arrive by 6:00 at the very latest.

Jamie Gallagher: Ok. Drive safely. Is Dad wearing his glasses?

Dad: We will. He is. We look forward to seeing you.

Jamie never imagined that he and Eve wouldn't be on speaking terms when Thanksgiving arrived. But regrettably, in the two weeks since they last saw each other, he hadn't reached out and neither had she. Jamie did consider giving in, as was his wont, and he even picked up his phone on multiple occasions with the intent to apologize. But every time he did, he was met with the reminder that Eve wasn't calling him either. And so his pride wouldn't allow him to make the first move, not after the beating it took in ten years with Lucy.

Instead, he went about his life, preparing for the dinner

party he'd offered to host for the holiday. It was a family affair, including Lucy and, by extension, Tyler; his own brother, Casey, and, by extension, his husband, Jelani. Lucy's sister and niece were there, along with their parents, and perhaps most notably, Jamie's parents were on their way, too. Jamie extended the olive branch to his mother against his better judgment, figuring if she really wanted to be in Jack's life, now was the time she'd show it. So as much as he might've wanted Eve to come, he didn't *need* her there. He had his own demons and distractions.

With dinnertime approaching, Jamie had taken to setting the table while his guests argued about whether to continue watching football or commence with Christmas movies. He wasn't surprised when he heard the opening to *Home Alone* in the background. Lucy eventually came to help, though he hadn't asked for or wanted it, but he didn't say anything when she began to place plates and utensils among the food dishes.

"This all looks so good," she said, her eye seemingly fixed on the macaroni and cheese.

"You look like you're salivating," Jamie said, making his way around her.

She grinned. "Sorry. Just hungry."

"I've been sneaking little bites of those collard greens Jelani made," he admitted. He looked around to verify no one was listening, fearing he'd be in trouble for eating early. "He put the jalapeños in 'em. They're so good."

"Well, now I know why you volunteered to set the table," Lucy said.

"It is my house. I don't know who else would do it."

"I'm here," she said, sounding offended that he hadn't considered enlisting her. "I know this isn't my home, but it's not all on you just because we're here. We agreed to keep doing this as a family."

Jamie's stare darted to Tyler, sitting comfortably in Jamie's living room. Jamie did agree to this, solely for Jack's sake, knowing it meant being cordial toward a man he wished he had nothing to do with. It was something he prepared for. But it still struck a dissonant chord to see Tyler in his home, fraternizing with his family members. "Yeah . . ." Jamie said, scratching his eyebrow with the knuckle of his thumb. "I agreed to a lot of things."

Lucy nodded. "I really appreciate you having him here," she said, her voice hushed as if it were a secret that Jamie hated him. Them. "I know how hard all of this has been on you."

"I'm all right," he said with a shrug and an empty smile. As a reflex, he pulled his phone from his pocket, quietly praying that Eve had contacted him, perhaps changing her mind at the last minute. It was a foolish wish, but also his last hope. "I'm gonna get the turkey," he said, turning for the kitchen before Lucy could respond.

There he found Jack, conspicuously quiet as he hovered over the dessert table containing all the pies and cakes awaiting dinner's end. "What are you doing?" Jamie asked.

Clearly startled, Jack immediately turned to his father and was just as quick to deny any wrongdoing. "Nothing."

Jamie laughed at the guilt painted on his face. "Well, do me a favor and stop breathing on the pies and take those pitchers of lemonade out to your mother."

"Yes, sir."

"Be careful."

"I will."

As Jack disappeared and Jamie went to the oven to retrieve the centerpiece of the meal, he could hear Lucy calling everyone to the table. It was amusing how she insisted on being cohost, despite his objections, as if they were still some happy couple. And in this case, *amusing* meant "exasperating."

But he ignored it to get on with his day. The sooner dinner started, the sooner it would be over. He brought the turkey to the dining table, much to everyone's delight, while they passed around plates and platters of the ancillary dishes. Honey-baked ham and buttermilk fried chicken, sweet potato soufflé, collards and cornbread, green bean casserole, brussels sprouts, macaroni and cheese, roasted corn pudding, eggplant dressing. A full banquet of colors and aromas before them.

"Luce, where's your wine?" her sister, Alexis, asked halfway through the first helpings.

"Oh, I . . . I was just gonna have some lemonade," Lucy replied.

"Really?" Alexis pressed, touching the back of her hand to Lucy's forehead. "Are you okay?"

"I'm fine," Lucy said, glancing at her and then at Tyler. "I'm his designated driver, so . . ."

"Oh, come on, you're not leaving for hours," Casey cut in. "Live a little."

Lucy glanced meekly around the table before looking to her fiancé again, receiving an encouraging nod in return. "Actually," she said, turning her attention to Jack as she stroked the back of his head, "I . . . am pregnant."

There were a few small gasps, followed by *oh*s while most everyone simply congratulated her, but Jamie felt like he was seeing double. The other voices, their laughter, it became a buzz of distorted noise. When they finally raised their glasses to the happy, expectant couple, he could feel Casey's comforting hand touch his back. But it only amplified his anguish. Because he was certain that his brother wasn't the only person looking to him, watching him unravel over the revelation.

"Jamie," his mother called out to him. He eyed her, praying she wouldn't embarrass him. "Is there any cranberry sauce?" she asked.

"Right. I'll get it," he said once his head stopped swimming long enough to form words, desperate to escape the table, and thankful to Diane for providing an excuse.

Jamie slipped into the kitchen and went to search the refrigerator for the dish Lucy's dad had prepared. But really, he stood in the doorway, taking long, deep breaths as the cool air washed his face. He exhaled shakily, the urge to call Eve only deepening. Maybe if she'd come to dinner like he'd asked, this announcement wouldn't have hit him nearly as hard. Or maybe it would've, and both of their nights would've been ruined. And maybe that was asking too much of her. But he wished like hell that she were there. After months of feeling so alone after he and Lucy were done, she came along, damaged and cold herself, and it felt like she'd saved him in some tiny way.

He closed the refrigerator door, ready to uselessly check his phone for the fifth time that day, but before he could disappoint himself again, Casey came strolling into the kitchen with his full plate. He didn't say anything, but offered a sympathetic smile and some turkey.

"I'm all right," Jamie said. He'd claimed as much at least three times that evening, and it sounded like more of a lie with every instance it crossed his lips.

"It's okay if you're not," Casey said, keeping his voice low. He leaned against the sink as he stared at his sibling. "She's a piece of work."

"I'm not . . . It's not that," Jamie said, shaking his head. "I'm over her. I think. I just . . . didn't see this coming, I guess."

"She's been screwing him for how long now? What'd you think was gonna happen?"

He half-heartedly chuckled at Casey's plainspokenness. "I didn't think about it."

"Well, I guess it's a good thing she hasn't been on your mind."

"Not at all, really."

"The opposite of love is indifference, isn't it?"

"I've had other things to occupy my time."

Casey quirked an eyebrow. "Can I ask you something without you getting defensive?"

"That is not how you start a question, Casey."

"When are you gonna get her out of that house you're still paying for?"

Jamie laughed again, because he knew precisely what was coming, and he was glad when Jelani joined them, allowing him to evade the question. "Enjoying the show?" Jamie asked him.

Jelani rolled his eyes dramatically. "Chile . . . your mother is out there asking your ex about collecting child support," he said. "Lord knows I love a shady moment, but I actually could not bear the tension."

"Oh, that's funny, because I was just asking Jamie when he's gonna stop paying spousal support for someone who was never his spouse," Casey said.

"Like mother, like son," Jamie said. Both Jelani and Casey

had their food, and he regretted that he didn't bring his own. "I guess we're eating in here now?"

"Take mine," Casey said, offering up his plate full of everything. "Can we get back on topic, please?"

"Have you asked him about the doctor yet?" Jelani asked before taking a big bite of chicken.

"Shhh . . . I hadn't gotten there yet," Casey said. It was clear he was trying to be surreptitious about it, speaking in a hushed tone and averting his brother's gaze. But he'd failed miserably.

Jamie peered at the two of them. "The doctor?"

"Okay, don't be mad, but . . . Jack told us about your girlfriend," Casey said. "And we googled her. But I wasn't gonna bring it up until you did. I swear."

Jamie sighed sharply, feeling like he'd lost control of everything about this dinner he was supposedly hosting. "She's not my girlfriend. We're friends."

"Well, I hope you're working on that, because I like her."

"You don't know anything about her."

"I saw some interviews with her. And she looks good on paper."

Jamie frowned, unsure of what that meant. Then again, he never thought to google Eve's name. He didn't even realize that was a thing. "Better than Lucy, you mean?"

"Obviously that," Casey said. "But also, just, in general." He shrugged in what must've been an effort to make his stalking sound casual. "And she's gorgeous."

"She has a play coming to the Public next year," Jelani inserted as if none of them knew. "I saw it when it opened, but Amina Pearson is starring now."

"What a good excuse for you to *finally* come to New York,"

Casey said to Jamie. His eagerness would have been infectious if it weren't so annoying.

"We've lived there, what, three years now?" Jelani said. "And it's gonna be a woman that gets him to finally visit, isn't it?"

"She's gonna be so good for him," Casey said.

"Guys." Jamie cut in before his brothers' imaginations had him engaged before dessert. "I appreciate all of . . . whatever this is . . . but Eve and I aren't gonna be anything more than whatever we are. She lives in New York, she doesn't like kids, she's way out of my league . . ." He trailed off as he realized he was listing all the reasons he shouldn't have gotten involved with her in the first place, and he had to laugh. "It was a fling. It's over now."

Casey's face expressed disbelief before he could form the words. "So . . . is that why you told Jack about her?"

"Well, I also told him we were friends, so I guess delusion runs in the family."

Jelani snorted.

"Fine," Casey relented. "If all she did was take your mind off Cruella in there, then good for you. I suppose."

Jamie suppressed another laugh with a forkful of dressing, but Casey wasn't wrong. If all he got out of his time was Eve was being untethered from his relationship with Lucy, then it was worth it.

It wasn't enough.

But it was definitely worth it.

Thanksgiving evening persisted, with dinner and dessert consumed before guests dispersed around Jamie's condo to do their own things: the kids played *Minecraft* in Jack's room, while most of the adults did end up unenthusiastically rooting against the Texans by the end of the night, too full of food to engage in conversation or otherwise move. Jamie was hanging out on his balcony with some pecan pie, enjoying the warm November night. Until his mother came out to join him.

"Don't stuff yourself with pie," was the first thing she said upon invading his peace. "You're so trim."

Jamie inhaled at the sound of his mother's voice and released it slowly, mimicking his idea of a breathing technique. "I'll be all right."

Diane took the seat across from him. "Are you?" she asked. "All right?"

"Do I look that depressed?"

"No," she replied with a quiet smile. She gazed at him, the typical sharpness in her gray eyes having softened over the years, he'd noticed. Age had been kind to her, mostly in the ways where it pulled back on her most severe features and tendencies. "You look good, if I'm being honest," she said.

"Good genes, I guess."

"You were always a handsome boy," she said.

Of course she lived an alternate version of reality. People with sullied pasts loved to romanticize them. The fact was, between acne and uncontrollable hair and a nose much too big for his face, he was a terribly unattractive kid. He didn't grow into his looks until well after puberty.

"If you say so," Jamie said, returning to his dessert.

"But you are too nice." She'd been sitting at the table for less than a minute before finding a reason to criticize him. He should've seen this coming.

Jamie didn't look at her but continued to eat, responding with his mouth full. "Is that so?"

"I know you didn't want me here. Maybe there's no way around Lucy, but you didn't have to allow her husband into your home, too."

"Last time I saw you, you said I was too judgmental." She was so goddamn fickle.

"So you swing to the opposite end and let people walk all over you?"

"Jack deserves a Thanksgiving with his family. And however I feel about it, that includes Tyler now. And you."

Diane chuckled, her laughter sounding mocking. "Jack doesn't care about the difference between today and tomorrow. Don't make that child your excuse to be miserable."

"I'm not miserable," he shot back.

"Last time I saw you, you said no one is happy." She cocked her head, examining him in the dim light of the evening. "You really believe that's true?"

"I don't know," Jamie said, wiping his mouth of crumbs. "I hope not."

"Your brother's happy," she said. "Jack seems happy."

"I hope so."

"It doesn't take a lot for kids." When he gave her a dubious glance, she nodded in acknowledgment. "Yes, yes, how would I know. But kids are resilient. And whether you admit it or not, I was a good mother. For as long as I could be."

"Yeah, well, most people are good until they're bad."

"I don't know that that's fair," Diane said. "When someone does something wrong, it doesn't necessarily negate everything they did right."

"Maybe not," Jamie said. He chewed his lip as he grappled with the thought, taking into consideration that maybe he did judge people, situations, too harshly sometimes. His mother set that in motion twenty years ago. "I guess it depends on the impact of what you did wrong."

"I won't argue with that."

Jamie sat back in his chair, surveying his serene neighborhood, even quieter than usual due to the holiday. "Was it easy to start over?" he wondered out loud.

Diane shook her head. "It was easier than being unhappy. But no, it wasn't easy."

"I met someone," he said.

"Eve," Diane replied.

Jamie laughed in spite of himself, unsure whether to blame his son or his brother, probably some combination of both. "Yes. Eve," he said. "She ran away from her life, kinda like you." He stared at his empty plate, wondering what Eve was doing at that exact moment. "She didn't cheat," he went on. "She didn't have kids. It wasn't exactly the same. But she did just . . . leave. And I can't lie, I kinda envy it."

"Where would you go?"

"I don't know. Someplace I've never been. Just . . . be somebody else."

"Jamie." Diane reached across the table, but stopped short of touching him. "I don't know you the way I'd like to, so it's presumptuous of me to be handing out life advice. But I'm still your mother, and maybe, if nothing else, you'll be willing to learn from my mistakes. Because I wish someone had told me before I ruined everything: You don't have to be someone else in order to change. You're not stuck."

He made a face at the platitude. He didn't want to tell her how much he'd been thinking about going to college, too self-conscious to share his insecurity with someone he still considered a stranger. "It's never too late to be who I wanna be?"

"It's trite," Diane admitted, finally allowing herself to touch his hand, briefly, "but it's true. The hard part is actually doing it."

Sure, it was banal. He'd had similar conversations with friends in the past. But there was also something different about hearing it from Diane. Maybe he'd been aching for some motherly advice all these years; maybe he instinctively knew she had the experience to back up her words. Either way, he really wanted to believe it.

Before he could tell her as much, and acknowledge that Diane was perhaps not as bad as his anger over the years had led him to believe, Casey came outside to join them. And Jamie was surprised by his disappointment. Jamie loved his brother. His outgoingness, his supportiveness. How he always made Jamie feel less boring than what was frankly, probably true.

But the same part of him that had been starved for a mother was annoyed that the little bit of time he'd gotten with her had suddenly come to an end. She'd been at his home all evening and he didn't mind it; it even felt *right* in a strange way. But watching his mother and his little brother instantly slip into their zingy rapport, Jamie was almost jealous of the relationship they'd cultivated. Of course, Casey was much younger when she left and didn't have the same baggage that Jamie carried about it. But seeing them share a laugh and a cigarette made Jamie want . . . not that, but something like that for himself. He wasn't sure that he would ever get there.

But he wanted it.

By the end of the night, Jamie was thankful to still be in one piece, but he would definitely heed Diane's words and never put himself in a situation like this again. He felt a palpable sense of relief when his home was finally emptied and quiet, even if it was a mess of dirty dishes, half-empty alcohol bottles, and left-overs.

Once he'd gotten it all into the kitchen, at least, Jamie headed upstairs to check on Jack, unsurprised to find him asleep but fully dressed atop his covers. He carefully pulled off Jack's jeans and laid them in an open chair before properly tucking him in. The kid still had remnants of fruit punch and peach cobbler around his mouth, which made Jamie smile as he kissed him good night. He hoped Jack had a good Thanksgiving, if no one else had.

Jamie made a pit stop at his own bedroom to kick off his shoes. He'd been on his feet for much of the day and didn't realize how much they hurt until his bare soles touched the cool wood floors. Before he could make it back downstairs, there was a buzz at the door, and he figured one of his guests had forgotten their keys or their plate, something to that effect. He went to the security system to allow the caller back up, but he was instead met with the image of Eve standing in his building's lobby. She had her head lowered, so he couldn't see her face, but unmistakably, it was her. Her twisted-out hair, her Patagonia jacket, her shapely figure. Clutching a bouquet of flowers. He froze. He was so resigned to her rejection, he couldn't fathom her showing up now.

She rang the buzzer again, effectively jolting him from his trance, and he finally answered.

"Hey," he said, and when she smiled up at the speaker, his heart instantly started to dance in his chest.

"It's me," she said.

She couldn't see him, of course, but that didn't stop him from positively beaming as he replied to her, "I know."

CHAPTER 25

Flowers

EVE

Eve could only be described as "nonplussed" when she entered Jamie Gallagher's posh digs. She'd been leery of showing up alone at his "Liberty Pike" address in Franklin, Tennessee—like most places in the South, it sounded like somewhere she wouldn't be welcome. And when she pulled up to a building resembling a warehouse, she thought surely she was lost until she spotted Jamie's Silverado parked on the street. Now that she knew he had a private elevator entrance, all expectations were null.

Eve was nervous as she made her way onto the elevator. She'd spent the entire three-hour drive steeling herself for whatever lived at this address, be it Jamie's cold shoulder or Jack meeting her at the door. But now that she was seconds from finding out, the angst that kept her from accepting Jamie's invite in the first place was rearing its ugly-ass head.

Eve took deep breaths throughout the short ride to the fourth floor, her eyes nearly popping out of her head when the gate opened to a beautiful, lavish, *colorful* apartment, akin to stepping out of that old, achromatic Kansas house and into the magnificent land of Oz. She was again uncertain she was in the right place until she heard Jamie's footsteps—recognizable, even in this foreign setting—and soon enough, he was standing in front of her.

Her breath caught in her throat when she tried to speak, doubt and delight taking hold of her faculties in equal measure. He was wearing her favorite denim shirt of his, the one that made his eyes look like a summer day and his skin the way butter pecan ice cream tasted.

Jamie also appeared speechless as he pulled her out of the elevator and into his arms. He held her close, cradling her head, inhaling her. Eve closed her eyes at his touch; she wrapped her arm around his waist and rested her head against him, basking in his aroma of sweet potatoes . . . and the relief that he wasn't still mad at her.

Eve smiled meekly as they separated, handing over the bouquet of roses she'd picked out at Whole Foods the day before. She spotted the peachy orange blossoms amid the chaos of shopping for her Thanksgiving meal for one, and they made her think of Jamie. It was in that moment she decided she was going to drive to Nashville. To apologize? To grovel? To not be alone? She hadn't decided. But she missed Jamie, and the walls she had up weren't doing either of them any favors.

"These are for me?" Jamie asked, clearly confounded by the overture. When she nodded, he smiled wide. "I don't think I've ever been given flowers before."

Eve timidly averted his eyes, hers dropping to the glossy wood floor. She hoped that meant he would remember this. "Most men haven't," she said.

He examined the bouquet like he'd never seen a rose before, his dark blue eyes flickering as he took in the gesture. "Thank you." His earnestness was as potent as the aroma of the bouquet.

Jamie took Eve by the hand, and soon enough, he was leading her through a tour of his not-so-humble abode, Eve marveling at each room for different reasons. The decor, the sheer size. His master bathroom was as big as his entire cabin back in Gatlinburg. When she talked to him on FaceTime, she typically only saw his headboard and didn't think much of it. But his home—his real home—was truly splendid. Vast and vibrant, with high ceilings and exposed pipes, gorgeous granite countertops and spotless hardwood floors with an ecru tint. Brightly colored furniture and accented walls. Fascinating paintings and unique fixtures. In the wall space above the kitchen there was a striking sculpture of a full-sized bike colored in every hue of the rainbow; in the kitchen by the breakfast nook, next to a bay window, hung a small collection of ceramic plates obviously painted by Jack. And as if Jamie's home had read her mind, there was a painting displayed at the top of the staircase, a parody of Edward Hopper's *Nighthawks* featuring characters from *The Wizard of Oz*. His home had character that was often absent in swanky places like this. And it was certainly swank. She'd had her suspicions, but it was clear now that Jamie Gallagher, with his two pairs of jeans and twenty-year-old truck, was actually rich as fuck.

"My brother did most of the decorating," he said, seeming to intuit her surprise as he guided her to the next room. "He said this was too nice a place to let me ruin, so I basically wrote him a blank check and let him have at it."

Eve tried to seem unaffected, but inwardly, she was impressed by the flex. "He has good taste."

"I think he gets it from our mom. He's arrogant, but he backs it up," Jamie said. "Though I will say, I built all these myself." He pointed toward a room with three walls of built-in shelves.

Eve grinned as she walked in. It wasn't a huge space—a guest room in any other home—but it was filled with books from the ceiling to the floor, all color coordinated. Two big leather chairs the color of Christmas trees sat at the center of the room with a plush white-and-blue rug between them. The fourth wall was a window, overlooking the city of Nashville. Or Franklin? She didn't know. She didn't care. It was a perfect room. She was only a visitor, but she was already picturing herself cozied up in that room with some Toni Morrison and a mug of purple tea on a quiet Sunday. Her heart skipped beats just thinking about it. Being happy there.

"Your place is gorgeous," she said.

Eve stepped farther in to explore the titles decorating the space. She first noticed *The Road,* then her eyes settled on the shelf below it, full of framed pictures. Jamie with his son. Jamie with his son beside a wiry white woman sporting long dark hair, whom she could only assume was Lucy. His son with another white guy, the spitting image of Jamie, with short, wavy, sable hair and blue eyes—she had to look closer to make sure it wasn't just him at a younger age. "Your brother?" she guessed.

"Casey."

She skimmed the entire row of snapshots, most of them of his son, until one particular photo at the end caught her eye. The picture had been taken in Jamie's kitchen, it appeared; his brother, seated across from an attractive Black man with glowing light brown skin, sporting a salt-and-pepper 'fro and an immaculate smile. She recognized him as a professor and author she'd seen often on MSNBC, but she couldn't piece together why he'd be sitting in Jamie's house.

"How do you know Jelani King?" she asked.

"Brother-in-law," he said, a crooked smile on his lips.

"Shit."

She didn't really know much about Jamie's life. She'd insulated herself so much, she never even tried to imagine what it looked like outside of her. While being so desperate to avoid his son, she'd avoided him—his home, his family, his friends. And that said nothing of how detached she'd been from her own lot. She hadn't talked to her parents since July. She'd been living in her little fantasy for the past five months, blocking out the real world as best she could—ignoring that this kind of existence was untenable.

Jamie came to join her, guiding her through the names and faces of all the people in the other photos, and she listened, dutifully memorizing them in case she happened to cross paths with any at some point.

Back in the hallway, the room just across the landing stole Eve's attention. Even in the darkness, she could see the small figure covered by a cobalt-blue bedspread. Jack. Her stomach dropped, but she was physically drawn to the room like a moth to a flame. She went and stood in the threshold, and just the sound of him drawing soft breaths made her want to crumble.

She imagined her lost son's room looking something like this when he was Jack's age. Maybe even now. Featuring an iMac and a telescope, action figures and video game consoles. Eve's bottom lip quivered as she tried to push it all out of her mind, but it refused to leave.

"You can meet him in the morning," Jamie said from behind her.

Eve took a deep breath as tears burned her eyes. She attempted to collect her emotions before turning back to him, but they fell anyway, and she wiped them discreetly, pretending to scratch her face. "Okay."

"It'll be fine," he promised, nodding for her to follow him. "You're gonna love him."

"So who cooked all this food?" Eve asked. She stuffed a piece of cold turkey into her mouth before placing the remainder of it in the refrigerator. She and Jamie had used the past hour to clean up, and from what she could tell, there'd been quite a few people in attendance. It was probably for the best that she'd missed it.

"Everyone did," he said, also sneaking a few bites of leftovers for himself. "It was a potluck kinda thing."

"What did Jelani bring?" she asked, still tickled that he was part of Jamie's family. She couldn't wait to tell Maya.

"He made the collards. I think those are all gone, but he did the cabbage, too, if you're interested."

"I am," Eve said. Her Thanksgiving dinner consisted of a Big Mac and fries on her drive to Nashville, both of which were too salty. She looked forward to having turkey and dressing and everything else for breakfast.

"Come have some pie with me," Jamie said.

"Let me just get this washed," Eve replied, taking the turkey pan to the sink.

He held up a dish of some apple confection like his own siren song. "Better hurry up before I eat it all."

She rolled her eyes but appreciated that he knew precisely how to tempt her. She joined him in the breakfast nook, happily accepting the fork to carve out a sample of the pie. She promptly moaned as the combination of apple and cinnamon and dough hit her tongue.

"You're supposed to save that sound for me," he whispered, gazing at the side of her face.

"You don't taste like this," she said, smiling.

Jamie briefly left their setup at the breakfast table and turned on some music to accompany their cleanup. And in the end, Jamie was the one to wash the dishes, while Eve enjoyed various desserts as she strategically packed the refrigerator shelves with Tupperware. His fridge was huge, but she liked making a puzzle out of the containers, deciding which foods would be accessed most. She tried to imagine what Jack would like and put those in reachable places.

When she was done, she watched Jamie as he worked, silently scrubbing and scraping at the dirty plates and pans. So introspective. Eve loved that about him.

She was pretty sure she loved him.

Without words, Eve set down her fork and pie and joined him at the sink, wrapping her arms around his slender waist to hug him from behind. She closed her eyes as she breathed him in for the second time that night, pressing her cheek against the soft denim of his shirt.

"You're not just a fantasy," she whispered.

Jamie turned to face her. He placed a gentle, sweet kiss over the top of her thick hair, then rested his forehead against hers. He inhaled as she exhaled, and for a moment, for several moments, they breathed as one. And when he began to sway to the music, Ella Fitzgerald's rich, sultry voice filling the kitchen, they moved as one, too.

During the last two weeks, Eve had a lot of time to think about this—what it meant for him to let her in, for her to *want* to be let in. This still wasn't in her plans, but she was trying not to be rigid. Jamie deserved someone who would step out of their comfort zone. Or at least, to try. So she was trying.

CHAPTER 26

Black Friday

EVE

Eve awoke the next morning naked in Jamie's bed—a scenario she was all too familiar with at this point in their relationship, yet it couldn't have felt more foreign. The sun was beaming past his sheer white curtains to brighten the already vivid turquoise room. His cabin in Gatlinburg was dark—in a good way—and they lived among trees, where sunlight had to sneak through the forest to reach them. Even Jamie's bed back there was simple, close to the floor; this bed sat high, with a colorful duvet that complemented the walls. She felt like she was in some stylish boutique hotel as opposed to her friend's home.

She scanned the vast room for any sign of Jamie, but the silence answered her question. If he'd disappeared somewhere into his massive apartment, she wasn't going to venture to find him, lest she cross paths with Jack. She sat up with a sigh and immediately lay back down, laden with the very idea of his son. She'd had a restless night, lying awake thinking about it. Because it was one thing to *say* she would do this, but now that she was there, Jamie's kid a few mere feet away, her resolve had been replaced by sheer terror.

That was when she noticed the note sitting atop Jamie's pillow, his neat, almost effete penmanship bidding her:

Evie,

I'm glad you're here. Went to get breakfast. I'll also stop by your car to get your things. Take a shower. Take your time. You can meet Jack at breakfast. We'll go slow.

See you soon,
Jamie

She instinctively smiled at the message—the fact that it would've been easier to send her a text, but that wasn't Jamie's way.

She wasn't sure what compelled her—maybe it was as simple as being there in Jamie's home with his family—but in the moment, she suddenly felt the need to reach out to her own.

Fri, Nov 28 8:01 AM

Eve Ambroise: Hi. I hope you're both well. And that you had a good Thanksgiving. Would love to catch up soon. xo

She sent the text with no expectation of a response after she'd ignored her parents for so long. She decided to mind Jamie's advice and rolled out of bed to start on her shower. She did take her time, exploring the full size and scope of the bathroom since she had the opportunity. The two sinks evoked a strange flutter in her stomach as she daydreamed about one becoming hers at some point in the distant future. It also made her think of Leo and the home she left behind, and her giddiness faded.

Eve went through Jamie's things, noting how little of the broad counter space he occupied. His toothbrush, toothpaste, and floss. Shaving supplies. Soap, deodorant, and some Q-tips. She adored how simple he was—not in a pejorative way, but that it didn't take much to satisfy him; she admired it.

In her exploration, she even debated taking a bath instead of a shower. The tub sat just behind the vanity, a deep rectangular basin, big enough for Jamie to join her if they wanted. She was running her fingers along the gold-plated faucet when there was a knock at the bedroom door, and she froze in place, praying it was the older Gallagher.

"Dad?" a little voice called out. It was somehow confident and commanding, as if he knew his father was in there and should've been up by then.

Eve told herself not to move or even breathe too hard. *Be cool and he'll go on his way.* But if he didn't, she was standing butt naked in the middle of the bathroom with no cover. *Shit.* She quickly but carefully tiptoed into the bedroom to retrieve last night's clothes, inwardly cursing Jamie for leaving them clear on the other side of the room. She made her way back into the bathroom, closing the door behind her just as he knocked again.

"Dad, are you up?" Jack asked.

Stumbling into her underwear as she moved toward the shower, she desperately hoped the kid would just assume his father was still asleep and let it go. But no. Seconds later, Jack's little footsteps were in the bedroom and he was knocking on the closed bathroom door, thereby reducing Eve to a human form of that Michael Scott GIF: *No. God. Please. No.*

"Dad, are you gonna make breakfast, or do I have to eat cereal?"

Eve had no intention of answering, figuring—or rather, hoping—Jamie would show up and get his son before she had to reveal herself. But when Jack tried the door, finding it locked, she knew she would have to either respond or leave this child thinking his father was possibly in danger.

"Your dad . . . went out for a minute," she said from behind the door. "He'll be right back."

Jack paused before asking, "Evie?"

Eve squeezed her eyes shut, the awkwardness of it all making her want to disappear. Her heart started to race, and she worried that a panic attack was on its way, which only made her panic more. She exhaled hard and nodded as if Jack could see her, before eventually replying, "Yes . . ."

"I'm Jack," he said brightly.

She grinned, his sweetness having an immediate calming effect. "Hi . . ."

"Are you okay?" he asked.

"Yeah . . ." She fumbled to get back into the rest of her clothes without making too much obvious noise, and soon enough, with another big deep breath, she opened the door. "Hi," she said again, offering a strained smile.

Beaming, Jack waved at her. "Do you live here now?"

Eve laughed, the innocence of his question immediately disarming her. He was quite cute, his wide smile a mixture of primary and permanent teeth. His dark hair was a mess after a night of sleep, but she could tell it was one of those stylish tapered haircuts. He was very much an amalgam of his parents, favoring Lucy—based on her limited knowledge of what the woman looked like anyway—but had Jamie's eyes.

She wished she knew what her son looked like.

"No, I'm just visiting," she answered politely. She was wary of being cold toward him, but she also didn't want to be too warm, for fear of him getting too comfortable.

"Cool. You wanna see my room?"

She chuckled again, finding the random request amusing, while also knowing she couldn't decline. "Um . . . sure." Eve was surprised when Jack took her hand, and by some miracle, she didn't collapse at his very touch. But seeing his little hand in hers, that ache in the pit of her stomach seemed to take hold, insistent on reminding her of what she didn't have. But she would ignore it for Jack. For Jamie.

And for herself, because she simply could not be crippled by this any longer. There was too much at stake now.

A few hours later, Jamie, Eve, and Jack were sitting down to lunch in front of an assortment of leftovers from the night before, which Eve couldn't wait to dive into. But Jack was more interested in getting to know his dad's friend and what she was all about.

Despite their strange start, he seemed to like her—even if she didn't know much about Marvel or Twitch streamers or anything about karate, but she'd done her best to be honest and give him her undivided attention. Over breakfast, he'd educated her on all the different Avengers and why the DC characters couldn't compare, and she asked questions and took actual notes. She could tell he appreciated that.

"All right, so here's the deal," Eve said as she filled herself up with macaroni and cheese, which—based solely on the crust—she'd surmised was made by someone Black. "I'll answer a question for every forkful of vegetables you eat."

Jack looked at his plate with small portions of cabbage, brussels sprouts, and corn pudding. "Do sweet potatoes count?"

"Of course. But your fork has to be *full.*"

"Well, wait," Jamie chimed in, "what happens if you don't wanna answer something?"

Eve looked at Jack, the two of them shrugging in unison as if they'd discussed it beforehand. "That's not the deal," she said. "If he eats, I have to answer."

"All right," Jamie said. "Wish I'd known to try this a few months ago."

They began before their food could get cold, Jack settling on a series of generic getting-to-know-you questions as a warm-up. Eve's favorite sports: tennis and soccer, though she also liked to swim. Her favorite television show of all time: She said *Abbott Elementary* because she doubted he'd ever heard of *The Leftovers.* He asked whether she used social media, and she informed him that she had Facebook and Instagram, but only used them sporadically for work. Her favorite song—the truth being Al Jarreau's version of "Look to the Rainbow," but again, for Jack's sake, she picked something more popular: "For Good" from *Wicked.* It led to Jack touting the merits of his own favorite song, "Defying Gravity," and spirited discourse about the musical, which was a genuine thrill for a theater girl like Eve. All in all, the questions were simple, sweet, easy. She should've known that one would eventually come and throw her for a loop. And it did, in the form of a twofer, as he gobbled up the last of his cabbage.

"So do you have any kids?" Jack asked evenly, as he had no way of knowing the subject was Eve's Achilles' heel. "And were you married before you met my dad?"

Eve felt like the wind had been knocked out of her, and she had to take a deep breath as she was suddenly forced to think about her real life again. Jack had her mind so filled with superheroes and silliness, it hadn't crossed her mind in hours, much to her surprise, and now, she was struggling not to burst. She swallowed hard and visibly before softly answering, "No."

"No to both questions?" Jack pressed, oblivious to her turmoil.

"No to both."

"Do you want to?"

Eve inhaled again, the word *no* burning her tongue once again, but she exhaled with the realization that his plate was empty. *Thank god.* "You're out of questions," she said, smiling with relief.

"Oh man!" Jack sat back in his chair with a groan.

Jamie laughed at their exchange as he cut back into their conversation. "It's gettin' late anyway," he said, checking his watch. "You should get upstairs and pack for your grandparents'. Your uncles will be here soon."

"Can Evie help me?"

"Well, that would be up to her."

Jack immediately turned to Eve. "I know I'm out of veggies, so I probably can't even ask this. But would you be okay with helping me pack?"

She laughed at him and his wit, enjoying that he anticipated her response before she could give it. "We can finish the game while you pack," she agreed.

The two of them descended from the high-top table, all too happy to leave Jamie to clean up after them. But before they could disappear, Eve gave Jamie a small smile and a look—one that said, *Thank you for trusting me with your son.* Because after the way she'd acted, she would've understood him being cautious. But no, he gave her free rein to be with Jack however she needed. And that meant something. It meant everything, actually.

CHAPTER 27

I'm Glad You're Mine

JAMIE

Stop it, you're eating too much."

"I am not eating too much," Jamie said, laughing as he took in another scoop of pie. "You've had most of it."

"I've only had, like, three bites," Eve said. "Three little bites, at that."

"That's a lie, but I can go get some more if you want."

"No, I don't want you to move," she said, running her free hand along his bare back. He'd never be able to recount how they got this way, but they were down to their underwear, lotus positioned in the middle of Jamie's kingly bed, sharing sweet potato pie and ice cream. And he wanted to stay exactly like this for as long as possible.

"Well, then you gotta learn to share." Jamie cut another spoonful of pie for her, taking care to add a dollop of the homemade vanilla ice cream along with it, and he fed it to her, watching as her lips pulled the dessert from the spoon. "Maybe the problem is we didn't get a big enough piece."

Eve didn't respond but kept her eyes on him as he took another scoop. The gentle clang of the silverware against the ceramic bowl reminded him of when they first met. "Hey," she eventually said.

"Hey," he replied, his mouth full.

She offered a quiet smile before saying, "Thank you for letting me into your real life."

Jamie nodded but got lost in his musings for a moment. He wanted to say that he looked forward to her returning the favor, but thought better of pushing. Still, the way she grappled with Jack's questions about marriage and children hadn't left his mind. Was it unease about Leo? Was he not as good to her as she claimed? The way she avoided whoever this man was, Jamie worried that he was abusive in some way. Was he why she'd been so timid about sex? But her initial objection to meeting Jack made him think it was something else. A miscarriage, perhaps a lost custody battle. Maybe all of it combined. She obviously wasn't ready to speak on it yet, so he wouldn't ask her to. He didn't want to beg to be let inside. Not when she'd already given so much.

Instead of speaking what was on his mind, Jamie replied with a kiss. A quick one, but potent enough that he could taste the ice cream on Eve's tongue, noting the way the flavor of it managed to change inside her mouth.

"Let's go to Paris," he said as they parted, surprising himself when the words came out. He'd been toying with the idea of taking Jack for Christmas, and errant thoughts of inviting Eve had crossed his mind, but he'd never intended to actually ask her. Not after last time.

Eve responded with a brittle chuckle. "What?"

"For Christmas," he clarified. "You, me, and Jack."

Eve's brown eyes widened, and he imagined that the idea of going on vacation with him and Jack sent pure panic through her veins, but she recovered quickly, replacing her trepidation with a new spoonful of ice cream, taking the bowl from him altogether. "I don't know what to say," she admitted.

"If you don't want to, it's fine. Really," he said, trying to ease the pressure. "I didn't realize what I was saying. I know it's asking a lot."

"What's scary is that I kinda do want to," Eve said. She stopped avoiding his gaze with the ice cream and looked him in the eye again.

"Then what's wrong?"

"Being here with you . . ." She spoke slowly and deliberately. "It's made me think about my own life. How I need to get back to it."

He looked up at her, his disappointment palpable. "What?"

"I need to see my family," she said. "My friends. I texted with my parents earlier today, and they said they'd like to have me home for Christmas."

"And then you'll be back?"

Eve grinned at him. "Of course," she said. She reached out to brush his curls from his face and rubbed her thumb against the top of his cheek.

Jamie hated how scared he was that she would hurt him. How insecure he felt about her, about them, about love in general. He liked to think he was free from Lucy, and in most ways he was, but she'd done indelible damage to his ability to trust. He did his best to expel his cynicism and took Eve's open hand, kissing her palm.

"I think that's a good idea," he said. But then, unable to help himself, he asked, "Are you gonna see him?" There was a nervousness to his question that he prayed she would quell.

She replied with a sympathetic smile. "I don't know. I'm not sure I can avoid it. We still have an apartment together."

Jamie nodded.

Just when the silence between them had gotten loud, Eve spoke again. "It's not that I don't like kids." When Jamie quirked an eyebrow, she went on, "Leo and I . . . we'd been trying for the past couple of years. Unsuccessfully, obviously." She bowed her head, seeming to avoid his eyes again. "It took a year to get pregnant the first time, and I miscarried a week before my first trimester ended. Another six months the second time." She exhaled sharply. "When it happened again in June, I felt like I was broken. There had to be something wrong. With us. With me. And I just . . . didn't want my life anymore. So I left."

"I'm so sorry, E—"

"Please don't feel bad for me," she interrupted. "I'm telling you this because I want you to trust me. I need you to believe me when I say that I'm going home because I need to. Because I left the wrong way. And if we're ever going to be anything, it can't be because I ran away."

The ghost of a grin sat on Jamie's lips as both relief and pride echoed in his blue eyes. "If you didn't want me to fall in love with you, you're doing a bad job," he said.

"Stop. I'm a mess."

"And still, here you are," he said. "Stop selling yourself short, Evie."

"I'm not trying to," she said. "I think . . ." She paused. "It's just really hard to believe you deserve love when you hate yourself."

Jamie pulled her in close, closing his eyes as he drew in her aroma of amber and rose, lime and vanilla. He wondered if she felt their hearts beating together the way he did. "You deserve everything you want, Eve. And I hate that the world hasn't given it to you yet." He caressed her back as he spoke, her bare skin feeling like silk to his fingertips. "But . . . you know, in the meantime, Jack can make for pretty good practice. He'll be back on Sunday." He smiled when he felt the gentle bobble of her laughter. "We'll be yours. If that's what you want."

"I do," Eve said.

It was the food coma talking, probably, but her choice of words, *I do,* felt significant. Heady and deliberate.

"Is that what you want?" she asked.

Jamie couldn't remember the last time he really cried. Maybe when Jack graduated from kindergarten. He was reasonably secure in his emotions and certainly had nothing against it, but there wasn't a whole lot that moved him all the way to full-fledged, face-streaking tears. But this did. Because it was a little overwhelming to realize that just being open to Eve, despite how low and lifeless he'd been feeling when he met her, had actually paid off. No one got through life without at least a little damage, but being vulnerable anyway? That was where the magic happened.

He'd fallen in like with Eve somewhere in the woods, but this, right here, was starting to feel like love.

Jamie squeezed Eve tighter as he replied, "Of course that's what I want."

"I thought you were about to leave me hanging," she said as they finally separated. Her smile was infectious, irradiating an already perfect face.

"I wanted to make sure you weren't gonna change your mind and take it back."

"Now, wait a minute. Let the record show that I have capitulated on every single thing you've asked of me," Eve said.

Jamie considered that for a moment, and he couldn't deny that despite her thorny surface, she was mostly soft underneath, and she'd generally met him at least halfway. After some prodding. For the most part. "Except for Paris," he teased.

Eve closed her eyes as she laughed at him. "You're an asshole," she said, still beaming. "How about this: I'll spend Christmas in New York and New Year's in Paris."

Jamie didn't stop to wonder whether she was serious before already rearranging his trip in his mind. He and Jack could be at Disneyland Paris on Christmas, spend their week sightseeing, and start the year with Eve, maybe on the Seine.

"Before I let my mind wander too far, is this a tentative plan, or . . . a promise?"

Eve took his hand into hers, the glint in her eyes meaning much more to him than the foreign words that came with it: "*Je te le promets.*"

CHAPTER 28

The Ways of a Woman in Love

EVE

"Can I be messy for a second?"

Eve eyed her coffee mate with a crackling amusement as her grin widened. "Please be messy," she said. She was sitting with Casey at a chic little European coffee bar down the street from Jamie's while they waited for Jack to get out of school.

Before continuing, Casey peeked around the corner, assumably to ensure his husband wasn't returning to their table just yet. "Okay, be honest. How do we feel about Lucy?"

"Oh." Eve shook her head, needing a long sip of her chai latte as she tried to concoct a tactful response. "So to be fair, I haven't met her yet," she started.

"Count yourself lucky."

She grinned again. "You really are messy."

"I know you've heard things," Casey said. "Be honest, and don't hold back just because she's Jack's mother. I'm positive he's the only good thing she's ever done in her life."

"Oh my god," Eve said, outright giggling now. "I don't know, I guess I just . . . I have questions."

"Like why Jamie ever spoke to her in the first place?" Casey quipped.

"Well, yes. And I know there are sides to every story, but I just can't help but wonder how anyone could treat someone like Jamie the way she did." Eve gazed into her cup, her mind wandering, however briefly, to Leo, and imagining someone, somewhere saying something similar about her. "But maybe some people are just bad matches, and that's okay."

Casey stared at her, a combination of mirth and mischief in his blue eyes, "Mm-hmm. I see why Jamie likes you."

Eve was practically bursting behind the smile she was trying to contain. But she truly delighted in hearing that out loud; it made it feel real. "And why's that?"

"You have that sort of intentional, introspective way about you. Just like he does."

Before she could respond—not that she knew what she'd say—Jelani had returned, reclaiming his seat at their tiny table near the front window. "The bathroom remains my second least favorite place to be recognized," he announced, "topped only by my father's wake." He then flashed his gorgeous smile, effectively glossing over that grim little tidbit. "What'd I miss?"

"Not too much," Casey said. "Eve hasn't met Lucy yet."

"Oh, girl, consider yourself lucky," Jelani said.

Eve laughed at their identical responses, even if a small part of her worried for when her path did cross with Lucy Ewen's.

"I was telling Eve how this feels right, though," Casey said. "You know how Jamie tries to pretend he's not sophisticated, but, Eve, you're, like, exactly what I pictured for him."

"Oh yeah," Jelani agreed. "He gets to be the person he wants to be with you."

"You unlock his potential. Instead of caging it."

"That right there," Jelani agreed, pointing to his husband animatedly.

As flattering as that was, and Eve hoped that was true of their relationship, she wondered how they could possibly know that for sure.

"We googled you, by the way," Casey added, seeming to intuit her skepticism.

"And we will be at the Public opening night. Front and center," Jelani said. "I actually saw it last year at BAM. I saw it with my little sister and my literary agent, and we sobbed through the whole fucking final act."

Eve adored those kinds of compliments. "You better not just be saying that."

"Swear to God."

"He sees a lot of shows, but even I remember him lauding this and hating that I didn't get to see it," Casey confirmed.

"We're so excited for you," Jelani said.

"Not that we know you intimately or anything, but just to meet you and see who you are and what you're doing." Casey punctuated his sentence with a kind smile. "We're excited for you . . . elated for Jamie."

"Are we completely overwhelming you right now?" Jelani asked. "I know Casey can be a lot."

Eve watched, amused as Casey playfully plucked Jelani, and she took a beat to consider the question. "You're not, actually," she said. And no one was more surprised than Eve that she was being honest. But this felt good. As Casey said, it felt right. She not only enjoyed being let into Jamie's life this way, but craved it on some level. Even if the idea of meeting Lucy was quietly terrifying, she still *wanted* it. She wanted everything that came with being Jamie's partner. It was why she'd forced herself to meet Jack, and why she accepted the coffee invite from Casey, recognizing the importance of spending some time with Jamie's family while she had the chance. This was the life she'd imagined when she first met Leo, but it had always managed to evade her. It was finally right there in front of her, waiting for her to touch it, take it, embrace it. Besides, what was waiting for her in New York other than a mess? A bunch of people she'd disappointed? Stella. Her parents. Even Maya wasn't exactly happy that Eve's summer sabbatical had stretched through autumn. She fit like a missing puzzle piece in Jamie's world—a euphoric feeling when she felt so outside her own. And she was going to hold on to that for as long as she could.

CHAPTER 29

See You Like I Do

JAMIE

"Where are the marshmallows?" Eve shouted.

Jamie rounded the corner from the living room to join her in the kitchen, where he found her inspecting the pantry. "We . . . don't have any marshmallows," he answered gingerly. "Did you tell me to get marshmallows?"

She looked back at him, giggling at his appearance—he was unintentionally dressed in gold, with several strips of shimmering ribbon slung over each shoulder. "*I* got marshmallows," she said. "But they've disappeared."

"Oh, well." He turned for the living room. "Jack!" he called, then waited to hear his footsteps scampering toward them. Within seconds, the kid appeared in the threshold of the kitchen, covered in glitter from Christmas ornaments.

"Yes?" he asked innocently.

"Do you know where the marshmallows are?"

Jack looked at Eve and then at the floor. "All of them?" he asked.

Jamie and Eve glanced at each other, his conspicuous reply

quirking both their eyebrows. "Do you know where any of them are?" Eve asked.

"Some of them . . . might be in my room," he revealed. "But not all of them."

"Why don't you go get the 'some' that are in your room," Jamie suggested, shaking his head as Jack ran off. "I'm sorry," he told Eve. "I don't know what's gotten into him lately."

In an uncharacteristically breezy response, Eve just shrugged. "His dad's got a new woman hanging around, his mom's got a baby on the way. He probably just wants attention."

"You planned an entire evening for us with the tree and everything," Jamie said. "He's got plenty of attention. He's just bein' a little asshole."

Eve laughed. "Maybe if you weren't so busy with your girlfriend, you would've noticed."

"Fair point." He joined her at the stove, wrapping his arm around her waist as he planted a kiss on the back of her neck, her hair in its updo allowing him easy access. "I don't even need the hot chocolate," he whispered, enjoying the taste of her. He was about to say something more explicit just as Jack returned, forcing them to separate. They watched him place half a bag of the Kraft Jet-Puffed mini-marshmallows on the counter and then step back.

"I'll give you credit for not eating them all," Eve commented, snickering as she picked them up.

"That's one of your Christmas gifts," Jamie added.

Jack's eyes went wide. "What?"

"You got to eat half a bag of marshmallows and you're not gettin' in trouble for it. Merry Christmas."

"But Christmas is still, like, twenty days away."

"How about . . . happy Hanukkah?" Eve inserted.

"We're not Jewish," he shot back.

"So you *want* to get in trouble here?" Jamie asked. "I think you have a trip to Dollywood coming up that we can cancel if that's what you're looking for."

"I'll take Hanukkah," he said, quickly rescinding his sarcasm.

"And now you *have* to watch *Charlie Brown* with me," Eve said, grinning as she returned to the stove to finish their hot chocolate.

Jack groaned as though Christmas were being stolen from him. "Oh, man."

"You both should be ashamed that it's not already a Christmas tradition in your home," Eve said. She handed over the full mugs and pointed them toward the living room. "Back to work, boys." She followed them, but not before stopping at the sound system to commence the Christmas music, sending Donny Hathaway's heavenly crooning through the loft's speakers.

Jamie's living room was a mess of holiday adornments—white lights, gold ribbons, and iridescent ornaments. They'd picked out a ten-foot noble fir, which was now sitting in front of the balcony window, waiting to be trimmed, and Eve was more excited about it than Jamie had ever seen her about anything. He should have seen it coming when she spent the *entire* afternoon in Target, but he didn't expect the amount of zeal that came with that truck full of decorations.

He didn't expect any of this, in fact. Eve had come alive since meeting Jack. She was a natural with him, instantly; there was such ease to their conversations, because Eve did the opposite of what most adults thought to do—she treated him like an equal.

He didn't know if cures to grief existed, but if they did, it seemed that Jack might have been hers.

"I told you," Jamie whispered as Jack ran off to the bathroom.

Eve looked up from her box of decorations, grinning. "Told me what?"

"That you'd love him."

She only shook her head, clearly unwilling to admit that defeat. "Promise me you'll take a video of when he finds out he's going to Paris?"

"I will," he nodded. He couldn't keep his gaze off her as she went back to dressing the tree, and she seemed so relaxed. Maybe even content. So unlike the woman who came to dinner at his cabin back in July. "I'm proud of you," he said.

She looked back up at him, a wide, enchanting smile claiming her gorgeous face, and she nodded back. "I'm proud of me, too."

"I know he's good at springing things on you. So if any of this is too much . . . if a whole day at Dollywood sounds like torture . . . you really don't have to. You can stay here, put up your candles . . ."

"Jamie," she whispered, shaking her head again. "I'm here. I'm in this."

He nodded. "Okay."

"And truth be told, I've been waiting half my life to go to Dollywood. You're not gonna be able to scare me out of this."

Jamie laughed, though he hoped that those feelings applied to more than just Dollywood. "Okay."

CHAPTER 30

Once Upon a Christmas

EVE

Fri, Dec 19 12:27

Stella Fischer-Fox: Hey lady. Just checking in. I wasn't sure if you'd gotten my last couple emails so I thought I'd text you just in case. Hope your holidays are going well!

Mon, Dec 22 9:33 AM

Maya Baudin: Friend! I hope you have the MOST AMAAAZING time at Dollywood! Ride all the rides! Eat all the food! (I heard the food there is bomb.) Take all the pictures!!! Enjoy every minute, friend! Because dreams that you dare to dream really do come true!

Maya Baudin: In case you're wondering, yes I am high af

Maya Baudin: But I don't mean it any less!!!

Maya Baudin: Don't judge me. It's Christmastime

Maya Baudin: Most importantly I can't wait to finally see you again bitch!!!!!

Eve was genuinely thrilled when Jack asked her if she would come to Dollywood with them. She'd been waiting to experience the park since her childhood, and even though she never got that chance, she relished getting to see it through Jack's eyes. Christmas in the Smokies was Dollywood's annual holiday festival, and apparently, a spectacle not to be missed. Jack and his best friend, Riley, had been coming to Dollywood since they were five, and they enjoyed all iterations of the park, but their favorite, by far, was Christmastime.

They arrived just before noon that day, and thanks to their fast passes, the kids very quickly racked up multiple rides on every roller coaster available. Eve knew that in her younger days, she'd be right there alongside them, screaming through every dip and dive the rides had to offer. But as an adult, Eve only had the wherewithal to try each roller coaster once before her stomach started asking questions like, *Girl, what the fuck are you doing?* But luckily, at Christmas in Dollywood, nighttime was the pièce de résistance.

The park was brimming with Christmas lights, literally millions of them, casting something of a celestial glow over their evening. Riley had somehow convinced them to go on the Drop Line, a ride that took them nearly three hundred feet in the air, then quickly dropped into a free fall. It was awful. But for the few minutes they were suspended over the city, with the view of glittering Pigeon Forge, Gatlinburg, and all the mountains in between, it was worth the mild heart arrhythmia that came with the drop.

When the foursome was back on solid ground, they visited all the light displays, taking pictures among the many trees adorned in everything from red and green to purple and yellow. Eve snapped shots of Jack and Riley, still running everywhere they were allowed, because their energy was boundless. Riley was a cute little Black girl with dimples and big, curly hair, reminding Eve a lot of her nine-year-old self. She'd asked Eve to hold on to her purple-and-blue eyeglasses when they got on the rides, and Eve took care of them like precious cargo, wanting Riley to trust her in the same way Jack seemed to. Just a year ago, it would've been inconceivable for her to hang out with two little humans without absolutely falling apart. Her friend Wesley and his wife had twins two years ago, and at some point, she'd stopped answering his texts because she couldn't bear the thought of being invited to his home and having to be around those precious babies. What a difference a year made.

"I don't wanna leave this place," Eve said. She was clutching Jamie's arm as they strolled through a passageway of lights, archway after archway bedecked in green, purple, and pink illumination. Jack and Riley were just a few paces ahead of them, giggling through a series of silly selfies, but she and Jamie were in their own little world.

"I can't believe you've never been here," he said. "You stayed a whole summer with Miss Hazel and never came?"

"I wanted to. *So* badly. But my grandma was *not* one for crowds."

"That's true," he granted, taking a swig of his hot chocolate. "She would tell me she didn't mind individuals, but she sure couldn't stand people."

They both giggled at the anecdote. "Relatable," Eve said.

"Either way, it wasn't like I had friends to come here with. And I haven't been back since then, so . . . I've missed out."

"Well, I'm glad I could be your first."

"You're certainly that." She grinned, her gaze finding his as she finished her sentence. The twinkle in Jamie's eyes was one of the first things Eve ever noticed about him, but under the shine of all the lights, they were positively dazzling. She had to resist the urge to stop in the middle of the crowd and kiss him.

As they continued their stroll, Jack turned to them with Jamie's phone, walking backward as he captured the two of them on camera. "Dad, say something."

"You should probably watch where you're going," Jamie said.

"I'm good, Dad."

Eve waved to the camera as she held tighter to Jamie's arm. "Merry Christmas from Dollywood!" she shouted.

"Are you cold yet?" Jack asked, laughing.

"A little," she admitted. She spent the last month making fun of Nashville and its lack of winter weather, but she'd forgotten that East Tennessee, especially up there in the mountains, was a different story, and she'd been shivering since the sun went down. "But your dad's doing a good job of keeping me warm."

"Miss Evie, since this is your first time, what was your favorite ride?" Riley asked.

"I think . . . I've gotta go with Thunderhead," she said, winking at Jack. "It's a solid choice."

"Nice." Jack nodded approvingly.

It was his favorite ride in the park, a mammoth of a roller coaster, mimicking one of those old wooden rides, complete with that slow, heavy climb to its apex, followed by the heart-stopping drop down, before taking you on a wild ride through the trees. And it boasted the best views of the full park. They'd gone up for one last ride at sunset, and it felt like they were in some fantastic painting.

"You're a good sport," Jamie told her as the kids resumed ignoring them.

"A good sport about what?"

"You've been on your feet all day. The kids have dragged you to every roller coaster and bumper car, you did a full photo shoot at Dolly's house. It's been a lot."

She also stood in interminable lines for cinnamon bread—which, to be fair, was worth it—and ate Dippin' Dots in forty-degree weather. It was a relief when they rode the Dollywood Express through the park, not only for the reprieve for her feet, but because it gave Eve a moment to genuinely marvel at all the lights and sights. Somehow, the park felt large and small; she didn't understand how this behemoth of a theme park could be homey and intimate. There was always a bit of magic embedded in the playgrounds of the world, places designed to make children happy—and yes, boatloads of money—but the charm of Dollywood felt like straight-up wizardry.

"Excuse you. I'm genuinely reconnecting with my childhood over here," Eve said. "And I really did like that ride. Reminded me of the Cyclone at Coney Island."

"Just don't let Jack hear you," Jamie said. "Last thing he needs is news of another amusement park to conquer."

Eve smiled at the thought of Jack at Coney Island. "I have to imagine he'll be sick of amusement parks by the time he gets through Disneyland." Between Dolly and Disney, the kid was going to spend an entire week on roller coasters.

"The thing about eight-year-olds is they don't easily tire of the things they love. I kinda envy it."

"Fair," Eve said. "But I also think everyone should visit Coney Island at least once, so I will not begrudge him that."

"In that case, you'll have to take me there when I'm in town," Jamie said.

Eve sent a quizzical glance his way. "Oh, are you coming to New York?"

"Your play opens in May, doesn't it?"

"Oh. Yeah. It does."

"You thought I wouldn't be there?"

"I . . . hadn't thought about it." Her confusion morphed into a mixture of awe and excitement. "Really?"

"You don't want me to?"

"No, of course I do. I just . . . I don't know. I keep forgetting we can exist outside of Tennessee."

"A few weeks ago, you didn't think we could leave your cabin."

"Okay, well, stop bringing up old stuff," she said, gently swatting his arm with her open hand. They strolled another few feet before Jack stopped in front of them, using his camera to record the sparkling ceiling again. "I hope we get to see all this footage when you're done," Eve called out to him.

"I'll think about it," Jack said.

"He's very particular about his art," Jamie said.

Eve could relate. "Has he told you what he wants to be when he grows up?"

Jamie sighed thoughtfully before replying, and a visible puff of air followed his warm breath in the cold evening. "I don't think he's said anything more consistently than comic book illustrator. But I happen to think he's a pretty good writer, too."

"He definitely seems drawn to visual media."

"He's a good student, but all his teachers tell me how distracted he gets with the sketching and doodling."

"And he's so into the superhero stuff. I bet he'd be great at animation, too."

"He hasn't gotten into that so much yet. So far, he's been kinda old-school about it."

"Gee, I wonder where he got that from."

Jamie chuckled. "Why?" he asked. "Don't tell me that's another trick you have up your sleeve."

Eve snorted as she had to work to hold on to the mouthful of cinnamon bread she'd bitten off. "Absolutely not. I was just thinking about the next few months. I know his mom has him in the summers, but they're gonna have a new baby then. It might be nice for Jack if he has something to focus on."

Jamie looked at her like she had two heads as she went on to mention that she had some friends who would be able to point him in the right direction, perhaps at Vanderbilt University. She paused when she noticed his strange regard. "What's wrong?"

"No, I just . . . I wasn't sure I'd see the day you were talking about the future. And not just ours, but Jack's."

"Oh." Eve felt sheepish, shrugging it off as no big deal, but her cheeks grew warm as she wondered if she'd gotten ahead of herself. "I don't know if you've noticed, but I'm very good at overthinking things."

"No, I'm glad you've thought about it," Jamie said. "I went ahead and sent in my application to Vanderbilt . . . and NYU."

Eve went from abashed to beaming in a matter of about a second. "Yeah?"

Jamie replied with his own shy smile. "You said I could take it slow, so . . . Yeah."

"I mean, you're obviously not struggling to pay bills. There's no rush. You can just do summer classes if you want."

"If I get into Vandy, it does mean I can't come out to Gatlinburg as often as I was. Classes are evenings and weekends."

"Oh, then this is a terrible idea," Eve said.

"But . . . maybe . . . you can spend more time in Nashville, instead of out here alone." He sounded unsure of himself, but he quickly appended before she could respond, "If you want."

Eve hoped her smile was as bright as it was earnest. "Yeah," she said. "Maybe so."

Seemingly pleased with that answer, Jamie took her hand in his, the welcome warmth of his skin suffusing her entire body as they continued their walk. As they neared the end of the gallery, Dolly Parton's version of "All I Want for Christmas Is You" blared throughout the park, and Eve sang along, serenading him animatedly.

"You're adorable," he said, unable to suppress a laugh as his entire face turned a bright shade of pink.

Eve had never been called adorable before. It wasn't an adjective often applied to Black women—and certainly not ones too dark to pass the paper bag test. The farther you stood from whiteness, the less you were on the receiving end of cutesy descriptors. She appreciated it.

"All I want for Christmas is *you*," Jamie told her once the song faded out and "Joy to the World" took its place.

She regretted that they wouldn't get to spend Christmas Day

together. But this evening was doing a good job of making up for it, at least. "New Year's," she reminded him.

At the end of the gangway, where the crowd dispersed back into the park, Jamie turned to Eve, a grin on his lips, and Eve noted the way the lights danced on his face, making him look like a Christmas ornament. She took the ends of his jacket into her hands, gently tugging him closer. Neither of their smiles faded as Jamie tilted his head and cupped her face, pulling her in for a kiss. His lips covered hers, his tongue pushed them apart, and Eve let out a gentle sigh when their tongues touched, the heat between them eclipsing the cold air surrounding them. Eve's fingers crept up to Jamie's neck, coiling through his curls, as usual, while his hand wrapped around her waist and then slipped down to her backside, stealthily pulling her closer and giving her a little squeeze—as usual. It was a passionate and sweet kiss all at once. Dynamic and dizzying. A kiss that said hello and goodbye in the very same breath.

As a teenager, Eve thought of Dollywood as some enchanting land just beyond her reach; the adult in her had to believe that the enigma of whatever sat beyond those butterfly-adorned gates was more interesting than reality. But no, Dollywood *was* magical. It was her somewhere over the rainbow, as Maya had so aptly reminded her. Dollywood, and everything surrounding it, was where she'd fallen in love.

CHAPTER 31

Rose-Colored Boy

JAMIE

Eve gasped as they stepped into Jamie's apartment, practically hissing as she said, "There's someone here." The alarm in her voice as she stopped in her tracks sent a small chill down his spine.

With Jack asleep in his arms, he couldn't maneuver as well as he would've liked, but he intuitively cradled Jack's head and jumped in front of Eve until he could view the culprit: Lucy, asleep on his couch.

"Oh." He sighed, relieved.

"'*Oh*'?" Eve said. "You were expecting company at this hour?"

"She isn't company," he muttered. He went to the couch to wake his ex, and more to the point, ask what the hell she was doing there. He looked to Eve as Lucy stirred. "You mind taking him upstairs?" he whispered to her.

Eve looked like she wanted to decline, but she motioned to retrieve Jack just as Lucy sat up.

"I am obviously here to take him with me," Lucy inserted

into their exchange. "But I'm glad you feel so comfortable having someone I've never met haul off with my son."

Eve immediately backed off, and Jamie could only look at her apologetically. "I'm gonna take this chicken upstairs instead," she said of the Popeye's they'd stopped for on the way home.

"I'm sorry," Lucy said. "I've just been sitting here for four hours, and I'm a little frustrated." She stood from her seat to offer Eve her hand. "I'm Lucy."

Eve replied with a terse smile. "Eve."

"It's nice to finally put a face to the name I've heard so much about."

"Likewise." Eve glanced at Jamie again. "I'll be upstairs?"

Jamie nodded. But he felt something like butterflies when she gently rubbed his back and offered a quick kiss to his cheek, and then Jack's. "Don't eat all the red beans and rice," he joked as she passed. He sobered when he returned his attention to Lucy, standing there glaring. "What are you doing here?" he asked. "I told you I'd drop him off in the morning."

"You told me when?"

"When I texted to tell you we were gonna get home late."

"Oh, so then not at all."

"What?"

"I received no such texts. Or I wouldn't be here, Jamie."

He found that hard to believe, but he didn't feel like going through his phone to prove his point. Maybe it didn't go through. Another reason to hate his iPhone. "Fine. Miscommunication, I guess."

"Oh, how the tables turn," Lucy said with a smirk.

"What is that supposed to mean?"

"You ripped me a new one when I was late once—"

"Once?"

"Yes, *once,* without calling. Fourth of July. Now, here we are, you waltz in here at midnight with no apologies, no good excuses . . ."

Unwilling to let her win the argument, Jamie pulled his phone from his jacket and went to their text thread, where, indeed, he'd typed out an informative and apologetic message about their delay and suggestion that she keep Jack for a full week when they returned from Paris. Except he never sent it. "Shit." He inhaled, then exhaled, working up the volition to apologize to Lucy, despite her haughtiness. "I'm . . . sorry about that."

"So maybe now you can admit that it's entirely possible to get caught up in the moment and forget to properly communicate?"

"I don't think you wanna start lecturing me about what's proper." He was trying to keep his voice low for Jack, but he could see this conversation devolving into an argument quickly if they weren't careful. "You need anything else?"

Lucy stared at him for several beats, as if she were trying to anticipate his response before she could ask him anything. "She's pretty," she said.

"Very," he agreed, wondering where this was going.

"Where'd you meet her?"

"What do you *want*?"

"Only the same courtesy that's been extended to you. I shouldn't have had to hear about her from my son," Lucy said. "She shouldn't have been a surprise to me."

"You're right," Jamie said. "I should've given you a heads-up."

"Makes me wonder what kind of woman would be around someone's child without meeting the mother anyway."

"I know you don't believe in boundaries," Jamie said, gesturing for her to take Jack, "but I'm drawing one here. You don't get to talk about her."

"Say what you will—"

"Lucy, I'm serious. Your problem is with me. Leave it there."

Lucy seemed taken aback, but she complied. "Okay."

But before she could leave, Jamie decided to go ahead and rip off the Band-Aid since they were already in the thick of it anyway. "Listen, I was gonna talk to you about this in the morning, but . . . I wanted you to know that I talked to a Realtor. And in the new year, we're putting the house up for sale."

Lucy laughed. It was a sarcastic laugh, sounding derisive to his exhausted mind. "Wow."

"You and Tyler are more than welcome to buy it from me, but I think it's for the best at this point."

"I know I encouraged you to move on with your life, but I gotta say, I wouldn't have done it if I'd known this would be the result."

Jamie grimaced. "You wouldn't have encouraged me to move on if you'd known I'd actually do it?"

"No. If I'd known you'd start acting like an . . . asshole," she whispered the expletive as if Jack wouldn't hear it with his ear all of three inches from her mouth.

"We agreed on December back in June. It's December," he reminded her. "I do deserve to be able to move on."

"And what about Jack?"

"I agreed to this because uprooting him from everything familiar felt cruel. But he's had a year here. I think he's okay.

Children are resilient." As the words left his mouth, Jamie realized he was parroting his own mother. Though, to be fair, she wasn't *always* wrong.

"Unbelievable," Lucy sighed. "You spring this on me at Christmas? You want me to move when I'm having a *baby*?"

"A new baby seems like a good time for a new beginning," he said sincerely. If they'd had the money when she was pregnant with Jack, they would've been in Brentwood a long time ago. "I'll email you the Realtor's information. She can help you find a place if you don't wanna buy this one. I made sure she had some nice properties."

"I guess I don't really have a choice here."

Jamie internally scolded himself for finding mild amusement in her frustration. "I think three months should be sufficient? Or you can talk to Tyler and get back to me."

"Stop acting like you care what he thinks," Lucy said. "If you wanna be a dick, just own it."

"I'm not being a dick. I've bent over backwards to be accommodating to you. Against the advice of everyone I know. Even my lawyer said I was way too kind. Like I said, Luce. I just wanna move on. And hopefully never feel the way you made me feel again."

Lucy bit her lip and nodded as she inched toward the exit. A slow simper took the place of whatever sarcastic gibe she surely wanted to send his way. "Good night then, Jamie."

Jamie waited until she was on the elevator before pulling off his jacket and heading upstairs to join Eve. He found her straddling his lounger, plowing through her chicken strips like she hadn't eaten in a few days. He grinned at the sight.

"Sorry about that," he said. "It was my fault. I didn't send the message."

"Everything okay?" she asked, not looking up from her food.

"Yeah." He took a seat in front of her and rummaged through their selection to find the red beans. "She's just such a fuckin' hypocrite," he went on. "If I'd done half the shit she's pulled, she would've been asking for sole custody. And I would've deserved it."

"Well . . ." Eve exhaled, rubbing her thumb against her index and middle fingers to rid them of crumbs. "You let her get away with it, so what do you expect?"

Her tone was on the acerbic side, which left Jamie frowning as he stared at her empty box. Had the woman he spent the day with already disappeared? "Excuse me?"

"I mean she probably cheated on you because she knew she could." When he looked up at her, stung, she pulled back on the throttle. "I'm sorry. That was mean."

He tried to shake off the insult, because it had been a perfect day until then, and he knew the effect Lucy could have on people. "It was."

"I just don't like the way she treats you."

"So your solution is to match her energy?"

"I'm *sorry,*" Eve repeated, her bare foot reaching out to touch his knee. She smiled at him, much of the tension in the room ebbing with it. "I'm frustrated that our first meeting went that way. I wish I'd been more prepared, I guess. And part of me hoped, despite everything you've told me, that I'd like her?" Eve's stare flitted downward as she shook her head again. "She's Jack's mom, so I didn't want to hate her."

"It's okay if you do," Jamie said.

"Stop."

"Don't let her ruin today," he said seriously. "She doesn't deserve that kind of power."

Eve nodded but still seemed unconvinced. She plastered on a smile anyway and reached out to touch his cheek—the way she often did when she was trying to be soft. "I'm gonna miss you," she said. "You know that, right?"

"You say it like we're gonna be apart forever. It's only a week."

"I know. But I've been dreading it. Being without you is bad enough; adding my parents to the equation?" She released a sharp exhale.

"Are they that difficult?"

"I generally know how to be around them. I usually shrink myself to keep the peace. But the last time we spoke, I hung up on them. And that was five months ago, so . . ."

Jamie made a face as he absorbed the weight of such a thing. He'd also hung up on his mom, not so long ago, out of contempt, but even now, he wouldn't do such a thing. "Just remember Paris is waiting on the other side of it," he said.

"So long as they don't drive me to a psych ward first."

"They can't be that bad," Jamie said. When Eve eyed him, he ceded that she would know her parents better than he did. "Well, how do you think they'll feel about us?"

"I try not to think about it," she said, shaking her head. "I doubt I'll tell them."

Jamie tried not to be insulted or let his doubts swallow him whole. Based on what little she'd shared, it even made some sense. "Whatever gets you through."

She smiled sympathetically. "It's not you. It's them."

"I believe you."

She leaned across the distance between them to offer a kiss, surely meant to appease him, and the bar was low enough that it actually did. "I love you," she said, her brown eyes searching his. For what, he didn't know. He hoped she didn't wonder whether he felt the same.

But he was halfway waiting for her to realize her mistake. He wasn't surprised that she loved him—she expressed as much in a lot of big and small ways, which was why he never expected to hear it out loud. He liked when she surprised him.

"I love you, too," he said hoarsely, unable to contain the smile that wanted to burst past his lips. Eve smiled, too, the one that showed all her teeth and the small dimple in her right cheek. He'd seen it many times at Dollywood. That smile had quickly become one of his favorite things in the world, sitting alongside Jack's laugh and random phone calls from Casey.

He quietly nodded to himself as he thought about what a good day it had been. What a good six months it had been. And he liked to think the next year would be even better.

In just a week, they would get to begin their lives together.

CHAPTER 32

One Big Unhappy Family

EVE

The moment Eve arrived home, the profound sense of gloom that she left with all those months ago seemed to come right back. She used to adore Christmas in the city, but after the splendor of Dollywood with Jamie, New York City seemed anemic in comparison. The rainy weather didn't help, turning a normal twenty-minute ride to Harlem into an hour and a hundred-dollar Uber—shout-out to surge pricing—with nothing but her scattered thoughts as company. She tried to come up with a palatable story to sell her parents once she walked through the door, but everything about her disappearing act opened up a world of questions. So she figured it best to just let them ask and she would answer.

But when she arrived, there were no questions—not even the silent ones that only existed in her mother's eyes. They seemed to actively avoid speaking on anything of substance. They only said they were happy to see her alive, in the flesh—as if they expected some stranger to show up in her place. Then again, maybe one had.

Instead of interrogating her, they started in on their usual gripes with their neighbors: One of them couldn't control their dog, another had tacky Christmas decorations that were "ruining" the aesthetic of the block. Her mother went on a full rant about Michael and Doris Akinyele across the street, allowing their eleven-year-old to come home from school alone. They evoked images of Gatlinburg, and the petty grievances the Crockett's staff liked to share with her about their coworkers.

For the afternoon, Eve snuck away to grab lunch with Stella. She was Jewish and so unencumbered by the last-minute bustle of Christmas Eve. She was also, unsurprisingly, eager to see Eve's face; and ultimately, despite hiding from her for the better part of six months, Eve was happy to reconnect with Stella, too. They sat in a corner of Melba's, sharing a platter of fried chicken with a side of eggnog waffles for Eve, discussing the current state of the play Eve was supposed to be drafting. And when Eve admitted she wasn't done yet, she did not get the reprimand she expected from Stella.

"Do you still wanna go with our original plan, or should we reassess?"

Eve's first instinct was to emphatically confirm that she wanted to move ahead as planned. But she decided to reply with the truth. "I don't know. I'm excited, but I've also been distracted. And with the scrutiny *Gamba Adisa* is going to be under, I don't want to overpromise and underdeliver with the next."

Stella was nodding, but it was clear she did not agree. "Can I tell you something?"

"Of course."

"You're not going to underdeliver, Eve. Can we just, like, knock that thought away?"

Eve was irrationally annoyed that Stella couldn't conceive of her insecurity, especially as a Black woman in an *overwhelmingly* white space like theater. Yes, it was great that her agent believed in her, but she couldn't do so blindly. Of course, avoiding Stella instead of just saying these things probably didn't help. "It's not that easy. But I can try," Eve offered. "I promise that I'm in this. I'm gonna ignore all this fear and do whatever you need me to do."

"I need you to finish your fucking play," Stella said loudly as she casually deconstructed their last chicken wing. There was a warmth in her words, matching the smile that punctuated her sentence, but Eve also knew she was at least fifty percent serious. "But it's about what *you* want, Eve. You have a unique opportunity here, and I want you to be able to take full advantage of it. But I can't want it *for* you. I'm here to make your dreams come true, not the other way around."

Indeed, having two pieces premiere at the Public in succession could seriously bolster her career—and more frankly, get her to Broadway. But that meant actually finishing the second one. The last few months, she'd done a whole lot of play and no work on her plays, and now she was paying the price.

"If I can get it done by the end of January, does that give us enough time to stick to the original plan?" Eve asked.

"I think so. But please let me worry about that," Stella said. "Just do your thing. And maybe keep me updated."

Eve knew she was going to do everything but let Stella worry about that. Perhaps if she could finish sooner, it would alleviate some of the pressure to get the rest of the deal done.

Then again, she would already be pushing her limits to get it all done in just a month—especially when she had no idea what more she wanted to say. It was as though she'd hit a wall, unable to get past the mental block that was her pregnancy and her parents. She would have to really batten down the hatches. Focus. Which meant Paris was out. And the thought of breaking her promise to Jamie raised a whole different set of anxieties.

"I'm gonna have it to you in two weeks," Eve announced. She exhaled heavily and chugged her sangria, wishing it were something stronger. Something that would give her the courage to disappoint her boyfriend after all the work she'd done to stop disappointing him. But if anyone understood priorities, it was him, so she internally committed to this timeline—for herself and for her career, and even for Stella, who had been her patient cheerleader, despite Eve not living up to any of her promises to her.

Eve left lunch feeling chastened—and necessarily so. But there was a bright side: Stella revealed that there were whispers about *Gamba Adisa* being short-listed for an Obie Award, which was an illustrious accolade for Off- and Off-Off-Broadway plays. She'd never imagined her little run in Clinton Hill had been noticed by anyone, but just the possibility was enough reason to get her head out of the clouds. Her time in Tennessee had been fun—elevating—and she looked forward to going back eventually, but for now, she needed to attend to her job.

Eve used the rest of the afternoon to finish up her holiday shopping. She'd done most of it in Nashville, but her mother always only wanted her favorite perfume for Christmas, which was exclusively available at a little fragrance shop in Flatbush, which Eve made it to just before their early closing. She picked out a few incenses for her dad and a special treat for Maya at the dispensary nearby before heading back uptown.

She returned to her parents' just in time to sit down to Christmas Eve dinner. Her father had been proud to tell her about the bouyon bef he had simmering in the Crock-Pot all day, meaning she was obligated to try it. But they were already eating when she arrived, which only managed to make her feel more out of place.

"I didn't know if you were going to eat," Joan said when Eve stepped into the open kitchen. "We usually have to beg you," she added when Eve didn't reply.

Eve smiled politely. She'd gained weight in Tennessee and hoped she'd get a compliment or two from the people who'd been telling her all her life that she didn't eat enough. "Daddy told me he was cooking, so I ate light at lunch," she said. She filled her bowl with a hearty helping of the soup and looked around for some kind of roll or cornbread to go with it, but didn't feel comfortable enough to ask. Instead, she silently joined them at the table. As she took her seat, her mother reached out to pinch her face. "Ma . . ."

"Such a beautiful girl," Joan commented. "You see the way her skin bounces back?"

"You don't have to prod the girl," Roger said. "That's what happens at thirty-three."

"I'm thirty-four, Daddy," Eve gently corrected him.

"You know what I meant."

"Your hair has grown," Joan said, as if surprised. She pulled at one of Eve's untwisted coils until it stopped halfway down her arm, seemingly satisfied with the length. "Looks healthy."

"Thanks," Eve said, letting out an undetectable sigh as she started on her food.

"So," Roger started, pushing back from the table, "where are we with this next play?"

"Oh," Eve replied, observing as her father went to the oven.

She should have known they were saving the interrogation for dinner. She felt like she was back with Stella again.

"We assumed you stayed all this time because you were finishing up."

"I'm still . . . working . . . on the . . . third act," she answered slowly, purposely dragging out her words until she could see what her father was up to. He ended up bringing her not one, but two rolls. "It's not done, but I promised my agent it would be in two weeks."

"Well, that's a relief," Joan said. "You're gonna need all the plays your little mind can write since you've wrecked your engagement."

"Here we go," Eve said.

"Third act," Roger said. "Should be the easiest part. That's the end, yes?"

"Depends on the writer," she said.

Eve had yet to tell her parents that her current production would be premiering at the fucking Public Theater in the spring, but when her mother and father exchanged a look of skepticism, she decided to continue holding on to that news.

"I'm fine," she said. "Jesus, you'd think I would've earned at least a little credit by now."

"Leaky roof tricks the sun, but not the rain," her dad replied.

"You squandered your credit when you decided to set fire to your life and all your wonderful opportunities by not coming back for several months," Joan said.

"And I guess it didn't matter to you that I needed to," Eve said. "That I feel better than I have in a long time."

"Because you only enjoy wreaking havoc, Eve. You always have."

"Joanie," Roger cut in.

"This is what she does," Joan said. "Give her a little bit of freedom, and everything turns to chaos. The way she likes it, I'm sure. Even Leonardo, God bless him, didn't know what to do with her."

Eve was annoyed that she'd suddenly lost her appetite, because her food looked delectable—brisket and plantains, spinach and malanga, swimming in a thick, thoroughly seasoned broth—and she really would have liked to enjoy it. But instead, she sat there mindlessly picking her bread into tiny pieces, determined not to let this force her into backsliding.

"How many good, single men do you think are out there?" her mother asked.

Eve had to suppress a smile when she thought of Jamie.

"*And* he's Catholic," Joan continued. "God knows they don't come around often. A family man, willing to take care of you."

"Ma, I'm barely Catholic myself, and I don't need anyone to take care of me. Please stop acting like he was a saint."

"I should have known," she said, shaking her head in disappointment. "You never even wore that ring. That beautiful ring."

"She knew she was settling when she accepted it," Roger commented as he inhaled another spoonful of soup.

Eve looked at her dad, always the more sensible of her parents when it came down to it, feeling betrayed by his assessment. "Daddy."

"It's true, sweetheart. I've no idea why you chose him. Perhaps you were too scared to marry someone with a backbone—"

"And there's my cue." Eve stood from her chair, much in the same way she had the last time she was there, ready to hightail it out of there. "Thanks for dinner, guys."

"But you didn't eat."

"Where are you going?" Joan asked.

Eve shook her head, lacking an answer. Maya was busy for the night, and there was no one else she felt comfortable dropping in on without more notice. But she'd rather figure it out on the way than be in the house with them for a second longer.

After a bit of consideration and a lot of desperation, Eve ended up back at her old apartment in Brooklyn. It was probably the last place she should've been, but Leo was in Jersey with his mom, as he was every Christmas, so it was her best and only option. Technically, it was still her place—her name was still on the lease, and her December rent payment cleared on the second of the month—so she rationalized it by saying she deserved to be there.

Still, when she walked in, she felt like an intruder. She could smell the sweet remnants of honey and pears from whatever Leo had cooked that day for his family dinner—*pettole,* if she had to guess, which was a favorite of his southern Italian clan. She pictured him at the stove, toiling with the giant ball of dough until he had a pan full of the fruity fritters, while she watched in awe.

The rest of the house appeared largely unchanged. Pristine. Boring. Same as she left it. Where the slate-blue walls and smoke-gray furniture once seemed understated and timeless, they now felt glum and sterile. The apartment had none of the color or personality that Casey had given to Jamie's place, nor the quaint charm of her grandmother's cabin. It was no wonder she was depressed here.

The foyer still prominently displayed a picture of her with Leo, the two of them on vacation in Rio, the snapshot from a boat ride they'd taken to Ilha Grande. She knew Leo well enough to understand why he didn't move that daily reminder, that relic of their relationship. But she wished he had.

When she reached the bedroom, seeing their neatly made bed, with one side turned down, ready for him whenever he returned, Eve finally sent him a text.

Wed, Dec 24 8:42 PM

Eve Ambroise: Hey, just FYI, I'm in town. At the apartment getting my stuff now. I'll be around until next week if you want to talk.

With that, Eve continued into the closet to grab her larger luggage and promptly began to collect her things. It was after 11:00 p.m. by the time she finished sorting through her jewelry, shoes, and dresses, filling two Samsonites, three Telfar duffels, and a Louis Vuitton trunk her godmother had given her when she went to college. She was sorely tempted to just stay there for the night; it was better, simpler, than trying to get a ride back to her parents' with all her things.

And just when she'd convinced herself that she wasn't overstepping boundaries she was the one to set, she heard Leo at the front door, his keys seeming to taunt her, daring her to try to hide from him for a single second longer.

She should've seen it coming. When he didn't reply to her text, she should've known he was on his way back to the city. But she was too preoccupied with herself to prepare, and so she froze the second she saw him. He was wrapped in a leather jacket and his favorite green plaid scarf with a red beanie covering his dark hair. Despite the distance between them, her at the top of their steps, him at the bottom, their eyes locked.

"Shit," he breathed, his expression projecting a curious mixture of excitement and doubt. She must have looked like she'd come face-to-face with a ghost, but he looked like he'd just been brought back to life.

"Hi," Eve replied, taking a few tentative steps down the staircase.

"You're really here?"

She frowned, stopping. "You didn't get my message?"

"I did, but . . . I guess I didn't expect to actually find you here."

"Oh."

"Are you staying?"

"No . . ."

"Oh."

"I was just . . ." Eve looked to the top of the steps, where two portmanteaus were waiting to be dragged down. "Why aren't you at your mom's?"

"My mom died in August," he said.

Eve's mouth dropped open as it felt like the wind had been knocked out of her, incredulous that something so momentous could've happened to him and she'd had no idea. "I'm so sorry," she stammered, feeling sad for him and for herself. She might not have loved Leo anymore, but she still cared about him, still knew how much it must have hurt to lose his most important person in the world. She wanted to ask why he didn't tell her, but it would've been a pointless, perhaps cruel question when she already knew the answer.

"I wish I knew what to say. How are you?"

Leo shrugged. "It's been a shitty year. I'm glad it's almost over."

Eve agreed. He'd racked up loss after loss—as much as she'd failed to acknowledge it, the miscarriages had happened to him, too—and then she did what she did, and then his mother. Now here she was reopening old wounds. "I'm so sorry for dropping in like this," she said.

"Where are you going?" Leo asked. He ignored her apology as his gaze landed on her bags.

"Back to the nuthouse."

He chuckled at her reference to her parents'. "But I mean after that. You said you were here just until next week?"

"Oh, I don't know," she said, stuffing her hands in her pockets nervously. "Back to Tennessee, probably. I owe Stella a play."

He nodded, scratching at his grayish scruff, and Eve knew he was waffling over whether to say anything further. Before he could get it out, she decided to walk back up the steps to retrieve her things, ill-equipped to handle this much awkwardness and guilt. But as she made it to the bottom of the steps with her last bag, Leo's big, exaggerated sigh, designed to stop her, did exactly that.

"What is it?" She was trying to be patient with him—for him—but she'd seen this show before.

"You can't just treat people like this, Eve."

She shook her head. "I'm just trying to get out of your way."

"You walk in here after half a year, rifle through all our things, take what you want, and now you're really just gonna leave again like none of it ever mattered?"

"I told you we could talk whenever you wanted."

"Well, I wanted to talk six months ago, so the least you can do now is stop rushing around long enough to face me."

Eve dropped her bag where she stood and raised her hands in surrender. "You're right. Please say whatever you'd like to say."

He peered at her in a way that felt condescending. "What are you doing, Eve? What is this?"

"I'm . . . moving out." She looked around at what she thought was obvious. "What else am I supposed to do?"

"But why are you leaving? You never gave me a good reason."

"Being miserable wasn't enough of a reason?"

"I mean, that's what therapy is for. That's why I kept begging you to try it. For real."

"Because I'd have to be crazy to wanna move on?"

"Because you walked around fucking catatonic for *weeks* after you had a miscarriage, and for the life of me, I can't figure out why that's not something you'd wanna talk to someone about," he said. "I know it can't be me, because God forbid you share anything resembling real feelings with me, but fuck, Eve. You couldn't let it be *someone*?"

Eve went from frowning to scowling as she listened to Leo bring up the feelings she'd tried to forget about. "You're one to talk about someone being catatonic," she said. "I had to drag you to every appointment. I had to force pills down your throat like a child. I wasn't your girlfriend; I was your mother. I was never interested in reversing those roles."

"Well, at least I'm better now. Did something about it. Instead of using grief as an excuse to stop trying."

"Yes, Leo, you're perfect now. Astounding that a straight white man in America is finally thriving."

"You know what, fuck you, Eve," he sent back, spinning on his heel. "So fucking arrogant."

"Excuse me?" she called after him.

"I said you're arrogant," he yelled, immediately turning back to her. "You think you're the only one in pain here. You think everyone's stupid but you."

"I don't think that," she said, her voice at a normal, earnest volume then. "I don't. I just don't think you realize how hard it was to be in this relationship sometimes."

"That's what I mean," he said. "You think I didn't notice you flinch when I touched you? How you hesitated whenever it was time to make any concrete plans for our wedding?" He closed his eyes, and for the first time in years, she genuinely wondered what he was thinking about. "I can't even tell you how many times I felt absolutely rejected by you and couldn't figure out why."

Eve bit her lip in another small show of remorse. "I'm sorry," she said.

"I don't even know why you wanted a baby so badly," he said. "You hurt people, Eve. It was just as hard being in a relationship with you. But I'm the asshole for trying to love you anyway."

"You weren't an asshole," Eve whispered. "I know you were good to me. You were." She nodded as the back of her eyes began to sting with unexpected tears. "But that doesn't mean I have to be tethered to you forever, does it?"

"No, you didn't make any vows," Leo said. "That was the plan, but . . . those change, I guess."

"They do."

They went silent, briefly, as Eve searched for something better to say than *sorry*. But she was.

"So . . . what," Leo cut into her thoughts. "You go back to

Tennessee forever? Do you just write your plays there?" It seemed like he was chiding her. "What's the new plan? Or does it not matter, so long as you're not here?"

She shook her head again, knowing she couldn't say anything about Jamie but feeling like she should. "I don't know . . ."

"Eve . . ."

"I met someone," she said, exhaling sharply once the words were out. "I didn't mean to. I didn't *plan* it. I didn't even know anyone lived in my grandmother's neighborhood. But he did, and . . . against all odds, we clicked."

Leo laughed, his hand covering his face, making his amusement seem all the more barbed. "Of course you did. Jesus fucking Christ."

"I know what it sounds like, but it really did just . . . happen."

"So you're going down there to live with him?" Leo chuckled again. "*That's* the plan?"

"I don't have a plan. I just know I was happy there."

"Yeah, because you were living in some fucking fantasy, apparently."

Eve winced at his choice of word, as it was exactly what she'd used when she was still trying to run from Jamie. She understood now why it bothered him, trivializing something that meant everything. "I don't know that this is doing us any good," she said. She picked up her bag and brought it to the foyer with the others, preparing to head out. But before leaving, she turned back to Leo with contrition in her eyes. "I really am sorry. For . . . everything."

CHAPTER 33

C'est la mort

JAMIE

What are you eating right now, Jack?"

With his mouth full, the youngster smiled brightly as he answered, "A croissant!"

"And you like it?"

"I love it," he said. "There's so much good bread in France, Eve!"

"But you know that we have these back home, right?" Jamie asked. "And that you've always refused to eat them?"

"The ones back home don't have chocolate in them."

"Some of them do," Jamie said.

"Oh. Well. I didn't know that."

Jamie laughed and turned the camera back toward himself briefly. "Four days in another country and the thing he's been most excited about is somethin' he can get at home."

"They taste better here!" Jack insisted, despite never having had one in the US. "This is the real thing."

Jamie turned the camera back on his son. "What else have you discovered in France?"

"Orangina!" Jack excitedly held up his bottle of the carbonated citrus drink.

"Anything not related to food?"

He gasped before replying, "Oh, I met Mickey and Minnie. And Buzz and Woody, and all the Disney princesses," he went on, his enthusiasm growing with each syllable. "They all spoke French! And there's a whole Marvel part of the park that we're gonna see today."

"Tell Eve about your favorite ride," Jamie suggested.

"Pirates of the Caribbean! Eve, it's the best ride," Jack shouted. "When you first walk in, you're in, like, this dungeon, and they show all these skeletons of prisoners that died in their cells. And then, the actual ride is this boat, but it's like a roller coaster, and it takes you through a whole exhibit and you see pirates and more rotted skeletons and shipwrecks and stuff from the movies. It's so creepy and cool," he said, grinning. "I can't wait 'til you get here so you can go on it with us."

"And how many times have you been on it already?"

"Six times!" Jack said. "And the line is always so long. But I promise it's worth it!"

"Today's gonna be our first day not going on it," Jamie commented to the camera, "so we'll see how that goes."

"I don't know if I'm gonna make it, Dad," Jack said with another big bite of his croissant. "I miss it already."

"We should actually be getting ready to go," Jamie said, "so I'm gonna hop in the shower. Say goodbye to Eve."

Jack waved at the camera with a chocolaty grin. "Au revoir, Eve! Joyeux Noël! Hope you're having fun in New Jersey!"

"New York," Jamie corrected him in a whisper.

"But Eve said she was flying to New Jersey."

"But she's from New York. They're very close."

"Okay, New York," Jack said. "I can't be expected to remember the states, Dad. I'm French now."

Laughing, Jamie turned the camera back on himself and blew Eve a little kiss, finishing it with a wave. "Merry Christmas. We miss you. See you soon."

Jamie hit send on the video to Eve as soon as he finished reviewing it for sound and content. His intent was to supply Eve with daily recaps, but he'd been busier and more exhausted than expected at the end of each day; plus, with the time difference, they kept missing each other's calls. Hopefully, a Christmas morning video from Jack would make up for it.

He still texted Eve frequently, regaling her with details of his adventures in a foreign country, discovering a different culture, fascinated by even the tiniest contrasts between France and the States. He told her of how he always attempted French when asking questions of the locals, but many didn't have the patience for it and generally ended up communicating in English anyway. He was also surprised that most French people didn't hate Americans as he assumed; in fact, many seemed to find him interesting somehow, wanting to know more about his life in America. The day before, walking through Montmartre, he'd met a woman with a son around Jack's age; they shared a cigarette while their kids played, and after telling her about his time at Dollywood, she swore her next trip to the US would be to Tennessee. He told her she might regret it, but she was convinced.

Jamie didn't mention in his texts how unsophisticated he often felt there, despite all the effort he'd put into appearing otherwise, from his elevated wardrobe to the upscale hotel he'd chosen. How surprised he was when Delta served dinner *and* breakfast on the plane. Or, conversely, how dopey he felt when he asked for ice water at a restaurant and learned how obnoxiously American it was. And maybe it was good that he had so much left to discover about the world, but he certainly wouldn't be reminding Eve that he was an absolute rube.

While Eve adored the video of Jack, she said what she really wanted for Christmas was FaceTime, and Jamie agreed they were past due for a catch-up. They'd been inseparable since Thanksgiving, and he liked life better that way. So on Christmas night, Jamie stayed up until 2:00 a.m., despite yet another entire day at the park, waiting for Eve to return from her parents'. And given what he knew about her relationship with them, he was fully prepared to lift her spirits, if need be.

"Did you open my gift yet?" Eve asked. Posted in front of a fuchsia wall in her best friend's apartment, she was beaming, wearing a Santa hat that barely covered her fluffy curls. Her merry smile lit up his iPad screen, doing everything in its power to close the 3,500-mile distance between them. He missed her, and the impersonality of video messaging only sharpened that twinge.

"I was waiting until I could do it with you." He proudly held the unopened package to the camera as proof. "You sure can wrap a present," he added, examining the lovely black-and-gold paper, a satiny golden ribbon tying it all together under an ornate bow. Even after traveling across the Atlantic, it was perfect.

Grinning, Jamie untied and began to strip the paper from the flat package. He let the wrapping fall to his bed and carefully opened the box, pulling from it a six-by-eight-inch wooden picture frame, painted lime green. His heart grew three sizes when he viewed the image inside it: a picture of Eve and Jack, posed in front of the Dollywood sign. Jack was wearing the wonderfully garish butterfly sunglasses Eve had picked up in the gift shop, and his grin, with all his missing teeth, was as wide as the frame. Eve, with her tongue sticking out and a smile sparkling in her eyes, looked so happy. Downright ebullient.

"It's perfect," he said. It was especially touching when he considered just how long she avoided even the subject of his son. Her heartache had dimmed her light, but he'd always been able to detect something in her beyond that sadness on the surface. It was a delight to witness her free herself from that pain.

Eve let out an audible sigh. "Yeah?"

He nodded, still studying the snapshot. They'd taken hundreds of pictures that day, and he loved them all, but this one, this gesture from Eve, was tangible evidence of just how far she, and they, had come.

"I'm so glad you walked into my life that day," he said.

"I'm so glad you saved mine," Eve said.

There was an immediate prickling in Jamie's cheeks, and a cursory glance at his image in the corner of the screen confirmed his pinkened face. He was uncomfortable with taking credit for such a thing. "Same here," he said. "I was just . . . existing. Jack was my life, he still is, but . . . it wasn't until you came along that I realized just how much I was missing out on."

Eve shook her head again, her bright smile dimming slightly. "I miss you."

"I miss you, too."

"I wish I'd come with you."

"It went that bad at your parents', huh?"

"I don't know," she said, her grin disappearing completely. "I'm not sure what I was looking for here. I thought I missed *them.* I thought coming home would smooth things over, I guess. But I should've known they'd never make it easy on me."

Jamie stared back at her, the dejection on her face making him wish he hadn't let her do this alone. They didn't know each other well enough for him to accompany her home, not really; but still, he should've. "Fuck parents," he said. "You already know how I feel about my mom."

"It's funny how when you're a kid, you think your parents know everything. We're deluded into believing they're always right. And it's a little astonishing to come to terms with the fact that they're just people, too."

"I worry about Jack realizing that about me . . ."

"You either die a hero or live long enough to see yourself become the villain."

"That's bleak," Jamie chuckled. "That's exactly why we don't do DC around here."

"For what it's worth, I don't think you, or Jack, have to worry about that."

"His mother, on the other hand . . ."

"I mean, no one's got it all."

They laughed, leaving Jamie sighing a bit wistfully as he gazed out the window ahead, the City of Light staring back at him. He wasn't used to anything so vibrant at three in the morning. When he stood on the terrace, he could practically reach out and touch the Eiffel Tower—it was the very reason he chose the Shangri-La hotel, and still, he sat in disbelief that he was here.

Before Eve, the notion had never even crossed his mind. Traveling outside the country was nothing more than an abstract concept, sitting on a shelf he always thought was out of his reach. Corny as it sounded, she'd actually changed his world.

"I um . . . I hope there's some way you can get your gift before you leave," he said, snapping out of his trance. "I can't exactly buy it on Amazon." Eve's face wrinkled with what he initially perceived as intrigue, until it clearly transformed into something else that he couldn't pinpoint but worried him all the same. "What is it?"

"No, it's nothing." She tried to muster that happy smile again, but it was only an echo of the one before.

"If you can't get it, it's not that big a deal. It's nothin' fancy."

"It's not that."

"Well, what's wrong?" he asked, an encouraging grin on his lips. "I'm realizing it's not as easy for me to read you in New York."

Eve scratched her forehead in a clear attempt at hiding her face before speaking. "How would you feel if . . . I come back a little later than we planned?"

Jamie smiled awkwardly, like she'd just spoken to him in French. "How do you mean?"

"I mean, I won't be able to make it to Paris." When he didn't respond, she went on, "And I'll probably need an extra few weeks to finish this draft, once and for all."

He inhaled sharply, feeling himself deflate with every word that fell out of her mouth. This was it. The moment he'd worried about since she decided to go home for Christmas. The nagging premonition that she would slip away from him was fulfilling itself. Her exciting New York life, her ex-fiancé, or whatever he was, had stolen her. It left his stomach churning. "I see . . ."

"I saw my agent yesterday, and she mentioned that my play

is in conversations for some prestigious awards. It's ridiculous, by my estimation," Eve laughed. "But shit, maybe it's not."

"Sounds like a big deal."

"It could be?" Her grin was slight and timid, as if she was waiting for him to approve. "I don't know, but I just—"

"I knew you were gonna do this," Jamie interrupted. "I fuckin' knew it."

Eve looked taken aback by his response, and he immediately felt like shit for being so severe. He wanted to be happy for her. He would've been on any other day. But he was self-aware enough to recognize that his patience was wearing thin.

"I'm not 'doing' anything," she said. "I just need to focus on work for a bit. But I'll be back."

"When?"

"You want an exact date?"

"Ballpark it."

"I don't quite know," she said. "I told Stella I'd have my draft done mid-January, so I should be able to come back to Tennessee for a couple of weeks after that. But then I'll need to gear up for *Gamba* rehearsals in February." She shook her head. "It's all a little chaotic, I'll admit, but until we figure it out, we can keep seeing each other on weekends. It can be just like it was."

"I don't want it to be like it was, Eve. I thought we were agreeing to move forward here."

"And we are. We will. But it's not like it would kill us to slow it down a little," she said. "I mean, six months ago, I was engaged to someone else."

Jamie couldn't argue with that. He'd always wondered about that random late-night call from her ex, and now, he had to question whether this abrupt change of heart involved him, too.

"What's so different all of a sudden?" he asked. "You've been there a day."

"I know. But being home . . . I'm reminded of what I left behind. It feels irresponsible to just pack up and leave again."

Jamie nodded. "Do you think it was irresponsible to get involved with me?"

"That's . . . not the word I would use."

"I see . . ."

"We moved so fast," Eve appended. She looked and sounded so regretful about it, he almost felt guilty. "And, Jamie, I love you. I meant that. But if we have any chance of making it, you cannot be the only good thing in my life."

Jamie stopped to consider her argument. It hurt, but she was right. And it wouldn't be fair to be mad at her for doing what was in her best interests.

But he needed to do the same. And maybe his best interests weren't in someone who constantly treated him, and his son, as auxiliary to her real life. "You're right," he said. "You spent six months telling me you didn't wanna be in a relationship, and I should've listened." He did feel guilty.

"That is not what I'm saying."

"No, I know. But . . . I think you're right that a break is probably in order."

It was Eve's turn to deflate, her wounded expression matching the way she'd made him feel. "But I'm not asking for a break. I just want to keep doing what we've been doing."

"A pause, a standstill, dress it up how you want. We're not moving forward, right?"

"But it's not forever. I just need time to do this, and then we can figure out the next move. The right move. For both of us."

"I *just* introduced you to my son, Eve." Jamie now scratched his forehead, attempting to hide his faltering facade. He couldn't figure out whether to be mad or sad. "I can't let him fall victim to your whims."

"I'm not sure that's fair," Eve said. "You have to know that I didn't agree lightly to meeting Jack. If you trusted me then, you should be able to now. I'm not Lucy."

"No, I'm very clear on that," Jamie said. "You're Eve, who told everyone in New York she'd be gone for 'three months,' and we see how that turned out. Ignoring your agent. Your parents. You run from things." He felt bad for holding that against her, but he'd seen enough of her fickleness firsthand to know he couldn't put faith in her promises. "I don't know how to trust that this isn't just you running from me."

"Wow." Eve laughed, but it was clear she wasn't amused, tears surfacing before she could say anything else. "Wow . . ."

Jamie looked down from the screen, the picture of her with Jack staring back at him, reminding him of what a good time they had together. Taunting him. Because before Eve, he couldn't pinpoint the last time he'd had fun. Of course, the joy of raising his son was unparalleled, but there had also been nothing quite like the small but potent thrill of being with someone he liked. The heart flutter he got when he caught her feeling the same. He hated that that wasn't enough; not for her, and not for him. But after Lucy, he simply could not risk being with someone who could hurt his kid.

"I'm sorry." He swallowed visibly, the lump in his throat making his voice hoarse. "But for so long, I've been so willing to accept whatever I've been given. Even these . . . little pieces of affection from you. I can't keep doing that to myself."

"I, um . . . I'm gonna go," Eve said. There was a tremble in her voice that broke his heart, and he continued to avoid the screen.

"I don't mean to be harsh," he said, "but—"

"No, I get it. You two enjoy your trip. And if you wanna talk after you get back . . . maybe after you've had some time to sit with it, I'll be here."

"Okay," he said, nodding. "You take care of yourself, Eve."

She ended the call without another word, the screen going dark just as traces of regret seemed to fill Jamie's ritzy hotel room. It wasn't lost on him, the irony of being in a place literally named for the idea of a utopia. *Shangri-la.* And here he was, entering his personal hell.

He hated irony.

CHAPTER 34

Mon, Dec 29 10:13 AM

Eve Ambroise: Hey, I'm not sure what your plans are, but I can be in Gatlinburg after the 1st. If you want to talk, or anything.

Wed, Dec 31 4:16 PM

Eve Ambroise: Are you just not going to answer?

Sat, Jan 3 7:12 PM

Eve Ambroise: Jamie.

Sat, Jan 3 8:14 PM

Eve Ambroise: Seriously?

Mon, Jan 5 9:03 PM

Eve Ambroise: Listen, I'm so sorry for every time I made you feel as though I didn't care. I recognize it's what's made it difficult to trust me now. But I'm literally begging you not to do this.

Tue, Jan 6 2:13 AM

Eve Ambroise: I feel ridiculous incessantly texting someone who clearly has no interest in responding, but I miss you. So much. Even the few minutes we spent on FaceTime were profoundly better than all the time I've had to spend without you this week. I fucked up. If you let me, I'll try to fix it.

Eve Ambroise: I gave you so much of me, Jamie. I couldn't give you everything, and I understand that's what's compounded my choice to stay. But I gave you what I could. I'm sorry it wasn't enough.

Eve Ambroise: But I didn't take the easy route. You pushed me, and I allowed you to, because I wanted this.

Eve Ambroise: You have to protect yourself. And Jack. I get that. After what you've been through, you should. So if you really think I'll hurt you, if you truly believe I'm bad for you, I'll accept that. It makes sense. It's just been a few months. We could move on fairly easily at this point. But Jamie, if any part of you still wants this too, then please talk to me.

Tue, Jan 6 3:12 AM

Eve Ambroise: I cannot believe you're ignoring me right now.

Eve Ambroise: Of course, I didn't birth any of your children, so I guess I don't get the same benefit of the doubt as the woman who cheated on you

Eve Ambroise: If I'd known this would be your reaction, I never would've encouraged you to grow a spine

Eve Ambroise: I hate that I ever trusted you

Tue, Jan 6 4:01 AM

Jamie Gallagher: Likewise.

CHAPTER 35

It Hurts Like Hell

EVE

As Eve's phone vibrated against her pillow, she opened her eyes to sunlight beaming through the windows after a long, sleepless night. She peered at her device to see the time and date: 9:41 a.m., January 12. She'd been holed up in Maya's guest room—which was really Maya's home gym—for a week now, unable to move much farther than the air mattress that inhabited it. She was living on a prayer that Jamie had come to his senses and retracted that last shitty text he'd sent—the only thing he'd said to her since tearing her heart in half. But the message that stirred her wasn't from him; rather, it was Stella, requesting a meeting that week, undoubtedly about the script she had yet to send her. Eve typed out a quick message—*When?*—and then threw her phone back on the bed.

In the week after New Year's, Eve had gone back to Gatlinburg, supposedly to pick up the few things she'd brought with her in June, but a small part of her hoped, however irrational, that she'd find Jamie there. That he'd returned from Paris early, even if only to come back to his cabin and ignore her. She could've taken that. Something to hang her hat on. Anything would've been better than the silence.

But he never showed up.

It was her own fault. She knew that. She understood it probably better than he did. She wished she could chalk this up to his jet lag—lack of sleep can make people mean—but she'd been too ambivalent for him to feel anything resembling secure in their relationship.

It was over.

It was hard to believe, considering their time at Dollywood. She thought she was getting a fairy-tale ending, Prince Charming and all that, but there was a reason she never believed in them before now. Even as a typical Disney millennial, she knew those stories were flights of fancy. She was the age of many of those princesses when she realized that reality was crushing and cruel; falling in love at sixteen was nothing but a recipe for disaster. Same for thirty-four, it turned out.

Eve returned to New York, having nowhere else to go, belonging to no one. It hurt to be in Gatlinburg, her apartment in Brooklyn was no longer hers, and her parents would just make her feel worse. So she went to the only place she felt welcome. While Maya had never been shy in telling Eve about herself—they first bonded after an argument in their freshman seminar—she was also incredibly generous with her love. Quite the opposite of Eve, who doled hers out in small doses, fearing what might happen if she gave it all at once. Clearly, a valid concern.

At Maya's, Eve did little more than sulk. Maya and/or Siobhan would come by her room every now and then, sometimes with food. Maya's little black cocker spaniel, Lil' Freedia, sat by her side for much of the day, which lifted Eve's spirits marginally. But for the most part, it was just her with her thoughts. She replied to a couple of texts, and only in one-word answers, just so friends knew she was alive. But was she? She was turning back into the woman she used to be. Not even slowly, but in a sharp, steady descent back into madness.

Mon, Jan 12 9:56 AM

Stella Fischer-Fox: Are you available today? If so, you are welcome to come to the office, or we can do lunch in your neck of the woods.

Eve wanted to blow off Stella for the hundredth time, but the wrench in her stomach told her it was time to face the music. Even if Stella wanted to drop her as a client, which she had every reason to do, avoiding her wouldn't change the outcome. So Eve agreed to meet at her office and finally forced herself out of bed.

Eve lacked the energy for hair or makeup, so she only pulled her hair into a ponytail, ignoring the frizz that she would normally try to tamp down in the name of professionalism. She used some Carmex to brighten her lips and wore her glasses instead of contacts in an effort to conceal the lifelessness. It was snowing, so she also didn't concern herself with dressing nicely—not that she would've anyway. Jeans and a sweater with some boots and a North Face coat she borrowed from Maya, as her own was packed in a duffel bag somewhere. She trudged through the slush to the Ralph Avenue station and took the C straight to Thirty-Fourth Street.

Stella's office was on the fourteenth floor of PENN 1, sitting just beside Madison Square Garden, and one of the sixty tallest buildings in the city. Eve typically felt like something of a big shot, strolling into this massive building to see her *agent*. On the agency's website, her name sat alongside a slew of Broadway heavyweights—directors and designers she'd dreamed of working with, other playwrights she admired. It helped her believe that her work was worth paying attention to.

But that day, she felt small as she made her way up to Stella's office, anticipating being dismissed. If she hadn't been so abruptly dumped just two weeks ago, Eve would've assumed *this* was the worst feeling in the world.

The receptionist at the Hayslett Group was a bubbly young Puerto Rican guy, Matthew, who dressed impeccably and always greeted Eve with compliments and coffee. Predictably, he skipped the flattery that day—it took only a cursory glance to assess that she was a mess—and sent her straight to Stella. He did have a flat white ready for her, complete with a heart rendered in the foam, but that just felt like a gesture of sympathy portending her dismissal.

"It's good to see you," Stella greeted her. She shut the door behind Eve and then took the seat beside her instead of at her desk. She stared at Eve, scrutinizing her with narrowed hazel eyes, as if she could figure out what the hell was wrong with her client through careful observation.

"Are you okay?" Stella asked, the bluntness in her Long Island accent surprising.

Eve wanted to say yes, hopeful that Stella would be polite enough to ignore the obvious lie. There was clearly *something* wrong with her. But before words could materialize, her eyes brimmed with hot tears and immediately spilled to her cheeks.

She swallowed hard, feeling frozen and overwhelmed as she simply tried to remember how to breathe. Tried not to be frustrated with her inability to control her own body as another panic attack took hold of her faculties.

Eve involuntarily balled her hands into fists and voluntarily squeezed her eyes shut. She then remembered what Jamie taught her and reopened them. She focused on Stella, the flecks of brown dotting her otherwise moss-green irises. The pattern in the wool of her juniper dress. The tiny diamond studs adorning her tiny ears. She waited for sounds—the chatter outside Stella's office, the ding of the elevators, the sound of sirens. There were always sirens in New York, from some distance or another. Quite the opposite of Tennessee.

Eve breathed slowly through her mouth, her gaze still on Stella as she worked to knock away all traces of panic. She hoped Stella understood that this wasn't intentional; she was genuinely suffering here.

Stella turned her entire body toward Eve, her stare softening into something closer to concerned. "Eve. What happened?"

Eve's instinct was to chuckle at the loaded question. Where would she even start? But her laugh came out as a tiny yelp, and before she knew it, her vision had blurred with tears again.

"You said you were distracted, but it feels like something else. Something . . . more? We can still put a pause on all of this if it's—"

"I think I'm losing my mind," Eve blurted. The second the words came out, she was gasping for air as if the very expression had taken it away. "I had a son when I was seventeen and my parents made me give him away. And I never stop thinking about him," she said, through gulps and sobs. "They sent me away and they took my baby, and they didn't care." She stopped speaking because her sentences were turning to gibberish beneath her tears. She just let herself cry.

Doubled over in her chair, she hugged her knees like her barely born son and allowed her weeps to fill Stella's small office, unconcerned with who might hear. She cried for the son she never got to know. She cried for her miscarriages. She cried for Leo. She cried for what she'd done. She cried for what she didn't do. She cried for finding Jamie when she had no right to be happy. She cried for losing him just when she started to believe she deserved that happiness. She cried for disappointing her parents and then alienating them. She cried for deserting her grandmother, even in her twilight. She cried for knowing some of these things weren't her fault, but needing to take the blame anyway. She cried for every moment she'd wanted to die over the past year, and for all the times she felt alive.

She was sobbing so hard, she wasn't sure she wouldn't pass out, but she was desperately grateful for Stella's embrace as she gently coaxed her to let it all out.

"It's okay," Stella promised, stroking her back. "You're okay."

As her wails slowly turned to sniffles, Eve felt empty. Not in a bad way, necessarily, but as if she'd gotten rid of this thing she'd been carrying for too long. Pent-up emotions that had been neglected for months, maybe years. Definitely years. Her face and neck were drenched, leaving her cold, but she felt . . . better.

"I keep fucking up," she said quietly to Stella. "I wanted to write. I tried to finish this play. But I feel like I have no idea what I'm doing."

"You put so much pressure on yourself," Stella lamented. "I don't even know if you're aware of it, but I wish you would give yourself a break."

Eve smiled sadly. "I tried to. When I left New York, I broke up with Leo." She waited for Stella to respond, but she said nothing. No judgment, no questions. Nothing. "I went to Tennessee to get away from everything that made me feel anything," she went on. "And then I met this guy. Jamie. And he did the opposite."

"That doesn't sound so bad," Stella said.

"I think I fell in love with him," Eve said, but quickly corrected herself. "I *know* I did. But then I came back home, and I'm realizing that I've been stuck in a holding pattern. And I don't have any business loving anyone right now."

"Says who?"

Eve sniffled. "Says him."

"I'm sure that's not true," Stella said. "Couples fight. Me and Jonah had an argument just this morning."

Eve shook her head, a fresh set of tears beginning to trickle. "He doesn't trust me," she said. She always figured Jamie would get sick of her; it was why she kept the wall up for so long. At least then she could say it was because she was an asshole. But things falling apart just when she was letting him in felt especially wicked. "And he probably shouldn't."

"You should go to him," Stella suggested. "Like in the movies. Go to Tennessee and give the big 'I'm sorry' speech. It's subversive because you're a woman apologizing to a man. Even if it does go against everything we stand for."

Eve chuckled, genuinely amused and appreciative of the laugh. But barring the fact that she'd already done that once, it would be an invasion this time. "I've thought about that, but . . . if he wanted to see me, he would've said so. He doesn't play games," she said, wiping more errant tears. "If he still wanted this, I'd know it."

It was that simple. Jamie was done. And with impeccable irony, he'd left her the same way she had Leo—bluntly, abruptly, and then going ghost afterward. Poetic justice, she supposed.

She fucking hated irony.

CHAPTER 36

The Bottom

JAMIE

Fri, Jan 16 3:44 PM

Casey Gallagher: Dude. I ask for pics of my nephew and you ignore me? Unbelievably rude.

Casey Gallagher: Also btw, mom has officially moved back in with dad. Hilarious. But I lowkey hope they make it? They're kinda cute, as it turns out.

Jamie awoke to the din of some relentless buzz, sending him shooting up from his couch in a stupor. With his head pounding, he wasn't quite sure the sound was even real until he recognized it as his doorbell, and he cursed the unexpected visitor. He padded slowly toward his security system, seeing Lucy and Jack waiting to be let up.

"What the hell?" he mumbled to himself; still, he let them in without comment.

He moved as fast as he could to clean up the mess of takeout containers and whiskey sitting on his coffee table, his son running into the apartment just as the clink of empty bottles hit the bottom of the garbage can. He was wholly unprepared to see Jack, or anyone else for that matter, but he plastered on a smile as the kid beelined toward him for a hug.

"Hey, you," Jamie greeted him, rubbing his back. "What are you doin' here, bud?"

"I live here," Jack said. He casually pulled off his backpack as they separated, throwing it on the breakfast table. "Is Eve here?"

Jamie's head started pounding even harder with the reminder that he'd have to explain himself to his son. Why the woman he'd suddenly brought into their lives was gone just as quickly. "Where's your mom?" he asked instead.

"She's coming," Jack said. "I think she's not feeling good."

"I'm feeling fine," Lucy called from the living room, though her tone said exactly the opposite. Once they were all in the same room, she appended, "Jack, do me a favor and go upstairs, sweetie."

Jamie tried to ready himself for the argument undoubtedly on its way, and he was sorely tempted to take another shot just to dull the aggravation that would come with it. As Jack scurried off, he regarded Lucy, noticing her protruding belly, which seemed to have doubled in size since the last time he saw her nearly three weeks ago. It felt like another punch in the gut. "What are you doing here?" he asked.

"Despite my best efforts, you do have physical custody of our son, so . . . I'm bringing him back, per our arrangement."

"But why today? You bring him back on Sunday, not Friday."

"You said I could have him for a week. Friday to Friday is a week."

Jamie sighed at the avoidable miscommunication. But then, he hadn't been very good at communicating as of late. "I can't have him right now," he said, plopping himself into the nearest chair.

"Are you sick?" she asked. "Is that why you locked me out of your apartment?"

"Lucy . . ."

"I didn't come to fight," she retorted.

"Good, because I don't have the energy to," Jamie said. He set down his metaphorical knife and surrendered his bad attitude. "I changed the code to my apartment because it's my apartment," he said. "I realized I can't just have you walking in here whenever you want."

"Is this about Eve?" Lucy asked. "Because I'm glad you're happy and all, but I'm not sure it's fair of you to rearrange our lives just for her."

Jamie rubbed his head, debating whether to be honest about Eve or tell Lucy to mind her fucking business. "It has nothing to do with her. It's about me, deserving privacy. I can't move on with my life if I keep letting you waltz into it whenever you feel like it."

Lucy also yielded, taking a tentative seat beside him. Ordinarily, she would've broken into a much longer protest, but it seemed that she really didn't want to argue. Jack was probably right that she wasn't feeling well. "I have something to ask you," she said.

"What is it?"

She looked nervous, which worried Jamie, his head thumping harder as he awaited her words. "We . . . found a house. I think."

He squinted at her choice of phrase. "You *think*?"

"It's not my favorite of the ones we've seen, but it's nice enough. Outside needs work. But it's got all new renovations inside, space for Jack and for this one," she said, stroking her belly, "and a good-sized backyard."

"And where is it?"

Lucy pinched her lips defiantly before answering. "Antioch."

Jamie chuckled at her reaction, spitting the word like it had ants in it. "Well, what's wrong with that?"

"It's thirty minutes from here. And from the school. And that's without traffic."

Jamie was already looking forward to putting some space between them. He deserved it and she needed it, apparently, even if only to get used to the idea of no longer relying on him. "It's not the end of the world," he said. "It just means planning better. Fewer impromptu visits, maybe."

"I'm sure you'd love that."

Jamie released a long breath, his impatience running neck and neck with his curiosity at that point. "So what does this have to do with me? Don't tell me you need more time in the house."

"I need a loan," she said, her copper eyes flitting to the floor as she bit her bottom lip. She sat back in her seat and cradled her belly, leaving Jamie wondering if the reminder she was with child was meant to evoke sympathy or something like it. She knew full well that he was going to do it, simply because he had the means, and he would never let Jack's mother languish. But he thought of Casey, and his mother, and even Eve, and he felt inclined to say no. How long was he supposed to take care of her? How long would he have to be the bigger person?

His stomach churned as his thoughts of Eve turned sour, still unsure, three weeks later, whether he'd made the right choice.

"Don't banks give out loans?" Jamie asked.

"For the down payment," she said. "We've got about fifteen thousand saved. Another fifteen would be a godsend right now. Especially with the baby coming."

"You don't have to keep reminding me that you're pregnant, Lucy. I have eyes. I have a heart. I know why you're asking."

"I feel lousy even asking, but I know—"

"You know I'd do anything for Jack, so why not take advantage?"

"Whoa," she said, clearly taken aback by his terseness. "If you don't want to, you can just say no. I don't need the shitty insults attached."

"Yeah well . . ." Jamie sniffled several times as he scratched the hair at his nape. "I guess I'm in a shitty mood."

Lucy frowned. "What is wrong with you?"

"There is nothing wrong with me," he said. "I just wish you didn't look at me like a cash machine."

"It's a loan, Jamie. I'm trying to get out of your house, like you asked. I got a job at Nashville General, so I can pay you back regularly. We just need some help."

It was tactless, but Jamie did inwardly question whether she had actually gotten a job. She'd stopped working when Jack was born and hadn't really looked back. "I don't have the energy for this," he mumbled, holding his hammering forehead with both hands. "Can you take Jack and just . . . go? Let me think about it."

"Are you sick?" she asked again. He could feel her hand on

his back as she asked, "Did something else happen with your dad?"

"No. I just drank too much."

"Well, that doesn't sound like you. What happened?"

"What happened?" he sighed again. His eyes felt so heavy, he wasn't sure they were open. "That's a loaded question."

"Is it?"

"What happened is . . . I have no idea how to be happy. Because you cheated on me, Lucy, and it fucked me up so much, I don't even trust what's in front of me." He looked at her, waiting for her expression to change. He knew her concerned act would last only so long as she felt superior to him. "I hate that you get everything you want."

She let her hand fall from his back. "You're a mean drunk."

"Please take Jack home," he pled. "I can't be around him like this."

"This isn't how I wanted things, Jamie." Her voice was so low, he could barely hear her over the pulsating. "I can't take it back. It's unfair that you're bearing the brunt of it. But I am sorry."

He didn't respond.

"When you stop feeling sorry for yourself, I hope you remember that you're the one who won. You have the money, you have all the power. I need your permission to have our son for longer than two days. Here I am begging you to help me buy a house. So no, I didn't get everything I want. I am paying for my sins. At a certain point, whatever's wrong with your life is on you."

Jamie nodded. "Which is why I changed the code."

"Fair enough," she said with a small, woeful chuckle. She carefully pulled herself up from the table and started toward the staircase. But first, she turned back to gaze at him. "Will you really think about it?"

They both knew he was going to give her the money, so there was no point in the charade. Noblesse oblige, as the French would say. "Please let this be the last favor you ask of me."

Sitting in his truck in the cold, Jamie stared at his text message thread with Eve, reliving the agony of watching her texts go from apologetic to apoplectic, all while he ignored her, having convinced himself he couldn't respond for his own good. He replied with something stupidly dismissive, just to make it stop, and he'd spent the last week trying, failing, not to regret it. But in fact, it was rather tragic to see their whirlwind romance draw to a close like that, not with a bang but a whimper of misery. It was probably in their best interests to go their separate ways, but Eve didn't deserve that. So, he sat there repeatedly typing and erasing messages, unable to find a simple, sincere set of words to convey what he needed to say.

He only wished he hadn't been stupid enough to involve Jack in this. He and Eve were adults; their attachment to each other would wane sooner than later. As Eve said, it had only been a few months. But he foolishly brought some stranger into his kid's life, knowing he was taking a risk, and wanting so badly to believe in it, in her, he did so without thinking of the consequences if it didn't work out. In the end, he was angrier with himself than with Eve.

He started again, typing a response—*I'm sor*—but then, again, erased it.

Instead, Jamie put his car in drive and took off aimlessly. He'd woken up hungry and hungover and got in his car with the intention of finding breakfast. Perhaps a Waffle House cheesesteak melt to work its miraculous healing powers. But his thoughts had him wandering, and before Jamie knew it, he was on I-40 headed west.

He didn't know what brought him to his dad's house; perhaps feeling lost, it made sense to make his way home. But there was a very specific longing that sat in the pit of his stomach, he realized, as he started up the walkway to his father's door. He just wanted a hug. Reassurance that he wasn't completely fucking up. As a parent, he often had to feign confidence, pretend he had any clue what he was doing at any given moment. But he'd run out of the ability to bluff. He just wanted his dad to tell him everything was okay.

But it was Jamie's mother who answered the door, looking like she was in the middle of a spa treatment. Her gray hair was wrapped in a towel, her clothes baggy and comfortable, and her face plastered in bright green goop. They were both perplexed by each other's appearance.

"Is . . . my dad here?" Jamie asked, feeling like a child as he said it.

"He's not, but come on in," Diane said, ushering him in from the thirty-degree day. "He went grocery shopping a little bit ago."

His dad was one of those types to wander up and down every aisle instead of making a list of necessary items. It always annoyed

Jamie and Casey, as it meant his trips to Kroger took actual hours.

"I had no idea you were coming," Diane said as they both settled in the den. "Your dad didn't mention it." She was hastily clearing the coffee table as she spoke, a small pile of candy wrappers, strawberry Creme Savers, sitting at the edge. Jamie remembered her always having a stash of them at the top of her dresser when he was a kid. He didn't even know they still made them.

"I didn't tell him I was coming," Jamie admitted. He felt like he was intruding.

"Oh, well. You're a nice surprise, then," Diane said, smiling at him warmly. "As you can see, we're doing absolutely nothing."

On his way in the room, Jamie did catch a glimpse of their sixty-inch television, where a commercial boasted a *90 Day Fiancé* marathon. Currently on the screen, a young interracial couple was pushing a baby stroller around a bagel shop.

"You ever watch this show?" Diane asked, noticing his regard. When Jamie shook his head, she said, "Some of the characters are absurd, but it's a very intriguing look at the different ways relationships can work."

"Sounds interesting," he replied apathetically.

When he didn't say anything else, Diane muted the TV and turned to her son with an eager smile. "You have something on your mind." It was a question, but it sounded more like a knowing statement.

Jamie unthinkingly started to grind his teeth as he decided whether to engage her. On one hand, she was obviously right. He had a million things on his mind. But he'd no intention of talking to *her* about it; he barely liked to acknowledge her existence. On the other hand, Diane had proven herself most useful when he was on the outs with Eve. Taking his mind off her, at least.

"I don't know if I wanna say," he admitted.

"Well now you have to tell me." She sat cross-legged on the sectional, offering him her undivided attention.

Jamie smiled, amused by how little she was affected by his enmity. "Well . . . I guess talking to you wouldn't be the worst thing in the world."

"Imagine that," she said with a grin.

"Please don't say anything like 'I told you so.' "

"I wouldn't dream of it," she said. "Just let the record show, people are capable of change. Even you."

He wished that were true. He really wanted it to be. "I don't know if I've changed so much as you've worn me down, but . . ."

Diane laughed. More of a giggle, really. "I'll take that."

"Is that how you got my dad back?"

"That's entirely possible."

"Seriously." He paused, realizing perhaps he'd driven to Memphis, unwittingly, to see his mother. "How did you come back from such an egregious fuckup?"

"Well, for starters, twenty years is a long time to hold a grudge," Diane said pointedly. "But the simple answer is I was honest. And I know you hate it, but your dad loves me. He just . . . forgave me."

Jamie let out a gentle chuckle. "I don't hate it."

"You do. And it's okay."

"I don't," he insisted. And he was pretty sure he was being honest. "I just can't relate, I guess."

"Well, you're a Pisces, so that makes sense."

"Horoscopes aren't real, you know."

"Says who?"

"Anyone with common sense. They're just generic enough to apply to anyone."

Diane paused and then exhaled, her gray eyes relaying a playful disappointment as she shook her head. "You're so cynical. Is that my fault?"

"Probably," Jamie said. "You ruining our family was my coming-of-age story."

"Would you have preferred if I'd died?"

"It might've fucked me up a little less," he said, both of them laughing. "Maybe I wouldn't have ended up with Lucy."

"Oh *god*." She groaned dramatically, sounding exhausted on his behalf. "Where did you find that awful woman anyway?"

Jamie wore a pensive smirk as he recalled crossing paths with Lucy on Honky Tonk Highway his first week in Nashville. "We met at a bar," he said.

"Of course you did."

"For what it's worth, we had a lot of good years together. And I wouldn't have Jack without her."

"While that's all fine, well, and good, Sammy said she didn't want to marry you, and I simply find that peculiar."

Jamie felt a sudden stinging in his eyes, fighting tears for reasons unknown. Something about his mother's words comforting him in a moment when he needed to be comforted. He liked the way she called his dad "Sammy," simultaneously bringing him back to his childhood and to Evie. He missed them both.

"Lucy went about it the wrong way," he said, sniffling, "but she was correct that we weren't right for each other. Might've saved me in the end."

"For the girl you told me about? Eve?"

"I don't think so . . ." He bit his lip as he tried to think of a way that could be true. "But who knows," he said. "Maybe so. Or maybe for someone else."

"Either way. You're probably right."

Jamie looked down contemplatively, noticing that at some point, he'd leisurely propped his feet on the coffee table, and he and Diane looked like two old friends chatting. "By any chance, do you remember when I got my acceptance letter from Vandy?" he asked her.

"'Course I do. Vanderbilt and U of M came on the same day, if I recall correctly."

"Oh yeah . . ."

"Why do you ask?"

"I applied again," he confessed. "And . . . I got in."

"Jamie!" She swatted his leg excitedly, and even under the green goo, her face lit up in a way that told him she was genuinely proud. Of him and for him. "That's incredible."

"I guess."

"I didn't even know that was something you'd been thinking about."

"I didn't either until . . ." He stopped short of mentioning Eve and shrugged to himself. "I'd been putting it off forever. Finally decided to just get it over with."

"I'm happy for you." Diane was nodding her approval. "Truly."

"Thanks . . . Mom." The word sounded foreign on his tongue, but he felt like he could get used to it. He wanted to.

"Is that why you're here? To celebrate?"

"The opposite," he said, still stewing in his vacillating feelings. Jamie wiped the corner of his eye as that tear he'd been holding on to threatened to fall. "I don't know. Just havin' a bad day."

"Okay," she replied, her tone abnormally gentle. "Is it okay if I celebrate, then?"

Jamie looked at her dubiously. "What does that mean . . . ?"

"I just wanna hug you."

"Oh. Yeah. Okay." Jamie was skeptical, but the two of them rose from the couch simultaneously. He wrapped his arm around her slight frame and instantly melted as she did the same. She smelled like green tea and strawberries, and it was as frustrating as it was heartening that she'd given him the exact thing he was looking for.

Jamie always thought of it as a cliché, but as it turned out, that didn't make it any less true: Forgiveness really is for the forgiver.

CHAPTER 37

The Climb

EVE

Wed, Feb 25 12:12 PM

Stefani Clemmons: Hey, sis. Just letting you know that Roundabout had to move us from the 12th floor to the 10th. Otherwise, we are ALL SET for rehearsals! I'm so, so excited to see your work in action!

Stefani Clemmons: Also, you're still not available Wednesdays, right? Want to make sure we have everyone accounted for as far as office space and time.

Eve Ambroise: Not on Wednesday afternoons. But I will 100% be there (and anywhere else you need me) otherwise. I can't wait to see you and *your* work in action!

"So. What's on your mind today, Eve?"

Eve stared at her psychologist, Dr. Garvey, for far too long, trying to conjure a suitable response. Because whenever she asked, the answer was essentially the same—Jamie. He'd been on her mind for two months now, which was the last time she'd heard from him. And each day was a little easier, the pain subsiding a little bit more, at least, but he wasn't gone from her head or heart. Not really.

But after her full-fledged breakdown in Stella's office, Eve knew she needed help. More than the temporary bandage that Tennessee provided. More than the balm of Jamie and his wonderful life. More than even the welcoming arms and support of her closest friends. She needed to heal. And she wasn't going to do that in Gatlinburg, with all those memories of Jamie plaguing her. She also no longer wanted to be alone. Maybe she never did.

So Eve firmly planted herself in New York. After a hellish search and a referral from one of the actors in *Gamba,* she was able to get into a cute enough two-bedroom in Crown Heights with lots of windows and a rooftop deck showing off Manhattan. It was barely affordable, but Eve had learned she couldn't put a price on her sanity. So now, two months into the new year, she had a play debuting in eight weeks, a new apartment to house all her troubles, and . . . she was trying therapy again.

Because Leo was right. Maya was right. Even her parents were right, to some degree. She couldn't keep meandering through her life half-fulfilled. She couldn't keep ignoring the pain eating away at her. It put her to bed and was waiting at the door when she woke up. It wasn't working, walking around like she didn't notice it following. She couldn't outrun it. So it was time to face it.

But having been in therapy for a few weeks now, it was grueling to sit there and examine it all. It felt like having open heart surgery without the anesthetic.

Still, she showed up every Wednesday at 2:00 p.m., ready to

do the hard work. After auditioning three other doctors Maya helped her find, she'd finally settled on this one, Dr. Jocelyn Kootin-Garvey. Eve had been very clear that she wanted a Black female counselor, the non-Black women of the past having failed her. She was lucky to be in New York, where that was an easier task than in a lot of other places.

She'd chosen Dr. Garvey because she specialized in trauma-focused cognitive behavioral therapy. But Eve also just liked the way she looked. She had a kind face, and she was well put together. She wore her natural hair cropped and dark blond, and she rocked a flawless red lip in her profile picture that immediately told Eve she knew what she was doing. In her videos, she spoke crisply. She was succinct but warm. She seemed like someone Eve could be friends with. And then Dr. Garvey made it clear in her first visit that they would absolutely *not* be friends, which Eve enjoyed, too.

Her office was painted a soothing sage green with walls full of books, which always put Eve at ease. Her furniture was contemporary but comfortable—big, cushy gray chairs sitting on a shaggy off-white rug. The space was big but still felt cozy, Eve noticed, as she sat there for almost an hour each week. She'd been with Dr. Garvey for only a month now, so they'd just scratched the surface of her many issues, but Eve liked her.

"I saw Leo the other day," Eve said, taking a deep breath. "Got some furniture from the old apartment."

In Eve's first two sessions, most of the focus was on her parents, which took up a lot of space, as they tended to do. Their last meeting was easier, as it was spent mostly on Maya and her other meaningful friendships. Proof that she wasn't all bad. But she'd been doling out information about Leo and Jamie little by little, not wanting to delve into her biggest mistakes. But it was silly to keep avoiding the reason she was there.

"You wanna talk about him?" When Eve shrugged, Dr. Garvey nodded and sat back in her chair. She crossed her legs and set her notepad in her lap. "Let's talk about Leo."

Eve didn't know whether to start with the good or the bad—not that there was a whole lot of either; for the bulk of their five years together, things were uneventful. Boring. They met, fell into mutual like, and they tolerated each other. He supported her financially while she was a fledgling playwright, and less so once she started teaching; she supported him emotionally while he processed the trauma attached to his father.

There it was, the parent thing again. In previous sessions, she talked with Dr. Garvey about how her parents' expectations weighed her down. But her parents didn't mean to. She understood that now. But it didn't make the damage any less harmful. Any more irrevocable. As the Philip Larkin poem goes, "They fill you with the faults they had / And add some extra, just for you." Leo's dad did it to him. Maya's dad to her. Jamie's mom to him.

It made Eve reexamine why she wanted to be a parent so badly in the first place. At seventeen years old, she would have done nothing for that child but ruin him. But there was something in her that felt robbed of the opportunity to try. To prove that you can be a good parent, a thoughtful parent, a gentle parent, even if you never had one. It was possible to break the cycle. She and Leo both believed that and desperately yearned for their chance.

"I should've been nicer to him," Eve finally said. "And I'm not saying that I was mean. I think I was kinder than I needed to be in a lot of instances." Dr. Garvey didn't speak, which Eve had learned was a habit of hers; she often allowed Eve to go on long streams of consciousness and gently nudge her toward her own conclusions. She'd ask questions, but they never felt like real questions. It was more like Dr. Garvey reading her for filth, under the guise of curiosity. Eve didn't necessarily like it—why was she depleting her savings just to listen to herself speak and potentially be insulted every ten minutes?—but somehow, perhaps due to her sheer desperation, it was working. So Eve continued.

"I just know that I probably wasn't fun to be around. If I were him, I would've dreaded coming home to someone who rarely expressed much beyond apathy. I didn't see it when I was in it, but knowing what I know now, I think it's kind of a wonder he stayed with me as long as he did."

"And what is it you know now?"

"Just . . . understanding what a relationship should look like. I've seen them from the outside. My parents, I think, probably have a healthy marriage. I told you about Maya and Siobhan. But I think I got a glimpse, from the inside, with Jamie, and that sort of genuine delight I experienced, it was always missing with Leo."

"Can I ask, what is it that made you want to be with him in the first place? Was it security?"

Eve turned sullen as she relived their so-called romance, how they found love in the wreckage of Leo's shitty relationship with his father. "I don't know," she said. "I think . . . some part of me was looking for a challenge. Or a distraction. After his father died, I thought it would be nice to be able to put him back together again. So I became his friend, his confidant, his caretaker.

I don't know if it was ever love. But there was a connection. Being there that way. That was intimacy you can't fake." She nodded as if trying to convince herself.

"And how long did this version of your relationship go on?"

"Too long. Probably . . . a year, year and a half?" Eve said. "I didn't enjoy it, but it was a good diversion. I could convince myself I was happy."

"What do you call 'happy'?" Dr. Garvey asked, jotting down a few more notes.

"Well . . . it was, you know, a partnership. We enjoyed one another's company, for a while at least. We traveled. We made 'couple' friends. We moved in together. He kept going to therapy. I wrote some plays." She smiled. "Things were normal."

"And you equate 'normal' with 'happy'?"

"I did." Eve nodded, feeling silly for it now. "I was getting the life I thought my parents cheated me out of. I was finally back on the right track. Husband, baby, career. All the things well-rounded women are 'supposed' to want. Because if you just want a family, you're simple. And if you just want to focus on your career, if you have no interest in children, you're too severe. You have to want it all, or you're broken. Walk that tightrope. And if you don't get it, you're a failure."

"Did you actually want *any* of it?"

"It's hard to say," Eve answered pensively. She shook her head. "I don't know when I decided I wanted a baby. I don't know if it's even a real desire. Do I want to be a *mother*? Would I grow tired of it, even if I love my child?" she asked, thinking of Lucy and the things Jamie once revealed about her. "I don't know if I want a baby or if I just wanted back what was taken from me."

"And was the miscarriage the first time you felt that unhappiness with Leo?"

Eve paused before replying, again, not wanting to give the easy answer. "Looking back, I was always unhappy. I was with him, I took care of him, because it felt like the right thing to do. You don't let someone drown if you can save them."

Dr. Garvey nodded again and then leaned toward Eve. "Have you ever thought about the mental toll you took on when you cared for this man at the very start of your relationship?" she asked. "You say you were fine at the time. Mentally sound. But think about having to walk around with an extra fifty pounds on your back for a year straight. At some point, you buckle under the undue weight, right? And then you add more. New job, new apartment, engagement, trying to conceive, marriage. That's a lot, Eve. These are all stressors, even if they're things you want for your life. And especially if they aren't.

"Add to that the devastating loss you experienced at *seventeen* years old," the therapist continued. The way she emphasized Eve's tender age made her feel genuinely seen. "You never got to properly process that. Now a miscarriage. And another. Eve, you have so much on your back, you can't even stand anymore. Going back to your metaphor—I have to ask, how do you expect to save someone else from drowning when you're underwater yourself?"

Eve's first instinct was to laugh, in part to keep from bursting into tears, but foremost, because she couldn't believe what she was hearing. She couldn't believe how much of a comfort it was to hear her therapist explicate it so simply. Giving validation to what she thought was true but always felt inept trying to explain to others.

At first, she really did hate addressing her so-called traumas. In her last session, Dr. Garvey mentioned that significant adversity early in life—her pregnancy and everything surrounding it—could create a vulnerability to major depression later, as it sets the nervous system to overrespond to stress. And after her previous experiences, particularly with Zoloft, Eve initially loathed being *diagnosed* with depression. But frankly, it was nice to have a name for her mood swings, her listlessness, her general bad attitude sometimes. Her panic attacks. To her surprise, therapy made her feel like she *wasn't* crazy. She'd started to understand why people did this to themselves.

"How . . ." Eve let out a heavy exhale as tears stung her eyes anyway, unsure what she even wanted to ask. She grabbed a Kleenex from the table beside her as she searched for the words. "How do I get rid of this ache?" she asked. "It feels like it bleeds into everything I do. It's inescapable."

Dr. Garvey sat back in her seat again. "What did you say about your parents when you first walked in here? How hard it is for you to move on when they won't acknowledge the problem?"

"I am acknowledging the problem," Eve said defensively. *It's me. Hi.* When Dr. Garvey only stared at her, she shook her head.

"Think about what cycles you might be perpetuating instead of owning, Eve. Your parents made their mistakes. And you've made yours. What now?"

"Even if I apologize to Leo, it's not going to fix what I did."

"It will not," the doctor agreed. "You walked out on this man who lost many of the same things you did. Nothing *fixes* that. Wounds heal; they don't disappear."

"I used him to make myself seem complete," Eve said. She rarely stopped to look at things from his side, too afraid of the truth she'd see. But there was no point in still running from it. "He deserved better," she said. "So did I."

Dr. Garvey scrawled a long note on her page and then looked back up at Eve. "Is that what you did with Jamie, too?"

Eve immediately turned fidgety, balling her damp tissues in her fist as she was forced to think about the havoc she created for herself by falling in love with Jamie Gallagher. She'd hoped they could delay this particular conversation a little longer—for when she wasn't still so underneath the situation.

"No. Like I mentioned, he was different, for sure." She sighed. "I went to Tennessee to get away from the noise of people and their opinions and their help. It's why I chose such a secluded place. But he lived right down the street, almost as though he was put there specifically for me." Eve chuckled at how ridiculous that sounded out loud, but that didn't make it any less accurate. "I was falling down this hole. Lost, sad, scared. All of it. And Jamie . . . caught me before I hit the ground."

"He did for you what you did for Leo," Dr. Garvey commented.

Eve never thought of it that way, but . . . "Yeah."

"Why do you think you weren't willing to let Leo do that for you?"

She shook her head. "I don't know. I guess . . . I felt I was the protector in that relationship," she said after careful deliberation. "Not that I felt he was useless, but maybe I didn't really trust Leo to be a safe harbor. Even when we were engaged, I put money to the side for myself . . . just in case." Dr. Garvey gave her a look that effectively said, *Yikes, sis,* but she spoke no words. "This was aside from savings, aside from money for the wedding," Eve added.

"He didn't notice?"

"He probably did," Eve said, recalling their Christmas Eve conversation. "But he never said anything."

"So with Jamie, you felt you could trust him?"

It stung Eve to think of the trust imbalance in her relationship with Jamie—so much of it was a mirror to hers with Leo. "Yes."

"And you said it was a sexual relationship as well?"

"It was. I'd never done anything like that before, casual sex. Before Leo, I told guys I was waiting until marriage because I was so scared to broach the topic."

"And your sex life with Leo?"

Eve made a face. "Functional?"

"Say more."

"We rarely had sex for . . . pleasure. He was on antidepressants, which basically killed his sex drive, and that worked well for me, because I wasn't interested anyway. Until we wanted a baby, of course."

"So you were both fine with the lack of sex. What was different with Jamie?"

"I told my friends it must've been the heat in Tennessee," she joked. "But I don't know, I suddenly wanted that . . . connection. I could feel myself turning cold, and I was sort of longing for someone to touch me, to just remind me I was alive. And Jamie seemed nice enough. Attractive. He could be that for me." Eve smiled. Sadly.

"Our first time was disastrous, because I was so out of my mind," she said, "but he was with me all the way. He was patient and honest. And when I finally decided I was actually ready, it was the most sublime experience." Eve paused to think about that moment in his cabin. "And I guess I had this realization that I've been missing out on so much by shutting down like this. Being afraid to feel things. Being afraid of my own body. And that's not to say I immediately unfurled, but I opened up in many different ways with him. And it felt good to do it. I liked who I was with him."

Eve was happy she could say that she was starting to like who she was without him, too.

"The thing is, I was so wrapped up in him, I wasn't really addressing my pain," she said. "I put it to the side so I could experience joy with him, but I still wasn't healthy."

Dr. Garvey grinned. "Would you rather be in Tennessee right now?"

"With him? I don't know. As much as I cherish what we had, even if it was only a few months, I don't want to be with someone who doesn't want to be with me. And I know he has his own story, his own baggage, and after having to pry me open, I do understand why he said, 'Enough is enough.' He's entitled to that."

Dr. Garvey nodded back. "So if he runs in here and pleads for you to come back?"

Eve's cheeks warmed at the mere thought. "The obvious answer is that I would go back in a heartbeat. Initially, at least," she said. "I miss him every day. I miss Jack. I miss Tennessee. Sometimes I wish I could've stopped time at the day we went to Dollywood. If I could've just stayed right there in that moment forever . . ." She trailed off as butterflies in her stomach reemerged with images of that night replaying in her mind. Walking arm in arm with Jamie under the cascading lights. Dollywood wasn't just an amusement park to her. Before she ever set foot inside, it represented an escape. A utopia, even.

Ironic that the literal Greek translation of the word was "a place that is nonexistent."

Once upon a time in Dollywood, she was almost happy. Almost.

"But now that I've had some space from it," Eve continued, "I'm not sure it's as easy as that. Because even though I understand it intellectually, I also know that I can't afford to be with someone who's going to emotionally lacerate me whenever he's feeling insecure. Not anymore." Jamie was gentle with Eve when she was hardened by her pain, and she would always love him for that—even if that love was finite. But it was time to focus on being gentle with herself now.

Dr. Garvey only nodded, but there was an undercurrent of satisfaction there, reminding Eve of the few times her mother's whisper of a smile would say she was proud of her. More importantly, Eve was proud of herself. She'd *finally* opened up to her pain, and she was already brighter and wiser for it.

"Before you get out of here," Dr. Garvey said, taking a glance at her watch, "we should talk about your assignment from last week. Where are we with Mr. and Mrs. Ambroise?"

CHAPTER 38

Come to Mama

EVE

A couple of days later, Eve was sitting at her parents' dining table for the first time since Christmas, studying them both as she waited for the correct set of words to find her. Ones that wouldn't put them on the defense, or start another argument with no resolution. It was the reason she hadn't done her therapy assignment the week before, and why she was so reluctant to do it now—she didn't have those words. But it was imperative to take her therapy seriously, and after the session she'd just had, Eve wanted to keep up her progress. So she finally asked to talk, and, to her parents' credit, they were quick to accommodate.

"So . . . are you going to say anything?" Joan asked after taking a long sip of her Earl Grey, her narrow brown eyes studying her daughter.

Eve shook her head, unconfident about where to even start. "I'd like to have an open discussion about what happened when I was in high school, Ma."

"I knew that's what this was about," Joan scoffed dismissively. "I do not have time to re-litigate this with you, Eve."

"Mom." Eve reached out to hold her mother's hand before she could get up, her eyes big and pleading. "Please don't make me beg you."

"Say what you want to say." Joan waved her off.

With a heavy and cautious breath, Eve began. "I say this knowing that me getting pregnant at seventeen was a shock to your system, and not something you could've prepared for. But I need you to know . . . I need you to listen when I tell you, how much it hurt that you and Daddy, without ever once considering what I wanted to do, forced me into a situation where I could neither get an abortion nor keep my baby."

"We're Catholic, Eve. Abortion was never going to be an option in this household," Roger finally spoke, his deep voice stern.

"I know that was the line you held, but can I just ask why you think children should have to abide by rules they never agreed to in the first place? Who gets to decide that I'm Catholic?"

"Your lineage decides," Joan said, a scowl hardening her soft features. "Our religion is a part of this family just as much as your last name and your complexion."

"The religion of our oppressors means that much to you?"

"It's the religion of our *ancestors*."

"And that meant I had no choice in the matter? I find it hard to believe you had a child just to take away her agency."

"You've made your choice, obviously," Joan said. "But at seventeen, your choices belonged to us."

"So if I'd gotten pregnant at eighteen, I would've been able to make my own? Because of that arbitrary line that makes eighteen-year-olds adults, a few months would've made the difference in me getting to keep my baby?"

"Please stop calling it your baby."

"He was mine."

"It is someone else's. You carried it, and then it was someone else's."

"Because you didn't give me a choice," Eve said. "And I don't know if it was a difficult decision for you and Daddy, but those nine months were unbearable for me. And having to watch my son taken away by strangers is the worst thing you could've done to me." Eve watched her father rise from the table, and she wondered whether this was the part where they kicked her out of their home again. Defiance was a cardinal sin in their household, and it was clear that asking for honesty fell under the umbrella of dissent.

But her father only walked away.

"Daddy?" Eve called after him.

Even her mother appeared perplexed. "Roger, where are you going?"

"I'm not doing this. You want to listen to her whine, you go ahead."

"Roger . . ."

"It's okay," Eve said. She was only surprised that it was her father and not her mother spurning her. Her relationship with Joan had always been fraught with tension, as Eve believed it was her staunch Catholicism that influenced her father. Over the years, he'd try to come to her defense, or at least be kinder about the topic when her mother was so unforgiving. She never imagined him being the problem when she finally gained the tools to approach this like an adult. Tears fell down her face before she even knew she wanted to cry; then she wanted to scream, exhausted of those tears. Another reason she hated therapy.

"Eve," Joan whispered, her gaze and her tone suddenly

softened. When Eve looked up at her, she nodded. "Say what you want to say."

She exhaled, having forgotten what they'd spoken of at this point. "I don't even know."

"Well, can I ask, what did you think you were going to do with a baby at your age?"

"Plenty of women have children young, and they go on to do great things."

"With great struggle."

"I've struggled anyway, Ma. I've been angry and sad." Her voice quivered, but she told herself to keep going. "I've been impenetrable to any man who's ever tried to get close to me. I've resented you and Daddy for half my life. All you did was make me not want to be honest with you or anyone else."

"Eve . . ."

"Leo and I had two miscarriages last year. And I fell apart because of it."

Joan paused. "You what?"

"I didn't want to tell you, because I didn't want lectures about premarital sex and all the things I was doing wrong to cause them—"

"Eve, I would never say anything like that," Joan cut in, her tone morphing into concern now. "I'm so sorry, sweetheart."

"I don't need you to be sorry about that. Anyone with an ounce of decency would be. I need you to recognize the damage you caused by making that decision for me." She wiped angrily at her face as she spoke. She still wasn't saying the right thing. Dr. Garvey told her that her healing couldn't rely on her parents' affirmation. But God, she needed it.

"You guys barely talked to me about it," Eve said. "You sent me to that dank, lonely house with Grandma . . . away from my friends, from you, for eight and a half months, with only a handful of dour phone calls and one visit to show for it. You wanted me to know you were disappointed? Mission accomplished. But you made me feel unloved."

"Oh, sweetheart. We wouldn't have been so worried for your future if we didn't love you."

"Being more concerned about a degree than my well-being isn't love, though, Ma."

Joan frowned again but nodded, seemingly accepting Eve's version of events. "But isn't there any solace in the fact that you've had a good life since then? You met a man who loves you dearly. If you cannot conceive naturally, then perhaps it's time someone return the favor you once bestowed upon another family. Adoption is such a beautiful thing, honey."

"Ma, stop it," Eve said. "This isn't a conversation about grandchildren. Or Leo. I left him because I didn't like him. He wasn't what I wanted. *This* isn't what I wanted."

"Well, what do you want, Eve? For me to change the past? I can't do that."

"I know you can't." She spoke quieter now. "I just want you to take responsibility for it. God forbid you admit you were wrong and just fucking apologize for it."

"Eve!"

"I'm sorry." She closed her eyes to compose herself. "I am. But so many times throughout my life, you've made me feel inadequate for not wanting the things you wanted for me. And if I could just have an acknowledgment—"

"Oh, sweetheart." Joan took her daughter's hand this time, wrapping it in her own. "No. Nothing about you is inadequate."

"Then why do I feel like this?"

"We did put a lot of expectation on you," she said. "And the pregnancy did shock us. We didn't know what to do. A baby having a baby. I just wanted you to have your life back. I didn't want to take away your potential."

"I wish you'd been willing to see it some other way," Eve said, sniffling back her tears.

"I do, too," Joan said. "Because I see this sorrow that I've caused. I heard it that night you called from Gatlinburg. I've seen my daughter only twice in eight months because of it. And I *am* sorry."

Eve looked at her mother—peered at her—trying to dissect her expression, her words, her touch, desperate to find sincerity there.

"I wish I had known better. I wish I'd known I'd be hurting you far more this way," Joan said. "Because that was never my intent, Eve. Your father and I, we were just trying to figure out what was best for you. And . . . and maybe we got it wrong."

As Eve melted into another fit of sobs, her mother released her grip and rushed to Eve's side of the table. Eve tried to wipe her face in preparation, but the tears only fell harder. And when Joan wrapped her arms around her, Eve let go. She fell into her mother's arms, the helpless child who'd been waiting for this embrace for nearly two decades finally fulfilled. And she wept.

It was two months past Christmas, but it was the best gift she could've gotten from her mother. She lamented that her father was unwilling to do the same.

But she would take this. She'd needed this.

Eve left her parents' not long after her productive heart-to-heart with her mom, as one of the other assignments from her therapist was weekly get-togethers with her friends. But before she could take off, Joan informed her of a package she had waiting in the coat closet. Eve couldn't imagine what would have been there—she'd stopped sending packages to their address at some point during the Obama administration. But when she retrieved the small rectangular box from the closet floor, it all came crashing back to her. Jamie's Christmas gift. Her name and his return address were written by Jack, and that ache she'd mostly gotten rid of had lodged itself right back in the center of her heart.

"What is it?" Joan had asked, noticing her smile.

"Just a Christmas gift," she'd said. They'd had a good talk, but she didn't have time to open up the can of emotional worms that was Jamie. "Thanks, Ma."

As soon as she was on the stoop, Eve began pulling at the box's tape, eager to see what Jamie had thought to give her back when things were still good. She opened the small notecard first, this one containing Jamie's handwriting.

It was pure coincidence that I found this.
Proof that you were destined to soar.

Her curiosity piqued, Eve ripped open the rest of the package. It felt like a book, the weight and size familiar, even if it made no sense that Jamie would give her something she already owned. But it was, indeed, a text she knew well. Audre Lorde's *Zami: A New Spelling of My Name*. But this version was different, both old and new. A first edition. First printing. Bound in the publisher's wraps, the cover red and purple—nothing at all like the more ubiquitous black-and-orange copy she owned.

Eve studied the book, its slightly tattered edges, the hint of smoker's scent. And inside the front cover, just beneath the title, there was an inscription and signature: *For Eve—Audre Lorde. Harlem 11/13/1991.* Eve gasped. Obviously, the book wasn't addressed to her specifically, but in a way, perhaps with a twist of kismet, she felt like it had been.

She had no idea where Jamie got it or what it might have cost him, but she wondered about it—and him—all the way to Brooklyn and beyond. It was the last thing she needed. In a moment when she was trying and succeeding at getting over Jamie, this only threatened to pull her back under. She had to remind herself that he'd done this before things fell apart. He'd made his feelings clear on Christmas, and everything prior was inconsequential now.

Right?

"Oh my god, whose bad idea was this?"

Thankfully, Eve's aimless thoughts were halted by the task at hand. Standing in the middle of some industrial kitchen in Brooklyn, Eve only smiled at her friend Nikole's complaint as she pushed her tomato chutney—which was starting to look more like tomato juice—around her sizzling pan. It was Maya's idea for their friend group to try a cooking class, and to be fair, most of them could use the lesson, as evidenced by how poorly it was going. But Eve wasn't about to sell out her friend like that.

"I just go where y'all tell me," Eve said.

"It was either Siobhan or Maya," their friend Wesley said knowingly. "You know they ain't happy unless they got us looking stupid."

"Can I just say," Brian piped up from the head of the class, "this was actually a good idea, for once?" Eve was just glad Brian was nowhere near her, as he and Maya had insisted on making the rest of them look like amateurs.

"You all are doing a *great* job," their instructor, Chef Delia, said. Her peppy tone and her inability to contain her laughter told them she was lying, but it was nice of her to say. They were trying—and out of seven of them, five were near failing—to prepare a three-course West African meal of potato bhajias, suya kebabs, and mandazi.

"All I know is I had nothing to do with this," Siobhan said. She was pointing her finger at those who'd brought up her name, and in the process, blinded the rest of them with her new engagement ring. "I wanted to go bowling."

"That would've been even worse than this," Eve said.

"It damn sure was my idea," Maya practically shouted. "Y'all know y'all having fun, so stop."

"If I'd known we'd have to cook before we ate, I would've eaten first," said Maya's cousin, Jason, from the station behind Eve.

"Made a pit stop at Chipotle or somethin'," Nikole agreed.

"If we had put a little more thought into this, I bet we could've finessed Maya and Brian into making this whole meal for us," Wesley said.

"They do get off on compliments," Eve said, leaving the small group laughing. "Definitely could've used that to our advantage."

"I wasn't gonna bring it up, but I really think Maya has an unfair edge here," Siobhan said.

"Yeah, her parents literally own a restaurant," Brian said.

"Just so we're all on the same page, we are sharing plates at the end, right?" Jason asked. "Because I'm about four, five seconds from snacking on these tomatoes."

Eve turned back to him, understanding his plight. "You know I have a Kind bar in my purse?"

"See, that's what I'm talking about. Women be prepared as fuck, man."

"You need to be more worried about those sad potatoes than some granola," Siobhan teased him, but he was already headed for the back of the room to rifle through Eve's bag for the snack.

"Can I just say how nice it is to hang out in person with you guys again?" Brian said. "It's been so fucking long."

"Thank you!" Maya said. "Eve been gone for damn near a year. I might end up playing in Australia next year. Wesley is about to have *three* kids ruining his life. Can y'all enjoy this and stop complaining?"

"Eve, you got a call coming in, babe," Jason called out. "You want your phone?"

Eve winced. "It's not my mom, is it?" Pleased as she was with the strides they'd made, she also needed space to decompress from their conversation, the situation, and the fact that her dad hadn't budged. Her friends were the best way to do that, and she didn't want her attention suddenly split.

"Name says 'Jamie Gallagher' . . ."

Eve shot her head in Jason's direction as if he were Jamie himself. He held up her phone as proof, and she could only stare, dumbstruck. Was he calling on purpose? Was he okay? Would this call make her life harder? Easier?

"Eve?"

"No." She shook her head, still trying to make sense of Jamie's sudden reemergence—as if he knew she'd just gotten his gift and was thinking of him. "No, I'll call him back." She glanced to Maya, at the cooking station directly across from her, hoping she had some inaudible sage advice to offer. She was the only person in the room who knew all the dirty details of her time in Tennessee, including how distressed she'd been over their abrupt ending.

What the fuck? Maya mouthed to her.

Eve shrugged.

"Call him back," Maya whispered.

Eve shook her head adamantly, not even sure how to approach going back down that road. But as she stared at her chutney and barely fried potatoes, she knew she would never be able to finish cooking, much less consume her meal, without knowing what Jamie wanted.

Fuck. She sure hoped Dr. Garvey wouldn't think less of her for this. "I'll be right back."

CHAPTER 39

Bday

JAMIE

The Public Theater

Feb 27

Subject: Alert! GAMBA ADISA Now Available

The Public Theater is excited to announce Obie Award–winning artist Eve Ambroise's GAMBA ADISA is set to premiere on Thursday, May 7, 2026. Inspired by the true story of slain activist Sandra Bland, Eve Ambroise's critically acclaimed play, GAMBA ADISA, is an emotive portrait of Black womanhood in America, as told by the pioneers of the Say Her Name movement. Featuring an all-Black female cast, including EMMY Award–winner Amina Pearson, directed by Stefani Clemmons, this is a must-see event.

Tickets are available now.

Jamie smiled at every word of the email he'd received from this place he'd never been to, or even heard of prior to last year, and while he'd no idea what an Obie Award was, or meant, he was certain Eve deserved one, because she deserved everything, and he was happy to see she was getting a fraction of that, at least. Getting that email was like seeing her name in lights. He was proud.

It also reignited a very specific ache that he didn't know still existed until he was confronted with her name again. Of course, he never really stopped thinking about her; he considered biting the bullet and calling nearly every single day since the last time they spoke. But he could never find a good enough reason to disrupt her life without knowing what to say.

That was, until now.

Jamie waited until evening fell and Jack was squarely tucked away for the night, not wanting to be interrupted, or eavesdropped on, for that matter. It was hard enough explaining to Jack why Eve wasn't in their lives any longer. He didn't want to give him any hope if the kid happened to hear them talking.

When he finally sat down to dial her number, he did so from memory. He preferred that method, as it kept important numbers at the front of his mind, since he hated to rely on the technology of it all. And when she didn't answer, he tried not to assume the worst. After how things ended, he wouldn't have blamed her if she never wanted to talk to him again. But it was equally as likely that she was simply busy. It was just around 10:00 p.m. in New York; for a city that never slept, it would make sense if her evening were just beginning.

Of course, that didn't stop him from staring at his phone, waiting for it to show any sign of life.

His heart nearly leapt out of his chest when it finally vibrated against the couch, and there on his lock screen sat a lone text from Eve:

Fri, Feb 27 9:03 PM

Eve Ambroise: Hey, did you mean to call me?

Jamie grinned at her response.

Fri, Feb 27 9:04 PM

Jamie Gallagher: I did. Are you busy?

Fri, Feb 27 9:14 PM

Eve Ambroise: Kinda. Will you be up later?

Jamie Gallagher: I can be. Whenever you have a moment. It's nothing important.

Eve Ambroise: Okay.

Eve Ambroise: I finally got your Christmas gift, by the way. It was perfect.

Jamie Gallagher: I'm so happy you liked it.

Jamie was relieved that she'd responded kindly; he hoped it meant, by some miracle, that she wasn't mad at him. Maybe she never was, or maybe she just wasn't anymore. Either way, it would make the wait for her call far less foreboding. He was even considering indulging in another slice of his birthday cake, courtesy of Jack, and maybe a couple of *90 Day Fiancé* episodes to pass the time. But before he even made it to the kitchen, his phone vibrated again, Eve's name and smiling face filling the display.

He was apprehensive again as he answered the call but did

his best to cover it with casual affability. "Hey." He said it as though they'd spoken yesterday instead of two months ago, like there'd been no space between them at all.

"Hi," she said quietly.

Jamie smiled at the sound of her voice, like music to his ears, featuring notes he'd missed hopelessly. "You sound different," he said. "Far away."

"I feel far away . . ."

"Where are you?" he asked, curious as to why she was whispering. Curious as to where she'd been without him.

"Brooklyn," she answered, sounding sad about it. "Where are you?"

"Nashville." It was difficult not to think of the last time she was there, wrapping gifts and baking cookies. The sex they had the morning he left for Paris, and how he would've made it last forever if he'd known he would end up doing what he did. "I haven't been back to Gatlinburg since . . . us."

"Oh."

There was an unspoken question lingering on Jamie's lips, wondering whether she was with her ex, but his inability to move forward, to trust that she was done with this guy, was what got them there in the first place. "You said you were busy?" he asked instead. "You didn't have to call right now, you know."

"I'm at a cooking class with friends," she said, chuckling. "More specifically, I'm sitting in a bathroom stall while my friends are out there cooking."

"Really?"

"Yeah."

"Are you sick?"

"No. I just didn't wanna wait to talk to you."

"Oh." Jamie's heart was fully racing, his voice turning hoarse as he tried to hold back his emotions. He thought he knew what he would say when they spoke, but now nothing would come to mind except the pure elation that she was eager to talk to him, too. "How long did you stay in Gatlinburg?"

"A little over a week. It was lonely without you."

He nodded. "Same reason I couldn't go back."

They went quiet for a moment, and he just listened to the sound of her breathing. It reminded him of all those times they'd lain in bed together, reading. They were good at not talking. It never felt uncomfortable. Even now, when it should've.

"I've missed you," Jamie said, so soft it sounded like a whisper.

He could hear her sniffle. "Me, too."

"I shouldn't have said what I said."

"No," she agreed.

"It's just . . . I didn't wanna get hurt."

Silence.

And then, eventually, she replied, "I know. Me neither."

"I'm sorry," he said. He was clutching his phone like it was her hand, desperate for her touch. God, how he regretted the time he'd wasted, being hurt when maybe he could've been happy.

It was so hard to know the difference between being smart and being scared.

"Jamie?" Eve called out.

"Yeah?"

"I should go," she said, sniffling again.

"Oh."

"It's not you," she added. "It's just that . . . I should get back to my friends. I thought maybe you wanted something specific."

He did. He wanted her. "I just . . . wanted to hear your voice, I guess."

"I wanted to hear yours. And to wish you an early happy birthday."

"Can I see you?" he blurted. He couldn't risk letting her get off that phone without asking. He could live with it if she said no. Hell, if he were her, he probably would've. But he couldn't live another day holding back for fear of what she'd say. Not when he already had proof of how good they could be together when they both let their guards down.

So he was handing her the opportunity to hurt him, knowing now, the reward was greater than the risk. And maybe, God willing, she just wanted to see him, too.

Eve sighed sharply, and Jamie steeled himself for her turndown, but she only responded with a simple, direct question: "When?"

CHAPTER 40

Miss You, Goodbye

EVE

Eve found this particular ride to Gatlinburg much easier than the last, her sadness exchanged for the confidence she'd been lacking for so many months now. Excitement tickled her toes, and she wondered if this was what Jamie felt when he was driving in from Nashville on Fridays. It was quite different—quite nice—not to be the one waiting. It was a heady tonic, knowing the person you're desperate to see is at the other end of the journey. It was no wonder Jamie did it so readily every weekend.

Unsurprisingly, Eve's heart beat faster when she reached their street and spotted that old Chevy sitting in the driveway. It put her at ease, that small sign that he was still himself, yet her pulse quickened anyway. That was the effect he had on her.

Eve pulled in and parked beside Jamie's truck. She glanced into the passenger window, recalling her first time riding with him—when he rescued her from a particularly jarring panic attack. Maybe it wasn't the healthiest thing in the world, being secluded in this place, but it—*he*—was what she needed at the time.

With a smile on her lips, Eve hopped out of her rental and

smoothed her plaid shirt, figuring it wrinkled during her travels. She got a quick glimpse of herself in the reflection of her window, her 4C hair still neatly in its high puff, with the headscarf she used as a headband perfectly in place. She grabbed her purse and headed up the walkway toward the staircase, her toes still tingling with every step she took. It all felt simultaneously familiar and foreign.

Reaching the steps, Eve stopped in her tracks when she realized Jamie was standing at the top of them, waiting for her. Her breath caught in her throat as she took him in. Him and that lazy smile. He was wearing her favorite denim shirt with the sleeves rolled up, showing off just enough skin. He hadn't shaved in about three weeks, she could tell, and his facial hair was perfect for it, all the different hues of gray complementing the blue. His hair looked wet—darker, wavier than normal—and she wondered if he'd just taken a shower. She couldn't wait to smell him again. His scent, the comfort of it, was one of the things she'd missed most.

Grinning, she dropped her bag and started up the steps to meet him. Jamie was already headed down, and they met somewhere in the middle. Each seeming to know what the other was thinking, they didn't waste time with words; instead, Jamie immediately leaned down to kiss her. It was sweet—soft—at first, in a show of both affection and atonement. But as Eve's fingers found his hair, as was her wont, he deepened the kiss, and it felt like he'd literally taken her breath away. As he tenderly slipped his tongue into her mouth, he hoisted her from the steps and into his arms. Eve broke their kiss, only briefly, to laugh when she felt herself lifted into the air, but she was quick to catch up, wrapping her legs around his waist.

She'd almost forgotten how good Jamie was at this. He kissed like it was breathing for him, so utterly natural. She never wanted to stop. And they didn't, even as Jamie turned and headed up the steps, his hand square on her back, keeping her safe as they moved. Their lips never parted for anything more than small breaths of air. Within seconds of seeing each other for the first time since the last time, they were in a full-on lip-smacking, tongue-wrestling make-out. It was as though they hadn't seen each other in ten years instead of ten weeks.

Soon after they made it inside, Jamie practically threw Eve onto the bed, and he hastily joined her. The room was already pleasantly warm, thanks to a small fire in the hearth, but it turned hot as soon as he made his way on top of her. He removed the scarf that dressed her neck like he was unwrapping a gift, his tongue then diving for her skin. He kissed her chin and along her jawline and back down again, taking care to cover every inch of her. He unbuttoned her shirt, releasing a series of low moans as he moved down her chest until his tongue was tickling her cleavage. He was careful and slow to pull down the cups of her bra to reveal her breasts, licking his lips at the sight of them, propped up by the underwire, her dark brown nipples stiff, before taking one into his mouth. He rolled his tongue around one bud and then gently tugged at the other with his teeth before repeating. He bathed them with long licks until they went soft and then hard again, all while Eve tangled her fingers in his feathery curls.

She had been thinking about exactly this on her flight. Images of him devouring her made the wait much shorter. She anticipated him being so eager to see her, there wouldn't be time or need for words, and he'd delivered tenfold, not taking a single second for granted.

Eve had every intention of returning the fervor, and she needed to get to him before he did his thing; otherwise, she'd soon be useless. As Jamie sucked on her tits like they were his dinner, she tugged at his hair, attempting to redirect his focus. He obliged, returning his kisses to her lips, allowing Eve to undress him, her fingers blindly fumbling with the buttons of his shirt. As soon as it loosened, she ran her fingers up his bare back and down again, the lines and curves of it so familiar to her, it made her warm inside. That dimple where his backside began, she'd studied it in their previous life together. She attempted to push down his jeans but didn't get very far as Jamie moved back down her neck, seemingly oblivious to her efforts.

He pulled up from her briefly, licking his swollen lips as he caught his breath and kicked off his shoes. But his eyes stayed on Eve's, his hungry stare making her squirm until he pulled her to the edge of the bed by her leg, leaving her giggling with glee as he pulled off her boots. She unbuttoned her jeans, and he removed those, too, his smile widening as her sheer teal thong stared back at him. He was climbing back onto the bed when her foot stopped him; she wiggled her toes at the button of his pants, and he took the hint, stepping out of them posthaste.

Eve grinned, admiring his naked form as he returned to her, welcoming him between her legs as he resumed his kisses. His tongue tangoed with hers, his erection teasing the inside of her thighs as his fingers dipped inside her underwear, the index and middle penetrating her wet center, eliciting a fervid moan.

"Jamie," she whispered against him. Her mouth fell open as he went deeper, as his lips moved downward, latching on to her throat, and it was clear that he was going to do everything in his power to make her forget her name that night.

When morning rose, Eve was the first to wake, peeling her face from Jamie's chest after hours of skin-to-skin contact. She had a headache that felt like a hangover, which was apt, as she'd been fully intoxicated by the man beside her. Her entire body, even her jaw, was throbbing, and she couldn't bring herself to move; she simply stared into the distance, enjoying the view of the trees, the sun peeking through the forest of branches. The promise of spring was in the air, green leaves just beginning to sprout. She'd heard that it tended to snow well into March here in Gatlinburg, but Eve imagined flowers would start budding sooner than later this year. She wished she would be around to see it.

Yawning, she ran her hand along Jamie's torso, reveling in the feel of his warm skin beneath her fingertips. She loved watching him in slumber; it made her giggle, in fact, the way he slept so still, like a corpse. Then again, he was probably spent, too.

"What are you laughing at?" Jamie asked. His eyes were still closed, his voice thick with fatigue, and she delighted in every bit of it. She'd missed waking up with him.

"I'm laughing at you laying there like a cadaver," she said, smiling as her fingers continued through his slight tuft of chest hair.

"That's probably because you almost killed me last night."

"Fair enough."

"How long you been awake?"

"Just a couple of minutes," Eve said.

Finally opening his eyes to the day, Jamie turned to her, amusement claiming his sweet face, the only evidence of his thirty-five years showing in the small wrinkles that started at his eyelashes and reached his temples. He squinted too much, and he smiled even more. Evidence of life lived. Despite his protestations to the contrary, he'd been happy before her; he could be again. She hoped.

As Eve's mind wandered, Jamie leaned in for a kiss, and the second their tongues touched, he eagerly began to move on top of her. Eve was quite happy to kiss him, morning breath and all, more than she should probably ever admit, and as his lips traversed her body, the more the tickle of his tongue on her stomach made her laugh, the less she wanted him to stop. But she hadn't prepared for this to be the only item on their agenda all weekend.

"Wait," she said. She touched his left shoulder, reminded of their first time together as her fingers involuntarily scrutinized the shape of his muscles. And same as then, she was questioning her own hesitance.

Jamie stopped and he stared, his blue eyes catching the morning light, resulting in a playful gleam. "What's wrong?"

Eve grinned at his concern. But she could also feel him teasing her, and she needed to get from beneath him before she gave in again. "We don't have anything for breakfast," she said.

"I guess it's a good thing you're the only thing I wanna eat."

Her face grew warm, and even her cheeks were sore from smiling so hard. "You're a mess."

Jamie leaned in to give her neck another kiss, long and tender, before pulling back again. "I brought you some food."

"Your penis doesn't count as nourishment."

He made a face. "I'm gonna refrain from making the joke that I seem to fill you up just fine," he quipped. "But no, I stopped at Whole Foods on the way up."

Eve grinned again, appreciating that he had both the forethought and the recollection that she hated the entire selection at Food City. He knew her well, which she had never been able to say about a man before. Or anyone, really. Maybe Maya. Maybe it was why she couldn't shake the feeling that all of this was a mistake.

"Hey," Jamie beckoned her gaze. When it landed on him, she could tell he was studying her. "What's wrong?"

"Why do you think something's wrong?"

"Because I don't know where you are right now," he said, his thumb caressing her arm. "But I wish you'd take me with you."

She replied with a quiet smile as she touched his scruffy cheek. "I've just . . . missed you."

"I missed you, too."

"And I don't wanna spend the whole weekend just doing . . . this." She gestured at their setup in his messy bed of crumpled sheets and discarded clothing. She cherished the weekends where they did nothing but this, but if they went back to it, if she spent too much time in his arms, she was positive she'd slip right back under. And all the work she'd done to free herself would be rendered futile.

"Okay . . ." Jamie nodded and left a chaste kiss on her lips before slowly rolling back to his side of the bed. "Whatever you wanna do is fine with me," he said. "We can just stare at each other all weekend for all I care."

Eve traded her musings for another smile. Because she was happy to do that, too. And she did stare at him for a long time. Her eyes fixed on him, she wondered what he was thinking, questioned what he saw when he looked back at her, was curious what he was hoping for at the end of these two days. She wished she could see into his mind. She imagined he'd yearned for the same on so many occasions, back when they were . . . whatever they were.

She reminisced as if it were so long ago. But in a lot of ways, it did feel like another life. She was so different from that woman. But he seemed very much the same, and she wasn't sure what that meant. If anything. It still stung, the way things fell apart between them, and it was hard for her to push down the pain. To pretend she didn't blame him for her unraveling when he abandoned her, even if it was her own fault for relying on him so much in the first place.

"Where have you been?" she eventually whispered. That was what came out of her mouth, even though she meant, *Why did you leave?* She searched his eyes for the answer to that question instead. If only she could erase the last two months and they could just pick up where they left off.

"I've been . . . home," Jamie said, a small, sheepish chuckle following. "Just working. Taking care of Jack. Back to life before you."

Eve nodded against her pillow.

"I thought about calling you every day," he said. "But then I thought it might be cruel to pull you back in—to even attempt it—if I wasn't sure what I wanted."

She looked down, not guiltily, but knowingly.

"I read your dissertation."

Eve narrowed her eyes at him. "You did not."

"I did. All two hundred and seventy-eight pages," he said. "Never imagined I'd spend my nights learning about the intersection of film culture and social activism in Liberia and Ghana, but . . . I'm glad I did. I love how much I learn from you." He punctuated his sentence with a doting gaze as a tiny smile claimed his face, manifesting as a twinkle in his eyes more than a twitch of his lips. "And then I just happened to come across the news about your show, and I had to call you," he said. "I just . . . saw your name, and all of a sudden, I knew what I wanted."

Eve didn't know how to respond. How sweet it was to hear him say that he wanted her. To know he hadn't really discarded her. After all the pain of the last two months, the loneliness and the regret that had tried its best to swallow her whole, being with him, like this, felt like a balm for the wound that was left when he shut her out. She leaned in to kiss him softly. Briefly. Her lips saying what had been on her mind since they laid eyes on each other the night before: *I'm home.*

Jamie quietly groaned at the touch of her lips, and then again when she pulled away. "Where are you going?" he asked, sighing as she climbed out of their bed. He reached out for her, but she was already gone and slipping into her panties.

"Go get our food," she called back to him.

While Jamie headed outside, Eve started scouring the cabinets for breakfast items, deciding on some grits Jamie had left over, while hoping he had bacon among his purchases. She was pleasantly surprised when he returned with a cooler full of groceries—mostly fruits and vegetables, but also steaks and bacon, eggs, bread, and juice. Enough to get them through the weekend and then a little more.

They flirted their way through breakfast prep, sharing little touches and kisses, as well as strawberries and blackberries, while Eve cooked their grits and Jamie took on the duty of bacon and toast. And mostly, there was that comfortable silence between them again, their actions taking the place of words, giving a quiet ease to their morning. The way it used to be.

Jamie stopped for a moment as the bacon sizzled to watch Eve, walking around in his shirt and basically nothing else, leaving Eve feeling self-conscious with his attention on her. "What?" she asked.

He shook his head, grinning cheekily as he popped a cherry into his mouth. "Just got a text from my mom. She told me to tell you hi."

Eve turned back to him, her eyebrows raised. "Your mom?" She smiled tentatively, unsure how he felt about it. "The one you don't speak to?"

He laughed. "We've been speaking a little more," he said. "Her and my dad came to visit for my birthday. They're watching Jack this weekend."

Eve nodded slowly as she stirred her grits, pleasantly surprised by this news. But the mention of Jack made her ache again, pangs of sadness settling in the pit of her stomach. "I'm really glad to hear that," she said, ignoring the pain. "I'm proud of you."

"I'm taking it slow," he said, leaning against the counter as he looked to the floor. "But I held that grudge for too long. Casey said I needed to forgive her, and he was right. Insufferable as he is, he's *usually* right."

"How does it feel to have her back in your life?"

"It feels . . . good?" He said it with a slow smile, as if he was just now realizing it. "I always felt like I had a part missing. And to be able to move forward and welcome her in. To feel like I've got a handle on this thing with Lucy. It's nice."

Eve nodded again, understanding him far too well. She went back to the stove, but only to turn it off—she didn't want burning food to interrupt what she was about to say. With Jamie watching her, she nimbly pulled herself onto the open counter space next to the refrigerator. "I have something to tell you, too."

Jamie's eyebrows quirked with silent intrigue. He stood in front of her, his hands resting on her thighs. "Okay."

"I started going to therapy," she revealed, her voice low as she avoided his gaze at first, focusing on his hands instead. She let the words hang in the air, feeling her heart beating in her ears as she tried to convince herself to keep speaking. That she—that *they*—needed to have this conversation.

He smiled. Again, the kind that put a glitter in his eyes. "I'm proud of *you*," he said, his thumb still rubbing her smooth skin. "I really am."

"After what happened with us, I really . . . lost it." She had to consciously suppress the humiliating image of her weeping in Stella's office. "I couldn't avoid it anymore."

Jamie nodded. "I'm sorry. I didn't know."

Eve shook her head. She'd chosen how to respond, and that wasn't on him. "We talk about you," she said with an inkling of a smile.

"Oh." He chewed at his bottom lip, his brows knitting then. "I don't think anyone ever wants to be on the receiving end of 'I talk to my therapist about you.' "

"Probably not."

"How bad is it?"

"There's no good or bad. Just the truth."

"Okay . . ."

"I had to discuss why I was so scared of letting you all the way in," Eve went on. She focused on the freckles on his nose as she spoke, because she couldn't handle his stare. Not now. Because for half a year, those eyes had begged to know her, and now that she was finally giving in, she couldn't watch as that earnestness decayed and turned to pity. "And the truth is, it was because I didn't want you to know I had a baby at seventeen." Her bottom lip began to quiver before she could say more. "I had to give him up for adoption."

"Eve." Jamie exhaled shakily as he took one of her hands.

"It wasn't just the miscarriages that sent me here. It was the combination of all of it. I felt like my parents had stolen my baby, my fiancé couldn't give me one, and I was reeling." She wiped at the tears that had begun to fall; they came faster than she could express her thoughts. "I'm so fucking tired of crying," she said, laughing at herself.

"It's okay."

"I don't even know what they named him," she said. "And I know you're not supposed to know, because there's no way you can ever move forward. But sometimes—most times—I feel like I never left that hospital room anyway." She stopped and sighed, knowing she was laying a lot on Jamie's doorstep. He squeezed her hands but bowed his head and simply listened to her.

"I came here because this is where my parents sent me when it happened," Eve continued. "They didn't want their friends to know. Their church." She rolled her eyes. "They hid me here. And I wanted to hide here, too. In the end, I guess, it's what brought me to you." She inhaled sharply and exhaled slowly, trying to recount the last year of her life without having to relive it. "And meeting you, it was . . . it was a breath of fresh air, to have someone who didn't know. I just wanted you to see me without this tragic backstory. I wanted a relationship . . . I wanted a *life* where I wasn't attached to my grief. And I know now that all it did was put a wall between us, and that wasn't fair to you. It wasn't fair to me. I fucked us up."

"No," Jamie cut in, looking up at her. "I put so much pressure on you."

"You just asked me to be good to you." She smiled glumly. "And I didn't always know how to do that." She closed her eyes as he kissed her left hand, and she ran her right over his lowered head. He was kind. And he was beautiful. And all of this only served to remind her that she probably never deserved him in the first place.

"I'd been trying to make sense of the shit my entire life," she said. "I didn't wanna be defined by it, but I let it consume me anyway. And then, the right set of words from the right person made me realize this wasn't my fault. At seventeen, I deserved to be supported. Not discarded. But my parents didn't know how to do that. And it wasn't their fault either. Not really." She shook her head as she smiled at him. "We're all just trying to do our best, right?"

"Yeah."

Eve nodded. "So . . . I just thought you deserved to know," she said, putting a cap on the conversation. "It was such a small thing in hindsight."

"It's not."

"No, what happened wasn't," she agreed. "But the reason I kept it from you was. You would've understood. And instead, it became the reason you couldn't trust me."

Jamie looked up at her with guilt sitting in his eyes. Turns out, she would have preferred the pity. "I do trust you."

Eve snickered. "You shouldn't."

"That's not true."

"I know you want to," she said. "I know you wouldn't be standing here if you didn't at all. But you needed to trust that I wouldn't hurt you, or Jack, and I couldn't give you that. I'm sorry I gave you this so late."

"I don't care how long it took," Jamie said. "You needed to grieve, and I didn't give you that." He swallowed visibly as he shook his head. "I wish I'd seen it. I wish I had been . . . I don't know. Better. Softer. Easier. You didn't deserve that. And *I'm* sorry."

Eve let out a small hiccup as she failed to hold back more tears. Instead, she felt all of her resolve crashing around her, because it just felt so goddamn good to get this off her chest, to be free from the weight of this unnecessary secret and allow Jamie to finally, fully see her—unstable, sad, and all. And to receive an apology she never needed or expected, it left her feeling hopeful, confused, relieved, and aggrieved. Trapped in all her spiraling emotions.

Jamie wiped her tears as they continued to fall, and she nodded, appreciating the affectionate gesture. "We should eat," she said, sniffling as she used her knuckle to clear her waterline. "I should've done that after breakfast."

"No, I'm glad you didn't wait." He wrapped his hands around hers and rested his head against her chest. "I don't know what you're looking for at the end of this weekend, but . . . for me, this feels like a new start."

Eve nodded again—not in agreement, but in understanding—and she came so close to telling him how badly she wanted that to be true. She took a deep breath before asking, "Do you see us going back?" Now it was her turn to beg, her brown eyes pleading with the top of his head for an answer to their central dilemma. "Or maybe I should say, is there a path forward for us? In your mind?"

Jamie shuffled his bare feet as he mused, and she could tell that nerves were inhibiting him. "I don't know," he finally answered. "But I'm open. To trying."

"Can you . . . see yourself moving to New York in the foreseeable future?"

"Well. No, probably not before Jack goes to college."

She figured as much. And the idea of a ten-year long-distance relationship was agonizing. "You know my play just moved to Off-Broadway, which is a pretty big deal for me," she said. "And against all odds, my next play is supposed to debut there right after that. So I need to be in New York right now." Because as much as Jamie felt like home, at some point, everyone has to leave the nest. "I *want* to be there."

"I see."

"So . . . I don't know."

"I mean, shit. That's great, Evie. That's incredible."

"It is," she agreed. She felt a flutter in her stomach, his use of *Evie* reminding her of the start of their relationship and all the best parts thereafter. *Eve,* she'd learned, was generally reserved for when he was disappointed in her. She wanted to hate him for making her yearn for a nickname she thought she'd buried with her grandmother. Instead, it had only endeared him to her more. "But I don't know what to do here," she said. "Do we meet up in Gatlinburg every few months?" She tried to smile at the thought, but her mouth wouldn't cooperate.

"That could be fun."

"We can visit each other every weekend."

"We can," Jamie said. "Or . . . maybe that's a step back."

"Maybe it is," she said. "And I don't know if I have any interest in going back."

Jamie nodded, too, but she couldn't tell whether he really understood how conflicted she was here. "The path forward doesn't sound easy," he said. "And with everything happening for you, I completely understand why you aren't particularly interested in goin' down it."

"But I am. It's just . . ."

"I get it," Jamie said, looking down again. "It's funny, because I was always so scared it was Leo in the way. Because Lucy had been in mine for so long. And being with her . . . it feels like it eroded so much of the good in me. My patience, my willingness to be really vulnerable. My confidence. I haven't been who I wanted to be." There again was that slow, unsteady sigh before he looked up at Eve. "I'm glad you started therapy," he said. "I'm happy for you. Even if it means the end of us."

"Jamie . . ."

"This isn't self-pity talking. I'm serious." He squeezed her knee as he gazed at her. "You've been holding on to so much. And I'm so sorry I added to your burdens. But more than anything, I just want you to be free from it all. However you need to get there."

Eve nodded as more tears sprang to her eyes, still unable to hold his gaze. This was the most honest she'd ever been with him, with anyone, and it made her realize why she'd spent so much time lying and avoiding and running. This shit hurt.

"So then . . . I guess we go our separate ways?" Jamie asked.

"I don't want that," Eve said, the quickness with which she responded a resounding denial.

"What do you want?"

"I don't know." She sat with it for several minutes, and Jamie let her, seeming to understand that she needed the silence. He always did.

"Things are going well for me," she finally said. "And you can't be in New York particularly often when Jack lives here. So. Yeah." She exhaled sharply. "Maybe this was just supposed to be a few good months. You were there when I needed something. And I was the same for you. But maybe it was never supposed to last forever."

"Maybe." He reached out to brush away another tear that had fallen down her nose, and he smiled sullenly.

"You can tell me if you don't agree."

"No, it's that I do agree," Jamie said. "I don't think either of us will ever be satisfied with some intermittent relationship. Not after what we had. And what's the use in pretending for a few months, just to let it fizzle out later? This is your time, and you can't squander it worrying about whether you're disappointing me." He then nodded emphatically, as if he'd settled on a resolution for both of them. "We had what we had."

Eve sniffled, some part of her wishing he could've convinced her otherwise. But prevailingly, she was proud that she was no longer willing to sacrifice her personal and professional growth for someone she loved. She no longer needed the distraction of a charming neighbor to get through the day. If six months was all she got to have with him, she would take that. She would cherish it. But he wasn't the only way to be happy. He couldn't be.

She nodded, too. "We had what we had."

In her old office at Fordham, Eve's mother kept a cheap little plaque with some pseudo-philosophical quote hanging over the threshold of the door. Her mother thought of it as a bit of sage advice for her students—a reminder for each time they stepped out into the world. Eve always considered it hollow, at best—until now, that is, picturing the words as she dismounted from the counter, preparing herself to walk out of Jamie's life. This time, on her own terms.

> **Leaving home, in a sense, involves a kind of second birth in which we give birth to ourselves.**

CHAPTER 41

Back Where You Started

JAMIE

Fri, Apr 10 1:31 PM

Lucy Ewen: Please tell Jack I love him and I'll miss him dearly. And to be good for his uncles. I know you'll tell him all this yourself, but make sure he knows I said it too?

Jamie Gallagher: Lol ok. I will.

"I can't wait until you get a new car," Casey said. "The fact that I still have to use an aux cord in here is egregious."

"We don't *have* to listen to music, you know."

"You really live like this, huh?" Casey reached across the console to grab Jamie's iPhone. "Do you even have music on this thing? I still haven't figured out why you bought it."

"For your information, I do," Jamie said, snatching his device back as they stopped at a red light. He opened his music app and chose an old Ray LaMontagne album for their ride to Jack's school. "Now finish your story."

"Oh, I was basically done," Casey said. "I've learned the hard way that Jelani's gonna do what he wants to do. He's so stubborn sometimes."

Jamie glanced at his brother, waiting for a punch line that never came. "And you think you aren't?"

"That's not the point here." As they resumed their drive, Jamie's phone pinged, signaling a new email, which Casey took upon himself to investigate. "*NYU Office of Admissions*? Excuse me?"

Jamie bristled, annoyed by both the sender and the fact that his brother was now aware of it. "Gimme that."

"What is this?"

"It's nothing," Jamie said, trying to reach across the car while keeping his eye on the road. "Gimme my phone."

"Dude, no," Casey protested. "You applied to NYU?"

"No, I did not."

"Is this for Jack?" He frowned and then gasped. "Is this from Eve?"

Jamie rolled his eyes. "Give me my phone, Casey."

Instead of acquiescing, Casey ignored him and proceeded to read the message. "'Dear Jamie. Congratulations! I am delighted to inform you that you have been selected for admissions to the BS in Leadership and Management Studies program at the New York University School of Professional Studies Division of Applied Undergraduate Studies for Fall 2026.'" His voice managed to go up an octave with every other word he read. "Are you fucking kidding me?" he shouted.

Jamie glared at his brother. "It's nothin'."

"What are you talking about? This is huge."

"It's really not."

"I didn't even know you applied to anywhere but Vanderbilt. This is amazing."

Jamie applied at Eve's suggestion, figuring, if nothing else, it would be cool to say he got into NYU, even if there was no way he could actually attend. But now, it just made the pain of their breakup even more acute, and he wished it were something he could've quietly ignored.

"I'm not going to NYU," he said. "I just wanted to see what it would take to get in."

"And now that you know, you're not gonna take advantage of it? You've wanted this for so long, Jamie."

"Yeah, but . . . Vandy was always the real dream. I was never gonna be able to live in New York for nine months of the year. And especially not now that me and Eve are done."

"What?" Casey chirped. "Since when?"

"Since December. Since March. I don't know."

"What did you do?"

"I didn't do anything," Jamie said, dodging a punch to his shoulder. "It just didn't work out." He tried to sound nonchalant about it, but he suspected his broken heart was betraying him.

"Bullshit," Casey said. "She adored you."

Jamie frowned, doubting Casey could come to that conclusion in the little time they'd spent together. "You met her, like, twice."

"I don't care. I saw it," Casey said. "And you, her, so what the hell could've happened that was so bad in three months?"

Jamie shook his head. "We didn't wanna be in a relationship one weekend at a time. And she has everything going for her in New York."

"And . . . you think Jack wouldn't like New York? Or what?"

He sent his brother another sidelong glance. "Unless I can convince Lucy to move there with me, I'm not sure how that's gonna work."

"You think he'd be the first kid to live a few states away from one of his parents?"

"I can't do that to Lucy."

"I believe I sat in a courtroom last summer where the state of Tennessee literally said you could."

"Casey." Jamie turned solemn, the way he did with Jack when he had to be firm. "It's not gonna happen. I'm not taking my kid from his mother."

"You're not taking him away. You'd just be doing something for yourself for once. Do what you want. Not what you think you have to do. You don't get extra points for getting through life unhappily."

"When you have kids, you'll understand."

"I hope I never understand *this*," Casey grumbled, clearly disappointed to hear it all.

And Jamie hated disappointing him. He spent most of their lives trying to hide the hard stuff from him, taking care to protect him when their parents wouldn't. Tried to be the perfect role model for him when their parents couldn't. But try as he might, Jamie could never hide this heartache from his perceptive little brother.

"I knew this wasn't your usual, thoughtful quiet," Casey said, gesturing in Jamie's direction. "You seemed melancholy."

"Things don't always work out the way you want them to," Jamie said. "But for the next nine years, Jack is my *only* priority."

Jamie could feel Casey's stare boring into him. "Have you ever heard the 'hole in the sidewalk' metaphor?" Casey asked.

Jamie looked at Casey again as they pulled into the parking lot of Jack's school, joining a long line of cars awaiting the children's release. "I don't think so," he said, squinting in the afternoon sun, wary of where this was going.

"All right, well, it's a poem by the lady who plays Sister Berthe in *The Sound of Music*—"

"Why do you know this?" Jamie interrupted.

"Shut up. Because it's good. So the poem goes, 'I walk down the street. There's a deep hole in the sidewalk. I fall in. I'm lost, I'm helpless. It isn't my fault. It takes forever to find a way out,'" Casey began to recite quickly. Perhaps trying to get through it before Jack emerged. He repeated the same line about the sidewalk, with only slight variations of the narrator falling into the hole and obviously recognizing their destructive patterns, leaving Jamie feeling like he was listening to a broken record.

"Okay," Jamie cut in again, "I think I get it."

Casey hushed him. "I'm almost done. 'I walk down the same street. There's a deep hole in the sidewalk. I walk around it,'" he said pointedly. "And finally, 'I walk down another street.'"

Jamie gazed intently out the window, internalizing the allegory and how it related to his own life—and even those around him. "Okay," he replied quietly.

"I don't know if Eve is on that different street," Casey said. "Maybe you move on, maybe you try again. I have no idea. But I just . . . I don't want you to get stuck again, Jamie."

"I don't want to either," Jamie said, thinking about how hard it had been to get over Lucy. Hell, the only reason he *really* did was Eve. What was he supposed to do now? Move on to someone else? That sounded like falling in the same hole. "I'm tryin' not to. I've been making amends with Mom. I'm finally doing this college thing that's been plaguing me for twenty years now. But with Eve . . . I don't know. We agreed to move on."

Before he could say any more, the doors to the school went swinging open, and classes full of third, fourth, and fifth graders flocked outside, searching for their parents' cars. Jack found them quickly, seeming to add a little pep to his step once he realized Casey was with him.

"I didn't know you were gonna be here!" he greeted Casey brightly. "Dad said you were gonna meet us at the airport."

"I was, but I decided to come in a little early to hang out with your old man," Casey said, helping his nephew into the back seat. "Uncle Jelani is still gonna meet us in a couple hours. His layover's at six."

"What time will we get to LA?" Jack asked, the excitement in his voice not fading.

Jamie looked at Jack in his mirror and simply chuckled. "And hello to you, too, bud."

"Hey, Dad," he replied nonchalantly.

"How was school?"

"It was good." He was already pulling his juice box from his backpack for his afternoon snack as he spoke. "We didn't really do anything except hang out."

Casey and Jamie exchanged knowing looks, Jamie glad to know he was paying tuition for his son to "hang out." "I'm guessing you don't have any homework for the week then."

"Nope," he said with a grin. "But we have a Spanish test the day we get back."

"Oh, we're gonna have to put your Spanish to the test while we're gone then," Casey said. "LA is a great place for that."

"Mrs. Bermudez said Los Angeles literally means 'the angels,'"

Jack said. "I never really noticed it was a Spanish word until she said that."

Casey smiled back at him. "Maybe we should take you down to Mexico while we're there," he suggested, looking to Jamie. "If that's cool with you, Dad."

"You can do that?" Jamie asked.

"Oh yeah," he said as if it were the simplest thing in the world. "Drive down to San Diego for a day or two, and from there, you can literally walk to Tijuana through San Ysidro. We can hop on some bikes and explore the city."

"Whoa, that's pretty cool," Jack said.

Jamie was genuinely delighted that his son would get to see another country while he was gone. Once upon a time, he and Eve discussed taking Jack somewhere for spring break, and he regretted that it obviously wasn't going to work out that way. But at least Jack was still getting his trip. "You ready to add another stamp to your passport?" Jamie asked him.

"You should come with us, Dad," Jack suggested, his mouth full of fruit snacks as he spoke. "We already know you're not gonna do anything while I'm gone."

"I have to work," Jamie sent back as both Jack and Casey laughed at the cold reminder that he was back to his old habits, no real life outside of his son. "But I'll be fine," he said. "You guys have fun for me."

But Jack and even Casey were right; he really did need to do something about that. Find himself a different street.

CHAPTER 42

Farther Up the Road

JAMIE

It was a sweltering, sunny Friday as Jamie trudged up the driveway to his former abode, practically glaring at the place as he drew closer. That awful red color. It was a minor miracle they'd been able to sell it as is.

Just as he made it to the front door, the sound of another car's arrival turned him around. He expected it to be the Realtor, Melanie, as they were scheduled to meet soon, but instead, it was Lucy in Tyler's car. Jamie let out a heavy exhale, bracing himself for their inevitable tension, but he painted on a pleasant face and went to greet her.

"Didn't expect to see you here," he said. He offered his hand, helping her out of the SUV in all her eight-months-pregnant glory, looking like she'd swallowed a watermelon whole.

Lucy sighed so loudly it sounded like a growl. "I packed a box full of Jack's old baby toys, but they're not at the new house, so I'm hoping we left them here."

"You could've just called, you know," Jamie said, escorting her up the short incline to the door. "I would've brought 'em over on Sunday."

"I didn't even know you were gonna be here." She was wiping the sweat that had already formed on her brow as she watched him unlock the door. "Why *are* you here?"

"Melanie's on her way," he said. "Handing over the keys today."

She nodded at his answer. "I'm too uncomfortable in my condition to feel sentimental about it all, but maybe you can be nostalgic for the both of us."

"I'll try," he said. He let her in ahead of him, the two of them finding the empty home already stuffy after just a few days without the air on.

"Jesus." Lucy frowned at the nuisance. "It's hotter in here than outside."

"You stay here," Jamie offered, directing her to stand in the open doorway. "I'll go look for the toys."

He started with the closets at the front of the house and worked his way back, involuntarily recalling the many big and little moments they shared there during the years. Moving in with the few pieces of furniture they could afford at the time; Jack's first big-boy bed; him learning to read, and then his first day of school; their parents coming into town when he graduated from kindergarten, staying in their new home for the first time; the way Jack would go sit in their closet and draw his comic books for hours, calling it his studio. Jamie couldn't help smiling, thinking about it all.

But then, his smile fell when he started to remember the bad times: the fights, the silences, the dearth of anything resembling passion.

It had been a long time since he called this place home, but he could still appreciate the sentiment attached to officially closing this chapter of his life.

Jamie eventually found the box in question in Jack's old bathroom. One of those last-minute things that got left behind, he presumed. Most of the toys would go to Lucy and Tyler's new baby now. Jamie considered himself happy for them these days, relieved that Jack would have a sibling to walk through life with, the way he had Casey. He found himself grinning again as he headed back to the front of the house. Lucy had made her way to the kitchen, where she was using the counter as support for her back.

"You all right?" Jamie asked, noting the anguish on her face.

"I'm miserable, but it's fine." As she stood up straight, she recognized the box in his arms. "You're a lifesaver."

"It's nothin'." He went to join her, setting the box on the counter between them. "How much longer do you have?"

"A little over four weeks," she said, exhaling. "She's due Memorial Day."

"Well . . . I can't imagine what it must be like in this heat, but you're handling it like a champ."

Lucy smiled. "You're kind. I'm just glad I don't have to go through the whole summer like this. I wouldn't make it."

"I'm sure you'd be fine," he offered, leaving the two of them gazing at each other for longer than they had in years now. It was a rare moment of warmth between the exes, which only gave way to awkwardness when it went on for too long.

"Well," Lucy was the first to say, "I . . . should get outta here. It'll be time to pick up Jack soon."

"Right," Jamie said, glancing at his watch. Jack had been

enjoying their new house all week, making for a good distraction from Eve, just as Jamie had run out of answers to his questions about her. "I'll see you Sunday then." He started to pick up the box to walk it to her car, but Lucy stopped him.

"Also," she started carefully, "I know it isn't my business, but I've wanted to mention this for a while now. Because you seem . . . sad. And I don't really know *what* happened, but Jack says Eve hasn't been around in a while. And I know you were happy with her."

Here we go, he thought. "Lucy . . ."

"I'm not . . . I don't mean to be intrusive," she said. "I just want to say . . . to *remind* you, I guess . . . not to let what I did ruin what you could have with someone else. Just in case you needed to hear it."

Jamie chuckled wryly at her lecturing him. After everything she'd done. "Believe it or not, everything isn't about you."

Lucy smiled tensely, rubbing her belly as she nodded. "I know that. This has nothing to do with me, really. Except that it's you. And I know that hurt . . . the kind of hurt that I put on you . . . it doesn't just disappear. It festers. It makes you scared to try again. And I know you wouldn't have let her meet Jack if it wasn't real to you. So whatever it is, I don't know if you got cold feet or what, but . . . if it's something fixable, I do hope you try to fix it."

Jamie was annoyed that she'd struck a nerve, considering their history. How he wished he could take her advice and go live happily ever after, as she'd somehow managed to do.

"Can I ask you something?" he said.

"Of course."

"How did you figure it out? What told you that Tyler was the right one?"

"Oh, wow." Lucy leaned against the counter once more and inhaled sharply. "I don't know that I can say I have anything figured out. I'm just happy, I guess."

"But we were happy once, weren't we? How'd you know he was different?"

"Well, you don't *know*," she said. "I just . . . trust him."

Jamie nodded slowly. He trusted Eve. He was learning to trust himself. But none of that fixed bad timing. None of that moved Tennessee any closer to New York.

"I wonder if some people are just in your life for a little while," he said. "Maybe they make it better and they move along. And it's no less impactful just because it only lasted a few months. You know?"

"Maybe . . ."

"I'm happy with the time Eve and I did get."

Lucy cocked her head and smirked. "That's bullshit."

"Excuse me?"

"You seem miserable, Jamie."

He laughed. "*You* seem miserable."

"Right now, that is true," she granted, gesturing to her swollen belly. "But my misery will cease in thirty days. You don't have pregnancy as an excuse."

"Yeah . . ." He scratched at his beard as he considered how honest to be with the woman in front of him. It was rare that they got along this well, and his candor could put her off easily. "I won't pretend I haven't considered picking up and leaving and taking Jack with me. But I don't think I have the strength to fight you on that."

"Well, no, you can't just take him," she said, her tone surprisingly airy. "But if you wanna go be with her, you should. You keep putting off what you want for other people. For Casey, for me. Now for Jack. But he deserves a dad who's happy. And he should know what it means to go after what you want."

Jamie wondered if that was how she rationalized what she did. "Is that right?"

"We wanna protect them so badly. And you've been so good about that," she said. "But the truth is, you were right to kick me out of here." She grinned when he looked up at her in what was surely shock. "You were. And as Jack gets older, his life is only gonna get harder." Lucy shrugged casually. "He's survived the last two years of us being apart, seesawing between these two different households. Two different states wouldn't be the hardest thing in the world."

Not that he needed it, but Jamie could feel his chest open up as he recognized Lucy was giving him permission to relocate to New York. "I don't know." Jamie sighed. "I'm sure it would build great character, but . . . taking him away from you, from his friends, his school . . ."

"To be clear, we're splitting custody in this scenario, right?"

"Of course. But that's significantly different from being a twenty-minute drive away."

"It is," Lucy said. "It would be. And I'm trying to be supportive, but you're the only one who can decide if it's worth it. If *she's* worth it."

Jamie wondered whether Lucy was only saying this because she felt she owed it to him. Whether she'd considered the ramifications for Jack, constantly flying back and forth between parents. Before recently, he'd been on a plane only a handful of times, and now they'd potentially be asking him to fly several times a year. To have two sets of friends. Full seasons away from one of them. Separate lives.

"I just don't wanna fuck him up," Jamie said, feeling farther from an answer than ever before. When he didn't think it was possible to take Jack from Tennessee, the path seemed clear. He couldn't be with Eve. But now, he had options.

"I know," Lucy said. "But if what I did didn't ruin him, you're probably okay."

"Well, the jury's still out on that. He is a little weird."

Their laughter filled the house before dwindling to comfortable silence and tender smiles. Nostalgia really was a potent son of a bitch, because for just a flash of a moment, Jamie forgot that this woman had emotionally demolished him just two years ago. He could only remember why he'd loved her once upon a time.

Thankfully, Lucy grabbed the toy box, effectively capping their conversation before his memories could betray him any further. "I know you're not gonna make this easy on yourself," she said. "If you don't wanna leave, don't. You have a good thing here, and it'd make all our lives a lot easier if you stayed. Plus, the grass isn't always greener," she reminded him. "But, you know, sometimes it is."

CHAPTER 43

Ain't a Sin to Win

EVE

Wed, May 6 1:54 PM

Leo Coletti: Hey. I know it's not until tomorrow but I just wanted to wish you best of luck with everything. Or I guess they say break a leg in theatre.

Eve Ambroise: Thank you, Leo. I really appreciate it. And I'll take both. 🙂

Eve pushed a long, tense breath through her lips as she waited for Dr. Garvey to come take her seat. It had been a few weeks since they'd seen each other—the doctor had gone on vacation to visit her daughter and newborn granddaughter—and now Eve worried the rapport they'd established would be affected by their time apart. That Dr. Garvey would be disappointed by her updates, as it hadn't been easy navigating life without her. She wasn't sure she was ready to be back under the microscope.

"It's good to see you," Dr. Garvey said, her tone chipper as she claimed her chair. "You look wonderful."

Eve smiled wide, appreciative of the compliment. She'd gone back to putting effort into her appearance, and it always elated her when people noticed. "Thank you, thank you. And how was your trip?"

"Entirely too short, but sweet," she said before shifting to business gears. "Now, if I'm not mistaken, you have quite a big event coming up soon? The Public is no small affair."

"Listen, *Hamilton* premiered there," Eve said. "I'm spiraling a little."

Dr. Garvey raised a surprised eyebrow. "Is it the typical nerves that come with doing something new? Or are we talking a Ted Lasso–type breakdown?"

Eve laughed at the unexpected humor. "Um. More the former than the latter," she was relieved to say. "Though I've been having trouble sleeping again."

The doctor was already writing notes on her pad. "And what are you thinking about on these sleepless nights?"

Eve winced. "About what happens if the audience at large doesn't like it. Doesn't get it. You know we only get one shot, and it better be impeccable." Her tone was suggestive, and as the words left her mouth, she realized precisely why she'd needed a Black therapist. No one else would understand what she meant; no one else on earth experienced that particular convergence of racism and sexism that Black women faced—the misogynoir of it all. No one else could be *we*.

"That's indisputable," Dr. Garvey said. "But as you've told it, people have already seen your work, Eve. It's the reason you're opening at the Public Theater. It's proof you didn't throw away your shot."

Eve grinned at the reference. "I know. That's what I keep

telling myself so I can feel better. Because if this goes well, we could go to *Broadway*. That's the dream," she said. "But if it doesn't . . . if I fail, I don't know. I might have to start coming in here twice a week."

Dr. Garvey offered a smile instead of a full laugh. "And in your mind, what happens when you fail? What does it look like?"

"Poverty," Eve said. "I don't know. I guess I worry that I'll have to start from the beginning. Or I'll have this stigma attached to my name. 'Oh, she didn't do well there.' And maybe I'm overreacting, but it's easier to prepare for it than to be smacked in the face by it."

"Does that change the outcome? If you prepare for a win, are you scared you'd lose?"

"Well . . . no."

"I know you don't want to be disappointed," Dr. Garvey said. "That sits in all of us. But you get to concoct any internal narrative you want. I'd love for you to ask yourself why, in your wildest dreams, you're not winning."

Eve bit the inside of her cheek as she recalled Jamie challenging her with something similar. "Is that my homework for this week?"

"That depends on what else you'd like to get off your chest. I remember you mentioning workshopping your next play when this current one goes live."

Eve tensed again, worried about disappointing her with the next topic on her list. Dr. Garvey never expressed anything of the sort, only encouraging her to find ways through her litany of issues. Still, it weighed on her before every session. Would today be the day she was too much for her therapist? She'd been at it for barely four months now, and she could tell she was gaining more confidence in her choices, slowly but surely, but she looked forward to the day she stopped being so concerned with what anyone else thought of them. Even her doctor.

"I actually . . . decided to push back my next play."

Dr. Garvey was visibly surprised by the news, her eyebrows lifting slightly. "The one you went to Tennessee to work on?"

"Yeah. Between moving and opening this play, and just . . . everything, my creativity was suffering for it, and I don't think that rushing, just to get to the next milestone, was going to serve me. It was just creating more anxiety in the end, so I decided to hold off. At least until this one is on solid ground at the Public."

"I imagine that was a hard decision. I know you were excited about the opportunity to debut successively."

"It wasn't a hard decision at all," Eve was happy to say. "It would've been nice, but I much prefer where I am mentally without that extra stress. I was surprised by how easy it was to tell my agent, 'Hey, I don't think I need to do this. I don't *want* to do this.'"

Dr. Garvey smiled. "Sometimes that's what it feels like when you've made your peace with something."

"When the hell did that happen?" Eve joked.

"What'd I tell you when you walked in here back in February?"

Eve rolled her eyes playfully as she quoted Dr. Garvey's mantra like a kindergartner reciting the Pledge. "That if I did the work, I'd see results."

"Imagine that."

Eve grinned.

"Have you heard from your dad lately?"

"Not a word," Eve said, looking down at her bright pink Rothy's. "I haven't reached out either, though."

Dr. Garvey scrawled a note in her book before responding, "You wanna say more about that?"

"Nope."

"What about Jamie? Have you heard from him since your last . . ."

Eve's cheeks began to tingle the second her thoughts shifted to him. "He texted last week. Sending well-wishes ahead of all the chaos. I'm sure he'll reach out tomorrow, too."

"That's nice."

"He's a nice person. Usually." Eve was tickled that she could make Dr. Garvey chuckle again. "I just said, 'Thanks,' and left it at that," she added.

"And are you trying to *seem* unfazed, or are you really okay with how this has all turned out?"

"Oop, not you trying to read me, Dr. Garvey," Eve said, laughing. "No, I'm fine. It hurts every now and then if I think about it for too long, but I really do feel like I'm miles away from where I started."

"You do seem very calm. Centered . . ."

"Your impact," Eve said, grinning. "But since you never tell me what I'm supposed to do, I keep trying to do what makes the most sense. And it seems to be working. It was another situation where I was able to look around and say, 'I don't need this.' Even if, in this case, it *was* something I wanted." Again, Eve looked down contemplatively as Jamie's lovely face flashed across her mind. "Jamie and I ended on a good note. Even if I'd like to talk to him every single day, it feels healthier that I was able to make a clean break."

"It may be," Dr. Garvey said in her usual composed timbre.

Eve laughed, though frustrated by her therapist's reply. Or lack thereof. "You're always so indiscernible when I talk about Jamie."

Dr. Garvey smiled at her observation. "That bothers you?"

"Yes! I'm flailing here."

"You're not," she assured her, still cool as ever. "You're not. And indeed, it is not my job to be prescriptive. The adoption, everything with Leo, your parents, to a certain degree—those are all parts of your past, and when you walked in here, you needed help navigating away from that trauma. You've gotten those tools now," she said, offering another soothing smile to her patient. "As for Jamie, if he's going to be part of your future, you have to get there on your own, Eve."

"That sounds like a ploy to make me keep paying you," Eve said, only half-kidding. "Do you at least have an opinion on him?"

"I do. I have a lot of opinions on all my patients' lives. That's human nature. But that's not going to help you, is it?"

"I know. You're right," Eve relented. She already knew what she wanted, so another point of view wouldn't *really* help. There was a good chance it would only confuse her more. She just wanted to know that her doctor liked him. That she'd approve if she took that step backward into a long-distance relationship she'd never *really* be satisfied with. "I'm just so curious."

"I will tell you something that I think you should hear. Something I've wanted you to come around to understanding without me saying it outright," Dr. Garvey said. "But sometimes, abstract lessons don't work, and we just need to hear things straight up. If you don't think you're ready to be in a relationship right now, by all means, please enjoy being single.

Please. But this journey you're on," she said, looking straight into Eve's eyes, "it should be about striving for progress, not perfection."

"Ms. Ambroise?"

Eve was so engrossed in her phone, looking for a text, an email, literally any sign of communication from her dad, she almost missed the knocking at her temporary door backstage at the Public. She was sharing a greenroom with her play's director, Stefani, where the two of them had just finished with makeup ahead of press. When Eve looked up, her mirror showed the reflection of the venue's house manager walking into the room toting a lavish flower arrangement.

Eve laughed, already taken aback by the gesture. "These can't be for me."

"Your assistant told me it was imperative that they were delivered to you personally."

"Thank you so much, Megan," she said, watching her set them on the vanity. It was a stunning—and large—bouquet of deep purple ranunculus with a card tucked among the dark buds. Eve waited for Megan to disappear before plucking out the note, eager to see who they were from.

If I'd had a granddaughter, I would want her to be like you.
I'm proud of you.
And so is Hazel.

I better see you soon,
Jill

Eve held the card to her chest, unable to hold back her tears. Not that she needed it, but it was a poignant reminder of what her time in Tennessee meant to her; not just now, but also seventeen years ago. She spent half her life avoiding the place that made her and then remade her. She was living testimony of the power of a praying grandmother, and how those prayers still protected her now. Eve only hoped Jill was right that her grandmother was proud; she hoped Hazel would have forgiven her the way Eve had managed to forgive herself.

"I just know I ruined my makeup," she mumbled, searching for a tissue to dab the corners of her eyes.

"Are you talking to yourself?"

Startled again, Eve shot out of her seat to see her agent walking through the opened door. "Stella!" she squealed. "You're here!"

"Of course I'm here! The whole office is camped out in the third and fourth rows." Stella was beaming as she pulled her in for a hug, the two of them shrieking over their triumph.

Stella squeezed and didn't let go until Eve joked that she was having trouble breathing. But when they pulled apart, they were each on the verge of more tears—happy ones now.

"Thank you for not giving up on me," Eve said. "But I wish you'd shown up sooner, because my eyeliner cannot handle this much crying," she added, kidding. "Shit."

Stella shook her head as she helped Eve wipe her face. "You're perfect."

"I'm not," Eve said with a bashful smile. "But . . . I'm much better than I was."

"The problem is you never knew how good you were in the first place," Stella said, handing over a small black-and-gold gift bag. "But I am *so* proud of you, Eve. I'm proud to know you, to represent you, and to bear witness to who you're going to be."

Eve peeked into the bag, a personalized leather-bound notebook staring back at her.

"For the next one," Stella said. "But only whenever you're ready."

"Okay, but be honest," Eve said, back to gently dabbing her waterline, "you were gonna let me go that day I came to your office, right?"

Stella made a face. "What?"

"If I hadn't broken down into a million pieces, you wouldn't have dropped me? I was sure that was why you called me in."

"Eve, I just wanted to check in with you." Stella chuckled sympathetically at what was surely a tortured expression on Eve's face, and she hugged her again. "Oh my god. No. Eve. You really thought I was giving up on you *now*? I mean maybe if this debut doesn't go well," she joked, gesturing at the area around them. "But we've got at least a month before we know if this is a bust."

The two of them laughed, but Eve found real solace in Stella's answer. It was a relief to know that she wasn't going to be discarded for her mistakes, as she'd feared. As she had been, once upon a time.

During rehearsals, the cast and crew had come up with a preshow ritual that they'd perform just before curtain every night. Actors in musicals often chose to sing or yell or hum—anything to warm their vocals ahead of a long night of using them. Other companies played a quick game, like Hacky Sack, or went around the room to cite something they were thankful for. *Gamba Adisa* was a production featuring all Black women, mostly millennials, and so their ritual could only involve the queen of their time, Beyoncé, in one way or another. They decided that they would dance it out to the live version of "Church Girl" every night, and there was nothing more edifying than a stage full of Black women letting loose to a song meant to embrace the freedom of spirit and renounce the shackles of judgment. A song for saints and sinners alike, it was essential to spend those four minutes celebrating that duality living in every single one of them.

And afterward, Eve took advantage of the chaos to seek sanctuary in her empty dressing room and return to her own roots in the church. She had convinced herself she no longer believed, because religion felt like the excuse her parents used to banish her. But she didn't want that to be her excuse; she didn't want to have to run away from relationships, including hers with God, in order to feel whole. So she closed the door, turned down the lights, leaving only the bulbs burning in the vanity, and she began her own personal ritual.

"I know you're there, God. It's me. Evie. I know you've been with me, even when I haven't been with you. And I just want to say thank you. If it's not too much to ask, I'm thinking about sticking around. I probably won't stop by for church every Sunday, but I would like to talk to you every once in a while. I'd like you to know that I see you. I'm present. I'm thankful. A year ago . . ." Eve let out a sharp exhale. "Well, you already know who and where I was a year ago. But thank you for giving me the sense and the strength to get out of my own way. Thank you for showing me life beyond the confines of my grief and my fear. Thank you for reminding me how to love myself. I'm still scared sometimes. I'm still sad sometimes. But I'm no longer scared of being sad. I'm no longer scared of being happy either." Eve opened her eyes and took a deep breath, her lips curling into an uncontainable smile as she stared at herself in her mirror. "Thank you for showing me the difference."

Amen.

When Eve first heard about this opportunity, she was afraid to believe in it. Getting eight weeks at the Public Theater was a dream. The fact that it starred an Emmy-winning actress sounded like a lie. Eve had gotten lost in the surreality of it all and had to resist the urge to pinch her own skin at random moments throughout the night, not wanting to give in to her cynicism. When she walked onto the stage to a standing ovation, she thought surely she'd be waking up soon, all of it some fever dream from the broke and broken college sophomore who chose theater as a major just to piss off her parents. In the subsequent years, it became her therapy, the stories she concocted allowing her to express her feelings of despair and rage, to dress her wounds, to relay her experiences. Now that she'd been to actual therapy, she could do that with her work, but also, so much more.

At their last rehearsal, one of the performers came up to her to tell her that this play was going to stay with people. The reviews used words like *powerful, fiery,* and *startling*. She hoped they were right. She hoped larger audiences would see Sandra Bland the person, the woman, whose life was more than its tragedy, and how Black women claimed their joy and existed in spaces beyond the trauma they were forced to endure. If that happened, whether they moved to Broadway or not, she'd succeeded.

In other ways, she'd failed. While her relationship with her mother was improving, the one with her father was nonexistent, and despite having the tools to move forward without his acknowledgment, she refused to use them. She'd decided to be just as stubborn as he was, even if it hurt. On the brighter side, she was learning to process that hurt without having to pretend it didn't exist. It wasn't sitting somewhere rotting her insides; it was a scar, and as Dr. Garvey would say, those healed with proper care.

And she was allowed to drop off her baggage sometimes.

CHAPTER 44

Fairytale

EVE

After a round of press and pictures, Eve attended the afterparty at the Standard with her mother at her side, Maya and Siobhan somewhere close. She walked onto a rooftop full of people and their applause, and Eve was positive she'd never smiled so hard in her life.

She looked *good* that night, too. She'd chosen a gorgeous cocktail dress from Haitian designer Joelle Wendy Fontaine. Simple but striking, the bronze silk with its dropped waist and open back accentuated Eve's finest assets, from her sculpted shoulders to her toned thighs. She wore her hair in long freestyle cornrows threaded with gold and glossy makeup to complement her gilded look. Eve didn't even need Maya's seal of approval, but she'd gotten it via FaceTime before the show, and again in person. Even strangers were shouting compliments at her.

"You are fucking amazing," Maya screamed as she approached her best friend, looking equally fly—and very Zendaya-esque—in her violet suit and matching pumps. "Bitch, I cried from beginning to end."

Eve wrapped her arms around Maya snugly. "Thanks, babe." She beamed. "But you've seen this play, like, eight times."

"But not with Amina," Maya said. "I hope you're ready for *all* of the awards. Drama Desk, Tony, Emmy, all of it."

"You're so stupid," Eve said, her grin still as wide as her face. "Thank you. I love you."

"You want a drink?" Maya asked, pointing to the bar. "Let me get you something."

"You're gonna buy me a drink at the open bar?" Eve teased.

"Well, I was offering to stand in line for you, but shit."

"Come." Eve took Maya's hand before she could respond and led her to a corner of the massive bar. It had been roped off, just for her and the play's cast and crew.

"Oh, bitch, you fancy!" Maya shouted over the music. Eve knew that Maya was certainly delighted for her but also relieved she wouldn't actually have to stand in that endless line for liquor.

"We've come a long way from not being able to get into Tongue and Groove," Eve said, recalling their early days at Spelman.

Maya made good on her promise to get their drinks: a margarita for herself and a whiskey sour for Eve. And once they were in hand, she raised her glass to her bestie.

"I know you gotta be *exhausted* of people complimenting you, but I'm doin' it anyway," she declared. "To my brilliant friend. It's *amazing* to be in this maze with you, sis."

Eve nodded, trying to knock back her tears. "Same."

"Drink."

Eve giggled after downing the liquor in practically one gulp, knowing she would regret it later. "Wait, where's Siobhan?" she asked.

"Dancing with everyone." Maya gestured to the dance floor. "I needed you to drink so I could get you out there."

"Bitch . . ."

"Come on," Maya begged. "It's your party."

"It's not."

"It is. And I'm not letting you leave without shaking all that ass," she said, giving her backside a playful swat. "Come."

"I'll be over in a minute," Eve said. "I need to eat something first."

"I'm coming back in ten minutes. You better be ready."

"I will be."

Eve smiled, watching Maya groove her way toward the crowd, and took a much-needed seat at the bar, her feet killing her after hours of running around in four-inch Louboutins. She ordered some french fries and another drink while she waited.

She was enjoying the time alone, as it allowed her to observe the crowd, all the people who'd helped her vision come together, enjoying the fruits of their labor. She was proud—of them and herself. And she was several sips into a grapefruit gimlet when a voice interrupted her journey toward a nice celebratory buzz.

"Is this seat taken?"

Eve turned to the voice, prepared to tell its owner that the section belonged to production staff only. But she lost her train of thought, along with her breath, when she found Jamie staring back at her. She hadn't recognized his inflection over the music, and barely recognized him, looking positively dapper in a crisp black suit and tie. She was speechless, her dropped jaw slowly turning into a smile as her heart raced to the beat of "I Wanna Dance with Somebody."

"What are you doing here?" she finally managed to ask.

Jamie grinned as he unfastened his jacket and took the seat she never offered. "I came to see your play."

"You saw my play?" she asked, still staring at him in a mixture of awe and confusion.

He grinned at her bewilderment. "What'd I miss?"

She narrowed her eyes at him, feeling like this was some sort of practical joke. Her mind playing tricks on her, urging her to go ahead and pinch herself this time. How did he even get in without being on the guest list? She surveyed the crowded floor in search of Maya—she seemed like the most likely culprit. But perhaps he was just artful enough to slip in on his own. And if this was, in fact, a dream, she wasn't ready to wake up.

"You haven't missed anything," she said, drinking him in like he was the cocktail in front of her.

He gazed back at her, the two of them holding an entire conversation with just their eyes, their stares saying far more than words ever could. Their silent exchange was loud and intimate, and it made Eve smile until she was on the edge of laughter.

"You wanna dance?" Jamie asked.

"You dance?"

"I do. I have. With you."

When he stood from his seat and offered his hand, Eve stared at him amusedly, trying to devise some clever reply, something about being on display in front of all those people. But she couldn't think of anything she wanted to say more than she wanted to dance with this man. She accepted his proffered hand and followed him to the dance floor, then past it, until they were in the corner of the rooftop, away from the crowd of moving bodies.

"What are we doing?" Eve wondered, unsure why they

needed to be isolated from everyone else. She was trying to be done with that version of herself.

"We're dancing."

Eve was still confused, but when he extended his arm, she was happy to settle in his embrace, his right hand spanning her bare back, pulling her close. His left hand took her right and he began to sway, taking her with him.

Eve instantly felt at home again, there in his arms, and relaxed as he guided them in slow circles, completely ignoring the rhythm of the upbeat music. It betrayed every instinct she had, but still, it felt right. She wanted to close her eyes, trusting that Jamie would lead her where they needed to go, but instead, she got lost in his. Those lovely blues, so full of all his dueling emotions. He was content, with her, at least in the moment, but there was melancholy there. He was nervous, and yet so confident. There was that puckish gleam, but his earnestness was ever present. Maybe, in essence, that was Jamie Gallagher.

Her eyes started to water the longer she stared, her lip involuntarily quivering, and she forced herself to look away before her feelings could swallow her whole. She rested her head against his shoulder and breathed him in.

"Are you okay?"

Eve was quick to answer, nodding against him. "Yes," she said.

She wasn't sure if that was true. She wasn't even sure if she was standing on her own or if Jamie was holding her up.

"You still think there's no path forward for us?" he asked, his voice low, as if they weren't alone.

Eve looked up at him. "Is there?"

Jamie smiled as they continued to sway in semicircles, ignoring anyone else that looked on, probably wondering what the hell she and Jamie were doing. As far as they were concerned, they were the only two people in the world. "What did you think when you saw me?" he asked.

"I thought I'd missed you so much, I was imagining things," she said, thankful to know she wasn't.

Jamie grinned. "When I saw you, I realized exactly why I woke up this morning with the sudden urge to hop on a flight to someplace I'd never been. And I thought, 'I'd get on a flight every day for that smile.'"

Eve was on the edge of bursting into pure sobs. Still so confused about how she could possibly deserve this man. After all her guardedness and uncertainty, here he was, still wanting her.

She went back to his shoulder, her comfortable place, and even though they were spinning, it felt as though the world had stopped for the two of them. She could feel his heart beating against her cheek, and when she did finally close her eyes, she imagined it beating for her. "What are you doing here?" she whispered.

He drew a long breath before speaking. "'Once we recognize what it is we're feeling, once we recognize we can feel deeply, love deeply, can feel joy, then we will demand that all parts of our lives produce that kind of joy.'"

Eve looked up at him, his lips twitching with the hint of a smile as she recognized the Audre Lorde quote.

"We had what we had," Jamie said. "But what if we could have more?"

"Can we . . . ?"

"Well." Jamie looked around, as if someone might be listening. "Turns out I got into NYU, and it looks like me and my kid might need a place to stay."

A tiny whimper fell from Eve's mouth as she felt herself melting, helpless to stop it. What a terrifying, wonderful feeling, knowing how much she wanted this, and how much it would hurt if they managed to ruin it again. Because maybe it would never be as easy as it was in their secluded little neighborhood in Gatlinburg. But she couldn't keep fantasizing about failing. Not when she had all these reasons to try. They were a work in progress, not perfection.

"You're moving to New York?" she asked, her disbelief not releasing its hold.

Jamie's eyes skipped around her face, his excitement flickering and reflecting the lights of the city surrounding them. "If you'll have us."

"Of course I'll have you." She laughed and she was crying at the same time, just as Jamie's lips crashed into hers, a flutter of butterflies, maybe fireflies, stirring her insides, adrenaline racing past them. She had never done hard drugs, but she imagined this was what heroin highs were made of. Eve knew, right then, she wanted this forever. Of *course* she would have them.

As they pulled apart, Eve trying carefully to wipe her tears, she gazed at Jamie, already imagining calling him the love of her life anytime someone asked.

He was so handsome, all dressed up in his Tom Ford suit fitting him like a glove. Eve looked like royalty on her big night. They cleaned up nice.

But she preferred them messy.

"You wanna get outta here?" she asked.

Jamie responded with only a slow smile at first, their dance coming to a grinding halt until they were simply standing there. "This is *your* party. We can't just leave. Can we?"

Eve took a moment to survey the lively scene, her friends and family and coworkers, along with people she'd never know, dancing the night away. She suspected no one would notice if she disappeared. But this time, she'd be back; she was too happy with what she'd built to leave it behind.

Maybe fairy tales didn't exist. But that didn't mean she couldn't have a happily ever after.

Still beaming, Eve shrugged. "I've done it before."

ACKNOWLEDGMENTS

Mom. Even if you never read this book, I hope you know how deeply thankful I am for every ounce of you and your support. I know that I haven't made it an easy journey, by any means, but I hope I made it worth it. This book is for you more than anyone.

Family and friends. I'm sure this whole author thing was a surprise to most of you. Nevertheless, you supported me, often without knowing it, and you nurtured this talent long before I ever knew I had it. As my first teachers, confidants, and champions, you've shaped my life, my experiences, my perspective, and so, you are all indispensable chords in my voice as a writer.

Sarah Younger. My inimitable agent, from your masterful management of your inbox to your uncanny way of calming all my anxiety-riddled (and often nonsensical) fears. I had a dream of how this whole author thing would go, and that dream included you long before your full request landed in my inbox. From the bottom to the top of my heart, thank you for making it come true. Thank you to everyone else at NYLA, especially Nancy Yost and Christina Miller, for everything you do.

Esi Sogah. Thank you, thank you, thank you for taking a chance on this story. I'm still in disbelief that you actually wanted my (not so) little book. When I tell stories of my publishing journey, I tell everyone how you were at the top of my list. Every agent I spoke to, I said, "I want Esi Sogah at Berkley." The fact that it actually happened doesn't quite make sense, but I'm so grateful we ended up together. Your guidance, your skill, and your patience have already made me a better writer. You, Genni, and Sarah are the greatest team a girl could ask for.

The Berkley PRH team, including Kristin Cipolla, Ariana

Abad, Jessica Mangicaro, Tyler Simon, Christine Legon, Katheryn Gao, Megha Jain, Ashley Tucker, Rachelle Baker, and Colleen Reinhart. Dream weavers extraordinaire! You all have turned my words and hopes into a real-life book, and I do not exaggerate when I say that it means the world to me.

To the audiobook team. You brought my characters to life in ways I could never do! Thank you for your voices—literally.

Robin Williams. (Not the one you're thinking of.) This book genuinely would not exist without you. Thank you for trusting me, and thank you for propelling me into alternate universes. I owe so much of this to you.

Bim Adewunmi. You showed me the power of fandom and all the beautiful Black women in it. Thank you for noticing me and my work and for making me believe I could do this. To no one's surprise, in all your immeasurable wisdom, you were absolutely right.

My critique group. Lee and Tam, thank you, always, for your time, your honesty, your kindness. You helped make my book precisely what it is today. Sara, I know this genre isn't exactly your wheelhouse, and I thank you for always being so engaged, present, and candid anyway. You always guide me into the light whenever I start feeling that impostor syndrome creeping in. Tanisha, our taskmaster extraordinaire, where would I be without you? Thank you for inviting me into the fold. Thank you for keeping us in touch, keeping us organized, keeping us *us*. I am so excited to see you take Hollywood by storm (but also desperately need to see Aubra on my bookshelf soon). Thank you for your service. *wink wink* And to Noué, my kindred romance-writing spirit. From the first chapter I read of *Long Past Summer,* I knew I would forever be chasing your brilliance.

I'm awed that I get to exchange critiques with you, watch you blossom as an author, and follow in your footsteps. I love you ladies for showing up in all the big and small ways that life allows. I feel privileged to call you my friends, and I thank you for keeping writing a safe space for me. LATTIS for life.

Gretchen Schreiber. Not only have you changed my life, but you're changing the face of publishing for the better. Thank you for creating LitUp, thank you for believing in the importance of women's voices, and thank you for seeing something in this novel that was worth putting its name behind. I hope I make you (and Reese) proud!

Tolani Akinola, Margot Fisher, Allison King, and Bora Reed. LitUp has changed my life in a million and one ways, but the best one is that it gave me you lovely humans! I'm so proud of our journeys and amazed that I get to be in this maze with y'all.

My fairy god-authors—Dhonielle Clayton and Zoraida Córdova. How on earth do I thank you for sending me to Sarah? I'm forever ever in your debt! To Tessa Gratton, Natalie C. Parker, Melissa Seymour, Sarah Harden, We Need Diverse Books, and everyone who put anything into our retreat: Thank you! It was the experience of a lifetime.

Jasmine Thee Guillory. I still can't believe I get to call you my mentor! You gave me so much confidence in this story. I was at my wit's end, and then you saw it for exactly what it was, and I cherish every bit of what that did for me.

Diane Marie Brown and Breanna McDaniel. More mentors! Unbelievable! Thank you so much for your time and immense talent.

Jessica Watterson, Stacey Bell, Amy Dressler, MK Lypka,

and Wendy Shames. While our space and time together may have been limited, you all left an indelible mark on my manuscript, and I feel so lucky to have met you. Thank you. Truly.

Caitlin Harbin, Tyler Lea, and Nekisa Nabors. Your insight gave this book the exact touches of realism I'd hoped for. Your time and conversations are so appreciated!

Danai Gurira. The tenacious and talented inspiration for this story, among so many others. Thank you for encouraging me, both directly and indirectly, to keep writing.

Beyoncé. Anyone who knows me likely knew I'd thank the queen, even if simply for existing. But I am acknowledging her here for a very specific reason: *Lemonade*. I'm proud to say that masterpiece is an integral chapter in my origin story. Thank you for motivating me constantly.

And with that in mind: the Richonne fandom. Many of us have been together for more than ten years now. (Where did the time go?!) Birdie, Morgan, Kia, Mel, Nalo, Tashann, Abria, Krystal, Keyan, Sian, and countless others. My first beta readers, critics, and cheerleaders. Your kindness, your support, your critiques, and even your frustrations have made me an exponentially better writer. I had zero expectations when I fell in love with a fictional couple on a zombie show and posted my first story, and somehow, y'all turned me into an author. I rediscovered my love for words through you, and while I can never repay everything you've given me, I hope I represent us well. Thank you all.

Last, but never least, my precious Dylan. Thank you for sitting with me through every letter of this book. Thank you for giving me so much joy when I thought I had none. I miss you every day. You were the best boy.

Author photo by Greta High

Ashley Jordan (she/her) is a millennial from Atlanta by way of Brooklyn. She attended Spelman College, obtaining a degree in psychology and a lifelong love and appreciation for women's stories. While she currently works in public health, she has embraced writing as a hobby since penning her first short story in second grade. When Ashley isn't at her day job or writing, she is either at a Beyoncé concert, rewatching *Mad Men,* or arguing about basketball with anyone who will listen. In 2023, she became a Reese's Book Club LitUp Fellow.

VISIT ASHLEY JORDAN ONLINE

AshleyJordanWrites

AshleyJordanWrites.com